SHERLOCK HOLMES
THE WEREWOLVES
OF EDINBURGH

BEING

BOOK TWO OF THE UNPUBLISHED CASE FILES OF
JOHN H. WATSON, M.D.

M.J. DOWNING

BURNS&LEA

LOUISVILLE   NEW YORK

Burns and Lea Books
11018 Radleigh Lane
Louisville, Kentucky 40291
www.burnsandleabooks.com

Design by www.formatting4U.com

Sherlock Holmes and the Werewolves of Edinburgh/ M.J. Downing. -- 1st ed.
Ebook ISBN: 978-1-7339806-2-3
Paperback ISBN: 978-1-7339806-1-6

For Mackenna, who brings the light.

"...all his senses have but human conditions: his ceremonies laid by, in his nakedness he appears but a man."

*Henry V:*Act IV, Sc. 1,Line 105
—William Shakespeare

PROLOGUE

Midsummer, 1891.

As I set down another tale of Department Zed and the Logres Society it serves, I realize that it will likely never find a reader. If, in the future, this or any other of these cases should come to light, I hope that I will be forgiven for speaking with such candor about my own actions and those of my dear departed friend, Mr. Sherlock Holmes. Though we are men who serve justice through science and reason, these cases forced Holmes and me to venture into areas of the fantastic.

Even as a surgeon during the Afghan wars, I witnessed things that confound scientific understanding: men who survived wounds that should have killed them; others who knew with certainty their own time of death, or that of a friend; and others who possessed power, seemingly, to manipulate the very elements around them. And though I have witnessed more bizarre realities than I care to recall, even apart from my Department Zed activities, I still do not believe in magic, in the occult. That is, it is not part of my creed, though it is real. I am no religious zealot, but I do believe in the power that holds men together in the face of evil injustice. Call it God, if you will.

And here, with the mild winds of summer singing through my study window, I recall that wintry night in the streets of Kensington Gardens when Holmes and I started down the path of this strange case. It led us to the extremity of each nearly taking the life of the other, and perhaps it made us better men. Those with greater wisdom than mine will have to judge whether I am right.

1

PART ONE: "A BUSMAN'S HOLIDAY."

CHAPTER ONE

"Boxing Day,"
26 December, 1888.

Though the cold did not bite hard, Holmes's teeth chattered. His convalescence had not gone well, and he was anything but his usual, vigorous self. I had recovered well from our long battle against Moriarty's forces and was in peak physical form. Yet the number of undead I had dispatched had more than doubled since Moriarty fled our wrath. As active agents of Department Zed, Magnus Guthrie and I had put down many active zombies. With Holmes's insights, we identified many of the carriers of the brain-killing disease and took them out of circulation and into treatment. Still, we lost many due to the weakened states in which we found them and the dangers of blood transfusions. Many were too far gone and were, therefore, sent to their rest by the edge of the sword. By Christmas, we had dealt with London's active zombies, though Guthrie, Holmes, and I remained busy.

Other strange concerns cropped up nightly: reports came in of violent hauntings and strange creatures, things that preyed on the poor and the helpless. This made Holmes seem prophetic in his assertion that Moriarty had opened the floodgates of a dark tide. I had yet to run into the fiend with a bull's head who was said to haunt the sewers or the goat-man who supposedly haunted the rail yards of the city. Even young Bill Wiggins and his friend Harvey Brewer, two of Holmes's most well-connected and observant Baker Street Irregulars, had not seen these creatures, though they had heard tell of them.

All our cases brought with them the risk of injury or death. I

5

had almost lost Guthrie in a foray with some benighted monster near Wicklow, Ireland, at the beginning of December, and it yet haunted my sleep. My nightmares shifted from the Battle of Maiwand to howling monstrosities with grasping claws and mouths hungry for human flesh. Their names or kinds, I did not know. A year before, I would have dismissed them as childish fancies, boggarts from old tales. Yet I faced them often and killed them with my sword. With that reality so hard to accept, my sleep was, at best, disrupted. This disruption continued even when the nightmares receded, as I had taken up nightly lodgings in Baker Street again so that I could tend my patient, Holmes, when he would let me.

The day after Christmas, with Holmes still needing recovery, we found ourselves hunting for another nightmare creature. I had urged Holmes to wait for us in our growler, with Wiggins driving and Brewer acting as our rear guard. The coach's minimal warmth was a block away as we spied on late-night wedding revelers in a quiet Kensington suburb.

Reports of London's infamous Spring Heeled Jack had come in from all over England. The press had identified Jack as active in Liverpool in September, even before we'd quashed Moriarty's plans. And two more attacks came in London, arriving with Christmas, as though to warn me that this season of light had a dark shadow that stalked the proudly lit hearths of British homes. Having begun to spend more time with my estranged wife, Mary, I had hoped for a peaceful twelve days of Christmas, but it was not to be.

Holmes shivering beside me, Guthrie at my other hand, we hunted Spring Heeled Jack amidst the fine homes of Kensington. Our orders were to capture, not merely eliminate, this thing in which I did not believe. And as I watched the revelers stumble along to their rest, this thought brought me no comfort. My agitation mounted by the second. It was too late for carolers to be out, but holly and evergreen garlands adorned lintels, gates, and even the gaslights. The wedding guests of the wealthy Cadogan family, practically reeling in holiday high spirits, made up for the lack of a choir. They warbled carols loud enough to wake their well-to-do neighbors.

"Damn that racket," I mumbled, standing at Holmes's side.

"If Jack was out here tonight, their singing has probably driven him away, whoever he is."

Spring Heeled Jack, I had thought, was just another bugbear of popular myth, based on the devilish Marquess of Waterford some half-century ago. Yellow journalists had turned that man's antics into the stuff of scary stories to sell news copy. Spring Heeled Jack, the supposed Terror of London, made for no good reason to have Holmes away from his needed rest. I had told him to leave the matter to Guthrie and me.

"If the records of Department Zed are to be trusted, this is exactly the milieu that will attract Spring Heeled Jack," Holmes murmured. He shifted his weight and grimaced, having demanded far too much from his injured knee.

"You should not be out here, Holmes," I said, watching him bend to rub the joint I had wrapped for him upon his insistence on joining this fanciful mission.

Holmes's need for action, always greater than my own, caused him to suffer when he was forced to be idle, and I feared that the present need for inactivity would lead to an increase in his cocaine use. However, seeing him favor his leg, I could not help saying, "You will end up with a permanent limp, if you do not take more care."

"Yes, yes, but our orders to capture this Spring Heeled Jack fellow came from Gladstone himself. Otherwise, I would have left this to you and Guthrie, as I did that Wicklow matter," Holmes replied, his keen eyes studying the rooflines. "A further word from Mycroft, stating that the original order came from Omar Raboud, the Logres Society's occult advisor, made it nearly impossible for me to decline."

"Occult advisor, indeed—" I grumbled, before Holmes interrupted me.

"And the Logres Society member to whom Mycroft reports in Department Zed business. Do not forget that he is your superior, old boy. After your formal investiture this Epiphany, you will be working more closely with him. And please recall that as a mere active agent member of the Society, I am not deep in their counsels. They tell me no more than they tell you. Mycroft and

Gladstone have great respect for Raboud, and that alone is enough to warrant my doing my best to carry out his order."

"But Holmes, you do not even believe in Spring Heeled Jack," I remonstrated. "How can you take seriously an order to capture this fellow, when you do not even believe he exists?"

"My past beliefs matter little. We have evidence, do we not, of criminal forces employing the occult? People have reported seeing this Jack fellow, being threatened by him, and we have a sighting from a credible witness. Moreover, my past correspondence with Raboud tells me that he is quite sound in his reasoning, even if the area of his expertise makes you uncomfortable. I simply bow to the demands of my superiors and follow orders, as you do."

"Yes. Very well," I said, watching the last of the stately broughams pull away from the tall, red-brick Cadogan residence. "But can you actually believe that we will see Spring Heeled Jack? He is a myth of London."

"You ask me, I'd say this 'ere Jack fellow is just some 'ard-pressed acrobat who likes the ladies," Guthrie said, joining us and handing me a weighted capture net made of black silk cord. That night, nets were the only weapons we brought into the field. My sword and pistol had stayed at home, and without them, I felt incomplete.

However, when I took the net, the feel of it lightened my mood. I ran the slim, strong bands through my fingers.

"This is a wicked-looking thing," I said. "Do you reckon it is made to catch imaginary creatures?"

"According to Mycroft, it is made to hold a full-grown male leopard," Holmes replied, shivering and pulling his coat more tightly about his slender frame. "And, Watson, I try not to prejudice my actions until I have all of the facts. Just keep your eyes on dark doorways and gates. I'll watch the rooftops."

"Rooftops is right," Guthrie said. "When I was a lad, they told stories of 'im, this Spring 'Eeled Jack. Eight feet 'igh, 'e were, a shape-shifter 'oo breathed fire and could leap twenty feet straight up. And a right toff, too, in 'is dapper dress."

"Which, if memory serves me, were popular stories fifty

years ago," I scoffed. "Do we hunt an octogenarian 'peeping Tom'?"

Holmes grew silent, tense. Leaning forward, he whispered, "No, Watson. We hunt a predator, I think. Look there, at the far corner of the Cadogan house. Do you see him?"

All the house lights in the Cadogan home had gone. Light from the gas lamps on the street played in spots on the edifice, making shadows shift as a mild breeze moved through the bare branches of mature trees behind the garden wall. Following Holmes's gaze up to the third floor, I saw another shadow detach itself from a dark spot and begin to crawl, insect-like, across the brickwork toward a window.

"Strewth! Look at that!" Guthrie whispered, edging forward.

My first sight of Spring Heeled Jack brought back to mind every story I'd ever heard of creeping creatures that prey upon the young. With them came a shiver of the fear I'd known then, too, the fear of dark faeries and monsters stealing infants in the night. Thoughts of the creature I'd dispatched in Wicklow came back to mind, and it made my hands shake.

I took no delight in faerie stories. My father had been as full of them as my mother had been of tales of the knights who protected fair damsels from such things. Such fanciful stories I had sought to leave behind me when I left the Edinburgh of my childhood. Yet there he was, manlike in shape though impossibly long of limb, creeping across the clean brickwork of the stately home. How he clung there I could not tell, but he moved along on fingertips, knees, and toes with a preternatural ease, making toward the windows of the third floor. As much as I wanted to call the stories about him bunk and nonsense, there he was.

"Holmes... what is he? And how did you know he would be here?"

"I didn't know, exactly, Watson. But Jack, as Guthrie observed, is overly fond of handsome young women, and the Cadogan family has hosted a wedding party this day. Today's wedding was the toast of the holiday season, you know. I thought it likely, given the eyewitness report we had of his presence in Knightsbridge two nights ago, that we would see him here, if anywhere, this night. I'll wager that there are several young, comely women in each of those guest rooms. He tracks them, Watson, seeks to find them alone, and appears to have learned that a boudoir is a fertile hunting ground.

"Go now, men, carefully," Holmes went on, goading us into action. "You will need to move quickly. I'll keep up as best I can."

And Guthrie and I were off, on silent feet, staying beneath the shadow of garden walls where we could. It wasn't a long run, but I found it hard to breathe. I was in pursuit of a legendary creature as real as the netting in my hands, the ground beneath my feet. Even as I ran, I could see Jack moving from window to window, looking for one left unfastened.

Easy movements marked him, as though clinging to brickwork were as natural to him as breathing, yet his attitude was urgent. I heard a whining growl come down from his position. Part of me thought that, once we had him, I'd see that he was just a normal man with some contraptions that helped him stick to the brick wall like a lizard basking in the sun. I told myself that this was simply an evil man, a rapist, with remarkable climbing ability, nothing more. Yet my heart beat fast.

Guthrie bolted through the Cadogans' front garden before I did and deployed his netting with a mighty heave. It was a grand throw, and it took Spring Heeled Jack unawares, wrapping around his left arm and leg. Jack gave a catlike hiss as the weighted cords tangled up his hand even as he sought to dislodge it. And he fell, three stories down, to land with a slight noise of snapping branches on the ornamental boxwoods below a first-floor window.

Even before Guthrie could clear the eight feet across to him, Jack was on his feet, standing near seven feet in height, to judge by Guthrie's six-feet-plus. Jack tore at the net, and blue flame shot from his mouth, which stretched wider than any human mouth had the right to stretch.

"Damnation!" I gasped at the sight.

Guthrie did not pause. He tackled Spring Heeled Jack, throwing his heavy shoulder into Jack's belly. Jack bent and swayed under the impact but, to my amazement, gave no ground.

Instead, with a clawed hand, he slashed at Guthrie's encircling arm and tossed him into the boxwoods. Seizing the moment, I hurled my net, taking Jack around his head and shoulders. The net's weighted ends wrapped around Jack's tall, slender form. He let out another hiss as it tangled his limbs, and he dropped to the ground, tearing at the black cords.

I leapt atop him and tried to secure the netting tighter around the bizarre figure who thrashed in the frozen grass. Blue fire erupted from Jack's wide maw, again, and burned several net strands to cinders. He rolled me off to one side easily, as though I were a child, and aimed a slash at me, though it was pulled short by the netting. Jack fell back and turned on his belly to get his long legs beneath him and spring away, as was reported to be his wont, but I threw myself onto his back and pulled him over on top of me.

"Get the hood on him, man," I said to Guthrie in a fierce whisper, for we each had a heavy canvas sack to put over the head of our quarry. "I'll get his arms."

Jack's convulsions were more than a match for my strength, but I grappled with him, pulling at the netting to trap his flailing arms, trying to keep my own arms away from the razor-sharp claws that had slashed Guthrie's arm. Seizing Jack from behind allowed me to wrap my legs around his torso and hold him somewhat still. His strength was like that of a giant snake, fluid, constant, and overwhelming.

Guthrie was running toward us. I managed to get an arm around Jack's throat in a choke hold to stop him from breathing flames as Guthrie landed atop him and dropped a black hood over his head. Holmes was limping into the garden as well, a pistol drawn at his side, at the best speed he could make, and behind him stood our carriage. I had help aplenty, then, but did not need it, for as soon as the hood fell into place, Jack ceased his struggles as though poleaxed. He lay limp in my arms. Guthrie, fist raised to strike Jack a heavy blow, stood still, then dropped his arm.

"Blimey, Cap'n. 'E's out."

"How? Did you strike him when the hood went on?"

11

"No, sir," Guthrie replied, as I pulled the hood away and let loose of Jack enough to search for a pulse in his corded neck.

Jack's face, like a Punchinello puppet's, had a pronounced brow, nose, and chin. Though he could spit blue fire, he had a humanlike appearance, so I assumed he had a human anatomy, of sorts. I found no pulse, though, and the creature lay atop me a surprisingly light weight for one so strong. I rolled him over into the grass and sought elsewhere for a pulse or a sign of breathing. Neither was apparent.

"What's happened, Watson?" Holmes whispered.

"You must've broke his neck, sir," Guthrie whispered, shock mixing with hard admiration.

"Impossible," I hissed. "This fellow is—was—stronger than both of us together. He can't be dead. It's impossible."

"I beg to differ," said Holmes, "though I, too, must express surprise. I saw the last bit of your struggle with him and worried more for the injury you might take. And now look at him."

"The old man'll take umbrage, Cap'n," Guthrie muttered, remembering our orders from Mr. Gladstone.

Lifting Jack's head with extreme caution, lest he only feigned complete collapse, I pushed open one of his overlarge eyes, finding his catlike pupil fixed and dilated. Spring Heeled Jack was dead, though by what means, I could not say.

"Well, come along," I said with a sigh. "Let's get him out of this garden before anyone notices our presence."

***

Once in the carriage, I could not help but notice Holmes's agitation, no doubt at our—my—failure to capture our quarry alive. Wishing to lift the tense mood, I asked Holmes about the client I'd seen him interviewing late that afternoon.

"What became of your elderly gentleman?" I asked.

I was surprised by the serious look on his face as he answered, "Ah. That elderly gentleman was one Abel Cameron, who calls himself the King of the Highland Travelers; I am in no position to dispute his claim. The Travelers are a far-flung folk with ways that are distinctly their own. Mycroft sent Mr. Cameron to me because of a series of murders and stolen artifacts in their ranks."

"Mycroft Holmes taking an interest in gypsies killing one another and stealing pots and pans?" I asked, wondering how Mycroft Holmes even knew of the Highland Travelers. I knew of them from my boyhood in Edinburgh and considered them, at best, itinerant laborers. Holmes, however, ignored my dismissal of them.

"The murders of several of their clan heads were done in different parts of the country at almost the same moment. It was orchestrated. As to the artifacts, these have a magical property, one upon which, Cameron says, the fate of the Commonwealth rests," Holmes replied. "I simply cannot do the legwork the case requires, so I suppose it will pass to you and Guthrie as soon as tomorrow, if this business with Raboud goes well. It is rather a serious matter, I think, though I do not know the particulars of the missing items just yet. My visitor was unsure about giving those details to me. I trust he will be more forthcoming when you are able to look into the thefts."

"Wouldn't he be better served by the Metropolitan Police?" I asked.

"No, Watson. Mr. Cameron, and indeed the whole Traveler community, have a tense relationship with the Old Bill, as do other folk of similar kind: the Romany, Irish Travelers, and such," Holmes replied. "And since the crimes Cameron reports have an occult connection with the Travelers, Mycroft will advise you of your first steps."

"If it is a serious matter, I suppose it must come under Department Zed's business," I said with a sigh, "though I don't know why the Travelers would place such trust in me."

"They will, for Mycroft does, as do I," he replied.

"I recognize that D. Z. is supposed to handle such clandestine things," I said, "but I cannot help but think that, in me, they have a poor agent as their investigator. They would be better off with Guthrie here as our most active man in the field."

"As long as I can bash 'em on the 'ead, I do fine, but I don't have the mind and 'eart for such matters as you do, Cap'n," Guthrie replied with a smile.

But I had to question how great a mindset I had for further magical matters.

***

Taking the entrance through the cellar of 221B Baker Street, Guthrie and I hauled Spring Heeled Jack's limp form. He weighed no more than a child of ten. Passing through Mrs. Hudson's kitchen, we rushed up to Holmes's sitting room. Holmes led the way, his keen gray eyes staring at the corpse we bore. Leaning heavily on his cane, he directed us to place our burden on the Persian carpet in the center of the room.

"Now that I see him better," Holmes said, "I, too, wish that we could have taken him alive."

"I can only hope that this Dr. Raboud will be able to learn as much in a postmortem as he had hoped to learn in an interview," I said.

"Mycroft speaks highly of Raboud's ability and of how much good he has done for the Logres Society," Holmes said. "Whatever he is able to learn, I think it will benefit Department Zed. Clearly, we need someone whose métier gives him insight into magical creatures, do we not?"

"Indeed," I agreed with a sigh, "we do. I sincerely hope he has a forgiving nature in the matter of such creatures' capture. I do not know whether I am more surprised at Spring Heeled Jack's demise or at his reality."

With my growing knowledge of the Logres Society, I had learned that Department Zed was one of several of its active arms, tasked with occult defense. The Society had many agents and was widespread, though it always operated unseen, doing what good it could do for the well-being of people seeking to live in civil order.

Holmes assured me that Raboud was a reasonable, if passionate, fellow. He indicated that the man was rather hard-pressed of late, though, given the little information that Mycroft would share with him. Holmes sought to assure me that Raboud would see that I'd had no choice in the manner of Spring Heeled Jack's unexpected death.

Lifting Jack's body with ease to remove his clothing, we found that he wore no conventional undergarments and that his coat, shirt, and breeches were of a strange, light material that lost a subtle glow as we removed them.

"How light he is, yet in all other ways almost human in his form, though its—his—genitalia are rather, er, extravagant," Holmes remarked, looking at the lean, catlike physique.

"'E'd be the talk of an 'areem, right enough," Guthrie observed.

"Yes, he does seem rather well set up for procreation," Holmes mused.

All of Jack's features were nearly human, almost as though he were—had been—a living human caricature. The corpse had little, if any, fat on it. Spring Heeled Jack was muscled like a predator in its hunting prime. His hands alone were a marvel, with claws that, when pressure was applied to the last knuckle of each digit, extended and contracted in the manner of a cat's.

"What do you make of 'im, Cap'n?" Guthrie asked. "For certain, 'e bears no other wound, and I'd lay odds that 'is neck isn't close to broke. He looks 'ole as a man can be, sir."

"Whole, yes," Holmes interjected, "but a human male? No."

"I see what you mean, Holmes, but suggesting that this man isn't human is preposterous," I protested, though I had seen flames erupt from this Jack's mouth. I thought that merely the trick of a mountebank, though. I could not, however, mount a strong argument against Holmes's observation. Holmes must be right, though I could not bring myself to agree with his conclusions so readily.

"If not human, then animal? I think not. Perhaps your working taxonomy of intelligent creatures needs a third option, but I will not offer an opinion one way or another, Watson," Holmes said with a wry smile at my discomfiture. "But I must wonder what we might have learned from this creature, could we have spoken with him. I wonder if he even spoke our language. He is rather like seeing something from a dream...

"But we will see what Raboud says in a matter of hours," he added. "Guthrie, you may stand down now, sir, as soon as

Watson has a good look at those wounds on your arm. We will send for you tomorrow for the review of this capture. Gladstone, Mycroft, and Raboud will likely want to take your testimony separately."

"Yes, sir," Guthrie said with a nod, a scowl on his face. Pulling off his tunic and wincing as the dried blood tugged at the slashes on his upper arm, he added, "But you can be sure that they'll 'ear nothin' o' this as a failure on Cap'n Jack's part. I'll take my oath on it."

"Indeed you will, and then some, if Omar Raboud is as particular as his reputation has him," Holmes added.

"Come, my friend," I said to Guthrie, and soon I was cleaning blood from the three lacerations scored a quarter inch deep across the man's upper arm. A series of stitches in each pulled them together well, and I breathed a sigh of relief. If not for the stout wool of Guthrie's coat, Spring Heeled Jack might have cost him the use of his arm. And yet the orders under which we worked had insisted on capture.

"Do not worry over the matter, failure or not. These men know what they are about and have much to consider. Our efforts might not be success enough for them, but they were good efforts," I said, taping some light gauze over the cuts.

Guthrie grumbled a bit more, flexed his arm and said, "Officers and their bleedin' expectations, beggin' your pardon, sir. They just ought to think before they send a bloke out on such a mission."

"I agree with you and shall take that as a recommendation for my own conduct for future missions," I replied.

"Difference is, Cap'n, that you'll always be right next to me. It's them that command from the rear 'oo rile me."

"I can think of no other proper way to lead, especially headstrong lads like you," I chided him, though I knew well that, in a soldier's life, most leaders stood in the rear. "Now get some rest before I write you up for obstreperousness."

As he left the room, I turned to take the chair opposite Holmes.

"Your recovery could do with more rest as well, Holmes," I

said, waving aside the fog of Holmes's tobacco smoke. Another pipe and several ounces of tobacco lay on the table at his elbow. Holmes looked to be in for a night of deep thinking.

"I know, Watson, but do stop sounding like my nursemaid, will you?" he mumbled, staring at the corpse cooling on the rug in the center of the room.

"Well, avoiding sleep to worry over this matter won't help your leg mend," I protested.

"You are correct as usual, Watson," he sighed, "but I cannot help giving thought to the matter now that I see the creature that Raboud wished captured. You see, Raboud must have a strong reason for coming from Paris on this matter. If he wished to have this creature alive, there was some important reason. At the very least, I must consider that Spring Heeled Jack is, truly, a creature only known in the occult world. And if that is so, his activity represents a significant threat."

"To whom, Holmes?" I asked.

"That I cannot say, and I will not hazard a guess until I have more facts," he answered. "But, given the occurrences of late, I think I have erred in dismissing all occult matters as the work of charlatans."

"I cannot help but think you wrong there, Holmes," I said. "This business is strange, yes, perhaps even grotesque, with regard to this poor fellow, but I think that we will have a better explanation for Spring Heeled Jack's reality from Raboud, if he is as great an expert as you say."

"I've mentioned Raboud's vaunted reputation. But there is something more, something I'm just beginning to grasp, from what Mycroft reveals to me, slowly, about the Logres Society. In the past hundred years, Watson, despite advances in science and government, there has been a tremendous upswing in occult matters, growing in the shadows of all this industrial and civil productivity. It runs like a glowing thread through our history.

"And, as Mycroft explained to me, the Logres Society has sought to protect the innocent from those who will tyrannize them and who often use occult means to do so. Even in its earliest days, the Logres Society never faced such dark opposition to its generous aims as it does now, and Raboud has been instrumental in uncovering several attempts to ruin the Society. Our enemies, especially the ones in the deepest shadows, Watson, would risk much to bring us down. I must conclude that Raboud's insistence on a live capture means that he sees this creature as harmful to the Society's interests. I just cannot tell how at this point. What cause has activated this creature?"

"I certainly cannot say, but I am well aware of the Society's caution, especially in taking on new members," I replied, "though I chafe at the delay and the secretiveness of their ways. I just hoped—well, it isn't important."

Holmes turned his gaze to me and offered a smile of appreciation, albeit a sad one. "You hoped that a more timely investiture in the Society would help you where Mary is concerned," Holmes added. He pointed to my left hand, where I was toying with my wedding ring, revealing that my thoughts were on Mary. I pulled the ring from my finger, annoyed with Holmes's ability to read me. Holmes had it right: after our joint efforts in the so-called Jack the Ripper murders, I had thought by Christmas Day to be invested in the Logres Society. I hoped my joining that august group could give Mary a reason to see me in a better light, even if she was not to know its inner workings.

"I assume you still see to her treatments?" Holmes asked, pushing me to open up.

"Yes, every two weeks, and as you know, I take most of my meals there with her. We are doing well together, and I have hopes that I can move back home soon," I said. Mary's smiles warmed with each time I saw her, as though we were courting again. She kissed and embraced me, though I had not returned, as yet, to our marriage bed. Mary seemed well on her way to forgiving my blind stupidity in succumbing to my desire for Anne Prescott, Holmes's client whose merciful death at my hands had ended the so-called Ripper murders earlier that year.

"I hope to spend much of this Christmas holiday with Mary," I added, "for she seems to have forgiven me."

"That is good news. Have you forgiven yourself, old man?" Holmes asked, lifting his eyebrow.

"Perhaps, a little, though I still feel the wrong I did," I replied. "I still don't know what came over me, with Anne. I never wanted to hurt Mary."

"Do you think that you loved Anne?"

"Yes. Yes, I do—did—but it was wrong to do so. I look back on it and see the weakness in my character that drew me to Anne so strongly, making me imagine that she and I could live out some heroic fantasy life."

"Almost like magic, hmm, Watson?"

"I've never thought of it that way," I said, "but I suppose you're right. I cast that spell from the weakest, neediest parts of myself. Possibly, Mary sees that now and understands something of what happened to me, perhaps better than I do myself. I do know that I've always loved and needed Mary as my partner in life, and I owe her my best."

"You seek to give everyone your best, don't you?"

"Yes, and maybe that's why I dislike all this talk of the occult, magic, and strange eldritch creatures. It might all be well and truly real, but it offers too much enticement to the less honorable facets of a man's nature."

"You are less estranged from yourself, Watson, than you have ever been," Holmes whispered.

"Perhaps," I said.

"However, you cannot hide your grief about Anne, about your own failings. To be a man is to fail. You must take better care of your inner man than that, Watson."

"My griefs, like my shortcomings, I bear with all the patience I can, Holmes, and you would be better off to do the same. I see that you have been pushing yourself too hard. Your knee looks swollen again," I said, desirous of moving our talk away from my recent past.

"A short trip to Bradley's today for more shag," he allowed.

"Which Wiggins or Brewer or any of your Baker Street Irregulars about here during the day would have been happy to retrieve for you," I complained, rising to my feet, recalling that I was out of my navy flake. "And, judging by that pile of shag at your elbow, you don't look to be preparing to retire this night."

"Someone must keep vigil for our guest," Holmes said with a wry smile as he relit his pipe. "His oddities warrant further speculation, especially in connection with his presence in London just now. Raboud's home is in Cairo, but he happened to be in Paris when word reached him about Spring Heeled Jack. That proximity could be a coincidence, but I must entertain the idea that it is not, especially since the coordinated murders in the Highland Traveler ranks happened at approximately the same time."

"That is speculation bordering on magical thinking, isn't it, Holmes?" I suggested, surprised by such an astounding leap in his logic.

"Patterns, Watson. We must all beware of patterns, large and small. That is why I follow the grief columns in the *Times* as assiduously as the latest national and international news."

"All this speculation about magic, though, Holmes: it's a rather sudden departure from your usual way of thinking, is it not?"

"That term 'magic' grates on your sensibilities, as it does mine, I see. It is a prejudice, Watson, and I do not need to tell you what disasters await the man who cannot confront his prejudices, however rational they seem."

Holmes's solemn manner suggested that he had said all he was going to say on the subject for the time being. I shook my head, weary of speculation, and retired to my lonely bed for what remained of the night.

CHAPTER TWO

"The Feast of St. John the Apostle,"
27 December, 1888.

The next morning, the mystery of Spring Heeled Jack deepened. The corpse had withered into a sunken thing, like a mummy, and the clothes we had taken from his body had disappeared completely. Holmes made a tour of the sitting room with his glass, while I asked Mrs. Hudson about her movements. Our good landlady had slept "like the dead," she said, and had not stirred since nine o'clock, when we'd first set out on our mission.

I ordered our breakfast and returned to Holmes. After an hour of detailed examination of windows, doors, chimney, and carpets, he offered the opinion that no one had been in the room since he had finally taken some sleep around three in the morning. We sent a hastily written description of the "capture" and of this morning's events to Mycroft by messenger.

I fetched our tray myself and sat opposite Holmes as we shared a silent breakfast. Holmes remained in deep thought and would say nothing about my assertions that no human body could have mummified on its own in one night.

"What we see here certainly defies the biological sciences. As to the clothing, it was certainly there last night. Am I to conclude that magical faeries took it?" I joked.

Holmes merely stared at me without speaking and raised his eyebrows. At length he said, "While I dislike that term as much as you do, 'faeries' may well be the only explanation I can offer. A close examination of the carpet where the clothing had lain revealed only a fine dust, more of a desiccated residue, as though a liquid solution had dried. And you will note that the corpse's skin has become leathery, though I doubt the body weighs less than it did. Some other science, perhaps..."

Holmes did not finish his thoughts.

I awaited his dictum that the facts should focus us on the probabilities that remained to us in the absence of impossibilities, yet he said nothing more. As for my efforts, I applied Occam's razor to the situation, wishing to see that the simplest explanation—a thief in the wee hours—had stolen the clothing, but that left me with the unsettling terms of that thief having "spirited" the articles away. As to the seeming mummification of the corpse, no simple explanation offered itself at all.

It neared luncheon when Holmes alerted me to the sound of Gladstone's coach. I opened Mrs. Hudson's front door to Prime Minister Gladstone and Mycroft Holmes, with two other gentlemen in tow. The dour looks of all four, as I ushered them into the front hall, suggested that our early morning report about the incident had not been greeted with favor.

"May I introduce to you, Dr. Watson, our esteemed colleagues, Dr. Omar Raboud of Cairo and his able assistant Mr. Dibba Al-Hassan?" Mycroft said.

Raboud was a small, dark man, rather bottle-shaped, wider at the hips than at the shoulders. With long, black hair, he was clean-shaven, well-dressed, and bespectacled, frail and delicate in his person. His tailor-made suit of black gabardine made him look as though his middle were bandaged heavily, and I wondered if he had been injured of late. However, the hand he offered me, though slight, had a hard grip and shook with nervous energy. He reminded me of Holmes in his brisk manner and the intensity of his grip.

Raboud's attendant, Dibba Al-Hassan, clad in yards of good Scots tweed, was quite the antithesis of his master. He was one of the most heavily muscled men I have ever seen and one of the most ebullient. He stood at his master's shoulder, a beatific smile on his dark, bearded face. When I shook his hand, it was all I could do to return the pressure of his grip, which could have broken my bones like dry twigs. He doffed his bowler hat and sketched a short bow to me. He looked me square in the eye and seemed delighted to address me as "*efendi*"—a term of respect, apparently—in deep, merry tones.

Raboud gave me a polite, reserved "How do you do?" at the door, and the others greeted me pleasantly enough, though I could tell by their quiet manner that they were concerned about the interview to follow. Mycroft Holmes's keen eyes tracked from Raboud to me, as though Mycroft waited for something to go amiss. It was not to be a pleasant meeting, and my nerves were on edge as I escorted them into our sitting room.

"Passionate" was too mild a word for Raboud's reaction to the corpse of Spring Heeled Jack. He turned on me, his dark eyes alight with anger and swimming behind the thick spectacles on his prominent nose. As he then dropped to one knee beside the corpse of Spring Heeled Jack, his words hit me like a blow, shocking me into stunned silence: "Bungler! Useless butcher! How dare you claim the title 'Doctor'?"

Holmes came to my defense. "Dr. Raboud, please!"

"Am I to beg your pardon for rebuking a man who has undone much of the work I'd hoped to do, Mr. Holmes? In the past year, I have traveled thousands of miles and endured sickness and attempts on my life for this Society, and I am here to battle an occult threat that this magnificent being could have helped me identify. Several of our European agents have been attacked through occult means, and my own associate, Dibba, as close to me as a brother, took nearly mortal wounds in my defense so that I could be here and learn from this ancient and venerable creature," he said, thrusting a finger at the cold body.

I saw no evidence of wounds or any weakness in Dibba Al-Hassan, and I would not have called Jack magnificent, but Raboud's response quieted Holmes.

I'd taken complete responsibility for Spring Heeled Jack's death in the report I'd submitted, shielding Guthrie from any blame, as was my duty as his superior officer. I'd expected to be the target of Raboud's disappointment. But I was astounded at his vehemence.

I sought to make some measure of peace with this man. "Please accept whatever service I can render to help your colleague, Dr. Raboud. I assure you that if I cannot provide your associate with proper treatment, I will be sure that he finds the best care—"

"As if I would trust him to your so-called 'best' care," Raboud cried, rising to stalk toward me, lenses quivering. "Look what you did to this beautiful creature, with your brutal ways!"

The sudden shrillness in his voice stung my pride and caused my anger to flare again. I sought for patience to combat my own outrage. My only recourse was to keep silent and watch him as he turned back to the corpse. Thinking it best to trust to my superiors, I backed away from Raboud and the corpse of Spring Heeled Jack, wondering what Raboud knew about him to see Jack as a "beautiful creature." I found it difficult to think of a dangerous threat to London and its people as beautiful.

Gladstone said, "I assure you that my men are as baffled as anyone about this—this being's death. Given their efforts, I am quite surprised that they took as little injury as they did in the attempt to capture him. Surely you can see that this body is free from any marks of violence."

"I should not be seeing a body at all. It should have dissolved like the clothing you reported having taken from it. This creature's body still lies under enchantment by some dark mage. You fail to see so much," Raboud murmured, running his hands above the corpse, an inch above its skin.

The body then quivered and began to dissolve into dust. It was a sight I will never forget. I bore witness to a solid—if bizarre—body becoming dust before my eyes. Even Holmes emitted a startled grunt. Raboud nearly swooned while doing whatever he did to cause this reaction.

"Even in my weakened state," he cried, "I can tell that this poor creature died confused and helpless. He must have been compelled to act and bound by a curse that took his life when he was captured. What did you estimate as his weight?"

I knew that Jack had suffered no confusion about doing violence to Guthrie or me, but from my place in the shadows of the room, I said only, "Less than five stone: about sixty pounds or a little more."

Still thinking of that brutal attack, I was shocked to see genuine tears spring to Raboud's eyes. I exchanged raised eyebrows with Holmes. Raboud wiped away those tears with an impatient hand, shook his head, and gave a shuddering sigh.

"He was nearly a thousand years old, this one," Raboud murmured, "and someone in this wretched country had him under a compulsion. I thank Allah that he suffered no injury to his frail body, despite your barbaric methods. After he led so long a peaceful life, it was a vile sin to take from him what was his."

Had I heard him right? A manlike creature who lived to be a thousand?

No one raised a voice to question Dr. Raboud's assessment. His words were taken as fact, as preposterous as they sounded. As to Jack's being "frail" and having led "a peaceful life," such a creature, unless his physical makeup was just a matter of chance, looked to be a predator, prone to violence, like a leopard or tiger.

Gladstone cleared his throat as he and Mycroft exchanged wondering glances at Raboud's demeanor.

"Dr. Raboud, please forgive us for our seeming insensitivity to the loss you feel," Gladstone said in low tones. "You seem to know—that is, to have known—him."

"No, Prime Minister. I did not know this creature, but I know his kind. They are a special people and dwell in the fae realm, away from contact with men," Raboud said, placing the sheet with reverence over the outlandish face. "They are prone to being attracted to mortal women and so have removed themselves from contact with mortals. This is a creature known to my people as an *afreet*—what you would call a lesser djinn, I think. Surely you have read Sir Richard's translation of the *Arabian Nights*? It has been available for several years now."

Raboud appeared to settle himself with some effort. He stood with head bowed, as though in prayer for this "afreet" who could have killed me. After a long moment of silence, Raboud went on to address me in strained tones.

"I offer my apologies, Dr. Watson, for my outburst. I must seem terribly ungrateful," Raboud said, more in deference to my associates than to me, I thought, for he glared at Mycroft Holmes as he said it.

"I gladly accept your apology, sir," I said, though grudgingly, "and offer you my sincerest condolences. I simply do not know what to say about your observations about this, this..."

"Afreet," he whispered.

"He was a mighty man—erm, creature—in his way, far more powerful than my colleague and I. I give you my word that I sought only to capture him, thinking him a danger. But we had reports of his assaults on two women in a single night, reports which Mycroft and others have been at pains to suppress. I—we thought him only a danger. As to his age, sir, I cannot help but think that this idea of his being some sort of faerie—"

Raboud gave me a hard look, one that forced me to be quiet. His look told me that anything I had to say to him would make him angry. Despite my indignation, I decided to tread cautiously on the subject. Raboud's reputation in the Logres Society demanded that reserve, even if he seemed to resort to pure fancy in labeling Jack as something from a faerie tale.

"And are you such an expert of the creatures of faerie, sir?" Raboud shot back at me.

"Well, no, sir. I was just thinki—"

"Do not bother yourself with thinking, *Doctor*," he said, hurling the name of my profession at me like an insult. "You know nothing of the worlds that intersect with your plane of existence, despite the fact that you have just minutes ago taken the hand of a faerie in greeting."

I turned my glance to Gladstone and the Holmes brothers and found that all looked away, unwilling to meet my glance.

"I—I do not know—" I stammered, going red in the face like a schoolboy chastised by his tutor for some huge gap in memory that should have been well known.

"Dibba Al-Hassan is of a faerie race," Raboud said, turning his gaze to his associate.

Holmes looked at me, then at Raboud's friend, raising his eyebrows.

26

Al-Hassan, that broad fellow, turned a smile upon me and explained in soft tones, "Yes, I am of the *dweraz, efendi*. I think your word for my people is "dwarf." Many of us live in your midst, though we are of the *longaevi* and are slow to die. It is my honor to serve Dr. Raboud as I served his father and his father's fathers for seven generations back. Please, accept that my master is much upset by the magical compulsion forced upon this ancient creature."

"Seven generations..." I said, looking at a hearty fellow who appeared to be my age, mid-thirties—forties at the most—but who claimed to be more than two hundred years old.

Then I realized that, while Raboud had claimed Al-Hassan was severely injured, I saw no sign of injury or weakness. "And you have just taken injury in Dr. Raboud's defense?" I asked.

"Yes. A revenant attacked us, a *wampyr*, I think you call them. My wounds were nothing, good sir."

"A wampyr? A vampire?" I asked, incredulous, as any man would be to find out that the world of fantasy creatures was being spoken of with such seriousness. "And you are a... dwarf, one of the little—"

Mycroft Holmes interjected in a low voice, "Think more of Alberich in the Wagnerian Ring Cycle."

Our former prime minister looked on silently, with an interested, if surprised, countenance. I had fought alongside Gladstone and expected that he would say something—anything—in my defense, but he did not.

"Enough, Dibba," Raboud grumbled, rising to his feet and focusing his swimming gaze upon me again. But he had not let his anger go.

"Dr. Watson is no more than a bloody-handed enforcer, part barber, part policeman, like much of the medical community he represents," he claimed, addressing my superiors. "Butchers, glorified with the title 'Doctor,' who know nothing beyond that which they can carve away with their surgeries."

Then he turned a bitter look to me and addressed me as though I were a schoolyard bully. "Dr. Watson, I worried that you were using that vile weapon of yours, that sword of which I have read. That was one reason why I came from Paris in such haste when Mr. Gladstone cabled me about the increased number of sightings of this kind of creature. Surely, you can see that such a weapon possesses power and, as such, needs to be studied. Furthermore, my concerns about the sword and your use of it give me reason to oppose your admission to the Logres Society. What do you say to that?"

I had been dressed down by many a superior officer in my time, and in more insulting language, but never so unjustly. Raboud seemed determined to oppose me in any way he could. Clearly he had chosen to see me as worthless before even shaking my hand. His bitter contempt was unlike anything I'd ever experienced from the members of the Logres Society. And, as I looked around at them, I noted that no more voices were raised in my defense. My role in the Logres Society had grown tenuous. It seemed to me an undeserved, cruel blow.

I would willingly suffer no more, not without putting my fist through Raboud's face, but my respect for my so-called associates held me back from any aggressive action. My choice was clear. I pushed past Mycroft Holmes and Mr. Gladstone and left, taking my hat and coat from the stand by the door. The raised voices calling my name as I walked out the door could rail on, as far as I was concerned.

Mrs. Hudson met me on the steps, full of questions about the shouting. I ignored her as I sought to get out into the street. Thrusting the door aside with the energy of my agitation, I was shocked to cause a handsome young man to stumble and reel back onto the sidewalk. I caught his flailing arm, stopped his fall, and got him steady on his feet. He bore a briefcase in each hand and a sheaf of correspondence under one arm and was off balance, trying not to drop everything. He appeared to have come from Gladstone's carriage, in which Raboud had arrived with the others. Offering a brusque "Pray forgive my haste, young sir," I started to walk away.

"You must be Dr. Watson," the fellow said, his accent French, cultured. "I heard that you were a powerful fellow, and I see now that it is true." The papers under his arm slid out and showered to the ground.

His kind manner and tone forced me to stop and address him. I gathered the documents near my feet and could not help seeing the Logres Society letterhead. A quick scan showed me the names of myself and my associates, including Sherlock Holmes and Anne Prescott. The papers appeared to be accounts of our actions in the "Undead Client" case. Shuffling them into a more orderly form, I gave them back to him. He smiled and offered his hand before he bent to retrieve a briefcase. His grip was firm, and he met me eye to eye, but having seen the reports, I was even more intent on departure.

"I am pleased to meet you. Thank you for your kindness, but I imagine that your opinion of me will change, if you came in the company of Dr. Omar Raboud," I said. "I—I am taking my leave of those esteemed gentlemen. May fortune smile upon your work."

And with that, I managed to turn and stride away, hearing only his polite reply, "*Au revoir.*"

***

A fine group of colleagues I have, I thought, in full stride down Baker Street. A man ought to be able to count on his mates when he suffers the contempt of some "jack-in-office." But a weak protest from Holmes and a few raised eyebrows were all that I had witnessed in my defense, and these paltry things from men who had heaped praise upon my efforts to carry out their missions. *Their* missions: that was very much the rub that chafed my soul as I strode away.

And just to think, a gigantic dwarf faerie shaking my hand. Another, Spring Heeled Jack, crawling up walls like a lizard, living to be one thousand years old, and dying at the lightest touch. Preposterous! Of all the farcical nonsense! And worse, even Holmes was giving it credence, all because of the vaunted opinion of Omar Raboud.

Though the street around me shimmered with red and green decorations on doors and in windows, I moved like a black cloud through the gaiety of this, the third day of Christmas, intent on putting immediate distance between me and my "esteemed" colleagues. People bustled about their business with "Merry Christmas" wishes on their lips and smiles on their faces, while I strode through their midst like a blast of bitter cold air. All my presence did was to make them all seem merrier. I confess a feeling of kinship with Mr. Dickens's Ebenezer Scrooge, in that all I desired was to be separated from the kindnesses of my fellow men. It pained me to remember that hope I had dared hold, to be invested as a member of the Logres Society by Christmas. *Wait until Epiphany*, they'd said. *In Edinburgh*, they'd said, as though it were an honor for me to have it held there. Pah! I might have been born in that benighted city, but I would not claim it as my home.

My mother had insisted that my brother and I learn the twelve days of Christmas and the meaning of each day. As a child, I'd found it fun, a good way to keep the holiday spirit lively. Today was the Feast of St. John, he who had penned the Book of Revelation. Having endured Raboud's insults on that day, my mood was certainly apocalyptic.

The notion of Edinburgh and my childhood took me back to the recent past, where I had trudged up Arthur's Seat and spread Anne Prescott's ashes to the north wind. It had been the best I could do for her. The memory of the kindness in her eyes haunted me as I walked on with renewed energy to get away from Baker Street as quickly as I could. One comfort remained to me, and that was in getting home to see Mary. Thoughts of her sweet smile lessened the bitterness of my meeting with Raboud, so I determined to walk to Paddington and do what I could to make Mary's third day of Christmas brighter.

Several blocks later, a hansom cab rolled up next to me at the curb, and the cabbie, muffled up to his eyes in a thick tartan scarf of red and grey, called down to me in merry tones.

"In a bit of a hurry, aren't you, good sir? Do you need transportation?"

His words, in a deep, sonorous voice, sounded refined, and the obvious kindness in his tone surprised me. I turned and looked up at him with a shocked look on my face, I'm sure, for such an attitude from a cabbie was as odd a thing as a faerie. His lot were usually grim and grasping.

He was a strong-looking chap, with large hands and long black hair. I could tell from the look in his eyes that he was smiling, though his scarf covered his nose and mouth.

"Why, erm, thank you, no. No, I don't, actually. I—I'm afraid that you see me letting off a bit of steam, sir," I confessed, taking an immediate liking to this common fellow, though I didn't know him from Adam.

He gave a deep chuckle and asked, "The missus wound you up a bit? Your mates done a bunk on you, sir?"

"Yes, yes, something like that," I answered with a shallow laugh. "The privileges of those in high office, more to the point."

"'The proud man's contumely, the pangs of despised love, the law's delay, the insolence of office, and the spurns that patient merit of th' unworthy takes... '" he proclaimed in a deep voice muffled by the wool. "Ah, like a pebble in your shoe, aren't they?" he added with a laugh. "Well, don't let the well-heeled beggars get you down."

"I am behind my time in that, old fellow," I said, wondering afresh at a cabbie who could quote from *Hamlet* with such clarity. I had not thought that night of those lines from the Dane's great soliloquy, but they described, more or less exactly, what troubled me. I stopped and looked hard at this cabbie, wondering if his presence were mere chance. It had to be chance, I thought, unless it was fate or... magic.

Preposterous. "I think the walk is doing me good, as is your sudden kindness, of course," I said. I fished in my pocket and found that I'd come away without my usual pocket money. One lone sixpence I found, and I tossed it to him in thanks.

"Ta, guv," he said, snatching the coin from the cold air, "and a Merry Christmas to you."

"And to you, my good man," I said, watching him urge his horse back into the flow of traffic down Baker Street.

At that moment, I noticed a pair of men looking intently at me from the dark doorway of a corn-factor's office across the street. The taller one pointed to me, and the shorter one pulled

31

his arm down. They were both dressed in plain brown suits, without ties, like tradesmen of some kind, for they wore work boots as well. The intervening traffic was heavy enough that I did not get but two quick looks at them between the vehicles on the street. And when in a break in the traffic I had a clearer sight, they were both gone.

"Perhaps I should have taken the cabbie's offer," I mumbled, drawing a strange look from a well-dressed couple walking arm in arm. I pushed on and hurried past them.

Later, still in Baker Street, I caught sight of those same two men watching me from an alleyway as I passed. I turned my eyes from them and crossed to their side of the street, taking the first left turn I could. When I gave them another glance, I saw that they had followed, so I hurried along and took a right turn which would take me to Marylebone and on toward Paddington. That they had marked me in a crowd along the sidewalk told me that I should proceed with caution and, if possible, determine their intent in a public encounter. It could hardly be robbery, in broad daylight, among so many people. Perhaps they followed anyone who left Baker Street. Was it coincidence that they had arrived on the scene after Gladstone and company did?

I made sure that they were still with me, marveling at their ability to blend with ease into the crowd. They weren't the usual London toughs looking for an easy mark, for I had put them through their paces, moving at a quick march. The typical London thug will look for an easier victim. Plus, from what I could tell, they had not the faces of ruffians. Theirs were bright and clean, though their clothing was rough.

Coming up on the Lamb and Flag public house, I turned in at the door and waited to get a better look at them. They stopped in their tracks, one older fellow, short, strong-looking and his younger, taller friend, both clean shaven. I motioned them to join me. The pub had a decent crowd for midday. If they failed to join me after an obvious invitation, their intent was hostile, and I would retreat to Baker Street instead of going home.

Going to the bar and ordering three pints of ale, I took a table in the middle of the floor and waited. When they came in, eyes scanning the room, I waved them over and said, "Gentlemen, do join me after all your efforts." And when the older man took off his hat, I finally recognized him. He was the King of Highland Travelers, who had come to consult with Holmes the very day before.

"Mr. Cameron, I believe," I said and gave my hand to the older fellow. He smiled amiably and returned my hand clasp with a hearty grip.

"Dr. Watson," he said, modulating his thick Scots brogue to speak to me, "please forgive this intrusion. This is my son and heir, Jamie Cameron."

"A pleasure, sir. Please, think nothing of it and join me in a bit of Christmas cheer. If you'd rather, I think this establishment offers a decent 'smoking bishop' or 'blue blazer,' if ale isn't to your liking." I desired to put them at their ease, for though their shadowing me was a bit odd, I gathered from their easy manner that they had no evil intent.

"Ale's all right with us, sir," young Jamie said, "and here's to your health and long days." He took a good pull at his drink. I did likewise, looking at the pair. They were the first Highland Travelers I'd ever met, and they weren't at all what I had expected.

"So, Mr. Cameron, what can I do for you and your son, that has you dogging my steps?"

"Well, sir," the older man said, "we know that you work with Mr. Holmes, right enough, and he told us that you'd be looking into our case, but we have reasons to ask you to avoid the case you're on."

"Your case or the one that I have been on of late?" I asked, wondering at this solicitous attitude toward me, as unknown to them as I was. Did they know of the cases of Department Zed? Perhaps they did, if they had followed Gladstone and company to Baker Street. Abel Cameron looked at the younger man, and they debated for a moment in a speech I could not follow; it sounded like Gaelic to me. After a moment, the elder man replied.

"Likely both," he said with a sigh. "Does it not seem too convenient that they have come to you both together?"

"And how do you know anything of my most recent case?" I asked, for Highland Travelers existed in a much different stratum of society than that of Raboud and the other members of the Logres Society.

"Well, sir, we have our ways of knowing things and many connections for which you'd likely not give us credit," the elder Cameron said.

"I see," I replied, though I knew enough distrust of all gypsy folk to think that that they were merely setting me up for some elaborate hoax. "I do not imagine you can know the particulars of the case I have been on, and I know little to nothing about yours, beyond the fact that it concerns murder and theft. Are you questioning my ability, gentlemen?" I wished to err on the side of caution.

"Nay, sir, for the Travelers have heard of the work you've done, and we respect it, since some of us share a bit of your mission, to put down the dark creatures that rise," the elder Cameron said in softer tones. He appeared to know something of Department Zed's functions, anyway, and it made me curious about the depth of his connection with Mycroft Holmes.

"So why wouldn't I be suited to look into any case that comes before me?" I asked.

"You are keenly suited to any case, sir, we know. As to our matter, we know why our artifacts were taken, but we do not know the names of those who took them and killed our people," Abel Cameron said. "But when we learned that it was you who were taking up this business, we were concerned that... that is, we were afraid..."

"That I would not be as successful as Holmes?" I offered.

"Just tell him, Da. The man has the right to know," Jamie interrupted.

There followed a brief but intense dialogue between the two in the patois used by Travelers. After a pause, the elder Cameron looked hard at me and then said to his son, "You tell him. You're the one with the Sight."

Again the occult raised its misty head in my presence, and I started to get up and walk away, for I was that tired of it.

"Gentlemen, I'm afraid that you—" I started, but Jamie reached across the table and grasped my arm. His strong grip shook.

"You must not take this path, sir," he said urgently. "Leave it to the others. Many actions will seem right and serve justice, but making the best choice, sir, in this case, would tax the soul of the best of men. And even making that choice will place a burden on you."

"Another burden, eh?" I interjected. "One you advise me to put aside, let others bear? If you know of me, gentlemen, surely you will see that I am not one to shift my responsibilities onto another man. It is a matter of honor."

"This business of ours, though, lies in shadow. We live in that shadow, were born to it, and know of the sacrifices needed," the elder Cameron said. "For you to carry on with our case will place you in the ranks of those who live apart, those whose lives are no longer solely their own."

"That isn't a fair burden, either," young Jamie added, "especially for one with so much to gain from the world of other men. Taking on our case, carrying it to its end, well, it could cause your life to burn and you'll be left with naught. That's more than we can ask any man. I've not seen all that can be, but on my mother's dead bones, I've seen that this case could be your ruin."

At his tense words, the hair on the back of my neck prickled beneath my collar.

"Hey, you lot," a voice called from the bar. "Pikies are not allowed here."

The barman and several rough-looking patrons had turned to glare at us. One of them had overheard the Gaelic patois and raised a cry against the Camerons. I started to rise in protest, but Cameron and his son got up and left without a further word, leaving me wondering about the manner of strangers I'd confronted today: a day of revelation, indeed. There was the calumny raised against me by the esteemed Dr. Raboud and the little defense I'd heard from my friends. I was known in my work by the Highland Travelers, however, who were looking out for my welfare. It was a confusing map to read, and I sat down hard to think about it.

I could not help but think that the Travelers were actually looking for a network of men, given what Holmes had told me about the murders all done at the same time in different locations. It suggested a fair degree of coordination as well as someone, some force, at its center to make it happen. Raboud's comments, though, had suggested that we were pitted against another mage. Both cases were connected, Cameron had said. As much as I wanted to think it likely, I didn't give it serious thought. However, Spring Heeled Jack certainly seemed to be a creature of the shadows, where the Travelers lived and moved, and the artifacts they'd reported stolen were said to have some occult significance.

I knew better than to dismiss any possible connection between Raboud's putative mage and the person coordinating the strikes on the Travelers. I had seen Moriarty work in a similar way, but neither Holmes nor Department Zed had found any trace of that monster in England or on the Continent. Perhaps another had risen to take Moriarty's place. I shuddered at the thought.

Raboud and my colleagues might not welcome me into the Logres Society, but I was committed to my work in Department Zed, and I wondered how I might discover a connection between both cases. That still seemed unlikely, about as unlikely as meeting a cabbie fluent in Shakespeare.

I sat thinking, indifferent to the comments of the men who remained at the bar muttering imprecations against Travelers and all who associated with them. It was just talk. I had a great deal to think about, and topmost on my mind was the increase in talk about magic that had come my way of late. It was being forced upon me, and I did not care for it.

I finished my pint before shouldering through the three or four bigoted Londoners who frowned on my going. I paid no attention to the vile names they muttered at me as I passed. But then one big fellow, some inches taller than I, laid a rough hand on my shoulder, and I reacted as I'd been trained to. With my opposing hand, I curled his fingers away from their hold on my coat in a joint lock that Mr. Uyeshiba, my sensei, had me practice often. Perhaps, in my frustration, I used more force than necessary. I earned his bleat of surprise and the popping sound of his shoulder dislocating. Twisting his weight around mine, I used his arm as a lever to spin him headfirst into his fellows. Three of them sprawled on the floor under his weight as I made for the door.

"That man has a dislocated shoulder," I said to the barman, in quiet tones, for I was deep in thought. "It had better be seen to, or he'll not be able to work and buy your excellent beer. Good day."

I carried on with my walk home, lost in thoughts and more than a little agitated by this magic nonsense and its sudden presence in my life.

CHAPTER THREE

"Further Revelation."

Much to my disappointment, Mary was not present when I reached our home in Paddington. I found a note affixed to the hall stand. It read,

John,

> *I am sorry to miss you today, but I couldn't remember if we had dinner plans this evening. Perhaps it was one of my spells, but I don't think so. I am feeling decidedly better these days, so much so that I have decided to take up Mycroft Holmes's offer of a brief holiday with his friend Mrs. Norton. His telegram came this afternoon, and Mrs. Norton bore letters of introduction from Mycroft and from Mr. Gladstone, so I know I can go with her safely. She is a delightful woman. I feel that I know her from somewhere, though she says we have not met before.*

> *She is here now, with that charming Commander O'Hara, to offer me the hospitality of her home and several theatrical opportunities over the next several days. It has been ages, it seems, since I have been to the theatre, and I am very excited to go. I hope you don't mind my being away for a few days of Christmas, but I think getting out will do me good, as does Mrs. Norton. And she feels certain that you will be able to join us one night, if you can be spared from your work. I've given my girl leave to go, though she has laid out your dress clothes in case you can join us. Please do, if you can!*

> *Love, Mary*

38

My first thought upon reading this was the possible risk to Mary's health if she were out of my care, even for a brief time. Mary had contracted the zombie infection from the evil Dr. LaLaurie during Holmes's and my fight with him earlier that year, and her condition was, in my opinion, still fragile. Though I had been giving her frequent blood transfusions to try to rid her blood of the infection—luckily, she had dependable donors in Holmes and Guthrie—I knew that I could only delay its effects. Eventually, it would take a toll on her brain; likely, in the end, it would cause her demise.

But Mycroft had been solicitous of Mary's condition. I knew I could trust that he had her best interest in mind in offering her this outing. Though I did not know who Mrs. Norton could be, I trusted Mycroft's judgment in pairing Mary with her. Perhaps she was a trained nurse, meant to look out for Mary's health in my absence.

I was, however, forced to wonder about the timing of the offer. Did Mycroft think Mary was in danger at home, now that Holmes and I were on a new case? Did he wish to involve her in a more observable routine where she could be protected from worry and from harm? The presence of O'Hara, whom Mycroft knew I considered beyond reproach, was surely a message to me that she was being shielded in this way. And perhaps Mycroft was right to do so.

In that thought, I settled my worries about Mary's absence, for I had reason enough to think her safe, for now. I took refuge at my old desk in my study, among the dust and cobwebs, thinking over all that had happened this day, Raboud's insulting manner notwithstanding. The odd occurrences of my return home gave me the sense that I had been caught up in a growing series of complications. Mary's use of the word "spell" had brought my thoughts back to magic, which I could not countenance, and it occurred to me that this was, as Holmes said, because of the negative associations I had from childhood with those words themselves. They did not belong in my world, for I had long ago separated myself from such ideas.

However, my experiences of late, when looked at with care,

told me that I had to borrow terms like "magic," "occult," or "supernatural" in place of better, more scientific terms. Clearly, Raboud's studies in the occult made him an expert about faeries, magical spells of compulsion, and such. And I had to face that this expertise made him a highly prized member of an august community, the Logres Society. I had seen much of the good that the L. S. had done for the poor in London during my time with Department Zed. And there were my own experiences too. To others, zombies were as outlandish a thing as faeries, yet I'd fought zombies, knew them as a real threat, whereas the man on the street would think them creatures of pure fancy.

But did that mean that I should take what Raboud said as fact or give any credence to the warning of Abel Cameron and his son? Zombies were one thing, but did their presence mean that I should give credence to magic? Faeries? Dwarfs? I stopped myself, remembering the incident earlier this month in Wicklow, where Guthrie and I encountered something that neither of us could explain but that had almost cost him his life. The murderous creature's last words to me had been ominous: "You will see. Dark things are risin', warrior; our time comes soon."[1]

In my hasty departure from Baker Street, I had brought with me the sword, Mustard Seed, with which I had dispatched many "occult" creatures. Taking it from its concealment under my greatcoat, I freed its bright blade from the night-black scabbard. The mere sight of that blade always demanded my utmost attention. I believed that it was the sharpest blade ever made, with an edge keener than my best scalpel yet as hard as diamonds. The very danger of that bitter edge sobered my thoughts, and I welcomed that. However, each time I used that blade, every zombie I killed, cost me something that I could not calculate.

Seeing my reflection in the keen blade, I saw Anne's death again. I wondered about Raboud's charge that Mustard Seed was an artifact of occult power, and I looked at the facts of that experience.

---

[1] find "The Wicklow Ghoul" at www.MJDowningsPlace.com

Anne, possessed by some dark entity, had been too quick for me. She had disabled Holmes, whose combat skills were much greater than mine. I'd observed her in action and knew that I was not capable, on the best of days, of beating her—or rather, that evil that possessed her—with sheer speed. Yet the swiftness of my strike, when I was forced to kill her, had been faster than I thought I could be. True, in the intervening time, my practice with the sword had shown my improvement. Yet, before I had gained some measure of mastery with it, I had done what was physically impossible for me.

Had Mustard Seed acted on its own power to give me the speed and strength to do that which I lacked the ability to do? Perhaps it had. At the time, I'd thought that Anne, somehow, had found a way to hold back the entity within her and give me more time. I could not explain it in rational terms. And there it was again: my vocabulary had not kept pace with my experiences.

Regardless of the dangers I might be facing, I decided I needed dinner and a relaxing pipe or two. This caused me to remember that I was out of tobacco and that Mary, bound on an errand with this "associate," had dismissed the cook for the day. So I lay my sword across my desk and prepared to leave. On this night, I was no one's warrior, unless I was Mary's, and I trusted that she was in good company. I left my home once again, walking far enough away from Sussex Gardens to find a cab, setting out across London again to James J. Fox's, a tobacconist in St. James's Street. From there, it was a short walk to a fine restaurant, the Criterion. Enjoying my meal there, I remembered it was the site of my first meeting with Dr. Sanford, who had introduced me to Holmes.

I took another a cab back home, wondering if I might sleep there this night. Going back to my things at Baker Street sounded a harsh note in my thoughts, remembering how I had left there, and I thought a night away would do me good. Truth be told, I was still a bit put out over Holmes's lack of a defense on my behalf.

As my cab rolled up to my door, I saw Holmes on my front steps, leaning on his cane outside my door. *I might well not get any sleep at all*, I thought. Seeing him forced me to remember

Mycroft's actions in taking Mary to safety, for his very look told me his thoughts: "The game's afoot, Watson."

"I hope your dinner at the Criterion was a good one, Watson," Holmes said instead, with a smile, as I stepped down from my cab, "and I infer that you have been by Fox's establishment."

His habit did not annoy me, then, for he knew where I would turn for a good meal, especially if I needed to treat myself, and as for Fox's, I had lit a bowl of that fragrant flake on my way home in the cab. Holmes knew about my preference for ship's tobacco and was familiar with which London tobacconists stocked it.

"You should have joined me in both, old man, rather than staying in the company of that loathsome little Raboud," I said. "You look as thin as a willow wand, Holmes. A full meal would do you good. As far as the flake is concerned, do come in and have a bowl. As you probably know, Mary is away."

"Yes, Mycroft told me that he would arrange for her departure, but he said nothing of its manner. As to my exhausted state, you may put that down to several hours of argument with our doctor of occult sciences," Holmes replied, waving away his need for better nutrition and a smoke. Any meals he took were small and quick, as though he lived on permanent military campaign. The look in his eyes and the set of his mouth showed that he spoke in earnest. "I came hoping that your o'erhasty exit from that contentious stage did not signify your abandonment of the play. You are needed in our ranks, sir. I fear that some game is afoot that will require all our combined ability to manage."

"I have no intention of abandoning my work in Department Zed, though I do not think that, with Raboud against me, I have any future in the L. S."

"I speak for Gladstone and our present leader when I say that we owe you many apologies for your treatment at our hands. We—I, really—did not offer as vigorous a defense on your part as was called for. I am glad to say, though, that through our efforts, Raboud's stance against you has softened, and he wishes to have you back, on certain conditions."

"What?" I cried, pausing with the key in my hand.
"Conditions? What manner of power does this Raboud hold that
defies a former—and likely future—prime minister of Great
Britain? And what of the conditions that we all went through this
past year? What conditions, other than working as I have done to
carry out the orders of my superiors, does Raboud imagine that I
will accept, Holmes? What hurdles has he set up for me? My one
desire, though, is to confront—"

I paused, for my front door opened with just the pressure of
my hand on the knob.

"Holmes, I—"

"Quietly, old man. You are expected, I see," he said, his
quick eyes scanning the darkness of my front hall. "Are you
armed?"

"No," I whispered. "Clearly, sword and pistol are not
required for dining at the Criterion."

"Well, we have my stick here. I only hope that it will
suffice," he said, handing it to me. "Sorry, Watson, but you are
the only one of us fit enough to 'welcome' an unexpected visitor
this evening."

Taking the stick in both hands, I entered the darkened hall
with Holmes behind me. As I did so, I recognized that I was
giving up the choice the Traveler King had offered me. Walking
into my own home put my feet on the path he had warned me
would lead to my ruin.

My senses sharpened, eyes scanning the darkness for an
unfamiliar shadow or furtive movement. I prayed a silent prayer
of gratitude that Mary was far away, in the company of our
female associate.

Ambient light from the street entered the kitchen through its
back windows and filtered into the hall toward my study and
surgery, but it wasn't enough to see anything clearly in my
darkened home. Nothing looked to be disturbed, and a quick
glance into my study on the left showed me that nothing there
had been touched since I'd left. Mustard Seed's blade shone in
patches of light that came through the front windows.

And then, a subtle sound, a light scratching on the tiled floor of the scullery, alerted us, and Holmes seized my upper arm. A low, hulking shape detached itself from the shadows of the kitchen. Whatever it was began to pant like an animal. The panting turned into a low growling, which no human throat made.

Holmes yelled "Watson!" and pushed me aside as that dark shadow—too solid now—sprang at us, so quickly that its outline blurred. All I could see for certain was its glowing eyes. It brushed by me as I fell. A bestial roar came from it as it struck Holmes, its blow taking him off his feet and propelling him out the front door to roll down my steps and land with a thud. I came to my feet within the darkness of my study, my hands groping for the sword that lay across my desk. As I took up that awful blade, that beast took a cautious step toward the threshold, toward Holmes.

"You may leave the way you came or die," I cried, and the horrid shape turned from Holmes to face me.

Though it stooped low, I saw its form in the gaslight that came from the street: manlike, though fur-covered. The remains of men's clothing hung, tattered, from its powerful limbs. Beneath those fiery eyes, its savage jaws hung open to reveal rows of sharp, white teeth and a lolling red tongue that, I imagined, longed to taste my blood. Its physical composition, a sin against nature, radiated evil. Nothing like it had I ever seen in my worst nightmares. It stepped toward me on wide paws, not human feet. Its rear legs were like those of a giant hound or wolf, and it bent low, as though to spring once again—at me.

"What in heaven's name are you?" I whispered, bringing the sword before me into guard posture. In less than a second, I saw the beast more clearly in the light that came in through my tall study windows from the gas streetlamps outside. The face both fascinated and horrified me: it was as though a man had been turned partly into a wolf. Its face alone, I thought, could induce insanity, for it made no sense, except a hellish one. Atop its torso, the wolf mutation became more human: wide, powerful shoulders and long arms, with a man's hands, fur-covered and tipped with long claws.

Its robust musculature sent a wave of terror through me, for

I thought it must possess power far beyond any man's, and its speed I had seen already. No stroke of mine would be quick enough, nor did I have speed to turn aside and avoid its next rush. Those horrible hands clutched before it as though preparing to rend me to bloody ribbons. Only the length of Mustard Seed stood between me and ripping death.

CHAPTER FOUR

"The Feast of the Holy Innocents,"
28 December, 1888.

Taking a step back with my right foot, I eased the sword over my head and let my weight sink down into my center. Combat I understood, even if this was likely to be my last one.

I watched its eyes, intelligent but evil, gloating over me, its intended victim. Its terrifying speed, sharp teeth, and rending claws were pitted against my only hope: the edge of the sharpest blade ever made.

At the first scratching of its claws on the carpet, the sword and I moved as one, and all my weight, strength, and determination were behind the only blow I would likely get. I stepped into its charge to cut directly into its face in mid-spring. It was as simple an act as breathing.

That blade flashed in the gaslight and bit through the maw and the vile head behind it, my stroke cleaving its head, neck, and trunk. Though its claws sought to tear at my belly, its growling ceased with an odd whine, as though it were surprised by the sword slicing through its body, down and out its right side. Mustard Seed sheared through bone, muscle, and shreds of clothing. The creature's foul blood sprayed me and the room behind me. For a fraction of a second, its eyes widened in shock, and then the sections of its body came undone, and it landed in two pieces on the floor.

As I stood back to look at the horrible thing that I had just killed, a trembling shook my limbs.

"Watson!" Holmes cried, on his hands and knees in the doorway of my study. "I feared that you were lost."

46

Words would not come to me as I went to help him to his feet, retrieving his cane, which I had dropped when I first fell. I lit the gas lamp in my study as the whistles of constables sounded in the distance outside. Holmes and I stood over the grisly mess that lay before us, the second outlandish corpse I had seen in a twenty-four-hour period. The world of the occult had come home.

"My God, Watson, what a creature!" Holmes muttered. "My very thoughts stagger and reel to accept the witness of my senses." His body staggered, too, as he leaned against me, staring at the unbelievable sight before us.

"Holmes, am I to believe that it is a... a werewolf?" I whispered, finding the term to be distasteful on my tongue.

"It must be. The lupine visage, retaining just a hint of a man's shape," he mused in hushed tones, bending low, his hands searching for his magnifying glass in his pocket. "'O brave new world, that hath such people in't,' if 'people' or 'person' is the right word, Watson," he muttered. "Creatures of faerie and nightmare flock around us, it seems. What will we know tomorrow as real?"

He spoke my mind, certainly, for though I had responded to the threat that this thing posed to life and limb, I wished to doubt the evidence before my eyes. Yet I had inadvertently killed one so-called faerie creature and shook the hand of another who made that claim for himself. Perhaps I would need some of Raboud's expertise. I started to protest that I simply would not believe what I had seen, but then a new marvel occurred.

"Holmes, look," I cried, as the cloven corpse in its pool of dark blood shuddered and twitched and, with sickening speed, began to change. In less than a minute, what had been an over-muscled man and wolf hybrid became, instead, the sundered remains of a pale young man, none too healthy, judging by his pallor and overall filthiness. Patches of what had been gray-black fur turned into a clear ooze that soaked his clothing and mingled with the blood that soaked into the Persian carpet of my study.

"Sickening but fascinating," Holmes whispered, leaning down to touch the ooze, which he wiped off on the carpet quickly. "It tingles, Watson. I think we must be observing

47

something that William Rankine termed the conservation of energy and seeing a direct connection between the occult and the hard sciences. I wish Raboud were here to see this."

"Not a desire I share," I replied, nearly breathless. "Doubtless, this is another of his rare and beautiful creatures, yet one happy to rip out our throats."

"But, Watson, we witnessed it in as clear and deadly a laboratory as could be wished. He was not dressed as a monster. He was a man, then somehow changed his form, and, in death, reverted back to his normal shape, correct?" Holmes answered. "It leaves me at a loss for words."

"On the contrary, you've said a great deal," I answered, "though I myself have struggled. Our lexicon simply cannot help us. We have gone beyond what we think of as knowledge, certainly. That, by far, is the most troubling idea that confronts me now, even if we do have a bloody corpse on the floor before us.

"In the meantime, what do we tell the police?" I added, for I heard the shrill blast of constables' whistles closing in on us.

"Clearly a case of self-defense, though against what and for what reason, I am at a loss to say," Holmes muttered.

In the next seconds, the first of the Old Bill stomped through the front garden.

"'Ere! What's all this, then, Jimmy?" the first constable through the door cried.

From Spring Heeled Jack, to an irrationally embittered occultist, to gypsies and then a werewolf, indeed I wondered what it all was.

***

However, the police were happy to see the matter as self-defense. They weren't shy about piecing him back together to identify him. And one constable knew him immediately.

"That's young Arnold Pinder, what we wanted in the murder of that gypo fella just last week," he cried.

The "gypo" comment struck a chord in me, but I let it go as too far-fetched a connection to the Traveler murders. Common knowledge held that murder was a regular occurrence in the Romany camps. I could not rush to the conclusion that Pinder was wanted for the murder of one of Cameron's people. It left in me a shadowy wondering at that possibility, though, given all that had happened this day.

My attacker being wanted in connection with a murder, the Metropolitan Police were quite willing to accept his attempt on my life. And, while the matter of his death was extreme in their eyes, they poked about the bloody ruin of his clothing and found a garroting wire rolled in one trouser pocket, which they took as proof that he'd sought to kill me. The constable grew quite comfortable with Holmes's suggestion that Pinder had been "stabbed" as he attacked me. "Really well stabbed," I think, was the wording that pleased them all.

Pinder's remains were removed and his belongings taken to Scotland Yard for the evidence bin. Although his loose change was pocketed, there was one rusty-looking medallion that had been around his neck—I'd sliced the chain in two—that they set aside, along with his papers, "in case we find a next of kin," the constable added with a sudden solemnity. And we were released.

***

That evening at Baker Street was quiet and strained, with Holmes saying little if anything. I said less, thinking of the warning the Camerons had given me. If I told Holmes about it, I risked confusing the issues before us. If Holmes took the Travelers' warning seriously, as I imagined he would since he'd listened carefully to the case they'd put before him, he would likely tell me that I should stand down from everything and avoid the chance of disaster. These were weighty matters for me, for the witness of my own senses and a strong intuition informed me that the world of the occult and all it contained was real and active, enough so to take my life or Holmes's. So I could not abandon the challenges that faced me. At length, I decided that I needed to be honest with Holmes, especially in the face of all these occult matters.

"By the way, Holmes," I added before going off to bed, "I had a visit from your Traveler fellow Cameron and his son while on my way home earlier."

"Really, Watson? To what end?" he asked.

I told him in detail about our meeting in the Lamb and Flag. His keen eyes searched my face and hands, looking, I supposed, for any sign of my state of mind. I tried to make my face impassive and keep my hands still, posture relaxed.

At length, when I had finished my tale, he smiled and said, "Given Raboud's attitude toward you, old fellow, it might well be a warning to take seriously, even if it is born of this Jamie Cameron's supposed psychic power. At present, I cannot dismiss such warnings as I might once have done.

"I have entertained a similar thought about connections between Raboud's mage and the Traveler murders. Time will need to tell, in that matter. I've thought more, though, about the choice you need to make about the Logres Society, whether it has earned your respect enough that you still wish to join it."

"I am inclined to do no less than honor the commitments I have made in good faith," I said.

"I see no dishonor in avoiding ruin, Watson."

"And I see no honor in giving way to these occult-based threats, Holmes, nor in abandoning my colleagues to face them without me," I replied.

"As I understand it, the only satisfactory method that the Logres Society has for releasing people from its service," Holmes said, his voice quiet, "would free you from the burden of such a dishonor."

"How's that, Holmes?"

"To have your memory wiped clean of all that you have done in connection with Department Zed and the Logres Society, of all those you have known in your association with it," he whispered.

"Can such a thing be done?"

"Raboud can do it, or so I'm told," Holmes replied, his eyes meeting mine. I returned his gaze, wondering how such a thing could be done. I knew that it must involve magic. It was a sobering thought, one that had several attractions. Ignorance, especially of zombies, Moriarty, and Anne Prescott's death at my hands, might well be bliss of a kind.

"It would free you from any connection to this or to the Travelers' case and would remove the threat of ruin along either path," Holmes added.

"What? And give up all of this that I'm learning about magic?" I said, forcing a laugh.

Holmes smiled but would say no more. Perhaps he recognized my attempt at humor as a bluff. The idea of someone—especially Raboud—toying with my memory sickened me.

I retired to my bedchamber with the knowledge that if I did take the choice that Raboud's treatment offered me, it would cost me Mary as well as Holmes, for my association with Holmes had introduced Mary into my life. My choice had been made, it seemed, since I could not conceive of a life separated from either of them.

***

I did not know what time it was, but my room was dark except for a dim light that crept under the door. My dreams had been of the ruin my choice would make me face, and my sleep had been light because of them. I woke with ease when my window slid open: the curtains billowed out and let in a cold draft. I heard the soft thud of feet landing on the floor. I sat up, alert, and the heavy curtains parted. There, in the dark, stood Mary before me, clad only in gossamer veils that hid none of her desirable charms. She smiled at me and extended her arms, but I knew that it could not be she, as much as I desired that reunion. Mary coming in through a window made no sense. Alarms sounded in my head, and I sat up.

"Dressed so, in winter, Mary?" I murmured in a harsh voice, and in that instant the vision changed. Mary's shape wavered before my eyes and became Anne Prescott, her dark hair falling over her naked shoulders, her hands, too, reaching out to me. She came to me as she had on the only night we were lovers, silent, a sweet scent about her.

"How... what spell is this?" I murmured, feeling overcome by the wonder of this dream.

"Watson," she murmured and sat down on the bed at my side. Her hands caressed my face, making my skin tingle where she touched me, and she whispered, "Hush, my love."

"Watson! Beware!" Holmes cried, striding into the room, dressed as though to go out, his cane raised to strike someone. In that instant, Anne rose to her feet, her lithe form clear to me in the light from the sitting room. She gave a short, hissing scream, pulled her arms close to her body, and turned quickly on the very spot where she stood. Then she was gone, and both Holmes and I stared at the spot where she had been, now as empty as the night. He stood breathing hard, setting the cane down to rest his weight on it and wincing at the pain in his knee.

Then he went to the window and threw open the curtains, asking me, "What did you see?"

"It was Mary, first, then became Anne. Anne Prescott, in the flesh," I murmured. "But you must have seen her as well. She... no, I must have been dreaming. Why did she call me Watson, not Jack?"

Holmes ignored me and bent to examine the window lock and the sash. "Did you leave this window open before you retired?"

"No. No, I didn't. Holmes, was I only dreaming?" I asked, finally coming to full, sober wakefulness out of the intoxication of that vision.

"Dreams do not use windows, old fellow," he muttered, stooping down to the spot upon which Mary's and then Anne's tender, bare feet had stood. "Nor do they leave a tingling residue on the floor."

"You saw her, then, surely," I said, knowing that he must have, "for the light had illumined her before she..."

"Before she disappeared?" He finished for me. "No, Watson. I did not see Anne Prescott, but I'm relatively sure that you did, or were given to think you did. I saw a wan-looking creature, thin, with white hair flowing around an elfin face."

"What? What is happening, Holmes? And why are you dressed to go out? Is it morning already?" I asked.

"It is morning, very early. About three, I think," Holmes replied. "Guthrie has come for both of us. Get dressed for action, old man. I will fill in the missing details on our way."

"On the way to where?" I asked, tossing aside the covers and rising. If Guthrie were here to get us, something—a zombie rising, perhaps—had been reported, and we were needed in the field.

I dressed as quickly as I could, in my black greatcoat and bowler, being sure that I had my sword at my side, with a truncheon and my heavy pistol. I took long enough to jam some extra bullets into my coat pocket before I rushed out into the cold and into the black brougham that stood at the dark curb in front of 221B, Wiggins in the driver's seat and Brewer at the head of the horses. As soon as my weight hit the carriage step, Brewer leaped aboard and Wiggins whipped his team into motion.

Within, I took the seat next to Holmes and Magnus Guthrie. On the opposite side of the carriage, I saw Dibba Al-Hassan and the fair-haired, French youth—a man of perhaps thirty—whom I had nearly knocked down the day before. My discussion with Holmes about the appearances of Mary and Anne in my room would have to wait.

"Where are we bound, gentlemen?" I asked, rocking as the carriage made a sharp left.

"The Alhambra Theatre, Leicester Square," Guthrie said. "We've another go at catchin' Spring 'Eeled Jack."

"What? Another one?" I asked.

"There have been several sightings this year, further north," Holmes said, "though we seem to have an infestation of afreets."

"My master is there. He dispatched me to get help," Dibba said.

"And, if I may know, who is this pleasant young fellow, and what is he doing here?" I asked, pointing to the young Frenchman.

"Watson, Dr. Raboud's man Dibba Al-Hassan you have met, but please allow me to introduce you to Monsieur Jean-Louis Dupain, Vicomte de Repaix," Holmes said. "Raboud's student."

"We have met, after a fashion," I said, and extended my hand to the lad, who took it in a good grip, though I noted that his hands were soft, like a scholar's. "I am pleased to know you, sir. I must confess that I am surprised to see you again, especially in this capacity."

"I am excited to join your team, Dr. Wat—"

"That'd be 'Captain' to you, boy," Guthrie growled, insisting on his military understanding of our relationship. No matter his rank, Guthrie sees himself as a sergeant and me as his captain. "And you ain't part of this team, yet, far as I know." Guthrie, who was often taciturn when turned out in the middle of the night, seemed to take particular exception to Dupain, though I saw no real reason for it. Something else must have prejudiced him against the fellow.

"Watson," Holmes interjected, "as part of his willingness to support you for membership in the Logres Society, Dr. Raboud has stipulated that you are to take on his pupil, our young vicomte here, as your protégé in this investigation. He is to hone his skills under your command. If you—we—are successful in finding the foe who operates against us, Raboud will add his full support to your membership. I urge you to take it as an olive branch."

"An olive branch," I repeated, thinking it odd that my path to ruin would begin with magical visitations and offers of peace from a man who had treated me with harsh disdain. However, I would not ignore a summons from Department Zed, so I kept my seat and gave some thought to my new protégé.

"And what are your skills, lad?" I asked, wondering how I was to help this soft-handed young gentleman.

"I am sensitive to occult forces at work, which was how I was able to detect that a faerie creature was nearby when we were in Miss Irene Adler's dressing room at the theatre after the show," Dupain said.

Holmes did not even bat an eye at the familiar name "Irene Adler," but I started when I heard it, remembering that upon her recent marriage she had become Mrs. Godfrey Norton. Could it be that my Mary kept company with the infamous Miss Adler? I could not bring the matter up in the present circumstances, at any rate. I pursued my questioning of my new helper.

"And I am to train you as a member of my team because you know when magic is going on? I do not see how working with us will help you. Do you?"

"I am to take my place soon in the retinue of Chancellor Otto von Bismarck, as his occult advisor, and though I have studied extensively with Dr. Raboud, I lack, as you English say, the ability to 'think with my feet.' Perhaps Dr. Raboud wishes to expose me to encounters that are, um, more urgent."

"Perhaps you mean 'think on my feet,' lad," I said, "which you will have to do. And it will involve getting your hands dirty, as well, if we get a chance to catch another of these creatures. Spring Heeled Jack is stronger than both of us put together but as delicate as an orchid, according to what we have witnessed. I hope you can do more than sense magic. Can you cast spells, for instance, to stop a moving target?"

"I have no such skill, *mon capitaine*, but I did not know, sir, that you were an adept in the hermetic arts," Dupain observed with a smile on his face.

"I am not," I said with perhaps more force than necessary. "What makes you say such a thing, sir?"

Guthrie looked at me, his eyes searching my face. Dibba nodded and added, "Yes, *efendi*, I too can recognize the sweet scent of it about you still."

"I—well, it seemed so obvious to me," Dupain stammered. "Just now, I detect in you the power of contact with the realm of faerie. Such workings stay with you, like a—how do you say—"

"Like a tingling residue?" Holmes said.

"Yes, for when a faerie is summoned into this world, he must make for himself a shape, often, and..." He stammered to a halt, for I stared hard at him, as did Holmes.

"It takes a powerful man to make such a summons, however, Monsieur Dupain," Dibba said, "and I think someone that powerful would be better able to cover it. Yes, no?"

"I did just have a... visitation," I admitted, "but I am no such practitioner. What do you know of this practice? Why would someone work this sort of spell, or hex, or whatever, on me?"

"I—I only know what I have learned in my studies with Dr. Raboud, who is capable of such magics," Dupain replied, his voice unsure. "But if you could tell me what you saw, perhaps... ?"

"I witnessed the living presence of two women, both beloved, but one who is yet alive and another who is dead," I admitted. "I cannot speak for what Holmes saw."

"A lover, come back from beyond, perhaps?" Dibba asked, a smile showing through his heavy beard.

"I did not see either of the women Watson did," Holmes said. "I saw a diaphanous, feminine shape with flowing white hair and large, luminous eyes."

"And you, Dr. Watson, saw... ?" Dupain said.

"One woman I know, changing into another," I said, wishing to avoid any mention of Mary or of Anne Prescott. Dupain closed his eyes and ran a hand through his thick hair. He didn't say anything for a moment, and the carriage rumbled on. My curiosity was getting to me, for thus far, Dupain's explanation for what I saw and what Holmes saw was better than anything I could come up with.

At length he said, "It—she, I should say, for it was a feminine creature, as Mr. Holmes agrees—sounds like one of the *sidhe*. The *leanan sídhe*, perhaps, to be more specific, though who could have wished such a thing on you I could not say. Do you know of anyone who wishes you harmed or taken out of the way?"

"No," I said, though I was forced to think of the other occult creatures I'd faced recently. "Is this sort of faerie harmful?"

"Yes, yes, indeed. If it was a leanan sídhe," Dupain answered with a vigorous shake of his head. "She is said to seduce men with her charms and feed upon their life forces, as the wampyr feeds on blood. I must consult with Dr. Raboud about this further. I might be in error."

"We must table this discussion for now, gentlemen, for we are at the Alhambra's rear entrance, if I am not mistaken," Holmes said, leaning past me to look out the window. "Dibba, will you lead the way?"

"Most certainly, *efendi*," he replied. "They are together under lock and key, for there were no others in the theatre when I left them."

Dibba shouldered through a heavy entrance door, breaking out its lock and the jamb itself to let us into the building. "I fear that I will owe these good men a new door. I was forced to lock all doors when I left, to protect my master and his charming friend from any other harm. I think this afreet is still in the building." The sounds of a whining growl came to my ears as we rushed into the dark. Grinding, tearing noises I heard as well. I cast a look at Guthrie. In the light of the lamp he held high, he mouthed, "Jack's claws." He pantomimed the raking of claws on wood, and I shuddered at what we might find if Raboud and Miss Adler had been between those talons and the wood.

Dibba led us straight to a stout door, not far from the rear of the stage, upon which was stenciled "Manager." The creature had heard our steps, I'll warrant, for he was gone. It was a heavy door—to keep the cash box safe, I presumed—but its exterior surface bore deep gouges up and down its length. Spring Heeled Jack's claws had failed to penetrate it.

"Dr. Raboud!" the dweraz called in a bellow that boomed through the empty theatre. "We are here. Please, open the door!"

A woman's voice called, "Coming!" And after the shooting of various bolts and latches, the door opened. Clearer light spilled out onto the rigging and props behind the curtain of the stage, illuminating our faces and showing us the enchanting image of Irene Adler in a blue silk dressing gown, her chestnut hair loose and falling around her shoulders. Guthrie uttered an appreciative "Well..." at the sight. In her right hand, she held a small pistol of heavy caliber, a derringer. Its hammer was back, and she had been ready to use it. Behind her, Omar Raboud sat on the floor, his head in one hand while the other propped him up. He looked sweaty and drawn, and he was breathing hard.

I rushed into the room to Raboud's side, Dibba across from me, letting his master's weight sink into his arms. I scanned him for injuries and searched for his pulse. Raboud did not resist my "mere barber's" efforts. The pallor, the sweat, and his rapid breathing suggested that he might well be suffering from some coronary malady, but his pulse was steady enough that I put his collapse down to overexertion. And yet, in such a small room, I didn't see how he could have exerted himself in a physical activity that would have weakened him so, unless it was within a carnal embrace of the lovely Miss Adler herself. Somehow, I doubted it.

"Mrs. Norton, pray tell us what has happened," Holmes said, studying the scene before him. She looked at me and smiled when Holmes used her married name. That much told me that Mary had indeed been in her company. I could only pray that O'Hara still guarded my wife.

Then we all looked at the floor, where four small cubes of polished stone were in a rough rectangle in front of Raboud. They gave off a dim glow, but otherwise nothing seemed amiss in the room; there was no sign of any struggle.

"Dear Dr. Raboud sought to protect us from that Jack fellow, who only just left the door seconds before I heard your footsteps coming along the corridor," she explained. Her voice, though rushed, held no note of hysteria or terror. "After Dibba left us, we thought ourselves quite safe in this room. Then, not long ago, that thing found us. I thought it would tear the door to pieces and do the same to us, once it got inside. I think Omar sought to cast some spell to protect us in case it broke open the door.

"And you need not refer to me by that name, Mr. Holmes. I am no longer the wife of Godfrey Norton, although that name comes in handy from time to time." She managed a grim smile at the last bit of information.

"My apologies, madam," Holmes said. "Watson, can he be moved? We need to search this theatre."

"I can move him," Dibba said, starting to scoop up the frail occultist.

"No!" Raboud cried, struggling out of Dibba's grasp. He rose to his feet, though unsteadily, and said, "We must capture him. He... he is too..." With those words, Raboud passed out again. Dibba had him in an instant.

"What has happened to him, Miss Adler?" I asked.

"He placed those stones on the floor and started mumbling something I could not understand. The effort seemed to cost him so much that he was on his hands and knees. Those stones actually started to glow, but Omar became so weak that he could do no more."

"I have seen him use these before, though I know little of the theory behind them," Dupain offered. "But he was just too weak to manage it, I fear."

"We will look into it later," Holmes said. "Dibba, bring him along, will you? Miss Adler, we will need your knowledge of the theatre's layout to help us search. Along the way, I hope you can shed some light on your meeting here with Dr. Raboud."

As we left the room, I went in front, with Holmes at my side and Irene Adler just behind us. Guthrie served as rear guard for the laden Dibba and young Dupain. Out on the boards of the broad stage, we stopped, for Irene explained, "During my last song, I could not help but notice some disturbances in the box seats up to the right." She pointed to the highest row of scarlet-and-gold-trimmed alcoves above us. The house lights were down, except for one lone gas lamp near the main doors, so the chambers above us were dark. "I heard some men shout, there were sounds of a scuffle, and then a woman screamed. Right after that, a pistol went off in the same vicinity, and the theatre began to clear. I was rushed off the stage to my dressing room upstairs, and there, of course, were Dr. Raboud and his associate. There were police constables rushing about, adding to the chaos..."

"You said 'of course' about finding Dr. Raboud in your dressing room. Was he there by prior arrangement?" Holmes asked. I was wondering the same thing, for I had not thought of Raboud as the type to be in the company of theatre people, especially this infamous American contralto.

"Yes. You see, I had some correspondence which he needed," she said, as though this idea were mundane. "I think it is time that you come to understand more about me, Sherlock. But I gather that our attacker, though lured perhaps by the number of whores in the alcoves, was really after me."

"How did you reach that conclusion so quickly?" I asked.

"The Alhambra has," Holmes interjected, "since its reconstruction several years ago, become a popular trysting place between young, rakish West End gentlemen and the more polished of the prostitutes in this city. You recall Clovis Peters and Mary Kelly, perhaps?" To Irene Adler, he made a different point: "I wish to know more, when we have the time, about your arrangement with Dr. Raboud. Now, however..."

The matter of our discussion was interrupted by an inhuman shriek that came from the upper alcoves on our left, behind us. Miss Adler turned and got off a shot with her derringer. The report nearly deafened me, and I was amazed that she actually hit the afreet as he leapt from the second row of private boxes to the stage, some forty feet or more. However, the shot was not lethal: Spring Heeled Jack fell upon Guthrie from behind and knocked him flat. We all spun in that direction, and I took out my truncheon and moved to the stage apron to cut off Jack's exit into the seats. He took very little note of me or of Holmes, who put himself between Jack and the other stage exit. In the meantime, the afreet, nearly seven feet tall, stood glaring at Miss Adler with undisguised lust on his cartoonish face, apparently eager to leap at her. He mumbled words in a tongue I could not understand. Dupain stumbled back into the curtain and fell in its folds as Dibba, placing Raboud on the floor, stepped out to confront the creature.

Raboud's servant placed himself directly in the path that Jack would have to take to Miss Adler. Jack's right thigh was bleeding, but he moved as though pain meant nothing to him. And as he moved, Dibba spoke to him in a language that was full of hissing sibilants, the tongue of the afreets, perhaps. I again could not tell what was said, but it was clear from the afreet's rough responses that he thought little of Dibba's ideas.

A movement high and to my right caught my eye. Someone else lurked in the box from which Jack had leapt. I took out my revolver and moved so that I could glance up without turning my head.

Dibba's tone crooned on as he apparently sought to calm the creature. Jack only shook his head as though to rid himself of the sound of his own language. Then he spat blue flame a yard in front of him and raked his clawed hands through the air, as though warning Dibba. At the same time, the curtain in the box moved to the side, and an arm, therein, aiming a pistol, lifted from the shadows. It could have been aiming at Raboud or Holmes, but it wasn't pointed at me, until I shouted, "You, in the box! Drop your weapon or I'll fire!"

At the same time Jack leapt, the pistol on high turned in my direction and fired. The bullet dug a gouge into the wooden floor of the stage as I leapt off the apron. Firing back, I saw my shot go high, for the curtain jerked at slightly more than head height, I thought. At the same instant, I marveled at the afreet's leap, which crossed much of the Alhambra's spacious stage in one bound. He fell toward Dibba from the height of ten feet at least, but when Dibba caught the fellow in his huge hands, both Raboud and Dupain cried out. Spring Heeled Jack collapsed in the hands of the dweraz, dead. He dangled like a marionette from Dibba's upraised arms, though he had been struck no blow. With my pistol trained on the shooter's last location, I watched for any shot in return, though none came, and a door, somewhere, slammed shut.

No one on the stage moved except Omar Raboud, who had risen to his hands and knees to cry out, "No!" in tones of deep anguish. He collapsed in tears and covered his head. Instinct forced me to his side, so piteously he called, but I could do nothing to comfort the poor, frail man. As I sat at his side, bidding him take deep breaths, Holmes joined me.

"Watson, did you get a look at the gunman?" he asked.

"I saw only his arm and the pistol," I said, taking Raboud's pulse. It was rapid but constant.

"We had better get up there," Holmes said, and made his way off the stage, to limp up the aisle and into the box seats. I caught up with him in seconds when Dibba came to hold quiet words with his master.

"Turkish tobacco," Holmes whispered, sniffing the still air in the dark at the rear of the box. Only one door to the box seats stood open, and I reached it first, Holmes hobbling along in my wake. With pistol drawn, I entered the dark box, in which the velvet seats had been overturned. Holmes came behind me, fumbling in his pocket for matches. He lit the single gas lamp on the rear wall of the box.

"Careful, Watson. We must look for evidence."

At my feet, I saw a man's hat and picked it up. It bore a damaged brim where, I supposed, I'd inadvertently shot it off the fellow's head.

"Here, Holmes, what do you make of this?"

Holmes was on his hands and knees, picking up objects from the floor. He rose slowly, pains from his injured knee scoring deep lines of pain into his face.

"A homburg. Very fashionable, though ruined through your marksmanship," he mused. He turned it round and round, sniffing at the inner band. "Worn by a man who uses a tonic— rather a lot of it, judging from this—that is redolent of sandalwood. He, I suspect, was the man who smoked this cigarette, a Muratti, Turkish made, though widely used across Europe these days. And with him, a rather poorer fellow who smoked cigarettes he rolled for himself." Holmes held the hat in one hand and the cigarette butts in the other.

"Come, we must join our colleagues," Holmes said, and made his way back to the stage as I followed.

In the haste of our departure, I was denied the opportunity to ask Mrs. Norton, née Adler, about the whereabouts of Mary.

***

Back at Baker Street, Holmes and I wrote and submitted our reports of the incidences of the past twenty-four hours. These Guthrie gathered up and took to Gladstone in the hours before dawn.

I rested as much as I could, trusting that Commander O'Hara looked out for Mary's safety. I reflected that today, the fourth day of Christmas, marked the Slaughter of the Innocents. I found that ironic, given Raboud's sense of loss at yet another of his "gentle afreets." A rather large and important meeting was to be held at the Diogenes Club in the afternoon, where, Holmes said, I was finally to meet the highest echelon of the Logres Society in England. It looked to me as though the Logres Society, in London at least, found itself in crisis mode, for the urgent need for reports and the calling in of the small Department Zed team seemed as though they were expecting an assault. Even Wiggins and Brewer had taken up residence at Baker Street, having ordered their Baker Street Irregulars to scatter into the alleys and sewers of London.

Our lads drove Holmes and me in the growler to the Diogenes Club, where they were to make up a roving patrol of the Pall Mall area. Guthrie went with us to set up a rear guard in the walnut-paneled hallway of the Diogenes Club, where we met.

I was thinking that Raboud's stance toward me would be softened by the death of the afreet at Dibba's hands. Surely, he would see that the first afreet's death was not a matter of my doing. However, I would make no overt mention of it or suggest that Raboud owed me an apology for his abusive behavior when we first met, though, clearly, reality and common decency demanded it. Such actions should be unnecessary among colleagues. However, that meeting with the immediate leaders of the Logres Society showed me how wrong I could be.

At that gathering, I met the Sovereign of the Logres Society, Alfred, Lord Tennyson, the poet of great renown, whose works on the Arthurian legends had made him a household name. I found it oddly amusing that such a man would be the Sovereign of a society which took its name from King Arthur's legendary kingdom, Logres. Yet his stance in favor of women's rights, as well as his concern for the conditions of London's poor, made him, I thought, a fine choice to be "king" of this secret society.

A gentleman whom I learned was "Court Champion," John Fitzwilliam Clayton, Lord Whitefell, stood at Tennyson's side. Whitefell bore on his back an ancient sword in a battered scabbard, held in place by a green baldric draped across his strong torso. At the Sovereign's other side stood the Seneschal of the Society, the legendary Sir Richard Francis Burton.

Much to my surprise, though apparently not to Holmes's given his cool demeanor toward her, the adventuress Irene Adler stood among the elite of the Logres Society. In a day dress that matched the emerald of her eyes, she rubbed elbows with Sir Richard and Lord Tennyson as though they were old friends. Dibba Al-Hassan and Jean-Louis Dupain stood near Raboud. He started the meeting by determining that the leaders of the Logres Society should leave London as soon as could be managed, for occult forces had targeted its members in a manner that suggested a planned assault. Those least able to defend themselves should go into hiding, he concluded.

"Omar," Whitefell said, looking down at Raboud, "If there is a focused attack on us, surely we would have had evidence of it before now, beyond the few assaults reported by our agents in Europe and the Near East."

"If I may, my lord," Mycroft Holmes interjected, "intelligence has reached me that several more of our operatives in Berlin, Vienna, and Brussels have gone missing, along with their immediate families, and the disappearances are all linked to a similar time within the past two days. We are attempting to assess the damage, but I have put all of our operatives on the alert and sent into hiding as many of our associates as I have been able to reach."

"Begging your pardon, Lord Whitefell," Holmes interjected, "but there was an operative of, I think, German extraction who was at the Alhambra last night, perhaps two. One man shot at Watson, though his first aim was likely at Raboud, Miss Adler, or me, before my friend drew his fire. And we have evidence of another with him. His origin is pure guesswork, on my part, but we might well be seeing that human agents manipulate Spring Heeled Jack, which would point to a network.

"I think Raboud's caution is wise. Someone drew us there. Like as not, these Spring Heeled Jack incidents have been designed to call us out, to force us to expose our presence. Specifically. Someone knew that Raboud, at least, would be at the Alhambra last night, and I do not think their intent was less than murderous. Given the coordinated movements against us, near and far, I suggest that Dr. Raboud is right, except in labeling this movement as solely occult. Might it not be political as well?"

No one grumbled about it, for Holmes was right. Thinking of all I had been through since Boxing Day, I had the distinct feeling that someone or some group drew a noose about us that they intended to close by New Year's Day. The memory of the network that had apparently killed the folk of the Traveler clans came back to mind, yet I said nothing about it, since my suspicions had not facts to connect their case with the Spring Heeled Jack business. Holmes, too, would have that thought in mind.

Raboud added, "Two afreets have been held under spells of compulsion, with an intent to target Miss Irene Adler, I believe. She was a guest at the Cadogan residence when the first afreet was deployed, and she bore a letter that was crucial to my plan for learning the identity of the person at the heart of our opposition. Furthermore, yesterday, a Loup-Garou Curse was used in an attempt to kill Holmes, and I still contend that this man, Dr. John Watson, is the most likely suspect," Raboud said.

"I beg your pardon?" I asked, unsure that I should trust my own ears. Raboud went on as though I were not in the room.

"He bears a weapon of obvious occult status, as powerful as the faerie blade, Galatine, that Lord Whitefell bears as Court Champion. And my associate here, Dupain, tells me that even before coming to 'aid' us last night, he had summoned a faerie creature to do his bidding."

"Omar," Tennyson said, "we have all been briefed about this information, and those of us who know and value Dr. Watson think it more likely that he was the subject of an assault by some dark faerie force last night. That is his report. As for this weapon he uses, you have only to consult with Mr. Uyeshiba about its provenance. Mustard Seed, if it belongs to anyone, belongs to Mr. Uyeshiba. Will you not take a better view of Dr. Watson on the basis, at least, of my support?"

"Thank you, Lord Tennyson," I murmured from my place next to Lord Whitefell.

"Prudence dictates that I do not, my lord, and my dedication

65

to the defense of this Society and its members, I hope, makes my opposition just as important as any man's report, even yours."

"Steady, Omar," Lord Whitefell said in a low rumble at my side. Whitefell stood several inches taller than I, and even if he hadn't been wearing a legendary broadsword across his back, he would have seemed formidable. "By common understanding, we know that these compulsions of faerie spirits present a serious threat to this Society and all the good it can do, and there is no cause to think that Dr. Watson's being a victim of a loup-garou attack makes him the orchestrator of that threat. He would hardly attack himself, now, would he?"

"I contend that the loup-garou attack was meant for Sherlock Holmes," Raboud countered, "and this Dr. Watson knew that he had nothing to fear from such a creature when he had the weapon at hand to defeat it. Besides, he arranged for his estranged wife to be absent from the house when Holmes arrived. Dr. Watson merely mistimed his arrival. He may well be as bold and dangerous as he is clever and well-hidden."

"In that, Omar, you are in error," Irene Adler said. "I arranged for Mrs. Watson's absence, on a matter of an interior investigation ordered by Lord Whitefell."

"She has it right, Omar," Whitefell said.

"Be that as it may, my lord, no one on record has defeated a loup-garou with a sword—until Dr. Watson did. There are so many things happening around him that he is the obvious center of action, and he is nearly a complete unknown to us."

"He is not, to me," Holmes said. "He is not one to meddle in the occult at all."

"I will wager the same, though I have little history with the man," Irene said. "I have worked as a clandestine operative of Lord Whitefell at your very side, Dr. Raboud. I stand ready to trust Dr. Watson."

"But, Sherlock," Raboud replied, ignoring Miss Adler, whose presence at a Logres Society meeting was becoming less of a mystery to me, "by your own report, you state that Dr. Watson consorted with the Highland Travelers, known traffickers in hedge wizardry."

"They only sought to warn him away from a case wherein he faces grave danger to his person," Holmes said in my defense. "As far as I know, Dr. Watson has never had contact with the Travelers before. As for his loyalty, he has carried on with each task given him, far less concerned with his own safety than with the welfare of this Society and the people who serve under him in the ranks of Department Zed. And yet you stand ready to support the investitures of both Guthrie and O'Hara, who are far less well-known."

"'Ear, 'ear," Guthrie mumbled.

"But, sir," Dupain said, tugging at Raboud's sleeve, "Dr. Watson isn't likely to be an adept, is he, sir? Not really, erm, I think."

"What do you mean, Jean-Louis?" Raboud asked, turning to fix a swimming gaze on his young charge.

"Well, sir, if I may, I read the same reports of the Anne Prescott case that you did, and I think an adept would have been able to release someone from such a state of zombie possession, just as you could, sir. I remember you told me, when Mr. Sherlock Holmes wrote seeking your help late last summer, that you could do that," Dupain explained. Hearing it, Raboud dropped his gaze to the floor and stroked his smooth chin.

Those words unbalanced me like a rogue wave striking a benighted ship in mid-ocean. I nearly capsized. The enormity of what Dupain had revealed made me dizzy, but my outrage rose up in response, and my fists clenched at my side. *Last summer.* Had Raboud wanted to, he could have saved Anne Prescott. With his help, she might, even now, be on the road to living her own life in Edinburgh. She would not have been in my life, true, but she might well have lived.

"You... you could have..." I said, starting across the room toward him, though I had not commanded my feet to move. My fists shook, and something like murder must have been written across my enraged face. Holmes laid a hand on my shoulder to halt me, but I pulled him along after me.

"Easy, old friend. I would have told you, but—" Holmes started to say.

Dibba sprang in between me and Raboud, and I grasped at

Raboud over the huge shoulder of the dweraz, who would not meet my gaze. Raboud started backing away from my approach.

Then Lord Whitefell's hand fell onto my shoulder and held me fast. He whispered to me, "I'm sorry. It was because of me, my friend, that Raboud was unable to respond to Holmes's letter. We all knew it and could do nothing. He has only just recovered enough to travel. I'm sorry. Please, Dr. Watson. Let it go."

My anger was fruitless, I knew, but its tremors still gripped me, and I stood glowering at Raboud, who read well the expression of my rage.

"You see," Raboud observed behind the insurmountable Dibba, "even now, among us, he shows his capacity for violence."

"I have tolerated as much from you as I can, Dr. Raboud," I said through clenched teeth. "You allowed a sterling woman—and many other innocent men and women—to fall prey to the most hideous depravity. Were it in my power to make you answer for it—"

"John," Irene Adler said at my side. She turned my head to face her. "What you went through on behalf of Miss Prescott, the costs you have paid, they are beyond what most people have paid to be in this Society. Only Raboud knows something of how you must feel, for he has paid a similar price in his recent attempts to locate Whitefell's son. I know you cannot see it now, but in time, you will. Please believe me."

Greater men than I had been bested by her pleading emerald eyes and her soothing voice. Given that she had taken Mary from danger and was a trusted colleague of the Logres Society leaders, I knew to trust her. I extended her the same trust that I did Mycroft Holmes, though in the case I have called "A Scandal in Bohemia," she had deceived Holmes and me earlier this year.

"Please excuse my behavior, Miss Adler, gentlemen," I managed in a husky voice. "I will endeavor to be worthy of your patience and trust, and I will do what I can to prove myself a friend to... all here, especially after the protection you, Miss Adler, have given my Mary."

"Yes, well," she said, "It is the least I could do, given our situation."

Raboud continued to glower at me. He certainly was consistent, for though he faced the doubts of his superiors, he still focused his animosity on me. And I wondered: Could it be subterfuge on his part? He was the only adept with the ability to do the sorts of things that had been done, and no one suspected that he might be at the center of the network set against us. I did not know how to go about it, but I would sound him out, if a mere man could fathom the mind of an occult master.

CHAPTER FIVE

"In the Company of Innocents."

"Dr. Watson," Tennyson asked as Lord Whitefell helped him don his long coat, "might I have a quiet word with you before I leave?"

With a nod, I walked with Whitefell and the Sovereign into the hallway, whereupon the great poet turned to me. "I've read that your meeting with the Travelers was with Abel Cameron. Is this so?"

"Yes, my lord," I answered, "and with his son Jamie. The old fellow claimed that his son has the gift of foreknowledge, sir. The Sight, the elder man called it."

I said this lightly, expecting a chuckle or a smile. None came. Both Tennyson and Whitefell looked hard at me.

"Can you give me a description of the Camerons, Doctor?" Whitefell asked.

"Yes, of course. They were dressed in old, brown tweed suits, and they wore heavy brogans. I took them for tradesmen, sir—plumbers, perhaps—until I spoke with them. The elder is a stout fellow, with strong hands and a clear eye. Both are clean-shaven and have sandy-colored hair, though that of the elder is salted with gray. The younger man is a slimmer version of his father."

Both men nodded and exchanged a meaningful raising of eyebrows. Tennyson said, "I am heartened to hear you say so, for those sound like the very men with whom Whitefell and I have had dealings. I must tell you that I place a great deal of trust in what they tell me. While the Highland Travelers do not live

70

exactly according to our laws, they are a people with a great depth of knowledge behind them. Travelers have learned to live in the world with great harmony, which has given them special abilities and very important charges to keep. I urge you to heed their words and give due consideration to the threat that you are under.

"If you would, I'd like you to put yourself under Lord Whitefell's protection. He has lived among the Travelers and knows their ways. Regardless of Omar Raboud's current resistance to you joining our number, I would not risk your 'ruin,' as Abel Cameron put it."

Both men possessed a depth and solemnity that made me want to treat them with respect, but I reacted with a nervous haste to say, "No—I mean, yes, my lord, and I thank you. You honor me with your concern. However, I must not put myself under anyone's protection now, for I cannot walk away from this investigation at this point, regardless of Dr. Raboud's disdain or of some vague threat that others have somehow seen in my future. Leaving the field now, I mean to say..."

"It isn't in you, is it?" Whitefell said with a hard grin.

"No, my lords, it is not."

Tennyson stared at me, a sad look on his face, and said, "There are not many men who can stare destruction in the face and keep calm."

"I can't say that I can, either, my lord, until such time as I see it. But I cannot abandon Holmes and Guthrie, in any case, any more than they would me. I am that much a soldier, still: I fight more for the men at my side than for any cause, even the lofty one that the Logres Society represents."

Tennyson smiled and nodded his acceptance.

"They work out to be the same thing, I think," Whitefell said, "and in the dangers that threaten us, locally and abroad, we have great need of men like you."

With those words, they walked away.

I returned to the meeting room in time to see Holmes withdraw into a corner, Dupain at his side. They were smiling, and Holmes took something from the young fellow and placed it in his vest pocket, nodding his thanks. Holmes saw me and beckoned to me.

"Watson, did I ever tell you about my brief tutelage under Auguste Dupin?"

"No," I said, holding back my true thoughts, for Holmes had only spoken of Dupin as a hopeless bungler in his methods of detection.

"Before my brief stint at university, I spent a season in his home, and that is where I first met Jean-Louis, though he was just a lad. Has it been twenty years ago now?" he asked, turning to the handsome fellow.

"Nearly so: sixteen or seventeen years since you took leave of us. You have become all that Uncle Auguste was, and more," Jean-Louis said, smiling at Holmes. My focus traveled back and forth between them. Clearly, there was more of Holmes's history to learn, as far as this young fellow Dupain was concerned, and I was glad that the direction of the conversation flowed away from me.

"Tell me, Jean-Louis, how is your mother?" Holmes asked. "And why have you changed your last name?"

"Madame Céline is as well as she can be. Now she abides in greater comfort in our ancient estates in Repaix," Dupain replied, with a dip of his head and a slight blush of color on his fair cheek. "We took our older name again when we left Paris."

"I am heartened to hear of the return of good fortune to your family, Jean-Louis," Holmes said. "When I left you last, your family was in need. I was sorry to go."

"Yes, but we were fortunate. One of Uncle Auguste's last cases, serving the court of Frederick III, did great service to our station, and through that favor we were able to return to our ancient home, though reduced in means. Not all losses can be restored with a single stroke of good fortune, after all. However, that favor was to the Bismarck family, from which developed further connections. So here I am, hoping to finish my training and take up my place in Chancellor Bismarck's retinue."

"I hope that the time you spend with us helps you," I said.

"I am sure from your reputation, Dr. Watson, that my work

with you will help me learn to employ my few gifts," he said, giving me his brightest smile. His quick eyes searched my face. "The quest for justice follows many paths, and like all members of my family, I am deeply drawn to mystery. I look forward to this more active phase of my training, Doctor."

"'E'll need a good bit of toughenin' up, Cap'n Jack," Magnus Guthrie said, having joined our group. Irene Adler and Raboud, who had been in conversation over the letter she bore for him, had approached behind the bulk of Dibba and stood close. I gathered that we were about to receive our orders and steeled myself for Raboud's further disdain.

"I know that you are less than happy under my leadership, Dr. Watson, since I doubt your fitness. If you wish to leave our ranks, I am quite willing to offer you the sort of release that your knowledge of our work demands," Raboud went on. "I trust that Holmes has mentioned something of it."

"He has, Dr. Raboud," I replied with as much courtesy as I could manage, "but I assumed that if I chose to walk away from my work for the Logres Society, I might remain in Department Zed."

"That is not a choice open to you, for the good of the Logres Society. However, if you do wish to leave, I will take your memory of all that you have been through over the past year or more."

"You can do that?" Adler asked. "Rather, I suppose I should say, should you do that?"

"It has been done before, for the poet priest Gerard Hopkins, as you may recall, at his wish. And, I hope, to his greater ease in his decline," Raboud added.

"I had not realized that he chose that route," Miss Adler murmured. "God be with the poor man, but surely his melancholia and his physical decline made such a radical step necessary. Dr. Watson is a man in his prime, a man of great accomplishment, of value, to us and to society. Your procedure would estrange him from people who are of significant importance in his life, such as Holmes and Magnus Guthrie there, to say nothing of his wife. He has yet to celebrate his first anniversary, however much uncertainty he faces there."

"No. You may keep your magic," I said.

Raboud favored me with a half-smile and squinting eyes. Given my mood, I would have rejected any offer he made to me, even a generous one.

"As I thought," Raboud murmured, daring to draw close to me. "With each word, you reveal that I am right about you. Of course you would not give over your position. How else could you work within the ranks of my beloved Logres Society to bring it down?"

His obstinacy made my anger flare.

"If you think that I would voluntarily turn you loose to wreak havoc in my memory, Dr. Raboud," I said, "you are sadly mistaken. You were too weak to work your magics last night, and I doubt you could work them now, as you claim in your offer."

Raboud looked away and took a step back, acknowledging that I was right.

"You challenge me and sully my name and reputation in a community I respect," I continued. "I will remain in that company and offer you my services, yet I will demand the satisfaction of hearing your apology before this court when my word proves truer than your esteemed occult knowledge."

"Bravo, sir!" Dupain cried, his face flushed, stirred by my rebuke. His fist punched the air in youthful enthusiasm. His reaction sent a round of laughter through all there, except Raboud, who glowered at his charge, though he relented for once in his attack upon my character.

Turning to take all of us in sight, Raboud took his stance as our captain.

"Receiving Lord Whitefell's report of the Spring Heeled Jack incidents alerted me to the fact that some new occult adept was at work in London, though I did not realize the extent of the danger facing us at the time. Now, learning about the compulsions those afreets were under and learning about that person's ability to cast the awful Loup-Garou Curse tells me that we face someone who has sought to draw out members of the Logres Society, someone who uses dark powers in secret. Someone we have yet to identify, someone with many allies, it

seems. Someone, close enough to know of our movements, who
seeks to bring harm to our Society. We are each a key part of the
defense we must mount against this force.

"Doctor, I considered you and this weapon of yours the
source of any new occasions of the occult violence that has
occurred. Others here tell me that I might well have been wrong
about that. We shall see. It seems that you and I are very much in
each other's lives now. Be sure that I will sound your depths,
uncover your secrets, whatever I can learn. This I shall do even
though, as you force me to admit, Doctor, you find me in a
weakened state. If you stay with our ranks, you will bear the
burden of my doubt about this dubious sword of yours and about
your motivations. Yet I must trust you to lead this investigation,
especially since Sherlock Holmes still suffers from his injury."

I learned something about Raboud then, for he addressed
me, for the first time, in tones of something like respect. He was
cold and observant now, where before he had been angry,
contemptuous. I saw that he was a man who had the ability to
master—or at least disguise—his emotions. I could not tell
whether, having heard other opinions supporting me, he was
thinking about changing his attitude toward me, or whether he
thought me a great threat still. For my part, I had no secrets that I
would withhold from him.

"Your weapon, please, Dr. Watson," Raboud demanded,
again in the attitude of command.

"Surely you would not disarm a man whom you send on a
deadly mission," Holmes protested, leaning heavily on his cane
to take weight off his knee.

I handed my sword to the Egyptian. Raboud pulled Mustard
Seed partway from its scabbard and ignored Holmes's protests.

"You dispatched the loup-garou with your sword, Doctor,"
he said, his eyes large and still behind his lenses.

"Yes, though I had time to do nothing else. I feared that he
was about to set upon Holmes. I was not carrying my pistol," I
explained.

"Typical firearm ammunition would have no effect upon
one so cursed, if indeed what assailed you was a loup-garou,

what the English call a werewolf," Raboud said. "In fact, your sword should have proven ineffective as well. Perhaps if you had been wielding the sword Lord Whitefell carries, Galatine, one would have expected it to serve your need. It was made in the faerie realm long ago and is a bane to all enchantments."

"But surely, Dr. Raboud, this sword's sharpness made it suffice. It has no magical properties of which I am aware; it doesn't glow or vibrate or seem to have anything to set it apart from other blades," I replied.

"Of which you are aware, you say," Raboud said, something like a gleam in his magnified eyes. "Dark magical artifacts place demands on us. They feed upon our strengths, our abilities, our substance. They grant us abilities we do not have, but the abilities only stem from the black magic with which I charge you. Only a dark adept would know that, heretofore, no loup-garou has ever fallen to a sword's edge. That you were not killed in a werewolf attack could well argue that you are such an adept, wielding powers that are at your command."

"But, Dr. Raboud," Dupain broke in again, "wouldn't he have been more likely to have let the beast kill Mr. Holmes? Then his powers would not have been exposed."

"Perhaps you are right, Jean-Louis. But such a thought leaves us with the idea that if he is not an adept, he is a very different sort of man, our Dr. Watson, able to use so magical a weapon and not let it use him."

"Perhaps, Doctor, I am neither of those. Perhaps it was luck, training, and the keen edge of this weapon that prevailed," I countered.

"Nevertheless, it was a feat of magic—black magic, as I see it. I will expose you, sir. You may count on that."

I saw in his eyes that Dr. Raboud believed in his certainty. I did not understand why he would start his thinking about me in the place where he had, but I could not change the way he thought. I could see his logic, but it was the most maddeningly perverse logic, because it simply denied who I was, or who I thought I was. My one choice was to prove myself loyal to our cause and follow his orders.

"What do you need me to do?" I asked Dr. Raboud. It gave Holmes a smile, and it seemed to confound Raboud for a moment, though I did not intend it to.

At length, his hands shaking—demonstrating his uncertainty, I thought—he gave me back my sword and handed to me a letter with its wax seal broken.

"My powers, as you saw last night, are not where they should be. Since I cannot divine the identity of our foe with certainty," he said, fixing me again with his pointed gaze, "we must consult with those whose powers are, presumably, fully functional."

"Not Dupain?" I asked, wondering who else in London might be qualified. I hoped he didn't mean the Travelers, for I had no idea where to start the search for them. According to Holmes, they rarely stayed put long enough to be found.

"Ah, no. Dupain, though he is a skilled scholar, lacks the abilities of a true adept. I wish you to begin your search with a man who is in the midst of founding an occult order here in London, one William Wynn Westcott. This letter, from a powerful adept, will serve as your introduction to him. With the name of Anna Sprengel, you should gain his immediate trust."

"Who is Anna Sprengel?" I asked.

"My mother," Miss Adler said.

Holmes, rarely taken by surprise—within my hearing, anyway—let out a bark of laughter and asked, "What?"

"Sherlock," Raboud said, as Adler turned a wry smile toward my friend Holmes, "Miss Adler took great pains to collect this missive from her mother, a much-revered woman in my craft, to provide you and your team with an introduction that, I'm certain, will guarantee Mr. Westcott's assistance. I have been planning this stage of the investigation for days now, from as soon as I had my summons to come to London. Please try to follow along closely."

It was Holmes's turn to deal with Raboud's insulting manner. Raboud explained that we were to find Westcott and determine, with his help, if any practitioners in London had enough power to manage the sort of enchantments we had experienced. With Westcott's help, we were to carry on investigating any persons who set themselves up as agents of the darker arts.

It was sound procedure, I thought, but Holmes drew me aside and said, "I wonder if you might excuse me from this duty, Watson. I wish to have a quiet talk with Miss Adler. Besides, I might just slow you down. Please call for me later at Briony Lodge. Do you remember it?"

"Certainly, Holmes," I replied. "You need to keep off that leg for a time, anyway."

Miss Adler took Holmes's arm, smiling at me and saying, "Good luck, boys. We look forward to hearing from you later. And do not worry about Mary. You will see her again, when you come to Briony Lodge."

I returned Miss Adler's smile, thinking about seeing Mary again soon. However, I recalled that Miss Adler had taken my wife with her as part of an internal investigation ordered by Lord Whitefell. Yet Mary knew nothing of the inner workings of the Logres Society or of their mission, beyond my role in Department Zed. I saw no reason for Mycroft or his associates to question Mary, unless of course it was to learn more about me or to offer her a role in the Logres Society as my wife. Though that thought cheered me to a degree, I could not shake the vague sense of dread it left in me. Dread notwithstanding, I could only take the next step into uncertainty.

CHAPTER SIX

"Innocent Victim."

A bright sun warmed the chill air of the fourth day of Christmas as we journeyed by coach to the High Street in Ealing. Guthrie sat at my side, eyeing the Iron Chancellor's young protégé with disdain. With the slender Dupain seated across from me, next to the quite substantial faerie-being Dibba, I sought to get more familiar with my young charge.

"So, Jean-Louis, are you familiar with protocols for questioning people?"

"No, Monsieur Watson, I—"

"When we're in the field, lad, we refer to 'im as Cap'n Jack, see?" Guthrie interrupted him. Guthrie rarely took his eyes off the lad, unless it was to engage in some jest with Dibba. Those two had become fast friends, the marine and the dweraz, though I could not see how it came about. Guthrie accepted Dibba's explanation of himself as though they were of the same regiment. But Guthrie remained cool to Dupain.

Dibba cast a sidelong look at Dupain and smiled. "Yes. Cap'n Jack, we name him."

"Our intent must remain foremost, as well as the secret nature of the Society we represent," I said, ignoring Guthrie's point of order. "We must not be rude or forward, except to the point of our need. Westcott is a person of some importance, and his reputation as a Crown coroner is one I've even heard of. If Frau Sprengel's letter has the desired effect, he must be made to see us as trusted agents of those in higher positions of power."

"Which we are," Dibba caroled with enthusiasm.

"Indeed, sir, though we must not name them," I said, urging caution. "And we wish to learn the name or names of any of his acquaintances in the magical community who might be this dark mage, as Raboud calls him. Dupain, let him speak freely. As Holmes has taught me, sometimes letting a man simply speak his mind without pressuring him lets him reveal more than he might wish to. We must remember that the person we seek may be a trusted friend of his whose dark practices are not out in the open."

"Ah, yes, *mon capitaine*," Jean-Louis replied. "We let him tell us more than he would reveal, yes?"

"Something like that," I said. "We must not allow anyone to know of Miss Adler as the daughter of Anna Sprengel, for fear of that information becoming public. In keeping that secret, we help Miss Adler maintain her public persona and her clandestine status with the Society."

"She is a most beautiful woman, so strong in herself, yes? No?" Dibba said with a wide smile. "What a lover she would be."

Guthrie chuckled at this, and Dupain blushed as he smiled.

"I daresay that we can think of her in better terms than the merely physical," I murmured, stilling Guthrie's laugh. "She is a woman of consequence and untold worth as well as a colleague we must hold in high esteem—though that auburn hair, those eyes, like green jewels—well, never mind."

Dibba shared a wide smile with Guthrie, somewhat at my expense, and said in solemn tones, "Yes. And we must not mention her statuesque figure, no?" I was forced to nod *yes* to this statement of truth, though I refused to say more. Guthrie and Dupain laughed loudly at this until I was relieved by our arrival at Westcott's address.

As we made ready to exit the carriage, Dupain put out an arm to stop me.

"Something is wrong, *mon capitaine*," he hissed. "My mind... itches. A magical work goes on within. I can feel it, and it is dark." He took a step out to the running board of the brougham in which we rode, looking like a pointer about to flush game. He shook his head as though it pained him to do so. "Dr. Watson, it is horrible," he whispered.

"Could it be Westcott himself, in some of his private resear—" I started to say.

Then the sparrows that flocked in the tall hedges for warmth erupted into the air around us in panicked flight. The door to the Tudor home opened abruptly, and two women bolted from it, falling to their hands and knees in the front garden. They were oblivious to our presence, for they looked back into the house as though they expected some horror to reach out and claim them.

"I go first," Dibba rumbled and leapt from the other side of the carriage, pelting toward the open door through which the women had fallen.

"Guthrie," I cried, "take Dupain and get those women clear. Then look for a back entry while I go in after our friend."

Unhooking Mustard Seed from its hanger as I ran, I raced forward on Dibba's heels. This dwarf was quick and remarkably agile. Three steps at a time, he cleared a staircase that emptied into a sitting room. I heard cries of pain as I followed Dibba. Someone upstairs stood in extremis: cries of excrucied terror were being torn from a man's constricted throat.

Dibba found the correct door as I rushed to gain his side. It was locked. No matter: with one hand on the knob, Dibba leaned back and threw his shoulder against two inches of solid English oak. Guthrie or I would have rebounded from such an attempt. Dibba's massive strength shattered the door, splitting it in two and sending the halves crashing onto the hardwood floor of a gentleman's study.

I rushed in behind Dibba and saw, to my horror, a man— William Wynn Westcott, I was forced to assume—hanging in the air near the tall, cross-beamed ceiling, in the middle of the room, his arms and legs drawn out away from him. With straining limbs, he fought against what appeared to be mere swirls of dark mist wrapped around each limb, pulling with a strength beyond the capacity of Westcott to endure. I feared those smoky tendrils would pull the poor man into quartered

81

pieces, though I could not think how. Westcott struggled so hard
that he wasn't even aware of us, and his cries and grunts of effort
told us he neared the end of his strength.

Just looking at the tendrils sickened me. My nose and throat
nearly shut down at the burning stench. If putrid meat were
burned in a sulfurous flame, it might give off such a ghastly
smell. I fought the urge to turn and flee from the room.

Westcott's twisting and writhing in the coils of mist had
been frantic when we entered, but just then his movements
stopped, and his limbs looked ready to give way to the cruel
strength that pulled at him. I saw his left shoulder dislocate and
heard a pitiful bleat of agony escape his gaping mouth, just as
Dibba leapt for him. Like Spring Heeled Jack himself, Dibba Al-
Hassan sprang on high, and my mouth gaped to see it. He
grasped Westcott around the waist, muttering words in some
language I had not heard him use, but the misty tendrils of raw
power lashed out at him, wrapped him in their coils, and threw
him down. Dibba thudded onto Westcott's desk. He rolled off
onto the floor, a mass of loose limbs and dead weight. The room
shook when he hit.

Guthrie's familiar, heavy tread rushed through the door
behind me, and he slid to a halt, a single oath bursting from him:
"Bugger!" My disbelief at what I saw froze me to the spot, but
Dibba's assault had taken something away from the force that
attacked Westcott, for Westcott sagged in the air, dropping lower
and sighing. How could a man fight this sort of power that came
from nowhere, tearing, torturing, malevolent?

"Your sword, *mon capitaine*," Dupain yelled, coming in
behind Guthrie. "Strike at the mist!"

I had little faith that such an action would accomplish
much, but even as I took Mustard Seed out of its scabbard,
Dibba sat up on the floor, shook his massive head like a wet dog
and cried, "No! Wait!" I had thought him dead, by the way he
landed on the desk and hit the floor, yet his eyes were bright
with the knowledge of what to do.

From an inside pocket of his tweeds, Dibba pulled a small
pouch, which he tossed to me, crying, "The powder within,

Cap'n. Toss it over him!" And once more, Dibba's deep voice intoned a chant, in Arabic, I think, for the name of Allah was raised again and again, as though in supplication.

Pouring half the contents of the calfskin pouch, a grainy, white powder, into my right hand, I cast it high over Westcott's struggling figure even as the tearing mist pulled at Westcott's limbs with renewed vigor and the poor man cried out again. The powder's larger particles fell more quickly, and on their way to the floor, they tore holes in the mist. A keening sound erupted around us, though nothing I saw in that room made it. And, as the powdery cloud of Dibba's concoction floated down, blue fire danced around the swirling mists binding Westcott's twisting form.

The keening grew to a high-pitched scream that emanated from everywhere and nowhere. It tore at the very air of the room, but whatever made it lost hold of its victim. At the rising of Dibba's chant, the same blue fire glowed into greater intensity and leapt along the trail of the mist. When that fire enveloped the length of those tendrils, a boom shook the whole house. Dupain shouted as though in fear or pain. Westcott was released and dropped, limp and heavy, into my arms. We hit the floor hard, and I let him roll away from me.

Dupain rushed to his side as I sought to rise and give Westcott medical attention.

"He breathes, *mon capitaine*," Dupain whispered. "You saved him."

"If not for this powder of Dibba's, I fear Westcott would be dead." I turned to Dibba, whom Guthrie had hauled to his feet. "What was that, Dibba, some sort of flash powder?"

"No, *efendi*. It is a mixture of blue ginger and salt my master uses from an ancient volcano, Emi Koussi. Most helpful for dispelling unwanted spirits," he said, massaging his ribs, which I was sure had been bruised, if not broken, by his fall onto Westcott's desk.

"And that chant, was it some sort of counterspell?" I asked.

"Ah, no, good Cap'n. It was a prayer. What other hope is there against things so dark?" Dibba answered, and again, I found myself out of my element. Magic, prayer, faith, were all terms that I typically did not use. Yet I recalled how, in desperation, I had turned to prayer in moments of great need, though I'd never stopped to consider whether my prayers would be answered.

But Westcott groaned at my side and his eyes fluttered open, and my thoughts turned to helping him. His shirt untucked, tie askew, Westcott's clothing was soaked with the sweat of his exertions, as though he had run miles, and I didn't think him conditioned for it. Like most successful men of middle years, he had grown stout and comfortable. His right hand reached for his left shoulder, and he groaned with the aching of that dislocation.

"Dupain," I said, "let him down onto his back, and slowly lift his left arm over his head. Westcott, you must relax and be still." With Dupain's help, I guided the arm up and back, as my patient whimpered. A sudden pop, the shoulder moved back into place, and we eased it down to his side. Westcott lost consciousness.

With Westcott's worst injury cared for, I returned to trying to make sense of the horror I had just witnessed. "Wh-what sort of magical spell was at work here?" I asked, turning my eyes to Dupain and Dibba.

Dupain only shrugged, giving me a wide-eyed glance. Dibba said, "Not a spell or a charm, but an evil thing that attacked him, sent by a mage of great power. It must take great hatred, Cap'n Jack, for a man to strike a bargain with a being so evil."

"I-I've never witnessed anything so..." I tried to say more, but no words would come. I recalled only the smell of the dark entity that had been forced out of Anne Prescott when I took her life. It had been quite similar to the stench the mist gave off. This entity must be even more demonic than the thing that had held Anne in thrall. That memory was always with me, though I'd never thought of it in terms of magic.

Westcott groaned and his eyes fluttered open. In a hoarse voice, he managed to say, "Whoever you are, I owe you gentlemen my life—unless, unless—" He stiffened against me, his eyes widening in sudden fear that we were the ones who had inflicted torment upon him.

"Rest easy, Dr. Westcott," I said in a low voice. "We came, seemingly in the nick of time, though chance brought us, you might say. My name is Dr. John Watson. These are my colleagues, Jean-Louis Dupain, Magnus Guthrie, and Dibba Al-Hassan, who is most responsible for freeing you."

His eyes glanced at each face as I gave them names, though he was still too weak to nod. The poor man closed his eyes and rubbed his left shoulder. He yawned deeply and then sighed, struggling to rise. We helped him, and Guthrie brought a desk chair, into which the victim collapsed.

He said, "I do not believe in chance, gentlemen, especially not in this situation. I was attacked by magical powers. You have the witness of your own eyes to tell you that. I can only conclude that you are here by virtue of some other power, to which I am grateful."

As loath as I was to use the word "magic," Westcott was right. We had just witnessed a magical attack, one as sickening as it was brutal.

"We have good cause to believe you, Dr. Westcott, though, for us, our presence here comes as a matter of chance. Guthrie," I said, looking up, "be so good as to fetch this man a brandy. I see several decanters on the sideboard next to the gasogene."

Guthrie brought over a small glass of dark liquid and said, "I'll go and alert his missus that the crisis is over, shall I, Cap'n?"

"Indeed. Good man, Guthrie. Dibba, are you not injured, man?" I asked, amazed again at his strength.

"No, Cap'n. I am not so easily hurt as men are," he said, standing behind Westcott. At that point, I believed what I'd been told about him.

"Dr. Westcott, if I may turn to the reason for our fortunate arrival, we are here with a letter of introduction from a person whose name I think you will trust, Anna Sprengel," I said. The name caused the Crown coroner to open his eyes wide and sit up straight. I handed him the letter as he eased back in his chair. He opened it and scanned its contents repeatedly, shaking his head.

"Now I am sure that you have come guided by a protecting hand. I—I do not think any man in England, other than my close associates, knows that name," Westcott said after a moment. "I came by it through great effort, so I think that you represent parties I must trust. But, Dr. Watson, have I not heard your name before? You are a physician and sometime colleague of the infamous Sherlock Holmes, are you not?"

"Indeed, sir, you have it aright, and our other colleague is Dr. Raboud," Dupain announced, looking on with excited joy at Westcott's recovery. Despite my amazement at all I had witnessed, my sense of caution returned at Dupain's slipup. I could not let the matter of our superiors become known and was shocked to think that Jean-Louis had used the name of Raboud so freely.

"Dupain," I said, trying to keep the harshness from my voice, "perhaps you'd be so good as to assist Guthrie in seeing to the ladies." I spoke with as much sympathy as I could muster, given my impatience with him. "The appearance of a handsome visage like yours will be a comfort and delight to them."

His smile disappeared then, and a look of anger, almost, replaced it. Clearly, Jean-Louis Dupain was unaccustomed to accepting orders from a superior.

As Jean-Louis left us, Westcott asked in surprise, "Did he mean Omar Raboud of Cairo?"

"Yes. Dr. Raboud is his mentor," I answered, seeking to stick to strict facts and not reveal too much about our superiors. "We are here on his orders, seeking the identity of anyone you might think of as a dangerous practitioner of magical arts, and our visit is the first step in our investigation of related matters."

"If you are associates of that mage, I am grateful. Dupain is a fortunate young man," Westcott said. "I must congratulate him on his success and press him for a meeting with his tutor."

"So Dr. Raboud's is a well-known name in the, ah, magical community?" I asked.

"Yes, but again, I would think the Englishmen who know that powerful name are few, though I see four here who think of him as a colleague. Extraordinary. I hope you can grant me my request to meet him," Westcott said.

"It is not in my power to grant your request, but I will pass it along. Now, could you tell me about this attack you've suffered? Is it not likely that the practitioner of dark magic we seek is the one who assaulted you?"

"Again, I am not much given to seeing pure chance behind it all, but I have no knowledge of my attacker. He—or she—is hidden from me, though someone who hated me must have been behind that ghastly summons. I was merely reviewing some correspondence about the physical location of our new temple, and then that chthonic entity was upon me. And though I hate to acknowledge it, such a working, though dark, was done with great skill or great power.

"I assure you that my colleagues, Mathers and Woodman, are well-acquainted with the members of our order. We know the ways of their workings, and no one I know has been associated with a force as dark as what attacked me. It was pure malevolence, Dr. Watson, a force driven by and through anger, bitter, hard resentment—almost vengeance, I thought it as it came over me. Truthfully, I know of no practitioner adept enough to work with such a force, unless it is Frau Sprengel, herself, or Omar Raboud, neither of whom is associated in any way with such dark magical workings, if reputations count for anything."

His words rang in my thoughts. Raboud had not appeared to know Westcott or his colleagues Mather and Woodman, but Westcott revered Raboud's name and reputation. Yet Raboud held me in contempt. True, his "watchdogs" Dupain and the dwarf were to be with me, but he had assented to Tennyson's request, so I was forced to concede that Raboud was willing to seek whatever was good for the Logres Society. That thought left me strangely angered.

Unless, of course, it was Raboud who had deceived the members of the Logres Society with his "good" works. Perhaps, if Raboud blamed them for the damage that he was supposed to have incurred in Africa on Whitefell's bidding, he was seeking revenge. As yet, I knew nothing of the details of his injuries; the topic must have been sensitive, for no one had spoken openly about them. At the very least, this was an idea that settled some of the anger that had begun to boil within me. I determined, at least, to let my suspicion of Raboud remain, despite the vaunted opinion that everyone seemed to hold of the man.

All these thoughts occurred in a flash of a moment, and I forced myself back to the task at hand. "Can you think of any practitioners of magic, at all, who wish you or your colleagues ill?" I asked Westcott.

"There are those, like Sir Alisdair Scrymgeour, who have opposed the start of our temple," Westcott said.

"Good Lord! You don't say! Scrymgeour?" I repeated. "It is not an appealing name." Even Dibba burst into a chuckle at it.

Westcott added, "A Scottish nobleman, something of a hedge wizard, really, adept at charms and potions, but a full member of the S. R. I. A., the 'Societas Rosicruciana in Anglia.' Actually, though flamboyant and outspoken, not a bad fellow, by reputation of his work in the community, but he is the only person to publicly oppose me or my colleagues. He is adamant that we do not pursue forming a temple in Edinburgh, which is part of our plan: the first here, then in Cardiff, then in Edinburgh. Scrymgeour has started a heated campaign against us, and I do not know why. I have only just received a letter from him demanding an audience with me and my colleagues.

"I've thought him just a bit of a hothead, really. I never took his threats to oppose our mission seriously. With the sway he holds in Fife, he stands in the way of our order setting up a temple in the north, but, really, I never considered him a danger. He has been too public in his opposition to our new order, and I do not think that he could handle an incantation as complex as that which assailed me out of nowhere."

"Nonetheless, we will question him. Perhaps he has associates you do not know, sir," I said, as Guthrie and Dupain admitted the womenfolk into the room. They came sobbing to Westcott's side, anxious to help him. The poor man looked done in, and I cannot imagine what the sight of him under attack had done to the women who had fled from it.

Westcott told me that Scrymgeour planned to stay at the

Midland Grand Hotel near St. Pancras Station. I decided to give
over any more questions and let his family help him recover.

"I would urge you to stay as safe as you can in the coming
days. I do not know what will come of our investigation, but we
will get to the bottom of this. May I assume that you have means
of defense against any further attacks of this kind?" I asked. "Or,
perhaps, my associates here"—I gestured to Dibba and Jean-
Louis—"can assist you."

"Oh, ah, sorry, *mon capitaine*, but I lack the practical skill,
though I know it in theory..." Dupain muttered in apology. "I
will be glad to help, erm, in any way..."

"Thank you, but I will manage on my own. I have
colleagues who will come to my aid," Westcott replied around a
deep yawn. He needed his rest.

"Ah, yes," Dupain said, seeming to grow more anxious to
help, "but perhaps I can make you a sleeping potion. These, I
have mixed for Mr. Glad—"

"That will be all, Dupain," I said, interrupting him before he
gave away any more Logres Society identities. "Jean-Louis, we
will let the matter rest with Mr. Westcott." I took his arm and
propelled him toward the door.

"Of course, *mon capitaine*," he said with a curt bow,
delivered with a neck stiff with defiance. We would have words
about this, I vowed, though I was forced to wonder if they would
do any good.

"Guthrie, a word in private, sir?" I asked, motioning him to
join me out on the lawn, as Westcott's wife and housekeeper
comforted the poor man.

***

I sent Guthrie to find Holmes at Briony Lodge, or, failing
his presence there, in our rooms at Baker Street. Dupain and
Dibba I advised to return to Dr. Raboud and report our actions as
well as Westcott's request to meet him. Raboud's orders,
however, stood against my own.

"We are to be your constant companions, Cap'n Jack,"

Dibba responded, "for though my heart reassures me of you, my master does not wish you out of my sight."

"*Oui, mon capitaine*, those are our orders, though I am in agreement with friend Al-Hassan," Dupain added as we rolled away from Westcott's home. "You are seeking Alisdair Scrymgeour at the Midland Grand Hotel, as Westcott mentioned, yes?"

"Indeed, and I am willing for you to join me in that, though I think it unnecessary, given Westcott's description of the man. But I must warn you that I must have a private word with Holmes as soon as I can, to which neither of you will be party. Am I clear on that?"

"Of course, for Mr. Holmes is a trus—" Dupain started to say and then closed his mouth.

"A trusted friend, and I am not, at least where Dr. Raboud is concerned?" I finished for him in words more heated than I had intended. "You are correct. And you will do well, young sir, to follow my orders promptly and take greater care about breaking the trust of Logres Society members and their identities. Do I make myself clear?"

"*Oui, mon capitaine*," Dupain said, blushing and dropping his glance to the carriage floor.

"Please, *efendi*," Dibba said, "forgive my master and his servants. The master's ways are peculiar, but I, for one, learned long ago to trust him, even if I fail to understand him. As for my young friend here, I have faith that he will try harder to contain his enthusiasm. We will have no problems about your words with Mr. Holmes, and you may do so in the tiniest whispers." Dibba clearly wished to give me a sense of ease.

"I apologize for my foolish behavior, *mon capitaine*," Dupain said in low tones. "I am too eager, I know, but this business fascinates me, and I long to prove myself able."

"Yes, lad, I know," I said, mollified by Dupain's pained expression. Determined to be more trusting than Raboud had been of me, I added, "I understand. When we meet with Alisdair Scrymgeour, would you like to lead the questioning, then?"

His eyes alight, Dupain agreed, asking, "May I know what you would have me do, sir?"

"I trust that your sensitivity to magical workings can tell you if he has recently used magic of the sort of that we witnessed today, correct?"

"*Oui*, sir," he cried. "You see, it leaves traces for days, when something like the hex that plagued Westcott is used with such malevolence. The taint of any magical working will stay on a man, and the darker it is, the more it will grate on my senses."

"Very well, then. If you detect such a taint upon him at our first meeting, I wish to ask first if he knew William Westcott," I said, underscoring the past tense. "If Scrymgeour sought to kill Westcott, a sense of his success might make him overconfident. So be sure to ask as though Westcott is with us no more. I will learn much by Scrymgeour's reaction. If you see that he is free of this taint, however, ask him how well he *knows* Westcott. That will convey your insights to me. Then you may leave the other questions to me."

"*Certainement*! Place your trust in me, sir," Dupain replied, seeming to puff up with pride. Dibba smiled and nodded, pleased that we were all on firmer footing.

***

We dined in the restaurant of the Midland Grand. I ate a light meal of soup and salad. I did not know what a denizen of the faerie kingdom would eat, but Dibba's bulk suggested that he would have a prodigious appetite. Surprisingly, he ordered a simple green salad and a glass of mineral water. Dupain, though, ate soup, salad, and a beef entrée, as if he hadn't eaten in days. I hoped he would not be too full if the matter of Scrymgeour's questioning led us into action.

Learning that our waiter knew by sight Sir Alisdair Scrymgeour, we made an arrangement with him to let us know if that man entered the dining area, so that we might make his acquaintance. At the first mention of the man's name, the waiter smiled and said, "Sir, the gentleman in question takes his meals elsewhere when he is with us, but he can usually be found in the hotel bar, where we stock some fine whiskies that appeal to his northern tastes. I will alert you to his entry when I see him."

"Yes, do so, but first send him a double portion of the bar's finest single malt, with our compliments."

The waiter, seeing no harm in my suggestion, became our accomplice and some forty minutes later came and told me that Scrymgeour had entered the bar. Our entry to the bar was timed so that we could see the double portion of fine scotch delivered to a striking figure of a man, who appeared ready to take the field of battle. No one took note of our entry, for all eyes were drawn to Scrymgeour.

Sir Alisdair wore a jacket of dark brown tweed, above a kilt in a tartan of such rusty, orangish red that it gave the impression of dried blood. His matching balmoral sat atop a mass of dark red hair above his well-trimmed beard. Sir Alisdair, a strong, fit man, looked as though he had stepped out of a painting of the Jacobite uprising, a sterling example of the Highlander. He had just removed the leather baldric which held an ancient claymore well over four feet in length. He leaned that weapon against a chair at his table. He also wore a dirk at his side and a staghorn *skean dubh* in his right boot top.

The lean, weathered face that he turned toward the waiter bearing his drink held a suspicious look at first, but then broke into a smile as the waiter motioned to us as the parties responsible for the scotch.

"Will ye not join me, gentlemen?" he called to us over the low murmur of twenty or so voices in the bar. Though he had a rasping, grating voice, Scrymgeour's cordial tones told me that, whatever had brought him from the wind-swept fields of Fife to London, it hardly seemed likely to be murder. He had the relaxed look of a man on holiday. He appeared tired, though. I noted, too, that he took the precaution of letting some of his drink spill onto his finger, so that he might test its taste before he asked us to join him.

Leaving our drink order with the waiter before we got to the table, we took seats on either side of the noble Scot. He rose and moved his sword, beckoning us to the empty chairs. He made sure to take a seat near toward the corner of the room, with no one at his back. He might have satisfied himself that the drink we offered bore no taint, but we had yet to gain his trust.

"You're on, lad," I whispered to Dupain as we settled in. He looked at me with a blank expression, like an actor who'd forgotten his line. His cheeks burning red, Dupain looked down at his hands, which lay on the table before him. I saw them shake. There was an uncomfortable silence.

So I cleared my throat and said, "Have we the pleasure of addressing Sir Alisdair Scrymgeour of Fife?"

"Aye, that ye have, gents. May I know your names?"

"Did you attempt the murder of Westam Willcott—er, William Westcott—this day, sir?" Dupain blurted out.

I held my breath, aghast at Dupain's ineptitude. Dibba, looking on with wide eyes, burst out laughing.

CHAPTER SEVEN

"Innocent Ineptitude."

Dupain had reduced my plan to rubbish. Scrymgeour studied each of our faces with a precise and humorous glance before he relaxed and even chuckled along with Dibba. They both appeared to enjoy my discomfiture as much as Dupain's fumbling interrogation.

"Now, I do know this Westcott gentleman, I will not deny. I've come to London to see that very man. But why would anyone attempt to murder Westcott, sir?" he asked.

"Sir Alisdair—" I began, before Dupain made the situation worse.

"Because you oppose his orderly approach to the occult arts with your own 'hedge wizardry'!" Dupain cried. Not content with his first blunder, Dupain seemed to think that voice volume obliterated stupidity. A ripple of laughter went through the room, though no one looked our way. Still, I was sure that the term 'hedge wizardry' had tickled the fancy of the urbane clientele of the Midland Grand bar.

Dibba laughed harder, drawing deeply on the unfortunate humor of Dupain's cloth-headedness. Sir Alisdair enjoyed the joke at our expense too, though he had to know that he was our suspect. Dupain had certainly warned him well and, likely, put him at ease. I closed my eyes and wished devoutly to be anywhere else. The lad's eagerness, combined with his total lack of situational awareness, had ruined any chance we had of getting more information of the kind we needed. I could only wish that I had ordered myself a double.

Our drinks arrived: Dibba's water, my own single malt, and a delicate glass of rosé for Dupain. Scrymgeour raised his glass to us and said, "I offer a toast to chance meetings, to hospitality—and to the time-honored tradition of putting your best man at the front of the charge!"

Laughing, he drank, as did Raboud's jolly servant. I drank in silence, and Dupain just managed to sip his delicate wine without spilling any.

"I beg your pardon for the faux pas of this... toddler, Sir Alisdair," I said, taking over the questioning, "but I assume that my colleague here has sensed that you have been involved in magical workings this day. He possesses a sensitivity to such things that I am supposed to trust, though his skills in questioning leave, well, everything to be desired. Suffice it to say that we have come from Westcott's home, where he was attacked today through magical means. He lists you among the opponents to his own efforts to start the Isis-Urania Temple, so we must question you about it."

"A better approach," Sir Alisdair said. "And your wee mannie here has it right. I have used various charms to protect myself, for I have been the object of someone's spells all this livelong day. What skills I have in protection I have put into place, though I daresay they will not be enough to combat the work of whatever black arts got the best of Westcott. He is skilled, sir, and I cannot match him with incantations."

"Perhaps," I said, "but you do stand in opposition to his efforts."

"Indeed I do, sir. However, that is only because his temple welcomes women practitioners. That will cause disaster if he succeeds in opening a similar temple in Edinburgh, as he wishes," Scrymgeour said. "As an adept, the man has no equal, but his new ideas would be a disaster in Scotland."

"I had not heard that Scots were in disfavor of women's advancement," I offered.

"And we are not," Scrymgeour answered with more energy. "I'm a great one for the lasses getting their due, under the law, but there's a power at work in my homeland amongst the witch-kind, especially the wandering folk, where the most common practitioners are women. Too many of them hold to the old ways that keep people in the dark. If the Romany folk gain control of some of the most holy sites, Edinburgh's so-called Arthur's Seat the most important, it will bring trouble. We simply cannot move as fast in that line of thinking as Westcott wishes. Therefore, I oppose him—for the present."

"Clearly, with the Epiphany plans for the Arthur's Seat meeting, we should bring this to the attention of Dr. Raboud," Dupain blurted out, giving me cause to wince.

"Jean-Louis," I growled over Scrymgeour's and Dibba's laughter at the embarrassment on my face, "we are not at liberty to announce the names of our associates in this matter, I'll thank you to recall. Utter not one word more, upon pain of battery."

His face going scarlet, Jean-Louis sat back in his chair, sufficiently admonished by my none-too-gentle rebuke. Our new acquaintance only sipped his fine scotch and nodded his head.

"Do not distress yourself, man," he said to me. "If ye are known as friends to Omar Raboud, you have my willing ear. His order harkens back, I believe, to Melchizedek. I've heard him speak in Prague and know him to be of great worth. Now, that is a mannie I'd give much to meet, e'en over Westcott, may his health be always good," Scrymgeour asserted, adding, "Ask what ye will."

Thus exposed, I thought it best to get back to the purpose of our call and be forthright with our Scots suspect. Besides, I had taken a genuine liking to the man. If he was lying about involvement in the attempt on Westcott's life, he was at least willing to brass out the meeting, and I respected that. It was the way of a soldier, an honorable attempt to stick to the truth, even if that required an ordeal. To me, it meant that Scrymgeour wasn't evil. That he added to the vaunted reputation of Omar Raboud, I would have to accept with grace.

"Have you not thought to work out your difficulties with Westcott face to face, Sir Alisdair?" I asked, thinking that he'd say yes.

"That's why I'm in London. He knows that, right enough, or

else you lads would not know my whereabouts. True, my
opposition to his efforts has been obvious, for it scares me to think
what the witch-folk and their Romany friends might try to do if
they are supported by his temple. They are, many of them, a
barbarous lot and need watching. But I have no wish to oppose
Westcott in the long view. So I've come to seek an audience with
him as soon as it can be arranged. If Omar Raboud is here with the
same purpose as well, then I ken that I'm in good company."

"I did not suggest that our purpose and yours are the same,
sir, but I think we are at least not enemies, if what you say is
true. But I wonder, sir: by 'Romany', do you refer to Abel
Cameron's people?" I asked.

Scrymgeour favored me with a long, slow look, as though
he were taking stock of me.

"Cameron is known to ye, then? And yet this Christmas
season ye travel to Edinburgh?" Scrymgeour asked.

"Yes, but in another matter, not Westcott's case," I
answered. He studied me for a long moment, apparently liking
this friendly game of guessing what was behind the blind.

"The Tinker folk, well, they are a different kind, sir, d'ye
ken? My mother's people, the Johnsons, were Travelers. They
do much for the folk of the Highlands. If ye get to Edinburgh
soon, with magical folk, ye'll know well enough the difference
between them—e'en the lowland Scots amongst them—and the
Romany folk. But Raboud, if he's bound for Auld Reekie as
well, he'll tell ye."

Scrymgeour's expression had changed after the mention of
the Traveler King. Still playing his game of planting ideas in his
talk to which I could react, he grew at last more relaxed, as
though among friends. He leaned forward at the table, eager to
talk, though he clearly had no notion of what to do with us.
Dupain he seemed to dismiss as a green youth who was just
learning my ways. But to Dibba, now, he spoke in another
tongue, which I thought might be Gaelic, and Raboud's servant
responded in kind. He favored Scrymgeour with his wide smile
and a hearty handshake as they spoke, and our guest relaxed
even more.

Noticing my glance shifting between them, Dibba explained, "This good man sees who—what—I am. He has been among some few of my northern kin. He asks about my service to my master, and I tell him only that I serve the Raboud family, nothing more, *efendi*."

Nodding my thanks to Dibba, I turned back to Scrymgeour. "I am glad to find you so amenable to us," I said, "though I am not part of the occult community, as Dupain and Al-Hassan are, in their different ways. We are more of an investigative team, working under Dr. Raboud's direct supervision—"

"What, like some sort of magical peelers? It's true that there's a surge of some kind in occult energy of late, and some measure of policing seems in order. I've heard rumors, too, of such a 'team,' as you put it, at work here and abroad. I've told ye of the reason for my visit. But what of you gentlemen? Are you, then, part of the official force to deal with crimes of magic?" Scrymgeour asked. He put me on the spot, having heard, like the Travelers, of Department Zed's exploits, though he knew not the name.

"Yes," I answered, seeing no use in denying it. "Those we serve would see justice done to all those who would use the magical arts to cause harm. We are looking for information on dangerous practitioners in London now, especially those who oppose such enterprises as Westcott's," I said.

"Ah. And since I set myself against Westcott, I'm a suspect," Scrymgeour said. "I've thought as much, but I cannot help ye there. Ye've no good reason to believe me, but I am not the malefactor ye seek. I know so little about folk who work the craft in these parts. I'm sensitive to power use, myself, though I'm just a simple 'hedge wizard,' as the lad charges. Ye have my word, though, that while I'm here in London, I'll keep my nose in the wind. There's much afoot, these days, and I'm glad to know you're around. Ye have my thanks, lads."

Scrymgeour drained his scotch, and I signaled the waiter to bring him another.

"But whoever is at work now," he continued, "has some good training, I'd say, for those in the dark arts often seek power, not skill, and are oft victims of their own spells. If this lad—or lass—is able to best Westcott, he also has skill enough to stay well hidden."

"Might those same, er, witches you mentioned be practicing in London as well?" I asked.

"I've no doubt that there's plenty of that craft at work in every corner of Britain, with their Romany friends, but unless ye wish to reveal the kind of things you're talking about, I cannot be sure. They'd not be likely to curry Westcott's favor, I'm thinking."

His manner made me think him a good risk, so I went straight to the one of the issues we'd dealt with. "Would the people you mentioned, the witches, be capable of casting the Loup-Garou Curse?"

Sir Alisdair's ruddy complexion drained of color in less than a second. He scooped up his glass and gulped down the expensive whisky. His hand gripped the scabbard of his claymore and shook with the effort. When he set the glass back on the table, I looked into the eyes of a terrified man.

"I would hope not, for such a person would have sold his soul for that sort of power," he whispered. "Ne'er before have I heard of such a thing in Britain."

"And yet I was forced to slay such a creature just yesterday, one that sought the lives of me and my colleague," I said.

"How could ye slay a loup-garou?" he muttered, his brows drawing together. Both his hands shook as he rested them on the table.

"With this," I replied, giving him a brief look at the scabbard of Mustard Seed within the folds of my coat.

"Then you, sir, are a man touched by God Almighty, or your weapon is God's own, I'm forced to think," he said in an awed whisper. "And please believe me, I do not want to count as your enemy, e'en if ye cannot call me friend."

"I am perhaps the latter, though certainly not the former," I replied. "I am merely charged with finding the person capable of casting such a curse. I can see that I've given you something of a fright, which I would not wish on a friend."

"Indeed ye have, sir, and I would be tempted to leave this city at once, were it not for wishing to hear Miss Adler sing here this very night. As it is, it will be my letter of explanation that Westcott receives on the morrow, not a visit. I'll keep clear of this business."

Westcott had said that he did not believe in coincidences in matters of the occult, and I was forced to see Scrymgeour's mention of Irene Adler as a gift to our cause. I'd had no idea that her performances would include the Midland Grand or anywhere else. Clearly, given her popularity and her need to attend to the Logres Society's mission, she would perform anywhere in London. If I could get her to speak to Scrymgeour, he might become a better ally than a suspect.

"I am acquainted with Miss Adler, sir," I replied. "Would you care to have a meeting with her on these premises after her concert?"

His hard eyes lit with joy. "For this fine dram, sir, I am already in your debt. A favor of that kind would make my debt to you unpayable. Can ye do it, man?"

"Given my ability to reach her, I can and I will. I count it a matter of honor, sir, and I trust that you will conduct yourself as a gentleman in her presence."

"Aye, sir. Here or in yon restaurant, at her disposal. Just to speak with her, face to face, would be a mighty gift. Music hath charms, ye ken, and that voice and those eyes of hers are full of magic. As for my conduct, if what ye say about your deeds of late is true, I would do well to keep to your good side."

"Then, sir, I will speak to Miss Adler on your behalf, I hope within the hour," I said, rising to shake his hand. "Now, however"—I nodded toward Dupain—"I must get this youngster home for his bedtime."

***

After we took our leave of the fearful but hopeful Alisdair Scrymgeour, I repaired to the front desk to learn if Irene Adler were already on the premises. The clerk told me she was not, as she was scheduled to turn the ample foyer of the hotel into a concert hall at ten o'clock that night. We had a matter of two hours, so I expected to intercept her, as well as Holmes, at Briony Lodge in a matter of much less time.

Dupain attempted to apologize, but I raised a hand and stopped him. I took my seat in the carriage and turned a stern glance to the man. "Dupain, your lack of preparedness for work in Department Zed is beyond my comprehension, considering the confidence Dr. Omar Raboud places in you. Further, I imagine that he knows this and has set you as a trap to deny my entry into the Society we all serve, for no amount of time will prepare you to be a member of that Society without bringing it to ruin with your ineptitude. You are not fit, man, but it is my job to make you so. And I will not fail. With this, I will need help.

"Dibba Al-Hassan, I have learned to trust your good nature, and I know that you have the gift of waiting in silence when matters that are not yours come before you. I now charge you with the additional task of keeping him silent," I said, pointing to the fallen countenance of Jean-Louis Dupain, "even to the point of clapping your hand over his mouth should I not give him leave to speak. Will you do this, yes, no?"

"Yes, *efendi*," Dibba said, trying not to smile at my use of his typical phrasing.

"You, Monsieur Dupain, when in the field, will respond with nods and head shakes unless I require you to speak. Is this clear?"

Dupain started to answer but then merely nodded, a mix of anger and shame on his youthful features.

"I completely understand that you will complain to Dr. Raboud about my treatment, and I intend to confront him with my complaint against him. In the meantime, watch, listen, and learn. Regardless of Raboud's assertion that you will not need it, you are to report to this address," I said, handing him a piece of paper with the address of the tea shop above Mr. Uyeshiba's dojo. "I will meet you there at eight o'clock tomorrow morning and get further help disciplining you to astute silence."

I spoke no other words until we drew near Briony Lodge,

where the front door to the white brick villa stood open. Irene Adler stood at the curb, ready to enter her waiting carriage. My heart leapt, for behind her stood Mary. Irene gave me a curious smile and drew Mary's attention to me as I dropped from our still moving four-wheeler.

"Mary," I cried, "I'm so relieved to find you at last. Your absence from home yesterday has had me on pins and needles of worry."

"Dr. Watson," Irene interjected, "I shall have Mary with me until matters in your home have been dealt with."

I nodded my thanks to her, wondering how I could tell her of the attack Holmes and I had suffered yesterday, though I knew that Wiggins and Brewer would be scouring Arnold Pinder's blood from my surgery floor and repairing what damage they could.

She greeted me with a pleasant smile and took both my hands in hers, but Mary did not move to embrace me. Her fair cheeks were red, in fact, as though I had caught her in a compromising situation. That, I put down to surprise.

"Dear John. I am sorry to have been a worry to you. I'm all right, really. Today, Miss Adler has told me that our home was the scene of a crime, though she has withheld the details to keep me from worrying. And she and I have had... quite a good deal to discuss, you know." She drew near, holding my hands in trembling fingers, and whispered, "And, my dear, we—just you and I—need to have a talk, soon."

"Of course, my dear," I said. "As you wish; when you wish."

CHAPTER EIGHT

"Innocence Tested."

"I fear you take us by surprise, Dr. Watson," Irene Adler said, reaching out to take my hand. "Mary and I have just become friends, having shared so much." Mary, I noticed, smiled at this, but it was a brittle smile.

"May I have a word with you before you depart?" I asked Irene.

"Yes, of course. Hastings, I will be another moment," she called to her driver. To me she whispered, "Mary knows nothing of my role in the L. S., of that be sure, but I must infer that you have come with business that concerns our needs."

As clearly as I could, in hushed tones, I told her all that had transpired and all that I hoped she might learn from Scrymgeour.

"Of course I will be happy to take that interview, and I must say that I am surprised by Dupain's ineptitude. You must feel it as a burden."

"Burdens are a working man's due, Miss Adler, though I thank you for your concern. And I thank you for seeing to Mary's safety, including keeping her well away from home."

She stared at me for a long moment, her eyes studying my face as though gauging my readiness. "You and I should talk, I think, prior to your reunion with Mary," she said. "In the meantime, I must pick up my agent and stage manager prior to my engagement at the Midland Grand. I bid you goodbye until the few of us rendezvous at a place to be named tomorrow. O'Hara will bring you word."

"Is Holmes within, still?" I asked.

"Ah, no. Sherlock found himself in need of quietude, which he could not find in our company. What I needed to say to both Mary and Sherlock was not easy to hear. I trust that you will find him, and Magnus Guthrie, at Baker Street."

With that, she mounted the carriage and her burly driver whipped up his team and rolled away. I returned with my charges to our carriage for the short jaunt to Baker Street. Dupain kept silent, his face a study in quiet concentration, as we rattled down Park Road with the dark reaches of Regent's Park to our right. Dibba's gentle eyes were closed, and he dozed easily, despite the bouncing of the carriage over the cobbled streets. My thoughts were of seeing Mary and wondering about the conversation Irene had held with Holmes and my wife that had affected them so. Holmes was usually not given to letting a conversation upset him in any way. And Mary—why, as I thought of it, she had borne the look of a penitent child whose mischief has been found out.

***

When we arrived at Baker Street, though, the front door of 221 stood ajar and the house in total darkness. Out of the carriage at once, I entered with haste and saw the door to Holmes's sitting room standing open at the top of those seventeen stairs. Dibba moved me aside and sprang up the stairs to the sitting room, determined to place his hardihood between his associates and any danger. Calling to him to take care, I kept pace just behind him and saw him stumble over Holmes's inert form, lying in the dark, just within the room.

"Lights, Dupain, Dibba! The gas lamps are by the mantel. Hurry!" I ordered, bending over Holmes, searching for a pulse in his neck. It was strong and steady.

When the lights came up, Holmes lay shirtless and shoeless before me. His trouser legs had each ripped at a seam, exposing his legs. Around his neck on a fine copper chain was a dark medallion, which I had never seen before. The times were rare when Holmes had appeared before me stripped to the waist. Had he always worn that medallion, I wondered? It seemed so unlike Holmes; sentimental, in fact.

"Holmes!" I called. He had no injuries that I could see, but as I lifted his arm, I saw beneath it a clear, glistening substance. I touched the substance, and a tingling ran up my fingertips, making me pull my hand back and wipe away the substance on my trouser leg. A shiver rose from my soul and coursed through me. Here was the substance that I'd seen in the wake of Arnold Pinder's postmortem return to human shape.

Even as I looked at it, it dried up and was no more. But its presence there, even briefly, shocked me to such a degree that I found it nearly impossible to deal with. It was the residue of magic. Holmes had been through a magical transformation, a thought which I desperately did not wish to believe.

I stirred myself to action. Chafing his wrists and calling his name soon brought him around, and his eyes fluttered open. The eyes were still his, grey, but less keen. He sighed deeply and stretched his limbs as if from a long, good sleep—itself an oddity for a man of such nervous energy.

"What happened, Holmes?" I whispered, watching him come around slowly. That he didn't awake in a state of terror gave me a sense of hope that nothing magical had happened to him. He looked as though he desired nothing more than to turn over and go back to sleep, but I would not have it. "Can you rise?"

"Dr. Watson!" Dupain called from the door of Holmes's room. "Here's Guthrie, in worse shape, I think!"

"Help Mr. Holmes to his feet, if you will, Dibba," I said to Raboud's servant. Running to Guthrie's side, I saw that he was out, too, as deeply as Holmes had been, though his face was bruised on one side. His pupils reacted to light, but the only sounds I got from him were deep groans as I tried to bring him around.

"Dupain, lad, be so good as to go downstairs and see if Mrs. Hudson is all right. I'll wager that you might need to rap on what looks to be a solid wall beneath the stairs. I can hope that she made it to that safe room before anything similar happened to her."

With a nod, Jean-Louis ran to do my bidding, and in moments I heard his knocking on the wall and his voice trying to coax our good landlady into coming out. When Holmes's hand fell onto my shoulder, I reacted with shock and wrapped my fingers around it without thinking, ready with a defensive wrist lock.

"Easy, old friend," Holmes said, alert now. "What has occurred?"

Letting go of his hand, I turned to see him secure on his feet, looking oddly in the peak of good health, Dibba behind him. Always pale, Holmes had lost a good deal of flesh over the course of the past summer and fall. Shirtless, he looked to have gained some of it back. In fact, he looked ready to step into the prizefighting ring, which I'd known him to do in the not-too-distant past. Despite my alarm at the substance I thought I had detected on him, I told myself that his convalescence accounted for his improved appearance. To see him restored at that moment, though, took me aback.

"I must ask you the same," I said, "for I entered to find you unconscious on the floor, and Guthrie injured as though from a fierce struggle."

"What is Guthrie doing here?" he asked as he squatted down with ease, placing his hand on Guthrie's shoulder as the latter sought to sit up.

"Careful, Holmes. Your knee," I protested.

Holmes turned raised eyebrows to me, looked at his knee, pushed up and down from the floor with ease, and said, "Hmph."

Guthrie held his head in his hands and moaned. Dupain entered with a distraught Mrs. Hudson at his side. She was wringing her hands and staring at the outlandish Dibba Al-Hassan.

"I sent Guthrie, some three hours ago, with a note that I needed to meet with you over an urgent matter," I said to Holmes. "He missed you at Briony Lodge and, as per my order, sought you here. I presume he didn't find you."

Holmes helped lift Guthrie to his feet. Dupain moved to help him, but Holmes appeared not to need it. I saw no limp or weakness in him at all. If anything, he looked stronger than he had for months, as though in the short time since our last moments together he had experienced a year of healing. Holmes, after placing Guthrie in a chair by the dark hearth, flexed and bent his once-injured leg with ease, frowning at the unexpected health in his limb.

Turning his scowl toward me, he said, "Watson, we have a mystery before us. This very day, as I returned in unhappy mood to this flat, I thought myself incurably lame, and now I feel, well, incredible. Perhaps your care has been more effective than we both thought."

"It seems miraculous," I replied. "One might say magical. Have you, perhaps, met with Dr. Raboud?"

"No, I came here from Briony Lodge, intent on getting away from a troubling woman. However, as good as I feel now, I am more amazed by my lack of awareness of how I came to be found unconscious, half-dressed, barefoot, unscathed, in the same room as my colleague who was obviously the victim of some assault. I have no memory after throwing myself into my bed, exhausted, just after sunset. Some two to three hours of my time is missing. This is unheard of, Watson."

"Englishmen walk in their sleep, yes, no?" Dibba offered with a palms-up shrug.

"Perhaps I—" Dupain started, before Holmes interrupted him with a raised hand.

"I do not walk in my sleep," Holmes said around a sudden yawn that belied his words. "I sleep quite lightly and wake at the slightest noise."

"If I may be so bold, Mr. Holmes," Dupain remarked, moving behind Guthrie to stand within the door to Holmes's room, "the mystery before us is complicated by the condition of your room." He retreated into Holmes's room, looking for the gas lamp, which he found and lit with speed and considerably more dexterity than he had managed in my presence all day.

The light revealed a room that had been torn apart. The bedclothes and mattress lay shredded and hurled into the corners of the room. Deep gouges ran across the shattered headboard, and I had the memory of the loup-garou's claws as well as those of Spring Heeled Jack. Holmes's dressing table lay on its side on the opposite side of the room from where it normally stood, his toiletries and washbasin reduced to broken bits of crockery and glass. I picked up Holmes's dressing gown, now somewhat tattered but whole enough to wear, and gave it to him to slip on against the cold breeze that came through the window's cracked glass.

Guthrie rose and came to stand at the door beside Dupain. The disastrous condition of Holmes's chamber held us entranced and terrified me with its implications. I told myself that if Holmes had been transformed into a werewolf, Guthrie and Mrs. Hudson would both be gruesome corpses. Holmes's glassy stare revealed that he was as much at a loss as I was. His demeanor unnerved me, for I was accustomed to Holmes thinking through every contingency. However, I determined to keep to myself that Holmes bore evidence of having been transformed into— something—and back into his natural shape. My lack of experience concerning all the faerie and magical influences thrust into my thoughts over the last several days left me adrift, rudderless. I needed to do something. I barked out an order.

"Those claw marks look like they could have been made by Spring Heeled Jack. Dupain, do you detect any traces of occult influences here?"

"*Oui, mon capitaine*, but they seem weak. I think neither man has worked with any magical force. I see—feel—no intent in them."

"Very well. Then search for anything that doesn't seem to belong. We must have some clue about how this happened," I said, desirous for some action that might help me make sense of this puzzle. Holmes appeared incapable of doing so. "Guthrie, can you add any sense to this?"

"Cap'n, I got no further than this," Guthrie said, standing in the doorway to the room, "when I came in from the stairs. I let myself in, downstairs, for no one answered the bell, sir. When I came into the sitting room, I saw this door just barely open, and when I knocked and stuck my 'ead in, somethin' hit me fast, 'ard, and I don't remember anythin' else until you brought me 'round, moments ago. So 'elp me, I don't know what 'it me, but it was that fast and strong, sir."

"And I didn't hear Mr. Guthrie, sir. Minutes before I heard his knock at the door, I heard the thumping and crashing of things on this floor, and I sought my safe room," Mrs. Hudson explained.

Dupain handed me a tattered mass of white fabric that had once been Holmes's shirt, which I held up by its shoulder seams, or what I could find of them, anyway. "Only ribbons and shreds, *mon capitaine*."

Holmes said. "Most peculiar. The violence done to this shirt, had it been on me at the time, would surely have left marks on my body, yet I have none. Do you see any on my back or shoulders, Watson?" he asked, pulling the dressing gown down and turning to expose his upper back to the lamplight.

"No," I said, seeing again that chain around his neck, "but I wonder about this medallion you wear."

"I gave him that, *mon capitaine*, a remembrance to him from my mother, with whom Mr. Holmes shared happier times when I was a boy," Dupain said. "My mother believed that it was a healing charm, of sorts. I was pleased to bring it to Mr. Holmes, when I knew that I would meet him as part of this final phase of my training. I am happy to think that it is perhaps, in part, responsible for his sudden renewed health."

"However grateful I am for the gift of it, such a claim is rather outlandish, don't you think, Jean-Louis?" Holmes interjected.

"I have borne it often, Mr. Holmes, since I was such a sickly child, as you will recall. When I no longer needed it, Mother asked me to bring it to you," the young Frenchman commented. "Perhaps Dr. Raboud, if you showed it to him, would be able to plumb the depths of its power. The shape on the back side of the medallion is supposed to reflect some story of the remarkable St. Francis, while the front side, I assume, shows his face in profile."

"Clearly, this medallion is the least of our worries at present, gentlemen, even if it is imbued with great healing powers. I've always said that Holmes's recuperative powers are rather incredible, but more incredible, still, is the mystery that confronts us in his person and his missing time," I said.

"How long, Mrs. Hudson, were you locked away in your safe room?" Holmes asked.

"Since shortly after your return, Mr. Holmes. No one else was in this house since you two left earlier today. And I didn't dare come out, even when I heard the knock on the door, which was Magnus himself," she declared. "I still remember those 'orrid zomblies from two months ago!"

"Zombies," Holmes corrected her. "So I must assume that I did this," he continued, with a gesture at the debris that had once been his furnishings, "though I am at a loss as to say how."

"It must be the adept whom we seek, yes? No?" Dibba offered. "This day, we have seen him strike at Mr. Westcott in a magical attack. Such a mage could strike any one of us with similar effect, no?"

I gave Holmes a précis of what we had seen happening to Westcott as well as an account of our interview with our one disappointing suspect, Alisdair Scrymgeour. Holmes's countenance grew darker as he took in all of my information. Whatever conclusions he was drawing, they were troubling, terrifying perhaps, to judge by the tension that mounted in his face. I wondered if he had intuited the solution to this puzzle and found it too horrible to share.

"Holmes," I whispered, drawing him away from the others for a quiet word, as had been my intent all along. "I begin to wonder if Raboud is behind this business. Although everyone seems to see him as trustworthy, he is the only powerful adept of whom we know who is in a position to do the Logres Society the greatest harm. Supposing that he can affect his environment through occult means such as those that afflicted Westcott, his power and reach are formidable. Do you see no cause to suspect him as the very dark power he sets us to find?"

"Given what I know of him, Watson, I cannot say much about his abilities, for I have never actually seen him work his arts. I have only read about the aftermath, which served justice and preserved the lives of many."

"Of his choosing, no doubt," I grumbled.

"Of the Society's choosing, Watson," Holmes corrected me.

"I simply cannot find cause to think him capable of such...
betrayal." Holmes's brow was darkening, as though other
thoughts intruded on the line of questions I had introduced.

"I don't know, Holmes," I muttered. "I certainly don't think
much of Bismarck's protégé, though, and I must wonder about
Raboud, too, if he chose this bungling boy to train."

"Raboud didn't choose him. Bismarck did, and he sought
out Raboud to complete the lad's training," Holmes replied.

"Then how does Dupain merit his standing in the Logres
Society?" I asked, thinking of my own difficulties getting onto its
lists.

"Mycroft told me that Raboud proffered the lad as someone
who could help the L. S. make peaceful inroads with Bismarck,
whose aggressive rule has been called into question by many
Society members," Holmes explained. His brow furrowed again,
and he turned away from me.

"What is it, Holmes? What are you thinking?" I asked, for I
had learned to accept his speculations as I did other men's facts.

"Perhaps I need to work on my own, Watson: separate
myself from your work on this case and pursue my own line of
investigation. Your questions have raised an interesting idea
which calls for several telegrams, many of which won't get
answers for days yet." He paused, stroking his chin. "I urge you
to stand down, at least until tomorrow. I will go and sound out
this 'hedge wizard' myself, if he remains at the Midland
Grand."

"But Holmes, how can you dare feel safe working alone?
You were found remarkably changed, and there was, on your
person, a clear, somewhat viscous, tingling residue."

"Do you think it was the same substance I found on
Pinder?" Holmes asked in a whisper.

"I—I cannot be sure, Holmes. It was only a trace, and it
dried quickly. As evidence, it leaves me with nothing, except a
mounting insecurity."

"About me, I imagine," he said. He toyed with the medallion
around his neck and closed his eyes in thought. He took it off and
stared at it, smiling at it as though in fond memory.

"Was she beautiful, Holmes?" I asked, thinking that he must be remembering Dupain's mother.

"Yes," he murmured, "and kind to the headstrong lad I was." He slipped the medallion's chain over his head. "This case is turning out to be quite a tonic for me, Watson. It has several enticing features and some far-reaching implications."

We were silent for a moment, still standing apart from Dibba, our landlady, Dupain, and Guthrie, though the latter stared hard at me. Holmes appeared to withdraw into his memory; his smile faded, and his brow darkened yet again. Since I lacked his ability to read the depth of emotions in the small changes in a man's face, I could not tell what he was thinking. At length, he whispered, "Tell me again where you met our Traveler friends yesterday."

I gave him the story again, and he listened with care, muttering under his breath, "Notting Hill, likely."

"Watson," he went on, giving me as keen-eyed a gaze as I'd ever seen from him, "in the next days, you will hear things that give you grave cause to doubt me, but rest assured that I am and have always been your friend and ally. However, I cannot stand with you and face this charge. As I see it now, I must pursue my own investigations, as I said. I urge you to stay within a larger group of our associates. Do all in your power to keep Guthrie at your side, or at least Dibba Al-Hassan, neither of whom are capable of betraying their word, the former through hard-won loyalty and the latter by his kind." He placed his hand on my shoulder.

"Very well, Holmes," I replied, "but I am at a loss as to how to take my next steps, without more from you. I simply cannot account for what's happened to you, though I am glad to see you strong again. Surely we should consult with Raboud, though I hate to admit it."

"Even though you doubt his intent?"

"Yes," I replied in a hoarse voice. "Raboud's reputation makes him the only resource I have in this matter. I would force myself to trust him, if he could shed light on what has happened to you. It is beyond my skill to comprehend, damn it. I hate being in this bind, but how else can we proceed?"

"With caution, with care, Watson. And, what's more, I need you to trust me now as you always have. I have a plan. Raboud needs you to train Dupain. Do so," he said. "This business will be resolved by Epiphany, I believe, though it will go hard from now until then. However, I must remain free to act in secrecy. It is time we used our enemy's methods against him. Steady on, Watson. Steady on. Trust me, and you might well grow to trust Raboud."

Holmes's words offered me hope, but they did little to allay my fears for him. Yet I knew that he was the most capable man alive, even if he had warned me that I would have reason to distrust him. He took my hand in his steel grip, as though to remind me of the bond of our friendship, and then removed himself to find undamaged clothing in the partially splintered wardrobe.

Holmes, I was sure, had some idea about what sort of thing had been done to him, and I reasoned that he was ready to seek out the Travelers, though I had no idea why. Perhaps he had a clearer idea about the identity of the adept working against us.

I put on as good a face as I could and made ready to send Dupain and Dibba back to the rooms they occupied, with Raboud, above the Diogenes Club. They were to meet me at Uyeshiba's dojo early the next day. Guthrie, with Dibba's trust, would remain at Baker Street with me, as surety of my actions staying under observation by some trustworthy agent.

I rested little, plagued by the idea of what Holmes had said about my doubting him. He was heading into danger, while I was to stay surrounded and protected. I had to assume that this was for my safety, though as I was burdened with my doubts about Raboud and with the warning of the Travelers, safety seemed an intangible thing, like a faerie tale.

CHAPTER NINE

"The Feast of St. Thomas à Becket,"
29 December, 1888.

The next morning, even lacking good rest, I kept my appointment with Dupain and my sensei, though the density of the fog that had covered London overnight almost made me late. Luckily, I found young Harvey Brewer with Bill Wiggins in the warmth of Mrs. Hudson's kitchen, and those two guided me to Master Uyeshiba's through the sewer tunnels.

Dibba and Dupain arrived late because of the fog. By then, I was deep into sword practice, moving through the katas, the set routines the master had taught me. As I went through the slow dance, I left Master Uyeshiba to take on his new charges.

The old man walked up to Dupain, looking him up and down as though taking stock of him.

"Your *ki* all wrong, boy." Here my sensei struck Dupain a short blow to his midsection, which sent the boy to the floor, doubled over, gasping for air. "When you rise, take hammer and pound pile of sand until you see straight." Uyeshiba brought the heavy hammer and dropped it near Jean-Louis's hand.

I'd been given nearly the same treatment under the old gentleman's rough tutelage. He had told me that my *ki*, my internal energy, was scattered and loose, and he'd prescribed the same solution: the hammer and the four-foot sand pile. After it had been knocked flat, a shovel lay nearby for the student to pile it up again.

To my surprise, when Uyeshiba turned to Dibba Al-Hassan, the old gentleman smiled and said, "Son of Earth welcome. Play on, as you like."

114

I concentrated on the dangerous edge of Mustard Seed, which flashed in the low light of the dojo as I flowed from one stance to the next. Having heard about my battle with Anne Prescott and her demise at my hands, Uyeshiba had claimed that Mustard Seed had chosen me as its master. In light of Raboud's charge that the sword was a dangerous magical artifact, I had to wonder whether Uyeshiba had not told me the same thing. After all, he had seemed to indicate a sense of agency in the sword, the ability to make a choice as to whom it belonged. Was this not an indication of magic? I had not considered it so at the time, but now I was forced to.

Given the events of the past two days, I seemed to be immersed in magical occurrences that challenged any definition of the word "magic" I had ever used. The loup-garou and the faerie visitor who had assumed familiar shapes to seduce me were both real, frightening things, seen with my own eyes and validated by others. I knew that I must ask Master Uyeshiba about this sword.

When the sensei had set my young colleague to working at the sand pile, admonishing him to put his back into it, he came to me to refine my technique, and I made so bold as to ask him outright about the power of Mustard Seed.

"Sensei, there is a man named Raboud, adept in the ways of magic, who tells me that I should be wary of Mustard Seed. He sees it as a source of magical power, one that needs to be understood before it is allowed to be used."

"Raboud, eh? Magic? What is this magic?" he asked, adjusting my hands on the *tsuka*, the grip of the ancient weapon. "You mean some other power than its balance, its keenness of blade? A sword is a thing of steel, of craft, not spells. That it belongs to you is no magic, just sense that foolish Englishman not see."

His bluff response was one I expected, but I needed more than a simple answer.

"Yes, sensei. But I am quicker with this sword than I was with the other katana I used. You have watched my technique improve because of it, I know. And I have come to trust this sword and its worth as a weapon. You might say that I have faith in it," I said. "Surely a work of craft can be imbued with a power that is not natural."

The sensei rapped my shin with a bamboo practice sword, a *shinai*, to show me where my stance ran too wide.

"You spread yourself out, ham-fist! There, better. Weight under you," he muttered, treating my overt concerns as incidental, not the purpose of our session. His keen eyes tracked my every move, and when I finished the kata, he motioned me to kneel on the tatami mat opposite him, while Dupain pounded away at the sand and the incredible Dibba balanced a hundred-pound dumbbell on his outstretched fingertips.

"You think Mustard Seed have power on its own? Kneel and put it on floor, butcher boy!"

I followed his order and placed the sword before my knees, thinking that finally Uyeshiba would reveal some obscure truth.

"Now, calm yourself. Close eyes. Put question out of mind. Sink into belly, into *ki*," he ordered. I put away all thoughts and centered myself, letting all of my tension go, letting myself feel rooted to the earth, as he'd taught me.

After a moment, he said, "Now, call on magic of sword. Make it to strike me."

"But—"

"Do it! Order sword to kill me! Now, barbarian! Command it!" he said.

"But to strike you, I will need to pick it up," I whispered.

"No! Use mind. Your sword is Mustard Seed. Use magical power in sword to make it move, oaf!"

I settled myself again and reached out in thought, in feeling, to the sword, knowing the touch of its grip in my hands, the coldness of the guard. I thought it through, felt the weight of the thing, the gathering of power as I drew the weapon above my head and struck at him. When I opened my eyes to see what I had done, I flinched and drew back, for the razor-sharp, chiseled point of Mustard Seed stood a hairsbreadth before my nose, unmoving, deadly, in Uyeshiba's capable hands.

He laughed so hard that he shook. Then he lay the sword back in front of me. "You British, so stupid!" he cried. "Think that sword can move without hand! Ha!"

"Yes, yes. I see, sensei. I see," I grumbled.

"If only," he said as his laughter ran on. "You think sword move on its own, huh, ham-fist? Sword need *this*," he said, grabbing my right hand in his left. With his own right hand, he pressed it against my chest and said, "And this. Sword not magic, fool. You *and* sword, ahhh. There is power when you become one."

Dibba had fallen onto his back with laughing at me. Uyeshiba pointed at him and said, "Son of Earth see it. Brings him much joy, see?"

"But how can I become one with a thing of craft, as you say, sensei?" I pleaded, determined to garner some meaning from the moment, something I could take away, other than being the butt of my sensei's joke.

"You do it all the time! Can you walk home in my shoes?" the old fellow asked, laughing still.

"Well, yes, if I needed to," I said, looking at the sandals he typically wore. "But then again, no, not in truth. They wouldn't fit me."

"Yes, but in your own shoes, can you?"

"Of course, because they—" I barked in frustration before the truth settled in me, giving me an even stronger sensation that I was rooted to the spot by my *ki*, my own body's energy, pushing down, connecting me to the great Earth beneath me. Of course I could walk anywhere in shoes that fitted me as if they were part of me. With new shoes, I merely had to break them in, so that I came to trust that they protected my bare feet from the roughness of London's streets. Somehow, Mustard Seed's construction fit me, and my habitual use of it gave me ability and power. To an observer, my achievements with the weapon might look magical, but my successes with it were really matters of who I was and what I did with it.

Was there no more to it than that? Faced with a question I could not answer, I focused instead on my *ki*, as Uyeshiba had insisted.

"Ahhh," Uyeshiba murmured. "See? Feel? Close eyes. They lie to you. How strong you are. Stay there, sink *ki* into the earth. You, like mountain, cannot be moved. See? Breathe deep.

Gooood," he crooned as I settled down once again, all my anger gone, replaced by the peace that lay always below it. At this point, a hand pushed hard on my shoulder as though to topple me over backward, but I did not move. That energy simply flowed into me, and I channeled it down. "Keep eyes closed; hold where you are," Uyeshiba ordered in a quiet voice.

Letting go of doubt, I concentrated, without tensing up, without the strength of my body but with the strength of my heart and soul. Hands pushed at me from one side and then the other. They lunged against my back, but I did not move. All the power exerted against me merely connected to my force, holding me to the Earth. I knelt, secure, immovable. Hands moved to the front of me and pushed harder and harder on my shoulders. I heard the grunt of effort behind them.

And then Uyeshiba's voice whispered, "Eyes closed, still. Touch, easy, the arms in front of you, and let all you feel move back against that flow."

Reaching up, I let my fingertips settle on the arms that pushed against me and simply let the force coming into me swirl down into my center, into my belly, though I knew no trace of strain. My body acted like a strong channel for a mighty river. I felt no need to resist. I was merely part of the flow, as a mill wheel moves a huge grinding stone with the easy but inexorable force of water.

"Stand and direct the flow of *ki* forward. Let that force move you," Uyeshiba whispered, and I rose to my knees and stood up. The hands pushing against me never relented, even when my sensei whispered, "Now, still rooted in Earth, walk forward. Let *ki* flow forward."

Doing so was easy, natural, like the breathing on which I concentrated as I meditated. I let the swirling power move forward as I followed Uyeshiba's suggestion. On gentle, easy steps, I went forward, unstoppable, until Uyeshiba called, "Stop. Open eyes."

There, before me, his mighty back pressed against the wall of the dojo, was Dibba, eyes wide with wonder, face streaked with the sweat of his efforts. Without any muscular effort at all, I

118

had pushed him up the wall so that he was on his tiptoes, weight almost off the floor. When I relaxed my arms, he sagged back to the floor, but his eyes did not lose their wonder.

"Truly wonderful, *efendi*," he said, giving me a bow and moving to stand beside the slack-jawed Jean-Louis, who leaned, breathing hard, on his sledgehammer.

Uyeshiba, at my side, whispered, "Magic? No." And he extended Mustard Seed to me. "When you are centered, in the heart of you, the sword acts only as extension of who you are. It fits you, like shoes. See?"

"So this sword... was made for me?"

"Same way as shoes. Shoemaker doesn't know this shoe or that shoe is for ham-fisted butcher boy, foolish Englishman. He makes shoes of all kinds. Sword maker only make one sword like this. Who knows why it fits foolish Englishman? It fits and does what you need. The more you use it, the better it fits. "

***

I left the dojo with Dupain and Dibba Al-Hassan, feeling more relaxed than I had in days. The fog outside, if anything, had grown denser, and the low winter sun lacked the power to dissipate it. Traffic on London's roads simply crawled along; at times, our cabbie had to leave his perch and lead his horse from the front, stopping often to run to the corner and make sure of the road signs. Dupain, exhausted, sat with his chin near his chest, asleep, while Dibba peered at the fog without.

"Cap'n Jack, this looks like a magical fog, yes, no? Do you ever see it this thick?"

"We are known for our fogs, true, but this one is blinding, I'll agree. Do you think it is the result of magic?" I asked.

"There are spells, I have heard, to cast a mist, but this is so large. It is everywhere, and I think it would blind even the person who made it. That is not good magic," he replied, reaching out of the cab to see his arm and hand grow dim before his eyes. The air temperature had dropped too, and it froze the fog on the exposed edges of the hansom cab. I wished then that I had not sent Brewer and Wiggins home that morning, for we would have fared better in the darkness of the sewer tunnels than on the roads.

Holmes had not yet returned when I'd left for the dojo. He was often out all night, and I knew that, with his sudden healing, he would be fine to investigate on his own, yet I wondered if this fog had helped or hindered his investigation. Though I had grown more settled, more confident as a result of the mystical event in the dojo, my inability to see three feet away from me seemed a fitting reality, the world matching my own inability to see where I was going.

I came to the decision, though, that I simply lacked enough experience with the occult to dismiss it or accept it. Fog, even a heavy one, would not deter us from returning to Baker Street. One step at a time was sufficient. I would make no decision on anything based on occult reasons. Not knowing what else I might witness as this case unfolded, I would stick to the tasks I was assigned and try to bring my bolstered confidence into my actions. My sensei had shown me that I possessed a far greater power in myself than I had thought possible. That power had come from me, was me, and that conferred a renewed sense of identity on me that I'd lacked since taking up the sword.

A cold wind rose from time to time, stirring the damp mist and sending it away in tatters and rags for odd moments before it seeped back around us. However, in one such wind, I saw that we had finally reached Baker Street and that a small party awaited us on the steps of 221. The briefly parted mist showed me that Irene Adler stood there, a distant, distracted look on her face that was at odds with the confidence I'd always seen in her.

At her elbow stood a tall, fair-haired gentleman in a drab brown suit, faded olive greatcoat, and bowler hat. I knew him, and a sense of warning rose in me. His presence meant that some criminal occurrence had touched upon this clandestine case of ours. Mrs. Hudson stood behind them in the doorway, wringing her hands. I suspected the worst with the presence of the Metropolitan Police.

I woke Dupain and secured his attention. Pulling him and

Dibba close to me, I said in low, clear tones, "Say no word of greeting to anyone, gentlemen. That tow-headed gentleman is Inspector Tobias Gregson of Scotland Yard. As far as the Metropolitan Police are concerned, we do not have a familiar relationship with Miss Adler. Not a word before we know what brings Gregson here."

The cabbie drew us to a halt before the familiar entrance. With the wind dropping again, fog settled around us all as we left the cab. Gregson's intelligent eyes squinted at me, and he nodded when he recognized me. Adler's face looked tired, drawn about the eyes, and her smile was brittle, a polite mask.

"Inspector Gregson," I called, stepping forward. "What brings us the honor of a visit from Scotland Yard's finest, on such a beastly day? And who, might I ask, is this charming young creature?"

"Ah, come now, Dr. Watson. Surely you know that face?" Gregson replied, drawing Irene forward toward me with a coarse hand upon her sleeve. She stumbled a bit but came nearer.

Of all Scotland Yard detectives, Gregson had the sharpest insights. I could only hope that Dupain remembered my instructions to hold his tongue. Gregson had the intellectual ability to sound a man like a bell, and Dupain was always too ready to be rung.

"You have a face a man might die for," I said to Irene, remembering what Holmes had said about her at his first sight of her, months before. I took her hand and brushed her gloved knuckles with a polite kiss.

"Do you not know the famous American songstress Irene Adler, sir?" Gregson interjected, watching for my reaction.

"Pleased to meet you, Doctor... Watson, was it?" she responded.

"Ah, Miss Adler," I said, keeping my eyes on her face, where any man would desire to look. "I must apologize. I did not know you were in town. Forgive me. My theatre attendance has been lax, of late. What a pleasure to meet you."

"Thank you, kind sir, but I fear that I am here at the request of Inspector Gregson on a rather unpleasant business touching upon your friend and associate, Mr. Sherlock Holmes."

"Surely, Doctor, you knew that Holmes went to the Midland Grand last night for the purpose of seeing this lady," Gregson said. Gregson was fond, Holmes had told me, of putting the parties of his investigation together and studying their reactions to one another.

"I did not know of his intent when he left last night," I said, feigning ignorance. "I assumed that he was off on a case. He had one minor matter with Miss Adler, some months ago, I think. Was the case reopened? I seem to recall that you were to be married, Miss Adler."

"Yes, but it simply would not do. Mr. Norton was a devoted philanderer rather than a devoted husband. It was over almost as soon as it began, though I'm flattered that you remember me."

"Well, I keep notes on Holmes's cases and, from time to time, chronicle them. But is not Mr. Holmes within? I rose early this morning to go to a small tea shop with our friends here. Ah, forgive me. I forgot to make the introductions."

Scrambling to find a suitable cover, I gave the proper names of my colleagues and told Gregson that Dupain was Holmes's acquaintance, that Dibba was Dupain's manservant, and that both were in town to celebrate the Christmas holidays with us. Simplicity in the ruse was needed. The situation Gregson presented challenged my ability to focus and find calm, but I was just able to do so by keeping as close to the truth as I could with him. My only hope was that I could keep Dupain's mouth shut beyond the context of general introductions, a hope that was dashed from the start.

"Miss Adler, how delightful to see you again," he cried, leaping at the chance to kiss her hand.

"Why, Jean-Louis, I had no idea that you were an admirer of Miss Adler," I remarked, giving him my knuckles in a sharp, hard jab to his shoulder.

"Oh, er, it was... Paris, surely, where I saw you in concert last... ?" Dupain said to Irene, surely aware of the sudden pain in his shoulder as a reminder of my standing order.

"A month or more ago, that must have been," Irene replied, giving the boy a polite smile and one raised eyebrow.

"Mrs. Hudson," I said, changing the focus of discussion, "could we impose on you for some tea for our guests in our sitting room?"

She jumped at my mention of her name but then opened the door to us. "Of course, Doctor. Just give me a minute." She led the way up the stairs to the sitting room. I was hopeful that the door to Holmes's ruined chamber was closed, still, as I had left it early that morning when I'd left to go to Mr. Uyeshiba's.

A quick survey of the sitting room showed me that Guthrie had departed and that all looked normal for a mildly untidy sitting room. My guests followed me, Gregson at the rear, studying us all. I seated Irene in the comfortable basket chair. Her face wore, still, the polite smile of a celebrity somewhat at odds with her adoring fans. She perched on the edge of her seat, as though she were in unfamiliar surroundings and unwilling to relax. We removed our outer garments, me taking care that the sword beneath my greatcoat remained unseen among the folds of dark wool. Dibba was the most relaxed of us all, taking a position behind Dupain's chair.

"Miss Adler, do you mind the scent of good Virginia tobacco?" I asked, thinking to take a relaxed attitude for the interview. I could sense an excitement in Gregson's manner. His smug grin showed that he enjoyed the act of throwing us all together.

"Not at all, Doctor, for my American ancestors were tobacco growers," she said with a pretty smile. Gregson drew a chair to Irene's side; I suspected this was so he could study our faces as we spoke. Clever fellow. I took Holmes's usual place and addressed Gregson as I rubbed out the flakes of James Fox's finest.

"So, Inspector, how can I be of service? You are here looking for Holmes. Is he working on a case with you?"

"He is wanted for questioning in a case of murder, Dr. Watson, a murder which happened last night in Miss Adler's rooms at the Midland Grand," Gregson said, turning to scan our faces in rapid succession.

"What?" I gasped, putting my pipe aside. I needed no acting to register shock. Fleetingly, I hoped that the murder victim was not one of our Logres Society associates. "You cannot mean it.

Holmes? The idea is sheer nonsense, Inspector. Whose murder? Why?"

"A Scottish nobleman, Sir Alisdair Scrymgeour, last seen by the Midland staff heading to Miss Adler's room, to which he had been invited by Miss Adler herself. Sherlock Holmes had been escorted to the same room by Miss Adler's stage manager some seven to ten minutes earlier. Holmes seems the most likely suspect, given that Miss Adler reported the crime only a few minutes later, after her arrival."

"That seems like a purely circumstantial timeline, Inspector," I said, "hardly conclusive to assign Holmes a motive for murder. I do not think that I have ever heard Sherlock make a reference to... what was the poor fellow's name?"

"Scrymgeour, Alisdair. Perhaps, perhaps not. Mere minutes are crucial in a murder, and I find that the motive often reveals itself in a study of the timeline. It shows the intent of those present. Miss Adler, would you mind detailing the events of your evening after the concert last night? In the meantime, I will have a look around, if you don't mind, Dr. Watson," Gregson said, rising from his seat.

"Of course not, Inspector. Please, Miss Adler, shed some light on this." With a deep breath, I had found enough calm to utter those words evenly. Gregson's intent, though, was to get a rise out of me, I thought. He stalked about the room, peering over the papers on Holmes's desk, poking through the correspondences stuck to the mantel with a penknife. Occasionally, he would turn to look back at me. I avoided his gaze.

Irene began her narrative in a calm voice, unhurried, though clearly she had given it word for word to Gregson already.

"I met Sir Alisdair, a devoted fan, by previous appointment in the hotel bar at the Midland Grand not five minutes after my last song. It must have been about 11:45. My driver, Tom Hastings, was with me, as he often is in the crowds after a concert, for safety's sake."

I realized that Gregson would have questioned Hastings as well and that Irene was giving me a clear sense of what Gregson knew of the case.

"When the crowd of my admirers made any private interview impossible, I suggested that Sir Alisdair take himself to my room, which the hotel had provided in the event that I did not wish to return to my own home at such a late hour. Such is my practice when performing shows in London or Paris, as I am usually in the company of fellow performers or friends."

"Were you expecting other company as well, Miss Adler?" I asked, attentive only to her words. Gregson was seeking to distract me by uttering small gasps of surprise and muttering words and phrases like "So?" and "Now, look there," as he wandered. I knew there was nothing about the place that I could not answer for or plead ignorance to. With each step, he moved closer to the doors of my chamber and Holmes's, and I prepared myself to show as much surprise as I could at the condition of Holmes's room. In the meantime, I focused on Irene's charming face—not at all a hardship—as she went on with her story. She smiled and gave me a sly wink to say that I played this game well.

"I had my manager and a female friend acting as my chaperones last night," she said, and I knew that the female friend was Mary. I could only hope to keep her apart from this business. "I expected them to be present during my interview with Sir Alisdair, but when I returned to the room, I found that they were not present. The door to the suite was ajar, and what I could see of the room frightened me, for there were splashes of blood everywhere, a window broken out, and the room a ghastly wreck. I went immediately to a hotel staff member for help, and he summoned the manager and the police."

"I assume, then, that those parties discovered the murdered man?" I asked.

"Yes," she replied, dropping her gaze to the floor and letting a note of horror enter her voice, "for I would not have dared enter such a scene of obvious violence. It was too awful to think of," she said, making her voice catch.

"There, there, madam. I hope that this doesn't upset you further, though I can tell that you are overwrought. Please, bear with me. Were you not aware, then, that Mr. Sherlock Holmes sought an interview with you last night?" I asked.

125

"Thank you, kind sir. No, for I did not yet know that he had met my stage manager and asked for an interview as well. It isn't uncommon, as I said, for several people to seek attendance at my after-show soiree," she explained.

Gregson's hand fell upon the doorknob of Holmes's room and he turned to look at me, clearing his throat. I returned his glance and waved him on, thinking that I would release the tension in me by registering shock and horror at the state of the room.

Upon entering with the tea service, Mrs. Hudson saw Gregson turn the doorknob to Holmes's room and cried out, "No, do not!"

We were all on our feet in the same instant.

CHAPTER TEN

"Murder in the Hotel."

Holmes's room stood mostly empty. Only the wardrobe with its cracked door remained in a swept-clean room. Bed, nightstand, and dressing table were gone. Gregson turned his keen eyes in our direction, but Mrs. Hudson was not to be outdone.

"The glaziers have only just left, sir. I hope the draft you caused has not dislodged the new pane. That putty is still wet," she said, treating Gregson to a reproving tone. I gave thanks for her coolness under pressure. She was most convincing.

"Sorry, ma'am," Gregson said, stepping back from the door. He gestured to the room and asked, "Has Mr. Holmes vacated the premises, then?" I wondered the same thing myself, though I had no doubt that Guthrie had been drafted by our most capable landlady in a massive cleanup effort just after I left this morning.

"Most certainly not," she snorted. "He knows when he's well-situated, does our Mr. Holmes. It just happens, Inspector, that he has finally taken my suggestion of some new furnishings, which I expect to be delivered by this afternoon. He also cracked the glass in his window yesterday with moving the headboard. The glaziers, as I said, have just put in a fresh pane not an hour ago. If you wish to verify my statement, sir..." This last word she uttered while giving Gregson a withering look, daring him to contest her veracity. He let her leave without another word and only then turned his attention back to us.

Relieved about not needing to explain Holmes's room, I turned to Gregson. "Given Miss Adler's testimony, Inspector, I

127

fail to see how Holmes is implicated in the commission of a murder. He was there, certainly, but—"

"I did not suggest that he committed murder, Dr. Watson, only that he is suspected and wanted for questioning," Gregson said, moving back to our company and pouring himself a cup of tea. "I, of course, who know Mr. Holmes only too well, realize that he is the most unlikely suspect for it, but for the likes of me, a common Scotland Yard drudge, the sparkling insights of your 'consulting detective' friend made me wish to question him as to how this poor Scotsman was killed."

Gregson changed his tune and his manner rather abruptly at that point, though he wasn't above trying to make us nervous. He took his chair again and clasped his hands in front of him.

"Sir Alisdair Scrymgeour's remains could only be identified by his attire, his kilt and plaid. He was torn limb from limb, almost in the matter of a Ripper murder, which I know from Lestrade was a matter of interest to both you and Mr. Holmes last autumn."

My own memory of Sir Alisdair had him armed and formidable. Whatever had torn him "limb from limb" had been something extremely powerful. I thought first of the afreet, Spring Heeled Jack, with his sharp claws, extreme strength, and speed, but I could not forget seeing the dreadful loup-garou, with its rending claws, snapping jaws, and even more prodigious strength. My suspicions about Holmes's magical transformation last night came back to haunt me, and I focused for a moment on the calmness of my breathing. I simply would not jump to a conclusion, especially about Holmes.

"The room was thoroughly destroyed. The amount of blood there reminded me of a Jack the Ripper murder scene," Gregson explained. "And our timeline suggests that Holmes might have been there at the time of Scrymgeour's death, which was brutal—though, I hope, quick. We know the victim was armed with a large sword he was seen to carry. Its broken blade suggests that he fought back, but the sword had no blood on it."

"So I wished to know of Mr. Holmes's ongoing involvement in the Ripper murders investigation and whether his pursuit of that killer led him to Miss Adler's room. How and why that murderer would target Miss Adler, I would give much to know, especially since she recently seemed to be the intended victim of a suspicious disturbance at the Alhambra as well. So I have brought her here, with Holmes's closest confidant, to learn what I can.

"I must say it is suspicious that we can find no trace of Holmes here, Doctor. Have you truly had no word from him? I have the testimony of Mrs. Hudson that she hasn't seen him since yesterday."

I sat in silence, staring at Gregson, who was clearly adrift in this matter. I realized, of course, that any typical police procedure would be insufficient.

"I have not seen him either. I simply never thought about it today, for I knew nothing of this murder, of course. As to the Whitechapel murders, we were never able to identify a single person involved. Like the Metropolitan Police, we were uncertain about the outcome of that case," I said, knowing that Moriarty was still abroad. "I did not think that Holmes still followed any leads in that case. Perhaps they only turned up last night, after he left my company."

Dupain, gratefully, had remained mute through all of this, his glance moving from face to face as he followed the conversation. He looked quite intent, though.

"Oh, oh! Please, Doctor, can you not help me?" Irene moaned, sinking her face into her hands.

"What is it, Miss Adler?" Gregson asked, moving to her side. She slumped forward and would have toppled out of her chair except for Dibba, who leapt to her side and caught her by her shoulders.

"Too much stress, I'd say," I offered, though I thought that she merely played upon Gregson's sympathy to bring this interview to an end. "Perhaps I should administer a sedative. Dupain, be so good as to call Mrs. Hudson back to us. I will need her help. Mr. Al-Hassan, would you be so kind as to carry Miss Adler to my room? I daresay, Inspector, that going over her testimony again, hearing of the brutality done to one or more of those who had gathered to meet her, was too much for her. I confess myself almost overwhelmed by the enormity of the situation."

Gregson stood back, a worried look on his face, as we carried out our impromptu scene of the delicate female overcome by emotion. He paced about as though he had no idea what to do. Whereas with my medical background, I had the perfect role: helper to the supposedly hysterical woman.

We carried our charade offstage, into my room, where Dibba placed Irene on my bed. Standing in the doorway, I made a show of retrieving my dusty medical bag and extracting a syringe and a phial from its depths. Dibba exited and closed the door behind him, leaving only Mrs. Hudson, Irene, and me in the room.

"A sedative, John? How delicious and how terrible," murmured Irene, opening her emerald eyes, which had a mischievous twinkle.

"Oh, there, I knew she was shamming," Mrs. Hudson whispered with a conspiratorial giggle.

"In such a sham, I doff my hat to you, dear lady," Irene said, "for the improvisation about Sherlock's new furniture. However, I shudder to think what this sign of feminine weakness will do to my public reputation."

My landlady waved both praise and concern aside, moving to stand beside the door and croon a Scottish lullaby for the benefit of the listening man whose shadow we could see below the door in the stronger light from the sitting room. Irene and I held a whispered conversation.

"I have no sedative to give you, even if it were called for, which I doubt, though I do not wish to cast aspersions on your acting ability," I said. "I do appreciate the moment to reflect on this matter with you."

"This Gregson is a cautious one," she whispered, "but you played your part well. Now you have all the pertinent facts, except this: Mary is safe in Briony Lodge."

"I knew she was with you earlier, but I avoided mention of her to keep Gregson off her scent, for she, I'm sure, had nothing to do with Scrymgeour's murder."

"Indeed, we want little of Gregson around. However, Mary was with me this evening. She and my stage manager, with whom I had a discreet word about her presence, went to my room with Sherlock, while I met that delightful Scot, the poor man."

"Mary was there during the murder? Was she—was there—"

Irene placed a strong, slender hand on my arm. "I saw no evidence that she met with any harm. But, John, we must go to her. Given the timing, she must have been present, or only just departed, when Sir Alisdair arrived at my room. My manager left her and Sherlock talking and ordered champagne and hors d'oeuvres for the evening. They may have had five minutes alone before my admirer joined them. I was busy for at least fifteen minutes before Hastings could get me away from my admirers in the bar. They were insisting on another song, if you can believe it.

"In any case, we must get back to Briony Lodge after we have spoken to Raboud. I dislike leaving Mary this long, since seeing Sherlock again yesterday has upset her."

"Why? Was she concerned about his condition?" I replied. "I can assure you that he was much im—"

"You really don't know, do you?" Irene interrupted me, surprise showing in her eyes.

"Know what?" I whispered, wondering why Mary would have been upset upon seeing Holmes at Briony Lodge. Perhaps, I thought, Holmes had relayed something to her about his plans in this case, and that had frightened her. I found this hard to believe. Mary had always had supreme confidence in Holmes's abilities.

"Never mind," Irene said, pushing past me and rising. "Now you must offer to escort me to my personal physician, which will be cover enough for Dr. Raboud, if Gregson insists on accompanying us further. We must get Raboud news of Holmes's disappearance and Scrymgeour's death. Let us make ready to leave."

***

Gregson, faced with Irene's suggestion that she had a condition requiring a visit to her physician on a monthly basis, discreetly bowed out of the investigation. "I will want to discuss Mr. Holmes's whereabouts again with you, Dr. Watson, after you have seen to this good lady's, er, condition. I will need you and your confederates here to come to the Yard tomorrow. If you have contact with Holmes before then, I expect an immediate telegram to that effect."

"Of course, Inspector," I lied with a solemn face, with no intention of keeping the appointment, if I could help it. I returned to the truth when I shook his hand and added, "I am as concerned to find him as you are."

As our hansom cab crept away through the fog, with Dupain and Dibba in another cab following, I asked Irene, "Are you worried about Mary having seen the actual murder? I assure you, she has been visited by extreme violence before."

"No. I have every hope that she left in the company of my agent before that grim scene began," Irene replied. "But whatever her past experiences, John, she would not have seen violence such as that which befell Scrymgeour. I can only hope that he died quickly. What I saw staggered even me. No, Mary would have departed to get away from Sherlock, especially after the uncertainty I'd put them through earlier."

"What uncertainty?" I asked, puzzled. "Again, you refer to something you think I ought to know already, but I have no idea what you are talking about." She turned from gazing at the blanket of fog, through which carriages, horses, and occasional faces appeared like moments from a dream. She gave me a hard stare. At length she nodded her head and sighed.

"No, of course you could not see that they may have been unfaithful to you."

I heard again Holmes's warning about learning things that would make me doubt him. Irene's stare grew more focused, but I would not meet her eyes. Taking a deep centering breath and leaning back in the seat, I gazed out at the blinding fog through which Hastings guided the horses at a walking pace.

"I doubt very much that such is the case," I said, though the enormity of her words threatened to induce a fog within me to match the one without.

"So Holmes has confided in you? I know Mary has not, unless she lied to me," Irene said.

"He warned me that I would hear things that would make me doubt him, but he asked me to trust him that these things were wrong," I replied.

Here was the reason, I thought, that Irene Adler had sought Mary out in the first place. Yet I found that I could not stick to a rational line of thought. I knew that Mary had always found Holmes compelling, though she had confided in me that he was too intense for her liking. Still, I had betrayed her; perhaps she had turned to Holmes, or had wanted to, as a way of hurting me. Such was not out of the realm of possibility.

"When is this supposed to have happened?"

"The night when you were with Anne, the night before the raid on LaLaurie's forces at Brompton," Irene said.

Holmes and Mary had been together that night, I knew, for when Mary had left me after hearing Anne's confession of love for me, Holmes had gone with her to keep her safe. I'd seen nothing in his manner afterward to tell me that he had done with Mary what I had done with Anne.

"I doubt it," I said again.

"Mary tells me that it happened," Irene replied.

"You know, though, from reading my reports, that Mary's mental condition is subject to effects from LaLaurie's zombie disease," I answered. "But all that doesn't touch upon the fact that this, if true, is a private matter between me, my wife, and my best friend."

"I fear it is a matter of concern for the Logres Society, especially for you and Holmes, who are highly placed," she said. "I act on orders from Whitefell and from Sherlock's brother, for the good of the Society. We could not risk this coming to you from Mary and potentially ruining yours and Holmes's ability to work together. You two are far too important in whatever else evolves in our long struggle, especially where Moriarty is concerned."

"Still, I wish you had come to me first," I returned, my tone growing bitter.

"Do you carry, still, enough guilt about your brief, ill-fated affair with Anne Prescott," she asked, reaching for my hand, "that you are blind to the reality that others might also have succumbed to such temptations?"

"What I have is less guilt and more sorrow," I returned, "and I would choose to bear my sorrows on my own, not in an official report for—but wait. Is this the reason that Raboud's contempt of me, his distrust in admitting me to the Society, was met with so little resistance?"

My anger began to rise. Holmes himself had said that I was owed a better defense against the occultist's charges. "Was Holmes confronted with this charge before you started questioning Mary?" I demanded to know.

"Not from me, though I believe that Mycroft brought it up to him," Irene answered, turning her eyes back to the fog that lay like a blanket across the carriage window. "And I cannot speak to the motivation of others, though I do know that they place, as I do, a great deal of trust in Raboud's opinion and counsel."

"So I am the last, really, to be briefed with this news," I said, "unless it has gone no further than the people you mentioned, who are very discreet."

"Well, Raboud knew—knows of it, and I suspect those who are closest to him have learned something of it," she murmured.

"Which undermines my authority with them," I said with more force than was, perhaps, needed. "Have you and your superiors not considered the danger in that? If my team members know that I am being investigated for the good of the society, they may question my orders, exposing us all to grave danger. The nerve of people in this damnable society of yours. No wonder Holmes has decided to pursue investigations on his own. No doubt, that is why he urged me to stay in the company of those I can trust."

Irene turned to face me and moved rather closer. "John," she whispered, "you are not taking this too well, I think."

"Please spare me the intended spell of your charms, Miss

Adler," I replied. "Thanks to you and your investigation of this matter, I have been separated from the one man I trust most, at a time when he needs me most, as well."

She crossed her arms, looked away, and said in cold, aloof tones, "Are you suggesting that my actions might have caused harm to this investigation?"

"Yes, I am," I said, and I turned her to face me. "You know full well that Holmes was at the scene of Scrymgeour's murder and that Gregson thinks of him as a suspect. By separating us, you have forced Holmes to work this case alone, without the aid of one who knows the dangers to which he has been exposed. If you and your betters had approached this business honestly, we might have faced it openly and avoided increasing the danger to us all."

"I cannot think of anything," she replied in her own anger, "that suggests I—or my superiors—have acted in a way to expose you or Sherlock Holmes to any danger greater than he has taken on in acting on his own."

"No, you would not think so, for you did not think to ask me about his condition when I saw him last. He was fully functional, as vigorous as always, maybe even more so, and I found upon his person evidence that he had been the subject of some magical incantation. God, what a fool I have been!"

"Magical incantation? Renewed vigor? What do you mean, Doctor?"

"Given the state of his room, the violence he did to Guthrie, and his miraculous recovery, I have grave reason to think that, indeed, Holmes is guilty of Scrymgeour's murder."

"How could any man kill another in the way that Scrymgeour was killed?" she demanded.

"No, you cannot see, can you? But you should know that I am, sadly, the only one, by Raboud's own admission, who can stop Holmes. For, if my fears are right, that tingling magical residue I found on Holmes's person yesterday is evidence that he has fallen under the power of the enemy we seek, that Holmes has become subject to the Loup-Garou Curse."

CHAPTER ELEVEN

"Little Room for Doubt."

Confronted with my suspicions, Raboud was much taken aback with my news of Sherlock Holmes's condition. He confirmed that in the aftermath of the transformation, the subject would feel euphoric and would also experience a profound healing of any physical malady or injury. He paced the length of the room in the Midland Grand where the murder had taken place. Adler stood at my side on the bloodstained carpet, while Dibba stayed with his back to the locked door. Dupain, having seen the evidence of murder, was being sick in the water closet.

Dried blood stained the carpet where Scrymgeour's corpse had been, and pieces of his shredded garments lay strewn near my feet. One of the bedposts and several chairs had been sliced to pieces or scored by the blade of Sir Alisdair's claymore or dirk in what must have been a heroic, if doomed, defense. The rest of the furniture was smashed almost beyond recognition. It looked like Holmes's room at Baker Street, except for the broad splashes of blood darkening to the colors of Scrymgeour's tartan. His death had been horrible, almost as horrible as the idea that Holmes, in werewolf form, might have done it.

"If what you suspect is true, Dr. Watson, all of us are marked for death," Raboud said. "I wish you had told me something of your suspicions earlier."

"Could you have stopped this?" I asked.

He looked at me for a long moment before he whispered, "No. No, it isn't likely that I could have, for my abilities, as you know, have been diminished. And if it was Holmes in werewolf form who did this, could any in the Logres Society, together or apart, have stopped him? No, Dr. Watson. Only you have the means and, I am forced to believe, the ability to do so."

"Yes, I do," I answered, "but I pray that such a test does not come to me. Had greater trust been placed in me, such as I deserved, had I been allowed to work with Holmes, I would have been in a position to do so. However, this extra investigation that Miss Adler carried on has separated us as well as weakening my ability to lead my team in the field. Your actions, as well as the actions of those who should have trusted me as much as you, have caused this. You have allowed Holmes to fall prey to this putative mage's curse and prevented me from being at his side."

Raboud shrugged his shoulders and said, "Protocol. We follow protocol in such situations, Doctor." His was the position of an officer whose command had failed its objective in the field. He bore my anger well, and this gave me a brief sense that he might be genuine. However, I was less than satisfied.

"Perhaps it is time to question such protocols, for they have led you to expose your best man in the field to dangers of which he is not aware and to turn loose a horror upon the world," I said, gesturing to the blood on the carpet and the destroyed furniture. Raboud, for once, had nothing to say, so I pressed on with my concern. "Holmes is formidable in his natural state. Would he retain any of his natural abilities if he were transformed into such a beast?"

"It is possible, I suppose," Raboud answered with a weary sigh, "but such information isn't readily available, Dr. Watson. Usually, the devastation of the Loup-Garou Curse leaves little behind in the way of information about how the curse interacts with its host."

"Can you give us any hope that Holmes can be cured of the curse?" Irene asked.

"Again, I suppose it is possible, if and when we learn the identity of the mage who cast it. But I do not know with any certainty, because the Loup-Garou Curse is so dark, so evil, that it usually ends in a situation like this," Raboud said, gesturing at the scene before us.

Indeed, the room's condition threatened to turn my stomach. Gregson had been polite when he reported Scrymgeour's death scene. Scrymgeour had been disemboweled, judging by the stench that remained. The cold air that poured through the broken window could not quite overcome it. Dupain had sickened from it immediately, and even Dibba had turned ashen-faced and stayed by the door. Irene, at my side, held a scented handkerchief to her nose.

"The Loup-Garou Curse can only be cast by someone in league with the blackest of infernal aid," Raboud went on. "And I am loath to believe that of Mr. Sherlock Holmes. Yet if all that you tell me is correct, I am forced to consider it. Further, it seems likely from what you say of Holmes's symptoms—missing time and sudden healing—that he has undergone some sort of magical transformation. I think we must assume that Holmes did this and that he is a victim of the dark mage who opposes us.

"I must congratulate you, Doctor. You have taken out one of our best defenders. I can only think that you will target Lord Whitefell next."

"Wh-what did you say?" I stammered. He had shifted so suddenly into blaming me that I had been unprepared for the insult. I should have known it was coming. "You cannot still think that I am your enemy."

"Please, Omar. This is ridiculous. Watson is Holmes's best friend. He would no more think to—" Irene interjected.

"You simply do not see it, do you, Miss Adler?" Raboud went on, folding thin arms across his narrow chest. "This man is quite capable of any action. He murdered the woman he used to separate himself from his wife and did so in a way that let the criminal, Moriarty, remain free. He used a Loup-Garou Curse to create a beast to attack Holmes. Now he has cursed Holmes, placing him to kill Scrymgeour, and will turn him against us as a weapon."

I gave a heavy sigh and shook my head at his stubbornness. "You are impossible to deal with, sir."

"Oh, am I? You think that I don't know that you are using Holmes because of his infidelity with your estranged wife?"

Raboud asked, in soft tones. More loudly, he added, "If I were you, Miss Adler, I would not let myself be alone with Dr. Watson."

"I have done so, and he has been, as always, a perfect gentleman," she replied.

"For now. No doubt he needs your fascination with Holmes to add to his control of the man."

Irene rolled her emerald eyes at Raboud's stubbornness. It had become a sort of mania, for Raboud, to bend his thoughts around seeing me as the source of his problems. Still, I knew my center and held my response to him in check.

"Dr. Raboud," I said in an earnest plea, "can you not free yourself from the destructive thought that I am your enemy? Will you not take my actions as earnest of my commitment to our common cause? We need you to lead us in this matter. You have stressed of late that your magical abilities are in a weakened state, but your intellect is sharp and your knowledge of occult matters is the best we could hope for as we try to identify our common foe."

"What of your other agents, Dr. Watson?" Raboud asked, his intent stare locked onto my countenance, his eyes searching for some reason to doubt me, I supposed.

"Other . . . my what?" I stammered.

"The gentleman, in the homburg hat, at whom you pretended to shoot in the Alhambra," Raboud spat back at me. "I caught sight of him outside of the Diogenes Club after my brief interview with Westcott this morning. Did you think me weak enough to fail to notice him and his Romany companions?"

Raboud had been followed, which meant that even now those men likely knew our whereabouts. My hands shook at the thought that the men from the theatre might be drawing a net around us, that we might even now be surrounded.

Dupain left the lavatory and came on careful steps to my side, having heard my exchange with his master. His look of fright suggested that he understood our situation. I looked at Irene and saw a frown of worry on her face as well. We had to make our forces secure and send away those not in immediate danger, while Raboud, Irene, Dupain, Dibba, and I sought some safe refuge. And I would take Mary with us, for her safety and my peace of mind.

"We have more than one enemy, or at least, our enemy has his own agents who can and will kill us or take us captive," I said. "Our lives will be forfeit, now, if we do not get to some place of safety, for I give you my word, Dr. Raboud, that the men who followed you did so without my knowledge. To think that we could have lost you, our chief defense against the occult, shakes me to my foundation. We may well, by this time, have lost Holmes, my Mary, or members of Department Zed, like Guthrie, O'Hara, and the lads Wiggins and Brewer."

"Please, Dr. Raboud," Dupain added, "listen to this man, trust his word. He speaks true."

"Yes, Omar. We need you to see this as true," Irene said.

With his eyes still intent on me, Raboud stood a moment in thought before he said, "I think that you are correct, Miss Adler, Dupain, that we should move to a place of safety. I intend to travel with Dibba to Penrith, in the north of England, this very night. There we will take refuge with Lord Whitefell at his estate. He is the only man I know who could possibly defeat Dr. Watson. In any case, Whitefell, Tennyson, and I must be in Edinburgh by Twelfth Night so that the Logres Society may go on. We simply cannot miss that moment, as I am sure Dr. Watson knows.

"However, I will be surrounded by my strongest, most trusted allies. I would recommend that Dupain and Miss Adler take the next train to the channel and leave England."

"No!" Dupain shouted. At Raboud's stern look turned in his direction, he pleaded, "I am learning so much, and I value my time with Dr. Watson. I simply cannot turn away."

Raboud turned his gaze to Irene, who said, "Omar, I am just as committed to the Logres Society, and as ready to face danger on its behalf, as any of us. Plus, I want to be there when you are forced to apologize to Dr. Watson. I am coming to Penrith as well, and I will stand with the others on Twelfth Night in Edinburgh."

"So, Dr. Raboud, what are your orders for me until I meet you at the train?" I asked, exasperated. "Is there any task that I can do for you that might help you see that I am not your enemy?"

"Yes. Find and kill Sherlock Holmes," he said.

"You cannot be serious," Irene said.

"But I am. Holmes is now a danger to the heads of the Logres Society. Logically, he must be eliminated."

"What of a cure for him?" I asked.

"The only certain cure for him is that accursed weapon that hangs at your side," Raboud answered. "Dupain, please go to the street and hail a cab to take us back to the Diogenes Club. And, Miss Adler, I still advise you to take the next train back to the Channel and leave these shores. There is no need to risk your loss to the Society as well as mine." With that, he swept from the room, Dupain running ahead of him to do his bidding.

***

Though every gas lamp in London had been lit by midday, the fog grew worse. Looking out the door of the Midland Grand, Irene and I seemed to be staring into nothing more than a filthy cotton wool, turning darker with the night. We found Hastings awaiting us not far from the hotel entrance, the carriage lamps two glowing orbs at either side of his driver's seat.

"That Dupain lad tipped me off you'd be comin' out," Hastings said, his voice nearly disembodied in the fog. "I'll need to walk the horses, guide 'em through this fog."

"I think I'll join you walking, Tom," I said, wishing to encounter any danger on my feet.

The mist was raw, cold, hard to breathe, but above all, eerie. Lights in nearby buildings took on a will-o'-the-wisp quality, alienating me from the London I'd thought I knew well. Faces of the few passersby appeared like phantoms at several feet away. Corners and street signs materialized before us at the same distance, seeming to spring from the fog as though they had forgotten to show up at their appointed places and were rushing to meet us as we came.

Hastings, though, like Bill Wiggins, had grown up on London's streets and claimed to know the feel of the cobbles beneath his feet. "Cheap shoes, sir, or none at all," he assured me. "You can set me down in London blindfold, and within six paces, I'll tell you where I am." I laughed at his joke but did not share his confident knowledge.

Irene soon alighted from the carriage and joined us in our walk, claiming a need to move to thwart the clinging chill. As we walked, she regaled me with tales of how Tom Hastings had helped her out of situations with fans who were more ardent than sensible. But while the two of them shared anecdotes—likely for my benefit, since I was sure they could see I was nervous—my attention was on shapes in the fog, shapes they didn't seem to see. Sometimes men would seem to draw near, becoming darker spots in the fog, and then fade away into the blackness beyond. And, as odd as it sounds, I could swear that I heard whispers near me, as though beings of mist spoke together near my ears, though in a language I didn't comprehend. Yet no one stepped forward. At some point, I began to walk with my hand on the cold *tsuka* of the sword beneath my coat.

But perhaps Hastings had seen something disturbing, for as she walked between us, Irene said, "What's wrong, Tom? You're positively fidgety."

"I dunno, miss, though I'm feelin' prickly all over. Must be this fog gettin' to me, like it seems to be gettin' to the good doctor there."

"Sorry, Tom," I murmured, unable to see whether he smiled at me or not. "I am as jumpy as a cat."

"Not to worry, sir. We're near Briony Lodge now, just within the next block. Three sets of 'ouse lights down from 'ere, on your right," he said.

"Tom, why don't you take the team to the stable and get yourself some dry clothing. Something warmer, too. You've been out in this beastly weather and I'll bet you're soaked to the skin. We'll need you to take us to Euston Station shortly, and then you can take some time off," Irene said, handing him an envelope. "I should be back in a few days."

His broad-shouldered shape moved off into the fog, as though man, horses, and carriage were being swallowed by the night. I noted a few human shapes moving past him, and in the light from one of the carriage lamps, I thought I saw Jamie Cameron's face. Startled, I stopped for a moment.

Irene took my arm. "What is it, John?"

"I thought I saw... someone I have only just met," I said. "Jamie Cameron."

"Really? You can make out faces in this?" she quipped. "And why would the heir to Abel Cameron be here?"

"Watching out for me," I murmured.

Walking on, we entered the glowing nimbus of a streetlamp, and just on the other side of it, I saw a movement. At the same time, a young man's voice behind me cried, "Drop to your knees!" From the other side of the misty globe, a hand and arm were raised, holding a pistol, its muzzle pointed at my head. Behind it came the shape of a homburg hat. I dropped, pulling Irene down with me as the flat *crack-crack* of the pistol sounded.

From outside the light, a dark shape flew through the mist and cannoned into the shooter. I pulled Irene behind me as I heard fighting: blows falling, men grunting and cursing, and footfalls running away. I rose, drawing my sword and pistol, moving toward them, but silence fell around me.

"John! Where are you?" Irene called.

"Here," I said, stepping back into the mist that glowed from the lamp. She entered it with me, and I saw that she held a derringer, cocked, in her right hand.

"Quickly, let us find the garden walls and seek your house," I said. "It must be only one or two away."

***

As a precaution, I asked her to wait while I opened her front door. I took her key and let myself in, sword drawn. My steps light, I managed to make very little noise as I entered the darkened marble foyer, light coming from the sitting room door to my right.

A quiet gasp from there had me on edge in a second. Needing to steady myself, I grasped the *tsuka* of my sword. I breathed in a deep, centering breath and stepped through the doorway into the sitting room. There, months ago, Holmes and I had found the picture of Irene Adler and Von Ormstein that was central to the case of "A Scandal in Bohemia." That seemed ages ago.

Tonight, in the light of candles and of the streetlamps through the windows, I beheld a tragic tableau: Mary stood next to the sofa, her hands covering her mouth, while Sherlock Holmes lay on that sofa, propped up on one elbow, his startled eyes staring at me.

"We heard shots," he said. "Has anyone taken harm?"

Irene, coming into the room behind me, stopped short. "Oh," she managed.

I held the sword at high guard. "Not that I know of, Holmes. Mary, kindly step away from him and go with Miss Adler."

"No, John, I will not," she replied in a shaking voice, moving to place herself between Holmes and me. "This isn't what it looks like, nor what, perhaps, you have been led to expect."

"You mistake my intentions, my dear. You are in danger," I said, keeping my eyes on Holmes's still figure. He watched me with intent eyes. In the flickering light of the candles, he looked nothing like the nonconformist parson he'd played the last time that his figure had graced that sofa. Indeed, he looked more like a lover still languid from the solaces of his beloved. That was a thought I did not wish to entertain.

"I aim to have Holmes, in whatever restraints can be managed, for the murder of Sir Alisdair Scrymgeour."

"Mary, kindly do as John asks," Irene added in a calm voice, extending a shaking hand to my wife. "Sherlock will come to no harm as long as we see no change in him."

Confused, her glance shifting between Holmes and me, Mary muttered, "Change? What do you mean, change?"

No one else said a thing. Mary took Irene's hand with only

mild hesitation, trusting her. When she moved to stand with Irene in the hallway, I took up a position opposite Holmes, to see him more clearly in the candlelight, wary of any sudden movements of my friend.

"Watson, I—" he began.

"Better it should be me here, perhaps, than Tobias Gregson, who is in on the case for the Yard," I interrupted. "You will need to answer to others for your movements last night."

"Ah, Watson, that I cannot do, though I desire to assure you that I have experienced no change since I saw you last. I am under the compulsion of a pact, with parties I cannot mention by name, to reveal nothing about my current condition—or, should I say, abilities." He finished with somewhat of a twinkle in his eye, which both annoyed and worried me.

"Perhaps you mean a pact with the Travelers, for I am sure that Jamie Cameron and several of his lads just came to the aid of Miss Adler and me," I said. "However, it would be best if you say little, Holmes, and please don't test me. I am rather overwrought at the moment. Those same agents from the Alhambra just tried to shoot me in the head. The leader appears to have purchased a new homburg."

"Being a slave to fashion might just be his undoing," Holmes said with a smile. "No doubt those men followed me here, though I know of no such plan of the Camerons to shadow my movements. Perhaps it is you they shadow, though the agents clearly thought you would come here, too. Cameron and his son, however, have a keen interest in you, I know." He sat up and placed his feet on the floor, which made me nervous. With his feet under him, Holmes is always dangerous.

"Um, yes," I replied, taking a step back. Then I whispered, "Holmes, do not move, if you value your life."

"Please, Watson. I know that I told you—"

"Just... hush. Be still," I said, my focus on any sign of forward movement from Holmes. I focused on my breathing, on the security of my weight over my center, and I felt no anger, only calm certainty. If he were under the Loup-Garou Curse, I could not risk him changing. I feared it with all my heart, for I knew that my only choice would be to kill him instantly, if only to save Mary and Irene Adler.

"Miss Adler," I said, keeping my eyes on Holmes, "I trust that among your things you have garments made of good, strong silk? Please fetch those so that we can restrain Holmes, unless you have lengths of chain and manacles on the premises."

"Despite my reputation, my tastes have never been so exotic, John," Irene said. Turning to a closet in the entry hall, Irene returned with a white silk scarf and bound Holmes's hands with it while he reclined on the couch. He never took his eyes off me while she secured him. She turned, then, to my wife and took her by the hand. "Come, Mary. We must tie his feet. Perhaps Hastings might find something more suitable in the stables."

Irene drew Mary away, the latter murmuring vague sounds of protest as they went to the rear of the house.

"May I rise, Watson?" Holmes asked.

"No. You may stay still or risk me executing Raboud's standing order to kill you."

"Well, Watson, I see that you have taken me at my word. And killing me would, I imagine, finally place you in Raboud's good graces."

"Perhaps, perhaps not. His mind is compromised of late. But just do not move."

"I'm damned if I know anything about this murder charge. Would you care to explain, or should I just move on to my heartfelt apologies for earning your doubt? I give you my word that on the night in question, last autumn, nothing untoward happened between Mary and me. As for last night, I had investigations that had me moving from Notting Hill to Bethnal Green until dawn. I have been among the Travelers, as you have so clearly perceived, but I came here, today, only to meet Miss Adler. I was surprised to find Mary here when I arrived, and she would not speak with me until shortly before your arrival."

"I rather think that none of that matters now, as long as you are willing to be bound and taken to Dr. Raboud. How—how do you feel, Holmes?" I asked. I chose not to take up the question about his time with Mary. If Holmes made an aggressive move,

I'd need all my concentration. I had never witnessed the change of a man into a werewolf—nor did I wish to yet—and if it happened quickly, I might not have enough time to defend myself. Holmes's posture, even seated, was now tense, on guard, as well it might be, with me standing over him in so threatening a manner.

"Other than feeling somewhat tired from a sleepless night, I am in excellent health," he said.

Without relaxing my guard—for I did not trust even the strength of silk to bind a werewolf—I said, "Raboud, Miss Adler, and myself can come to no other conclusion than that you, under the effects of a Loup-Garou Curse, brutally murdered Sir Alisdair Scrymgeour in Miss Adler's suite at the Midland Grand. And Gregson, though he knows nothing of the curse, wants you for questioning on that same charge, since you were the last person known to be with the victim before he was torn to pieces. Once you are secured, we will look to Dr. Raboud to exert some control over you and try to remove the curse."

"Well, that certainly explains your readiness to remove my head from my neck," Holmes said with a sigh. "I must, as always, commend your sense of duty, Watson, even to that end, for if I felt that I were subject to this Loup-Garou Curse, with no recourse of my own, I should ask it of you myself," Holmes replied. "However, I am under no such compulsion, Watson. My mind is my own. And I must tell you that I was not the last person to be with this Scrymgeour fellow, for I left Miss Adler's room seconds after Mary did, though secretly, through the hotel staff's exit. No one, as far as I know, saw me, so Gregson will not be able to place me in his timeline, though he is methodical.

"As to our foe, he plays a deadly game, does he not?" Holmes observed, leaning back slowly and laying his bound hands in his lap. "If I have been cursed, though, your most expedient end is surely to kill me now, here. I daresay that even Mycroft would heartily agree to that, for to risk freeing me exposes all the Logres Society to danger. And God knows, Watson, that other husbands who have cause to suspect another man of cuckoldry would do so, readily. The newspapers are rife with such tales. Even Lestrade or Gregson would likely see the justice in it. However, I daresay you'd be better served to untie me, give me a weapon, and dispatch me so you can claim self-defense."

"Don't talk rubbish, old man," I replied, never shifting. "As for the accusation of adultery, I am as guilty as the next man. You know that. And even if that charge against you is true, I stand here as your friend and one who knows that you, though dangerous like no other, represent our best hope in stopping our faceless enemy."

"Then it seems only logical that you would free me and let me do just that. I can tell you that if I was suffering under a curse, I am no longer, and within a day or two, at the most, I can put a name on our common foe. Then, if I am free, I can find a way to turn the curse upon our enemy. After all, a weapon can be turned on the one who uses it, and I have set in motion my plan to do just that. I simply need you to let me go and carry it out. I tell you this as a truth, as true as my assurance that I did not betray you with Mary, although she believes it happened."

"No, Holmes," I cried, paying little mind to his plans or the accusations he faced. This was my chance to guarantee his safety. "I will not waste this chance to make sure that—"

Screams and a wild braying of horses came through from the rear of the house, causing each of us to jump as though prodded with a needle. On instinct, I ran toward the cries, Holmes following. We dashed past a small library on our left and made for the kitchen visible in the rear, its outer door crashing open to admit Mary and Irene, screams issuing from their mouths. Mary, gibbering in terror, took shelter behind us as we met them there, but Irene pushed at Holmes and me to flee.

"It is Hastings!" she shouted. "The curse has him!"

"Behind me," I ordered as I sliced the silk holding Holmes's hands, "and get clear of the house. Holmes, arm yourself!"

My friend pulled a cleaver and a long, wicked-looking boning knife from where they hung on hooks near the sink behind us. He moved to the other side of a heavy oak butcher block table in the center of the kitchen. I would have plenty of room above waist height to ply my sword, but the narrow confines of the kitchen offered too many ways to block many strikes. Still, with an armed and ready Holmes by my side, I flushed with confidence to meet whatever threat came through the door.

In less than a second, my confidence waned.

Hastings, a man near Guthrie's size when in mortal form, was transformed under the Loup-Garou Curse into a frightening blend of muscle, fur, and speed. Tattered coat flying from gargantuan shoulders, he came through the door without making a sound, except for claws scrabbling on the stone flags of the floor. He took not a second, then bounded to his left, making straight for Holmes.

Even in our desperate battles with zombies, I'd never seen Holmes move so quickly, so fluidly. He dove forward to meet Hastings's charge, going low, under the werewolf's outstretched claws and snapping jaws. The blades flashed in Holmes's hands, moving more quickly than I could track them, as he turned over in his dive to strike at the underbelly of the horrid thing. The Hastings-wolf hybrid howled in fury and pain and landed in a ball, but he rose to his feet, his back against the sink. A thrusting kick from me sent the butcher block table across the floor to rest between Holmes and the monster. Having cleared enough room for a strike, I waited, poised, ready for Hastings's leap at me, which would give me my best chance to strike down at it. I saw that Holmes's cuts had served only to slash open what remained of Hastings's clothing.

Hastings, eyes glowing, snarled at me as he began to stalk across the eight feet between us. He wasn't about to leap. Before I could change position from high guard, he lunged forward, snatching my greatcoat in his left claws as his right swept up toward my midsection to rip open my belly. My only thought was to block that ripping thrust, and my sword moved at the speed of my thought, even as I heard Holmes's warning shout.

The werewolf pulled me closer as Mustard Seed descended, edge out, to meet the sweeping claw. Mustard Seed's blade bit through enchanted fur, flesh, and bone. The creature's strike cost him his right hand and forearm. His howling near deafened me.

In its pain, the werewolf released me, and Holmes threw the meat cleaver at the creature's head. Hastings took two steps back from the stunning blow. This was my chance: I did a full turn around my center and swept a stroke through the werewolf's neck, stopping his howl. The last blast of air from his lungs instead struck a mournful, fading note as he fell to the floor.

"Well done, Watson," Holmes said, already at my side.

"Thanks, old man," I replied, wiping the ichor off my blade on what remained of Hastings's trouser leg. "Your tossing that meat cleaver gave me the time and space I needed."

"Yes, perhaps. But Uyeshiba would be displeased with one thing."

"What do you mean, Holmes?" I asked, watching the werewolf transform back into pieces of Tom Hastings.

"I'm sorry about this, Watson, but you let down your guard," Holmes said. His right hook must have landed precisely on the tip of my chin, for all I can recall is a flash of light and then profound darkness.

PART TWO: "THE HIGH ROAD NORTH."

CHAPTER TWELVE

"Seeking Safe Passage."

My jaw and head, as well as my sense of pride, pained me, but Mary and Irene were safe. They had found me next to Hastings's body, with Holmes nowhere to be seen. Irene gathered from Hastings's person such things as might identify him: only a tattered wallet, the worn stub of a clay pipe, and some loose change from his pockets.

I was forced to lead the carriage to Euston Station on foot to take the last train to Carlisle, which I knew Raboud and his party would be taking as well. We barely arrived in time, the walking lasting twice as long as it would have on a clear night. However, I supposed that on foot we would not be followed, though since the fog stayed heavy, I could not be certain.

When we finally arrived at Euston, I found the telegraph office there and sent word to Commander O'Hara to have Wiggins and Brewer bury Hastings's remains in the plot near the graves of those we had lost in last autumn's battle with zombies at Brompton Castle. Irene had told me that Hastings had no living relatives, so I hoped that we were doing our best for him.

As we approached the ticket office, we met Dr. Raboud, Dupain, and Dibba, all standing amidst their luggage. Raboud wore a surprised look at our arrival.

"I see that you have not acted in accordance with my suspicions," he said with a wry smile. "Well played, Dr. Watson."

"I fear you will not think so when I tell you all that has happened since we left the Midland Grand," I said. While I told him all, I watched his anger build at my refusal to obey his standing order.

Irene, though, defended me. "Given that Jamie Cameron of the Highland Travelers came to his aid when those men tried to kill us, Dr. Raboud, you ought to see that as some proof that Dr. Watson is a man of his word. Tennyson trusts the Travelers, and they have made it their mission to protect Watson. They must have followed Watson since they first made contact with him. Can you think that they would not have informed Tennyson if they suspected Watson was their enemy?"

Raboud appeared to think about this for a long moment, until the ticket clerk interrupted his thoughts: "Sir, the train will depart soon. Do you wish to purchase passage to Carlisle?"

"Yes," Raboud said, "for all of us, please." Porters came for the luggage. The ticket agent informed us that only two sleeper berths remained and suggested that several of us would have to sit up in the dining car, for the second-class seats were all full.

"I will sit up," I said. "That way, Dr. Raboud can be certain that someone he trusts can watch me at all times."

The occultist nodded that such would be acceptable and said that he and Dibba would stand first watch over me.

Before we boarded, I took the conductor by the arm, led him aside and asked, "Is it possible that the Great Western will defeat the Great Eastern this night in the race to Scotland?"

"Why, there is no such thing as such a race, my good sir," the jolly little fellow replied with a twinkle in his eyes. A merry smile played about below his grizzled beard in his good-humored denial. "But I daresay we'll be out o' this ghastly fog 'fore the Flyin' Scotsman will."

I knew as well as the next *Times* reader that the two competing rail lines from London to Scotland held unofficial races in order to claim which boasted the fastest times. Word had it that wagers took place on either side of the Atlantic. Reporters in Scotland were known to dispatch telegrams to New York, Boston, and Chicago about the winners.

"I am no reporter, sir, nor railway official, but my business takes me to Penrith, just south of Carlisle, and I've boasted to the ladies," I said, grinning and pointing to Mary and Irene, "that the Great Western arrives in Aberdeen a good half hour before the Flying Scotsman."

"More like just under twenty minutes on average," he confessed, though he glanced about him in a nervous manner. "But I assure you, there is no race of any kind, sir. 'S matter of record, and our engine makes near seventy, whereas the Scot cannot pull more than forty-five."

"Exactly the source of my boast," I said, looking at the sleek, steaming engine. "And the solace of soft affections awaits me, should I prove correct in claiming that we will arrive in less than seven hours."

I gave him a knowing elbow nudge and a conspiratorial wink to cement my lie. And a lie it surely was. Mary had clearly been overwrought by the events of the evening; it had taken all Irene Adler's blandishments, aided with a little brandy, to prepare her for travel. As far as I knew, there was no chance of anything coming my way other than polite cordiality... and soreness in my head from Holmes's stunning right.

"Oh, ah," the conductor replied, his smile widening. "I cannot comment on any sort of race, sir, but tonight we are booked, for the most part, with families travelin' to Carlisle. So we will not be observin' the time scheduled for each station along the way."

"And no stop in Penrith, I suppose?" I added, taking two sovereigns from my pocket and casually examining them.

"Not a full stop, sir," he said, eyeing the currency, "except, perhaps, for those who can exit without any delay."

"We understand each other, then," I said, handing him the coins. "Another pair of these waits for you if you can find me a half hour before we reach Penrith, so that I might make ready."

"Yes, sir," he said, tucking the coins into his vest pocket. "And should I wire ahead for some overland conveyance to meet you there?"

"Indeed, and I shall see you further rewarded should you succeed," I returned.

"I should have word for you by the time we pass through Leeds, sir," the conductor said. "Ask for Mills 'ere if you don't see me." He gestured to a man standing nearby. Mills, having overheard my assurances, replied with a nod of his head, wearing a broad grin at the thought of two weeks' wages in his pocket by the time he reached Carlisle.

I boarded behind the rest of our party, conducting the ladies to their berth while Raboud, Dupain, and Dibba entered the other first-class accommodations. I then took it upon myself to travel through all the cars looking for homburgs and sniffing for the aroma of Turkish tobacco, but we appeared to have given those men the slip. Who they were, beyond confederates of the spell-slinging foe who plagued us, I had no clue. Holmes's hints had suggested that he'd be able to better identify them in two days' time. However, their presence spoke of a network of foes, and I recalled with dread the network of enemies, headed by Moriarty, that we had battled nearly a year earlier. If that vile man had returned to the scene, I would kill him without a second thought should he appear before me.

Yet the Holmes brothers and Mr. Gladstone had assured me, just a week earlier, that no sign of that arch-criminal had been seen in England or on the Continent. That meant, of course, that some other network opposed us. That thought brought me no joy. Magic was unsettling enough without a crowd of unknown assassins dogging our steps.

With Irene and Mary in one berth, I left Raboud, Dibba, and Dupain to sort themselves out in the other. I headed for the dining car, expecting to sit up for the first leg of the seven hours with at least one of the other men, hoping it would be the good-natured Dibba. I seated myself at the far end of the car, my back to a corner, away from four roisterous young men at the other end. At a glance, I took them to be military, from their manner of dress and their swaggering talk. If someone did attack me in the car, I thought, perhaps I could appeal to such strong, battle-trained men to join in my defense.

My double scotch arrived at the same moment that, to my surprise, Raboud entered the dining car, looking for me. Before he could join me, however, one of the young men at the far table pushed to his feet and stood in Raboud's path.

"What's this, then?" he cried. "Little wog is on 'is 'olidays, is 'e?"

He earned the laughter of his three companions and, emboldened by their support—and likely by too much liquor before he'd boarded at Euston—he placed a hand on Raboud's chest, holding the slender Egyptian in place. Raboud started, his dark eyes aswim behind those thick lenses.

Despite my distrust and dislike of Raboud, the term *wog* had me on my feet in an instant, remembering my strong feelings about the way enlisted men in India abused their native servants. I started down the aisle as the other fellows rose from their seats. Raboud seemed to withdraw into himself, casting his dim glance to the floor of the dining car. The bullyboys laughed and pestered the esteemed occultist, one of them going so far as to snatch the lenses from Raboud's nose and place them on his own.

The tall fellow loomed over Raboud, and I approached him quickly from behind. My left foot placed on the back of the fellow's leg, I jerked down on the collar of his jacket. Raboud's first persecutor fell onto his broad backside with a loud thump and groans of pain. The others stopped laughing and turned on me, ready to fight. The one nearest me hurled a looping punch at my head; I stepped inside it with ease. My swift blow to his lower right side widened his eyes, and he sank to his knees, the kidney strike removing his ability to rise, no matter how angry. He stared up at me, as did his companion with the aching rump.

"Gentlemen," I said, extending a hand to the fellow who still had Raboud's lenses in hand, "pray let me buy you a round of drinks."

At that point Dibba Al-Hassan filled the doorway behind his master and drew an appreciative gasp from all four of them, stopping their words of protest. Dibba placed his hands on Raboud's shoulders, gently shoving aside the tough who had stood behind his master.

"Sure, sure, guv," the one with the lenses muttered, handing them to me. I passed them back to Raboud. "We meant no 'arm, see? Just a bit o' fun, like."

"It isn't 'guv' but 'Captain,'" I returned, fixing the lad with a glare befitting one of that rank. "Please accept my offer of a quiet drink and consider it a reward for lessons learned, hmm?"

Dibba smiled at them all and conducted his master to the table I pointed out, where my own drink awaited me. The four rowdies took their seats as I returned to mine and ordered a round for them, along with the tonic water Raboud and Dibba requested. The boys were more subdued now, but they did acknowledge the arrival of their refreshments in a quiet salute, which I returned.

"Thank you, Dr. Watson," Raboud said, sitting opposite me. "I confess that your violence has its uses, though I knew that Dibba was a dozen paces behind me. You needn't have intervened on my behalf."

"Perhaps it was more on my behalf, as well as that of those lads," I said, disliking the Egyptian even more. "I couldn't have you turning them into toads or something more fitting, jackals maybe." This earned a laugh from Dibba, which made me smile as well. Raboud merely continued to stare at me, unaffected by his associate's ebullience.

"Let us pass on this mundane matter, then, and turn to the real reason I have sought you out: Holmes's assault on you, Miss Adler, and your wife," Raboud said, taking a sip of his tonic water.

"It was not an assault," I replied, "so much as a necessity to get me out of the way, since I was bound by your thick-headed order—sir," I replied. Dibba smiled at my rebuke and rolled his eyes toward the ceiling, earning a wry smile from Raboud.

"My associate, this inestimable dweraz, has been chiding me about my attitude toward you. And I have come to realize that perhaps, in my weakened state, I should trust his assessment of you more than my own," Raboud confided in a low voice.

"Very well," I replied, somewhat disarmed by his reply.

"You gave no thought to carrying out my order to kill him?" Raboud asked.

"Of course I did, but he wasn't... changed. He was Holmes as I'd known him, only more fit. I could no more have killed him than I could have killed Dibba—or you. And it was only with his aid that I was able to stop poor Hastings."

"Can you assure me that the discovery of the body of Miss Adler's driver will not compromise our investigation?" Raboud asked.

"Indeed, our lads are well versed in such matters, and Miss Adler tells me that Mr. Hastings had no family to miss him and raise any sort of alarm," I replied. "Commander O'Hara will oversee this, and Magnus Guthrie will contact me when he arrives in Penrith tomorrow."

While I could appreciate Raboud's sense of caution, I would be slow to believe that he had changed his stance on me. I was more grateful to Dibba, who had apparently taken my part.

I had been wondering, though, about the events of the evening, and my thoughts turned back to Hastings. Someone had chosen him and cast the Loup-Garou Curse on him. Hastings had been used as a weapon, intended to kill Irene, Mary, Holmes, and me. Where and when had the spell been cast on Hastings? And why?

It seemed reasonable to think that the man in the homburg was in league with the person who worked the magic, for they seemed to be in league with whoever was behind the attack of the afreet in the Alhambra Theatre. The homburg man, though, had tried to kill Irene and me outside Briony Lodge. Had those men not known that Holmes and Mary were within? Had they not known that the curse had been placed on Hastings? Perhaps, I thought, Hastings had only been intended to destroy Irene and me.

The question remained: by whom? Logic told me that the person who could do that, Dr. Omar Raboud, sat across the table from me, yet I found that I was quite willing to dismiss that idea. It had occurred to me before, but all that I had learned about Raboud, including his blind distrust of me, told me that his single-minded devotion to the Logres Society meant that he could not be the enemy I sought.

At that very moment, he reinforced my conclusion, saying, "I suppose that you understand Holmes is an even greater

159

danger, now, to the leaders of the Logres Society. Is it likely that he is in league with the mage who works against us? Since he entered your chamber so quickly when the faerie entered to seduce you, might he not already have known it would visit?"

"Preposterous. That night, before we came to the Alhambra, he was as shocked as I was and saw something different than I did, something which clearly upset him as much as this faerie business upset me," I replied. "Besides, Holmes is in league with no one, except himself, if you want my opinion. Holmes most often works alone. Me, he tolerates much of the time as a sort of barometer for what is 'normal,' mundane."

"Perhaps that is but a manipulation to cover his true intent, which is to do harm," Raboud insisted. "As a werewolf, his true intent will manifest in more ferocity. If you valued Holmes as a friend, even a manipulative one, shouldn't you have destroyed him when you had the chance? The danger he represents is incalculable."

"Yes, but if he is a danger, at least we have forced him from London. He will follow us, surely," I replied. "Besides, I must remind you that even if Holmes is a serious threat, he is not the one we need to find. Name that mage, as you call him, and we can eliminate all other threats."

Raboud's shoulders slumped, and he turned his gaze from me. When he did look at me again, I returned his stare until he broke contact.

"You are right, sir, though I wish I could argue with you. But I regret to say that I am no closer to identifying that person. Perhaps worse, your continued presence at my side argues against my certainty that you are my enemy. As Dibba has insisted, I have given you too many chances to do me harm, and you—"

"You needn't say any more, sir," I replied. "I am heartily glad that you have come to a better understanding of me. May I assume, then, that you are no longer opposed to my investiture in the Logres Society?"

"I—yes. You may count on my support," he replied in weary tones, his face marked with even greater fatigue than before. Losing his will to oppose me seemed to have drained him further, as though his anger toward me had given him the energy to go on.

"You need rest, Dr. Raboud," I said, "which I hope you can get at Whitefell Manor. Once there, if we can identify our foe, will we hold off on going to Edinburgh for the investiture ceremony?"

"No," he claimed, with something like a spark coming back to his eyes. "As many of us as possible need to be in Edinburgh by the fifth of January, for Twelfth Night. Have I not told you this?"

"You did mention it, but I assumed that with the threats against us just now, the investiture might be postponed or perhaps even moved to London," I said. I had never enjoyed the notion of going back to Edinburgh. I had been there not long before to scatter Anne Prescott's ashes, which was reason enough to avoid going back. However, there were older reasons to stay away from that city, reasons I did not wish to divulge. They were such that I couldn't think how to articulate them, at any rate.

"I think you have misunderstood something vital about our flight to the north, Dr. Watson," Raboud said.

"Then please enlighten me, sir," I replied, with more energy than I had intended, for in my confusion and fatigue, I could feel my resentment about the city of my birth adding to the tension I carried.

"Tennyson and the Court Champion, Lord Whitefell, have fled for safety to an area near Penrith, below Carlisle. That is where the ancestral estate of the Whitefell family rests, on the northern border of the Lake District. From there, Tennyson and Whitefell, at the very least, must go to Edinburgh. I take a risk in telling you this, but upon Dibba's word that you can be trusted, I will tell you: the Sovereign of the Logres Society must stand at the pinnacle of Arthur's Seat at precisely midnight on the fifth of January, the English feast of Twelfth Night, in order to take on the Mantle of Logres."

"What are you talking about? Some ceremonial robe, perhaps?" I asked.

"No, no," Raboud said. "The Mantle of Logres is a granting of special abilities—you might say magical abilities—that gives the Sovereign the insight needed to be a just and true leader. The nature of that gift manifests itself differently in every Sovereign, and it is essential to his or her rule. This season's investiture was set to happen the next day, the day of Epiphany according to Christian reckoning, only as a matter of convenience."

The convenience of the date, and the possibility that another place might need to be chosen, suddenly seemed far less important. "This is the first I've heard of the—what was it?"

"The Mantle of Logres," Raboud replied in low tones. He favored me with a tired smile. "I forget that you have had little tutelage in the workings of the Logres Society. Your exploits, rather than your training, have earned you the invitation into its ranks. But I must confess that your lack of knowledge about the importance of this ceremony only proves that you are not the enemy I had supposed you were."

"Perhaps you could . . ." I began, leaning closer over the table. Raboud looked at Dibba, who nodded. Taking a deep breath, Raboud began.

"You see, the true power in magical arts comes not in the casting of spells and such but in the attuning of an adept's ability to connect to the power that Allah creates in the world around us. The Earth itself features lines of energy, like those upon which the ancient pyramids of Giza are aligned. There, the god-kings of Egypt once drew upon that power to create a mighty empire, but that was for their own good, not for the good of their subjects. But there were others before them who learned to use that power for the common good, such as Melchizedek, the founder of my order."

"Do you mean the fellow mentioned in the book of Genesis?" I asked.

"Yes, indeed," Raboud said with a smile, "that very fellow, known even to Christians as the King of Salem, which is to say, the King of Peace."

"And this relates somehow to the necessity of going to Edinburgh," I stated, inviting him to avoid the history of his order.

"Edinburgh—Arthur's Seat, to be specific—is the northernmost point of a triangle of power that defines the ancient kingdom of Logres. Its other points are London and Cardiff. This knowledge, we have learned, came to the legendary King Arthur as a gift from the Light Court of faerie-kind, his allies of old; they granted him the right to rule in justice. Though evil pulled him down, the power remains. The Mantle of Logres is a name for the power itself, which comes into the one who places himself on Arthur's Seat and declares himself willing to use it for proper rule. The power flows to the north in winter, to London in spring, and to Cardiff in September, with the autumnal equinox."

As outlandish as Raboud's description sounded to my ears, it made a sort of sense in my heart. My intuition showed me that this was the reason for the Logres Society's mission: promoting civil order for common people, seeking their educational growth, and protecting them from occult threats and power-mad domination. His words gave me a new and sudden appreciation for magic, but those words were in conflict with my past, with the very reasons I desired to stay away from Edinburgh.

My agitation grew as I thought about my youth, my upbringing in that city. The clacking of the train wheels seemed to pound in my head. The sway of the carriage made me dizzy, and my hands clenched and unclenched as I held them together before me, seeking to be patient but losing any calm I could muster. Even Dibba's smile irritated me, as did Raboud's gentle gaze searching my face. I told myself that I should be happy to be given this view of the Logres Society, which I had given everything to defend.

"If only it were not Edinburgh," I said through my teeth.

"The city itself presents you with a problem?" Raboud asked gently. "I thought it would be all this talk of magical power."

"I was born in Edinburgh, raised there," I said, unable to control the exasperation that caught me up.

"This is a problem? I was born in Cairo, but I miss it, always. I feel as though I am more myself there than anywhere else in the wide world."

"I—I envy that sense of connection you have with your home, sir," I said, "but Edinburgh is clouded in my memory with cold, damp, and people trapped in their own foolish fancies. I believe, as Samuel Johnson did, that the only good thing to come out of Scotland is the road to England."

Dibba laughed at the old joke, but it seemed to lend more intensity to Raboud.

"Foolish fancies like magic?" he asked, studying me, his eyes enlarged by his lenses.

"Yes, because magic is a cheat, a sham that we inflict on ourselves, like overblown piety, like those stories of knights, quests, rescuing damsels..."

"But you have seen that magical power is real, Doctor," Raboud whispered, leaning closer, seemingly fascinated by my overwrought condition.

"Yes, I have seen it—as evil, as a power that draws men to it, like sex or strong drink. It draws them to their destruction and that of others," I claimed, my hands shaking.

Dibba looked on, smiling, as though he enjoyed the sight of me caught up in my memories. And indeed the floodgates had opened: I could have been back in my youth again, seeing my father, the would-be artist, succumbing to drink through the drudgery of a civil service job, married to a woman who demanded piety and practicality yet filled her children's heads with the fluff of chivalrous tales.

Suddenly, I could not bear even the thought of going back to Scotland, a damnable place of conquered people left grindingly poor, for the most part. Its people were forced to live with only dreams of freedom and of faerie magic. As a child, I had longed for the day when I could leave Edinburgh and identify myself as English, like my father. Here, though, I was being carried back to it, and that left me no peace.

"What do you want of me, Raboud?" I finally demanded, ready to defend myself from this thin, calm man who sat with peaceful hands folded before him.

"That is my question for you, sir: what do you want, Dr. Watson?"

"I want to be treated fairly, to do my work, to be shed of this case, this damnable, awful magic," I said, trembling with agitation. "I want to..." I did not know what else, though I bore it like a weight in my stomach. I could not vomit it forth and rid myself of that mass or of the taste of it that rose in my throat.

"I am sorry," Raboud whispered, "for I asked the wrong question. It wasn't the question of magic, for magic comes from the soul, which is not emotion any more than it is intellect. Magic is less illusion than a revelation of soul truths, such as that we are, all of us, connected. It is experienced in the power of a wish that most needs granting. Here is the question that magic asks you: what is it you wish for?"

A strange wave of dizziness passed over me, one that left me with a clearer sight of all that was before my eyes. That word, "wish," reached into me, caused tears to start from my eyes. They were old tears, as the one sob that passed my throat was the sound of an old, persistent pain.

Dibba reached across the table and placed a heavy hand on my arm. "Yes, Cap'n Jack. Yes, good."

The pain was good? Yet in that thought, turning to look at what I called pain, I saw only doubt, confusion, and old anger. And all of these began to dissolve with the suggestion that they were not mine to bear, at least not alone.

The weight in my stomach lifted, and that one sob turned into a deep sigh. The tension I typically carry in my shoulders and neck faded away. My hands stopped shaking. I realized that while I might be able to have some measure of control over my situation through breathing and meditation, through the discipline of the sword, through my work, my true wish lay beneath that. All I could do was accept it.

"I wish to know... that there is more, that there is meaning, that I am more than this sword and its burden. I wish to be... good. I wish to know who I am." The train wheels no longer grated in my hearing, and the rocking of the rail car soothed me.

"Then," Raboud whispered, "you have touched the place of magic in your life. I cannot tell you who you are, but I can tell you that you are not the man I thought you were and not the man you have thought you were. I know now that you were never my enemy, unless you are the most deeply guileful being under the sun."

"I am no more guileful than Dibba or Dupain. Yet I must tell you that I have doubts about that lad's abilities—although I'm sure his training has shown him to be a fine pupil of your studies."

"He proved himself... loyal to me, insisting on staying with my father when I set out for West Africa. In time, perhaps, he will become a great help to our Society," Raboud said softly, seeming to relax even more.

Glad that I was free from Raboud's malice now, I wanted nothing more than to stay at that table, though I was a bit embarrassed at having shown so much emotion. Thankfully, my companions did nothing to mark it, so I let it pass too. But then a sudden sense of fear passed through me.

"Dupain," I said with a start as an image of his frightened face flashed through my thoughts. "Where is he?"

"We left him sleeping in the berth," Dibba answered. "He was tired."

Looking beyond them, I saw that of the four men who had confronted Raboud, only three remained. "Your erstwhile attacker has left his companions. I think that Dupain needs watching."

Raboud rose with a sudden start, as though he sensed some danger, too. "Come, Dibba. We should check on him." Following them, I stopped at the ruffians' table to inquire about the man who had confronted Raboud. It seemed that he hadn't been one of their friends at all.

"Claimed 'is name was Maguire, sir, and bought us two rounds of drinks," one fellow confessed. "Seemed at first that we all knew 'im, but now not one of us knows where from."

"Thank you," I said. I was too distracted by their news to admonish them further about treating Dr. Raboud with respect. "Maguire," I thought, had joined their number under false pretenses, and given the situation, I imagined that he was part of our foe's network. Raboud and Dibba could take care of Dupain. I needed to find my conductor friend.

He was two cars ahead, in the salon, and he had the passenger manifest spread out on a table before him.

"One too many passengers on tonight's trip?" I asked.

"Yes, indeed, according to our last count," the conductor said, leaning back to look at me with curiosity in his eyes. "Now why is it, sir, that I knew that you would be involved in this little mystery, though I have accounted for all of your party?"

"Ah, my friend, trouble follows me like a faithful hound," I replied in joking tones.

Knowing that an impostor traveled among us set my curiosity on edge. His British accent had not matched the voices I'd heard from the Alhambra's balcony. Could he be feigning a British accent? Could he be in disguise? This speculation sent my mind to espionage rather than magic, which was somewhat comforting, in an odd way.

"I just wonder if you can see a Maguire on that list," I continued.

He stared at me for a moment, and I met him eye to eye. "Are you a policeman, sir?"

"No, I am not, but I do represent some individuals who do policing of a sort, though I will say nothing more of them," I replied.

He looked down at his list, then, and shook his head. "No Maguire here, sir. Should I initiate a search?"

"No, I think not. Chances are, I will run into him before you do, and you had better leave him to me. Whatever happens, my party will wish to disembark at Penrith, and I remain willing to pay for that privilege," I advised him. "Do we still have a deal?"

He considered me gravely. "Sir, I don't mind saying that you give me the collywobbles, for I sense something in you that is—"

"What? Dark? Distrustful?" I asked.

"No, sir. Intent, sir, and I think lethal," he said with a sly smile, "though perhaps not to me. You see, twenty years aboard this line and others has trained my eye. You've weapons about you, sir, under that coat of yours, but you bear them out of need, not to harm—I hope."

Searching in my pocket, I found two more sovereigns and handed them to him. "Me? Why, I am as docile as a lamb, sir. But I am armed—"

"Dr. Watson!" Irene called from the car door. "You are needed. Dupain, he—"

"Yes. Right away," I said to her. To the conductor I said, "Perhaps you should follow me, though not too closely. We might need your help." I did not wait to see whether he agreed.

CHAPTER THIRTEEN

"The Feast of St. Egwin, Protector of Widows and Orphans,"
30 December, 1888.

As soon as I entered the first-class rail car, I saw Mary and Irene Adler in the corridor. Mary stood with her hands over her eyes; Irene peered in over Dibba's shoulder. She saw, as I did, a pale, quivering Dupain, his left shirtsleeve blood-soaked and torn open. Dibba held pressure on the wound, in which a wicked clasp knife was still imbedded. Raboud called out the young fellow's name.

When I pushed past Mary and Irene and took Dibba's hand away, I inspected the wound and breathed a sigh of relief: the knife had penetrated just the bicep muscle, missing both arteries of the upper arm. I removed the knife, handed it back over my shoulder for someone to take, and let the wound bleed a little more. It was no deeper than an inch or so.

I turned to the anxious faces behind me. "He is in no real danger. The wound is not deep."

"Oh, you lot are a skilamalink bunch," the conductor muttered, sticking his head around the compartment door. "I'll fetch some supplies, shall I?"

"Thank you, my friend," I said.

"He's waking, Watson," Raboud muttered.

"S-sorry, *m-mon capitaine*," the lad stuttered, his eyes fixing their gaze on my face. "I am always becoming a... nuisance to you."

"Hush, boy," I whispered. "Lie still and let me bind my handkerchief around your arm."

"This knife," Irene said, "is a *navaja*, favored by the Gitanos, the gypsy folk of Andalusia. Hastings once carried one like that but with a plain wooden handle. This one is ivory."

"So it would appear," I whispered, taking the weapon from her again. The mention of gypsies reminded me that the Highland Travelers were not the only gypsy folk to be involved in this case. I sighed at my level of ignorance at what was going on—in this case, who the players were. Separated from Holmes's knowledge and insight, I could do nothing but push on.

I thought it better to concentrate more on the wound the blade had made. A touch along the blade's edge told me that it was quite sharp, which seemed at odds with the relative shallowness of the strike. The blow behind it had not been all that powerful, I thought, and might have been delivered by a woman or a child. A grown man intent on murdering Dupain would have skewered the arm entirely with such a blade.

The conductor returned with supplies, and I bathed the wound and wrapped Dupain's arm with gauze and tape. He lapsed into unconsciousness again, likely as much from relief as from the pain. I thought of the men and boys among my own colleagues whose similar wounds I had tended. An old soldier, like Guthrie, would have seen to such a wound on his own, but this lad, accustomed to a more sedate and studious life, was not ready for even superficial combat wounds.

"We should send him back to London," I said to Raboud. I had seen the lad's lack of preparedness for Department Zed work, and I had a desire to protect him from further harm. "Surely Bismarck would thank you for returning his protégé with fewer scars."

"Regardless of the Chancellor's wishes, the boy would not go," Raboud sighed. "The lad is devoted to you, Dr. Watson, as he was to my father or me. You observed his reaction to being withdrawn in Miss Adler's hotel room, yes? I fear that exposure to your leadership has given him fanciful, even romantic notions about the work he will carry out for the Logres Society. He simply will not leave his '*capitaine*' while this mission goes on."

Dibba nodded his assent, and Mary murmured, "It is true, John. Your men love you and will follow you anywhere, no matter the cost they bear."

Irene cleared her throat and tugged at the sleeves of Raboud and Dibba, bidding them come and have a drink with her in the club car. I turned to take Mary's hands in mine.

"I fear I have become rather another burden on you, John, dear," Mary whispered, letting me fold her into my embrace. "I really shouldn't be here, should I?"

"I would wish you far from harm, but at least here I can attempt to protect you. You see, dear, I have proof positive that I am rather a target for certain parties in this case—or cases, really. If you were in London still, I don't doubt that they would try to harm me by hurting you. I know that it is rather an inconvenience for you to be away from home, with borrowed things, but at least here I can see you safe."

Her head nestled into my shoulder, and I held her tight, grateful for this moment, despite all that I had heard. As though thinking the same thing, she murmured, "It is indeed a wonder that you would wish me safe, given what I have done."

"Mary, I will not pretend to judge you. I have no right, you know," I replied.

"Because of what happened between you and Anne. Yes, I know. I wonder, have you seen that it was a similar thing that happened with Sherlock and me, an error, a fantasy gone wrong in the heat of a very bad moment?"

"Yes," I said. Making her question whether it truly had happened would do little good. I could clearly see why she would have entertained such thoughts about Holmes, for he had been magnificent in solving a family issue for her. She had to see him as a hero. I certainly desired forgiveness for my foolish actions, and in asking that, I had to extend the same to her. Even if her betrayal of me was only a confusion brought on by her malady, it must have been what she had secretly desired for as long as I'd known her, though she would have had to wait forever for Holmes to recognize how she saw him. I suppose, in a way, Mary had wed both Holmes and myself, for, at our best, we are inseparable—or should be. Holmes's whereabouts and condition now were worries I could not shake.

"I think perhaps I'd better join the others, since you plan to stay here and watch your patient. He seems such a hapless youth," she said, reaching out to push the hair off his forehead.

"Yes, love. Go have a good talk with Miss Adler. I know that you are much in her thoughts and cares," I said, and sent her down the corridor. I watched her slender figure move away, noting how much I liked her walk; she turned to catch me at it and blushed. As she left the car, however, something like an odd ripple in the air passed between us, making me start in alarm. Its fading, though, was quick, and I thought it a trick of the shifting light in the rail car and my own need for sleep. Still, it was unsettling, and even Dupain mumbled something in his sleep.

***

Later, with Dupain resting more easily, I nodded, near sleep myself, with thoughts of Mary filling my imagination. When we reached our destination, I would place myself at the disposal of my superiors and be the best help I could in ferreting out this mage and determining the identities of the man in the homburg and of his minions. Beyond that, I looked forward only to returning home with my wife, even if it meant that my investiture in the Logres Society would be delayed or denied me altogether.

In the midst of such confusing thoughts, the conductor came to the compartment door and roused me.

"Are we making good time?" I asked him.

"Ah, yes, sir, but as to our fast run this night, I fear that we will fall short of our usual speed. That wretched fog we left behind with the city, but the Midlands have received a generous fall of snow this night, recent reports say, and the track conditions are suspect. We will make our destination, to be sure, but it will be slower going to the north, sir. It may be that we will even be delayed in reaching Penrith. Do you still intend to disembark there and seek overland transportation?"

"Yes, I do, and the fewer people who know of our intent, the better," I said.

"Very good, sir. Your foreign friends are dozing in the salon car, but the young ladies have locked themselves into their berth here. Perhaps you should take some rest, too, sir?"

"Thank you," I said. "I am fine with just watching over our friend here."

With Dupain in quiet sleep opposite me—I intended to wake him in an hour—I fell to considering how best to proceed. It might have been safer for Mary and Irene to have remained with Raboud and Dibba, but I saw no immediate need to alarm my wife further or add to her discomfort by having her return to the dining car. I considered the attack on Dupain and what it told me of our foe. If my young charge had awakened in time to see the attacker, he might have told us that the supposed Maguire had done it, but that would have made little sense, given Maguire's size. It made no sense that such a man would have made such a slight wound with that long, sharp blade.

And why Dupain? Was it because we had left him alone, vulnerable? He had no crucial role in the Logres Society, unless he had learned enough about the enemy to identify them. If, perhaps, he had shown too great an awareness of the enemy's identity, they would have wanted to eliminate him, even if their attack couldn't be made to fit the pattern of previous attacks.

The train rocked on into the night. The trees and fields I could see through the frost-edged windows turned white, and the cold that seeped into the car deepened so that my fingers grew chill, yet Dupain slept on. I considered waking him and joining the others, but I didn't. Something in his relaxed face made me unwilling to break the calm of his rest, for rest he needed, as did I.

Taking Mustard Seed off its hanger within my greatcoat, I laid it across my knees, the pommel toward the inner door of our berth. For a time, I mused on how Tom Hastings, in his accursed form, had moved to attack Holmes first in Irene Adler's kitchen. Had he been cursed to deal with just Holmes or all of us? I had to think that it was the latter. I wondered whether the leaders of the Logres Society were safe or whether Lord Whitefell, even at this moment, defended them from dreadful, unholy creatures.

That was a possibility, even if our enemy were on this train. Maguire might only be an accomplice, like the man in the homburg. Our enemy could move on many fronts, especially if the Travelers were right and it was all one case. Such an adversary would have accomplices everywhere, literally enchanted to do his bidding. The problem of fighting this unknown foe was that we fought against someone who employed magical means against which we could not adequately prepare. I knew, all too well, about facing an enemy who had plotted ahead of me, and I shuddered at the thought of what magic would add to the stress and confusion of tracking such a foe.

Raboud had been unable, as he said, to track our foe with magic. Even his seeming acceptance that I was not his enemy had seemed to weaken him further, and I wondered what he had gone through in Africa to diminish his powers to that point, especially at this time when we needed them so.

In these thoughts, I remembered that we had entered, some hours ago, the Feast of St. Egwin. I thought of how I had once been a sort of orphaned fellow who needed protection. My mother had stressed that during these twelve days of Christmas, when the season grows old, we should think of the needs of others. With too many "others" to worry about, I let my hands rest on the scabbard of my sword, seeking only to protect this orphan in my charge, for Dupain needed it.

He was clearly in over his head in his work with Raboud, especially in Department Zed. I still felt he should be sent home. Yet he was bound, like the rest of us, into this uncertain night and new day. In these unhappy thoughts, I drifted off into sleep, failing to maintain my guard.

***

I awoke with a start in pitch black: the interior lights had gone out, though the train sped on into the night. The only light came from the ambient glow of the snowfall outside. I heard

Dupain's slow, steady respirations. Another sound came, though, from the black corridor outside our locked compartment door. Furtive steps made the floorboards creak under a heavy tread.

The opposite side of the car must have faced an embankment of sorts, or else we passed under the shadow of overhanging trees, dark, deep, and wild. That made sense to me, given the heavily wooded country through which we traveled, the western edge of the Yorkshire Dales and the forests of the Lake District. As a Londoner, by choice, I might have been forgiven for shivering at the thought of the snowbound wilderness. But a deeper shaking took hold of my limbs, for in the same moment I saw through the door's glass that whatever had made the soft, heavy steps in the corridor appeared as a large form, darker than the night under the trees outside.

Red eyes squinted through the glass, and the handle to our berth began to turn. The sudden shriek of metal being torn like paper made me leap to my feet. Dupain, reclining to my left, let out a sudden cry and sat up with a start.

"Get up, lad, and get behind me," I whispered, and I clasped Mustard Seed with both hands, its chiseled point toward the door. When the lights flickered on for an instant, I groaned, for outside the door I saw what I had most feared: the excessive musculature and stooping head of a loup-garou. This one was taller, rangier than the two I'd killed before, and it bore no shred of clothing.

Its glowing eyes stared at us. The werewolf looked at me, at my sword, then turned its eyes to Dupain. Perhaps it was fear of the sword point that kept it in the hallway—I don't know—but it stayed still, watching.

Behind me, I heard Dupain begin to mutter, and his hand on my shoulder shook. He muttered in French, "No, no. Not yet," as the panic built up in his voice. But I focused only on the thing in the corridor, which began to ease the door open, its movements slow, cautious. Almost wishing that it would spring and release the tension in me, I lowered my center of gravity and breathed deep, knowing that I could not make a broad cut in the confines of a rail car.

Dupain's rising panic culminated in a wordless cry, the outer door opened, and before I could protest, the young fellow had hauled on the shoulders of my coat, pulling me with him out into the cold night.

Dupain screamed as we tumbled down a steep embankment, landing in a spray of snow, me trying to maintain a good grip on my sword so that it would not impale either of us as we fell. I slid to a halt some forty feet down the embankment, while Dupain landed with a crackling crash in a weedy thicket several yards below me. The train rattled on, and in my last glimpse of it, I was sure that a large dark shape dropped from it several hundred yards from us.

We were two men, ill-prepared, lost in a snowy wilderness, and we were being hunted.

CHAPTER FOURTEEN

"Fear and Fancy in the Wood."

Sheathing my sword, I ran to Dupain's aid. His left arm, he held useless, and I saw his bandage reddened with fresh blood. His knife wound had begun to bleed again. Noting the blackthorn part of the thicket, I did not doubt that he had been punctured by thorns, as well. The werewolf, I assumed, would have no trouble tracking us, with the young man bleeding.

"Here, lad. Take hold of my wrist," I said, grasping his right forearm. I hauled him out of the blackthorn bushes, pleased to see that he had not taken any serious lacerations in his fall, though he yelped where thorns poked his skin through the fabric of his shirt and trousers. Getting him on his feet, I wrapped my greatcoat around his shoulders.

"We need to move, now. Quickly, Jean-Louis."

Toward the west, all I could see were trees on small, rolling hills that seemed to melt in the distance into low-lying clouds that held yet more snow. On the other side of the tracks, a wild heath rose, snow covering it like a shroud. There was no good in going back to the track, for I did not know where we were, except north of Leeds. I thought little of our chances of flagging down the next train.

Being hunted, I wanted to move, not stay still and wait. The open terrain of the Dales on the far side of the tracks would allow us to see the approach of the loup-garou, but if we stayed there, we would be easy to see, too. Though I am no woodsman, I reasoned that we might hide better in the woods. There, we also had ready access to fuel for a fire, which we would need for survival if the wolf didn't get us first. The thought of it leaping on us from behind chilled me worse than the snow.

Thus far, though, this monster behaved differently than the two others I had faced. And given what Raboud had told me of the curse, I found any variation in werewolf behavior quite puzzling. That is not to say that I welcomed another encounter as a way to learn more about werewolves. In fact, I did not even know whether this one hunted me, or Dupain, or both. It did not matter much. However, the creature's seeming reticence to push its attack through the door and into the rail car stayed in my thoughts. It had not acted like Hastings or Pinder, stalking and attacking with immediate, murderous intent. That intrigued me.

But survival mattered most for now: the cold could kill us as well as the monster. Though freezing to death, from what I'd been told, would be a much more pleasant death than being disemboweled or having one's throat ripped out.

Hurrying Dupain down the slope of the embankment and into the thicker trees, I pushed away confusing thoughts and concentrated on putting some distance between us and our foe, if possible. I needed to find somewhere defensible, with wood for a fire, for I could feel my feet getting wetter and colder in my street shoes, and I reasoned that Dupain's were no better.

"Wh-where are we going?" Dupain stammered at my side, my coat draping his shoulders like a cloak. He clutched the bandage over his wound and bent his head.

"Just now, we are putting distance between us and the tracks, lad, distance between us and that which pursues us," I replied. "Can you tell me anything about the Loup-Garou Curse that might help us?"

"Alas, no, sir. My training with Dr. Raboud... concerns only my sensitivity to magical workings and how to detect them on people near me. I have little knowledge of the dark arts... and only in theory," Dupain panted, showing fatigue already. "But judging from Dr. Raboud's reactions to that curse, I think it a horrible thing, likely brought on by great hatred and perhaps a need for... awful revenge."

"Revenge against whom, lad?"

"Ah, only the enemy knows, *mon capitaine*," he replied, catching his breath. "But perhaps this revenge seems justified to our enemy. Perhaps the Logres Society has done him harm. Can you not see harm in the work of careless, even cruel, policemen, or worse yet, those who press the rigors of their faith or politics upon backward people?"

"True," I mumbled, "too true. I suppose I might never learn the motive that drives our foe."

"You might, *mon capitaine*, if we survive this snow. I—I am chilled to the b-bone," the youth said through chattering teeth. In truth, since we had seen or heard nothing pursuing us for some time, my main thoughts had also turned to our need to get warm.

"We shall have to see about getting a fire going. I hope to find a road that leads to a village, though I'm not sure of our location. Courage, young fellow, and keep moving with me," I said. I hoped a confident tone would give the lad a sense of hope I did not feel on my own.

***

We had come well away from the tracks, perhaps a half mile or more through difficult terrain, and Dupain shivered and gasped for air. The shock of his attack had weakened the lad. He lacked any level of conditioning to give him the stamina we needed to avoid pursuit for long. I had given him the wicked-looking *navaja*, the knife with which he had been wounded, for he needed some form of protection of his own, should we become separated in an attack. He clung to it with both hands as we made our way through snow and brambles.

The land about us rose and fell. Short, steep hills rose to jagged, rocky summits, and we wound our way between them. I sought to keep a westward heading, hoping to come upon aid of some sort, though I worried about exposing anyone with whom we made contact to the loup-garou that followed us. Once or twice, I'd heard some movement behind us, so as often as I could, I drew dried windfall across our tracks. And when a small stream trickled along at the base of a snowy bank down which we slid, I pulled Dupain into the icy water and waded away to our left.

The opposite bank rose up to a small knoll, this one crowned with a heavy growth of pines, and if we could gain it, we might, at least, find shelter beneath the pine boughs and let Dupain recover something of his strength.

My feet, too, were freezing, so we needed fire. Had I been on my own, I would have pushed on and followed the stream downhill, knowing that it would likely join with other waters and, perhaps, empty into one of the many small rivers that fed the lakes of the region. There, we would almost certainly find a village. But the lad stumbled and complained about the icy water.

"I know, Jean-Louis, but it hides our scent on the ground, I believe, and if we can hold out a little longer, we may well confuse the one that tracks us."

"It—it is awful to think of that thing out there, seeking us," he said.

As we moved down the river, I was recalling boyhood stories of witches and ghosts. We were, after all, lost in the woods. And I thought I recalled that running water was meant to be a protective barrier against magic. Hoping to take Dupain's mind off his fear, I appealed to his occult knowledge by asking him if this were true.

"It seems likely, *mon capitaine*," he whispered, "for water such as this is pure, and no evil hex or charm will hold up against it, though it makes my feet feel like blocks of ice."

"Sorry, lad," I replied, stepping out of the stream onto a large, icy boulder and extending my hand to him. "It is a risk, but if we can seclude ourselves in the pines on the far side of this knoll, we might make a bit of a fire and warm ourselves."

"But the fire, she will be seen, yes?"

"I know, I know, lad," I said, staying atop the bare rocks that led into the tree line. "But it wouldn't do to freeze to death, either. Any means of survival has its risks, but we must think of what we need right this minute. I have had some training along these lines, lad, though by no means enough to give me cheer at the moment."

"You—you are so good to me, *mon capitaine*," he said, clambering up to my side on the rocks. "It would have found me already and killed me, were it not for you. But given our mission for the Logres Society, should you not abandon me? I am no use to you, I know."

"Nonsense. We stand a better chance together," I said. "And Department Zed never, ever leaves a man behind."

"Yes, Magnus Guthrie says this about you," Dupain said. "Dibba, too, says this. He knows to trust you, despite what Dr. Raboud has said. I almost think that Dr. Raboud is—well, no. It cannot be."

So Dupain had begun to suspect his master, and I heard this just as I had decided to trust Raboud. It was strange to think it, but I said in truth, "No, Jean-Louis, Raboud is not our foe. I am fairly sure that no one in our circle is responsible for all the harm done."

"Ah, good. Of course you are right," he mumbled.

I gathered more windfall on my way through the pines and pushed ahead. The resinous pine needles that covered the ground would make a quick blaze, helping to dry the wet wood. We needed fire more than we needed to know more of our foe.

As I got a small blaze going and fed it with such tinder as I had on hand, I let myself wonder about this lad in my charge. Though Dupain had proven himself inept in the field, I granted that he must be intelligent, useful in some way, enough so to draw the eye of Chancellor Bismarck. In truth, I'd always seen Bismarck as an autocrat, bent on power, but a very careful man. What good he saw in Dupain was beyond me to grasp. But I had my charge to keep.

I bade Dupain strip off his shoes and socks and warm his feet, which he could barely do on his own. As he fumbled with his wet footgear, I searched for more windfall that I could dry.

"Did you see any sign of... it?" the lad asked as I came back to his side after a brief survey of the direction from which we'd come.

"Nothing, though I cannot see far amidst all these trees. We will press on, once our things are dry," I said, "for we must get word to Raboud and those who will await us at Penrith that we are alive and being pursued."

"I am sure that it is out there, still, watching us, *mon capitaine*. Such a horrible thing. What could it do but kill us?" Dupain said in quavering tones. "I am sorry to say it, but I know why it would seek to kill you. You have been attacked twice, and that makes sense, in a way. You are our best defense against it, given your skill and bravery. But why me? I am nothing, compared to you or Mr. Holmes—or to his brother, or to Tennyson and Gladstone. I am just a student. What threat do I bring?"

"I do not know, lad," I answered, thinking that Dupain had learned only too well of his own ineptitude. Shivering barefoot and pitiable by our small blaze, he certainly presented little threat. "Perhaps it isn't a matter of who you are but of what you know. Do you recall anything of the attack on the train?"

"No, *mon capitaine*. I wake to a noise and there is a dark shape—a tall man, I think—above me. I see the flash of his knife and I roll aside."

"That would have been the Maguire fellow," I muttered, "an impostor we discovered on the train. He did not press his attack?"

"Ah, no. My cries of pain made him flee, and next I know, your ladies are at my side."

But Maguire was a tall fellow, strong-looking. If he had intended to kill Dupain, it seemed to me that he would have done so quickly and easily. But I didn't pursue this thought. "'My ladies'?" I replied with a grunting laugh. "That they are 'my ladies' hardly seems the case."

"Oh, does it not?" he replied with a light laugh. "I have seen the way they look at you, *mon capitaine*. You have the choice of them, I think."

"Do not be absurd, Jean-Louis," I replied, turning away from his smile. "Miss Adler suggested that Raboud told you of my situation with my wife. Miss Adler is merely my colleague, who has befriended my wife, with whom I am making amends."

"Are you sure that such is Miss Adler's intent? She is a woman of the world, and no woman can abide a rival," he said. "In France, we know this: A woman such as Irene Adler plays a long game to get the match she wants. She keeps her rival close to her, in her power, as you say. And Miss Adler knows that Holmes is not a man to marry. He is wed to other, loftier notions, his passions for detection. My Great-Uncle Auguste was such a man, and he was no woman's idea of a lover or a husband.

"Miss Adler keeps your wife by her side, I think, to show you that she is a greater prize than your wife, who is pretty but who clearly wishes now to be joined with Sherlock Holmes instead or you. Your wife, I fear, cannot forgive you for your infidelity. Surely Magnus Guthrie has told you this? He understands."

"Well, lad, I haven't spoken to Guthrie about Mary and Holmes. And I don't see that you have read the situation correctly."

"Oh, no? Tell me, *mon capitaine*: did not Miss Adler make it her business to help you know of the transgression of your wife and Mr. Holmes?" Dupain asked.

"Yes, yes, but that was for my benefit, not hers, lad," I argued. "You may have the know of it in France, but among the English, things aren't that way." At least not with this Englishman.

"Ah, Dr. Watson, my mother was a beautiful woman with many admirers, and I grew to know many things about seeking, um, the solaces of a lover, as the old poets say," Dupain explained as he checked his stockings hanging above the fire.

To say that his words had no effect on me would be to deny that they offered a balm. It was a pleasant fantasy to think myself pursued by a woman like Irene Adler. But I had experienced something like that with Anne Prescott, whose beauty and passion had drawn me into visions of a legendary union. I tasted it ever so briefly, and it was taken from me. Men cannot have their deepest desires, and I knew this too well, where this lad knew nothing of the kind. I turned away from Dupain to see to the drying of my own socks.

"Are your socks dry, lad? We need to move soon," I said, inspecting my own shoes, which water and rough passage had near ruined. Dupain's were no better off, and I hoped we could find a village soon, preferably one with a cobbler.

"I did not mean to overstep my bounds, *mon capitaine*," the lad said, tugging at my sleeve as I rose.

"No harm done," I said.

Then I heard a fierce growl cut through the relative calm. An instant later, I heard the curious ratcheting sound of a *navaja* opening. I drew my sword, feeling for Dupain's arm to draw him behind me. That low snarl had come to us through the trees at our backs. I had heard nothing of the thing's approach and could see nothing in the relative darkness of the trees.

Its low growl repeated from my left, somewhere closer to the side of the granite we stood on, and still I could see nothing. A glance at Dupain showed the lad at my side, knife held out in front of him. His hands shook and his eyes widened with the fear that was upon him.

"Steady, lad," I replied. "Just place your back to mine and watch for the movement of any brush."

"I'm t-too terrified," he stuttered. "I cannot see a thi—No! Look! There, *mon capitaine*!"

I followed his pointing finger down and to the other side of the boulder atop which we stood. There, crouched low, its wide paws on the rock, the werewolf watched us. Had I not known the terror of it, I would have paused to marvel at this creature, this living weapon, for it was magnificent in its muscularity and grace of movement. It took two steps up the smooth rock, its eyes mere slits of red light in the night-black fur of the blended lupine and human face.

"Steady, lad," I whispered again, for Dupain, in his panic, bleated words in his native tongue as the werewolf took another step up toward us.

Though I was terrified, I knew that I had the better ground for any strike I could deliver with Mustard Seed. If it charged, I thought that I could meet it with a cut that would take its head. Yet I wasn't sure one strike would be enough. Seeing its savage

muzzle, with rows of bitter-sharp white teeth, was like facing a
tiger in its own jungle, the absolute physical master of its
domain. Any man would feel puny and worthless before it, and I
had only the trust in my sword and mortal skill with which to
face it.

But it did not charge. It crouched low and stared, not at me
but at Dupain, who peered at it over my shoulder. I, however,
kept my eyes on it, unblinking, seeking to settle into my center
as Uyeshiba had taught me, feeling the sword as an extension of
my person. Nothing mattered in that second but my connection
to the weapon and my easy breathing.

Dupain clutched, then, at the collar of my coat, and the
beast moved. It did not leap to attack but came fast and low,
clawed hands at its side. I struck, but it stopped short and pulled
back, and the chisel point of my blade only grazed the plates of
fur-covered muscle on its chest and abdomen. And before I
could recover my balance and strike it again, it hit me in the
chest and knocked me onto my back, into the dark recesses of a
pine tree. Dupain screamed as he tumbled away from me. And
though I was on my feet in an instant, the werewolf was gone,
leaving Dupain curled up on the ground, face down, holding his
hands to his middle. Recalling Scrymgeour's disembowelment, I
feared the worst.

I rushed to the lad's side, staying watchful for any sign of
the monster's return.

"Jean-Louis! Did it get to you?" I cried.

Dupain rolled over with pressure from my hand on his
shoulder. I saw blood on his abdomen, and he cradled his right
hand, but he was alive. I breathed a sigh of relief. "Here. Let me
see, lad."

Quivering with fear, he let me see his hand, which was
broken at the wrist. Several claw marks showed on his hand and
wrist; they bled, but not profusely. No doubt, I thought, the
wound in his arm would be open again as well. Why had the
monster left him alive?

"Strange that such a perfect killing machine would switch
to grappling tricks, is it not?" I muttered, sitting back from him.

"It took m—that knife," he muttered.

"Come, lad," I said, pulling Dupain into a sitting position, "let's get you ready to move away from here."

"Why would it just take the knife?" Dupain asked while I helped him with his stockings.

"If the man who stabbed you is also the loup-garou, perhaps he just wanted his knife back," I said, trying to make a semblance of sense of the facts I had. "Perhaps he resorted to werewolf shape only because his first attack on you failed."

I could not be certain of such a reading of the clues; why would a werewolf need a knife? My idea mollified Dupain, though. He fell silent, nodded, and pulled on one of his shoes while I tied the other.

What I did not tell him was that I wondered if this werewolf might be Holmes transformed. With his mastery of disguise, Holmes could have boarded the train as that Maguire fellow. This werewolf was not just a weapon, or if he was, he was a thinking weapon. That argued for Holmes, as well. The beast had avoided my cut at it, as though it had seen it coming, though my strike had been faster than flesh and blood could avoid, unless the creature had been Holmes transformed. His natural speed was beyond that of most men; as a werewolf, if indeed he retained his human abilities, he would be truly astounding. The last time I'd spoken with Holmes, he had hinted at his new abilities. Could Holmes as a werewolf make decisions beyond the will to murder?

Pinder had been a killer; Hastings had been a ruffian, at best, in Irene Adler's service, a strong-arm acting in her defense against admirers who became too demanding. Holmes as a werewolf would be superior in skill, if he retained any of his natural abilities once a transformed creature. Was such possible? I doubted whether Dupain would know, but questions burned in my mind. Why had the beast left us alive? It could have killed both of us. I could think of only one explanation: it was Holmes. However, that was a thought too ridiculous to utter. I would say nothing of the idea to Dupain.

CHAPTER FIFTEEN

"Some Yuletide Cheer."

We saw nothing of the werewolf for the rest of that day, and I ended by half-carrying Dupain, who had passed the point of his limits shortly after we extinguished our small fire and hurried off into the snow. The country around us opened a bit, but that just made us subject to the cutting wind that blew the snow in our faces as we plodded through drifts. The clouds stayed so heavy, full of the threat of more snow, that I had little sense of the time of day. Soon it felt like days, though I knew it was only hours, since we'd left the small comfort of our fire, though when we reached a road, the sullen disc of the sun overhead showed me that noon had come and gone.

To my great delight, I spotted a wagon of some sort coming toward us down the road at a slow clip. Drawn by the shaggiest horse I had ever seen, the conveyance looked for all the world like a bathing wagon, like a house on four wobbling wheels. And this contraption was driven by a man nearly as shaggy as the horse. It reminded me of a gypsy caravan, though it wasn't loaded down with the trappings of a camp. Its driver barely looked at me as I flagged him down and begged for help.

"Thank God you've come, sir. My associate is near done in. We must get to shelter," I cried.

His guttural reply might have been in Gaelic, I thought, or in some other little-used barbaric tongue; whatever the language, I had no idea what he'd said. He did, though, spring into action with an almost youthful energy, despite his obvious years, and helped me lift the slumping Dupain into the back of his odd conveyance.

"Can you get us someplace warm, sir?" I pleaded and earned another such reply as he scrambled about within the dark interior of the wagon. I saw by the light of his match that he had laid a fire in an old stove within. He beckoned us inside. His strength surprised me yet again as he lifted Dupain's drooping body into the wagon. The lad could hardly move on his own, as cold and exhausted as he was.

"Might I know your name, sir?" I asked.

"Dirkdiggin, Ah am," he said, extending me his raw, red hand. His grip was like steel, but the furrows of a smile creased his gaunt face beneath his beard, and there was a merry twinkle in his eyes. I told him my name, and he mumbled a reply around a hoarse chuckle. It sounded like it contained the words "freeze," "southerner," and "neighbors helping."

Soon he had shut us in a warming, dark interior that smelled of old dung and wool. It could have been just my fatigue, but I thought I detected the word "traveler" in his speech, though whether that referred to the Travelers or us as lost travelers, I could not tell. It mattered little, in any case, for he had offered us warmth and protection.

Dupain rested quiet on a pile of sacking, and I sat on a low stool affixed to the floor beside the small stove. There was wood enough to last for several hours, but even just being out of the wind, I felt I could breathe easier. Where we were headed, I had no idea, but an act of kindness such as Mr. Diggin had offered us would not, I hoped, turn to evil.

Thus far, our trip north had fallen far from the plan. I did not know where Whitefell Manor was, so I had to hope that Raboud and company waited for us in Penrith. By now, they had to know we were missing, but they might not have known when we'd left the train. Surely Mary and Irene would have heard the noise of our struggle and the conductor would have seen the opened outer door. But I had no way of knowing.

In the warmth of that odd wagon, I took some comfort in the notion that Holmes was the werewolf who had followed us off the train. Why he had not found a way to identify himself to us was unclear, but many of Holmes's methods were a mystery to me. The unescapable conclusion for me was that Dupain was a suspect, in Holmes's eyes, which I considered ridiculous. But the reality was that if Holmes were the werewolf—were Maguire—he would not have attacked Dupain on the train. Was the attacker a different person, an associate of my Alhambra assailant, the mysterious man in the homburg hat? That man had tried to shoot me down outside Briony Lodge, though why, I could not say. There were too many questions still, and I had too few facts to consider.

Of one thing I was more sure: Raboud and I would be on better footing. At our last meeting, he had seemed more certain of my honesty, even if the question of what I had wished was still a dark mystery to me. Somehow, Edinburgh lay at the heart of that mystery, and the peace I found in my heart was only because I knew that I wasn't bound there, at least not yet.

***

An hour or so later, the door to the wagon opened on a wonderful sight: The White House Inn stood before us. Mr. Diggin assisted me in getting Dupain within and into a room. The landlord told us the local blacksmith was usually called upon to set broken bones and asked if we wished for a doctor to be brought from Windermere instead. I gave the man my name and told him that I would tend to the lad myself but asked if any laudanum might be had locally. He promised to do what he could, and then he gave me the keys to the room in which we'd placed Dupain and to an adjoining one. Diggin disappeared before I could thank him or reward him in any way.

I turned my focus on Dupain. With the lad resting in a warm bed, I took his wrist in my hands and examined it. It was swollen, but it didn't look otherwise too misshapen. According to all I'd seen and heard, werewolves possessed strength enough to have torn the hand from the lad's arm. The precise break was further evidence that argued for Holmes as the werewolf who had attacked us.

Dupain studied me with eyes barely open and whispered, "I wish I were less in your debt, *mon capitaine*."

"Nay, lad. You owe me nothing. Any officer worth his salt owes his men everything," I replied. "I will have this set soon, if our landlord can find some laudanum. You'll soon be mended—"

"No—please, sir. No laudanum," he cried, half rising. A look of fear gripped him, as though I had suggested removing his hand. I raised my eyebrows in surprise at his reaction, and he subsided.

"I—well, I have never taken anything stronger than a glass of wine," he went on. "You see, my mother warned me that such things led to my father's death. I live in fear of them."

"Very well, Jean-Louis," I whispered, thinking poorly of myself for the way I had reacted to him many times over the past few days. "I will work with care and not cause you more pain than necessary."

We were fortunate that the innkeeper, Mr. Roach, kept a well-stocked supply of medicines on hand. We were presented with some carbolic acid, which I diluted immediately and used to clean the mild abrasions on Dupain's injured wrist. Then, without warning him, I began the process of setting his bones, stopping my pull on his arm only when I felt the bones fall back into place. Dupain bit his lip at the pain and gasped a few times, but he bore it well enough, though when I finally had the joint set to rights, he fainted away. I bound his wrist and hand and laid it out straight between two rough but clean slats of pine, to keep the joint still.

Then I left him sleeping and sought out my own room. Divesting myself of my outer garments and my sword, I went to make arrangements with Mr. Roach, whom I found behind the bar downstairs in as pleasant a pub as I have ever visited.

The landlord soon had me sitting by a lively fire with a pint of porter at my elbow and a view down the darkening, snow-covered valley below the inn. With Christmas just behind us and Epiphany days away, garlands of pine boughs and bright, prickly holly still graced his mantel. Candles twinkled on windowsills and tabletops. Sprigs of mistletoe hung from the dark, rough oak beams of the ceiling, inviting stolen kisses. All these sights reminded me of holidays in happier times. They left me, too, with the pleasant thought of traveling home this way with Mary.

"The Troutbeck Valley is the handsomest landscape in all

of England," Mr. Roach offered, following my gaze, which I had turned out the window. A man an inch or so taller than I, he had a broad, round, comfortable presence that fit well into my notions of a country innkeeper. His florid face held eyes crinkled at the corners with much laughter. He looked quite intelligent and seemed curious about our sudden appearance at his inn.

"During the Christmas holidays," he went on, "we don't get many visitors. Our one guest, before you two came, is the vicar's elder sister, who doesn't much socialize."

"Thank you, Mr. Roach," I said, grateful for the warm fire and for any friendly voice, no matter how inquisitive. "I wonder if you know of any means of getting word to Lord Whitefell of my presence here."

"Well, sir," Roach responded in a startled voice at my mention of the local gentry, "Whitefell Manor is some twenty mile north of here. I don't know of anyone bound that way, but I might send my boy, Tim, down to Windermere in the morning to dispatch a telegram on your behalf."

"If he is able, that would be much appreciated, and I would see him—and you—rewarded for your help," I said. He nodded and sank his bulk into a seat near me, his ruddy countenance bursting with curiosity.

"Of course, friends of Lord John Whitefell are welcome here, Dr. Watson, but your curious manner and circumstance of arrival here have me wondering what tale explains it all. You and yon injured youth, not attired for journeying in heavy weather, show up on my doorstep in a strange conveyance. Why, I simply must know how it comes to be."

"Of our business, especially with Lord Whitefell, I can say nothing except that the lad and I were waylaid by a person or persons unknown on our journey north. As to our conveyance, I assumed that our rescuer—Mr. Dirk Diggin, I believe his name was—was a local. I'd hoped to see him rewarded."

Roach's countenance drew down into a deep frown, and he stroked his chin as he thought. His eyes darted around the room, as though he searched his memory for the face of Mr. Diggin in this place. At length, he turned his gaze back to me.

"I know the face of everyone who dwells for miles about in all directions, and I would swear that I'd never seen him before," he said thoughtfully. "His horse looked familiar, though. That'd be Old Dolly. Belongs to Angus Scrobie, over Sadgill way. Puts her out on loan when a man needs to pull a tree stump. I wouldn't be surprised if that old cart she pulled was Scrobie's, as well. He's a right woolgatherer, is Scrobie. Lord knows where he came by such a wagon. But that feller driving it weren't Scrobie. That, I'll take my oath on. Leave me a bit, and I'll see what's become of him."

"Certainly, sir," I said, wondering if Diggin were one of Cameron's followers. Or might he have been Holmes? It was improbable, but possible: I had been duped many times by my friend's ability to change his outer appearance. But I knew one thing: Holmes would contact me, when he could, without exposing his plans to others. In the meantime, I packed a pipe and gave myself over to a well-deserved rest beside the fire.

***

Night had settled in by the time I took my dinner. I had looked in on Dupain with the housemaid, who took the lad a bowl of broth, some fresh bread, and a pot of tea. He was asleep, so I advised her to place them nearby. With a shy smile at Dupain's handsome features and fair hair, she did as I bid her, and we both left him to rest. He had no fever, I found, so I suspected that he would sleep until he recovered from his exhaustion. I closed the door on him and went back to the pub to take my meal of heavy stew and bread, which I set to with relish, watching fresh snow fall on the drive in front of the inn.

The locals who came in from the cold, shucking off coats and hats, stayed fairly quiet and distant from me, though I insisted on standing them a round of drinks as I sat by the fire again, nursing my feet and hands, which, having been soaked much of the morning in frigid temperatures, were raw and sore. I suspected Dupain's extremities to be in the same condition. I inquired of the men at the bar where I might find heavier cloaks, or coats, and boots for two. I was greeted with silence and shrugs from the three fellows with fresh mugs in their hands, but at length, Mr. Roach said that he would check around to see what might be found.

In the telegram message I composed for Mr. Roach's son to take to Windermere at first light, I requested some survival gear, as well as transportation from the Troutbeck Valley to Whitefell Manor, since, I supposed, all of our leaders and Raboud's party were gathered in safety there.

"I'm unable to account for your Mr. Diggin," Mr. Roach said, standing at my elbow, "but my Tim saw him driving Old Dolly back the very direction you came from, not minutes after he left you in my house."

"Strange," I replied, "but perhaps his errand was elsewhere and he brought us here out of kindness. I know nothing about him, but even though he isn't a local, he knew of this inn."

"Well, 'The Mortal Man'—our White House Inn—is well known in these parts," Roach said with a grin. "Perhaps he was just a traveler, passing through. Perhaps, too, his nag was a near match for Scrobie's Old Dolly. Though it is strange, as you say."

"Indeed," I said, agreeing with him and keeping my thoughts on the matter to myself, for I knew that Diggin— whoever he was or whoever had sent him—had saved us.

I knew from seeing Jamie Cameron in the fog, before we were shot at near Briony Lodge, that the Travelers kept watch over me. Had they sent Mr. Diggin to our aid? That seemed impossible, given that young Cameron hadn't followed me onto the train and wouldn't have known Dupain and I had left it. Could his "sight" have informed him? My speculation was useless. At least I knew that Whitefell Manor was only some twenty miles away.

***

Before the evening was through, Mr. Roach had presented me with a pair of worn but suitable lumbermen's boots that he had obtained from the local smith, who was about my size. These I took, along with a pair of woolen stockings belonging to the younger Roach, a handsome, well-grown lad, though not yet as large as his portly father. With these, I retired to my room, stopping to check on Dupain.

His door, I found, was locked from within, and his empty dinner tray lay in the corridor. I knocked, of course, but when I listened with care, I heard only what sounded like the soft sighing of a young woman. I remembered the housemaid's smiling appreciation of my young charge's beauty.

I backed away from the door, thinking to make no further noise. I left him—and her—feeling as though morning would see him able to travel with ease. I thought that he might even wish to return to the White House Inn when this matter was concluded, for the young woman, Adele, was a pretty thing and just about his age. The thought of two young people finding each other made me smile and contemplate my reunion with Mary. That was a wholesome thought, in this setting, and I hoped that Adele's solaces might be a balm for the lad's soul, after the trauma of the previous day.

Having consumed two more pots of Burton Ale in the course of my evening, I was soon warm beneath the covers, intent on sleeping well past the point of young Tim's departure to Windermere with my communiqué for Whitefell. With any luck, I would be able to stay in this marvelous spot another day, perhaps two, before carrying on to Whitefell Manor and taking up this business again.

It was not to be.

CHAPTER SIXTEEN

"The Feast of New Year's Eve,"
31 December, 1888.

In the small hours of the morning, I woke to the sound of a woman's scream and the slamming of a door. Outside my window, the eerie light of a snowy night showed me new flakes falling. Sitting up, I grasped the cord-wrapped *tsuka* of Mustard Seed and strode to the door. More voices joined in the uproar, and I was certain I heard Roach's voice among them shouting, "What is it, girl? What is it?" And other voices rose outside, shouts from the near distance.

I went back into my room to pull on my clothing and borrowed boots. They were snug, with the woolen hose, but I pulled them on, laced them up, hung the sword beneath my greatcoat, and headed for the stairs.

Gathered by the front door of the inn, Roach and his wife and son were standing around the housemaid, who had slammed shut the door and sat with her back to it as though she held it closed against assault. Roach, in his nightshirt and cap, knelt down in front of her, and I heard her gather breath through a terror-stricken throat.

"I'd ne'er seen 'im afore," she cried, "but my gran 'as, and I'm tellin' you, sir, that were Old Stinker 'f I ever sarw 'im. Eight feet tall, 'e was, black as night, wi' red eyes, an' 'e came at me with 'is 'orrible claws—ooooohh!"

"You daft child," Roach said to her, shaking her by the shoulder. "This isn't Whitby. Those haunts and bogeys of yours are just in your head! How did you come to be at my door this late, anyroad? You should've been home in bed hours ago."

195

The girl, Adele, dropped her pretty face into her hands and bowed her head, lost in fear. Roach turned and saw me, his face startled.

"Let me," I said, and knelt by Adele's side. I stroked her hair and crooned to her, "There, there, girl. Just tell me true what you saw. Was it Old Stinker?" That was one of the tales of witches and abnormal beasts I'd remembered earlier that supposedly roamed the wilds, killing livestock and waylaying poor, unfortunates abroad at night.

"Aw, Dr. Watson," young Tim said, "that's just some old story about a monster from over in the Dales, sir, near Flixton, where Adele's people are."

"Is what he says true, Miss Adele?" I asked in a soft voice, lifting the girl's chin that she might look into my eyes.

"Y-Yessir, your lordship, 'tis. That's what I saw, an' 'e was comin' for me," she said in a soft voice, choked with the tears of fright.

"Was your young man with you?" I asked, meaning Dupain. Her gaze fell to the floor and her cheeks flushed.

"N-no, sir. 'E was sleepin' as I left 'im," she whispered, earning a sigh of disappointment from the landlady and a shaking head from Mr. Roach.

"I believe you, child," I said softly. "Tell me, if you can, where the creature came from and where he went."

"I dursn't look where 'e went after 'e lunged at me, a'comin' from the corner of the inn, sir."

"Very well, child," I said, lifting her to her feet and pressing her into the embrace of Mrs. Roach. "I will see to this matter. Mr. Roach," I said, turning to him. "I will return as quickly as I can, but do not worry. I think I can clear this up."

"But how, sir?" Roach asked in an awed whisper. "If it was, er, like what the lass says?"

"Leave it to me," I said. "I hope to be back shortly."

I unbolted the door and pushed out into the night before he could protest further. I was growing more confident that this beast was Holmes, doing what he could to draw me out in order to make contact with me.

With the fall of yet more snow, werewolf tracks would be easy to find, for they would be fresh and undisturbed yet. In moments, I located the outlandishly sized paw prints, deep in the snow. Walking in them, I sought to wipe out any trace of what Adele had seen. Holmes must have stayed around, hidden in a thicket in the valley, awaiting deep nightfall to contact me. Granted, it was a risk seeking him out, but I wanted to confront him and let him know that I was aware of his presence, if not his plan. If I could tell him of our intent to push on to Whitefell Manor in a day or two at the most, and if I could convince him to go there as well, I might yet help him in whatever his aim was.

His spoor led me into a wood that stood above the inn on the slopes of the valley. He moved quickly, I thought, for the tracks were yards apart. Deer tracks I also saw, and these ran away up the slope at an angle from his tracks. And then I saw the first traces of blood on the snow. A shiver ran down my spine, though not from the cold; I was warm through with my exertions. I was chilled within by the sight of great gouts of blood, pooled in depressions in the snow. The deer, no doubt, had been attacked.

"Really, Holmes," I muttered, sickened by the thought of it.

Moving through the snow, I passed through a heavier growth of trees and heard the low growls of a beast. With them came the sounds of the beast feeding, and in seconds I saw him tearing at the carcass of a young deer, blood bright on his maw and on his terrifying claws. The deer's eyes and mouth were wide, still, and I shuddered at the thought that Holmes had begun to feed on it while it was still alive. It was dead now, though, and the savage jaws of the thing that was my friend tore at its throat with abandon. He didn't even seem to hear my approach.

Striding up to him, I gave him a hard push with my right foot, enough to topple him over, and cried, "Holmes! Get hold of yourself, man! You've got to get out of these parts before you have the whole of the Lake District up in arms and out for your blood!"

He turned on me, bloody maw gaping at me, snarling, jaws snapping, splashing fresh blood. His limbs were splayed out beneath him, his red eyes narrowed as though he would charge me. I unhooked Mustard Seed, scabbard and all, and fetched the beast a sharp blow in his snout. With a yelp, he bound backward, rising onto his hind legs, rubbing his muzzle with one too-human-looking hand.

"You were seen by that young woman," I said, pointing my sword, still scabbarded, at his face, appalled by what I'd seen him do. Even if it was just a deer, the savagery of his actions near made me sick, as did the stink of the poor animal he had disemboweled. "I cannot pretend to know what you are about, what plan you work, but you can do me no good by terrorizing the locals. It's bad enough—"

He sprang at me with a scything motion of his right hand, his own speed limited by the depth of the snow around his feet. It was obviously meant as a killing stroke, though, aimed to take my guts and add them to those of his prey. I moved without thinking, recognizing in an instant my own stupidity. Holmes as werewolf had chosen only to disarm Dupain. This creature's eyes glowed with the need to rend and kill.

This creature was not Holmes.

I shouted a wordless cry of pure effort and fetched the beast a harder blow with the scabbard, across its flashing wrist, and a second blow atop its head. I was moving more quickly than I would have thought possible. My blow dazed it a bit, and it dropped down onto all fours then, head shaking. I unsheathed Mustard Seed and cast the scabbard aside.

Having been foolish enough to think I knew something of werewolves, let alone that this hellish monster was Holmes transformed, I determined to lose no time and brought Mustard Seed high for a cut that would relieve this thing of its head. I struck fast, but the blade only bit through the snow and into the frozen turf beneath. The werewolf rolled away, despite being dazed, and sprang at me while my sword was stuck hard in the ground. It knocked me away from my weapon and hurled me bodily some ten feet back down the trail, where I landed and rolled many times. I fetched up hard against a gorse thicket, its branches snapping with my weight and with the Herculean force of the loup-garou's throw.

In a second it was on me, clawed hands pulling at the shoulders of my greatcoat to bring its teeth down to my throat. My hands on its neck, I resisted with all the strength I could muster. Its back claws tore the material of my coat to shreds, and it growled in such a way that I thought it laughed at me. My arms began to weaken against the pull of its massive strength. I was sure that the glow in its red and feral eyes mocked my struggle. Angrily, I brought my right leg up hard into its groin, remembering that it was part human. It moaned and howled in rage as I repeated my attack on the weakest point of male anatomy.

But, even in its spasms of pain, it never let loose its hold on me. Then it stopped using its rear claws to tear at me and pinned both my legs to the ground. It pulled harder again; the rear seam of my coat began to tear. It shifted its grip and tore away the upper part of my coat, lifting its right paw high above me, eyes gloating, tongue lolling, ready to taste my blood. I had no time to reflect upon my coming death. But a shattering report ripped the air, the loup-garou's head flew back, and it toppled away from me. Someone had shot it.

Rolling, slithering through the snow, I moved away, desperate only to put distance between myself and the wolf-man hybrid. Men's voices reached me, and I saw a lantern approaching up the trail I had come by. I scrambled along on all fours toward that light. They called my name, and I recognized Roach and his son. The lad, Tim, bore an old Enfield rifle-musket, which he struggled to load as his father, with wide, staring eyes, hauled on my hands to pull me to him.

"Not dead! Not dead!" I cried, wishing to warn them that the werewolf was invulnerable to ordinary firearms, though the cannon-like blast of the venerable black powder weapon still rang in my ears.

"I see that!" Roach cried, throwing a protective arm around my shoulders. Young Tim Roach stood above him, musket loaded again, its muzzle sweeping the area of my attack. "Though dead you almost were, I think. What the hell was—"

"No! I meant the beast you shot," I managed. "It cannot be harmed by ordinary means." That thought struck me, and I turned to look for Mustard Seed. It was stuck in the ground, still, some four or five yards from the bloody deer carcass.

The loup-garou was nowhere to be seen.

"It's gone, Da," Tim cried, still searching for a mark to shoot at, though he'd hit the beast square in the head. "'M sure I hit it, though."

"Yes, Tim. You did," I said, sudden relief making me so weak that I fell to my knees again.

Father and son stood over me, breathing hard. Tim kept the rifle half raised.

"Come," I said. "Help me retrieve my weapon." And they flanked me as my faltering steps took me to recover Mustard Seed and its scabbard.

***

The only thing I recall of the trip back to the White House Inn, which Mr. Roach again called "The Mortal Man," is the wracking chill that grew worse, sweeping through me. At some point, I blacked out, and they tumbled me into a warm bed. The next thing I remember is waking to the sound of distant voices.

"How in the name of glory could he go after such a thing armed only with that?" Mr. Roach was asking.

A voice I knew well, Magnus Guthrie's, answered clearly, "Well, sir, 'e's killed two such creatures with it before now, and I'm damned if I know why 'e didn't claim a third last night. 'E's that good, my captain is."

Forcing open my eyes, I saw Guthrie's face above mine, as he sat by my bed in the early morning light that filtered into the room. Dupain paced the room behind him, his splinted arm held close to his side and a worried scowl darkening his handsome features. In his good hand, he held my sword. The landlord stood behind them both. As I looked around, the sounds of the room also came more clearly to me.

"And it looks like he's back," said Roach. "I'll just fetch some tea for the three of you, shall I?"

"Thank you, Mr. Roach. Guthrie," I managed in weak

tones, while trying to rise on my elbow, "how on earth have you come so early? The boy can't have had time—"

"Nor did 'e need to, sir," Guthrie said, pushing me back down into the warmth of the mattress. "I arrived before first light and stopped the lad before he left for Windermere."

"But how did you know I was here?" I asked.

"Another 'n, Cap'n. Telegram, that is. It came late last night to Whitefell Manor," Guthrie said. "Came late last night, sir, an' I came quick as I could, sir. Got 'ere not much more'n two hours after you went out to face the beast. Found the 'ole 'ouse in an uproar, and this one"—he jerked a thumb at Dupain—"a'sleepin' through it all."

"Never mind about Dupain," I said. "He has come in for more than his share of difficulty thus far. But tell me, how are things there? At Whitefell, I mean? Are the others there and safe?"

"We've 'ad no word from the elder 'Olmes brother, but the others are safe as 'ouses, Cap'n. No alarms and everyone as comfy as can be, 'cept for Raboud, Mr. Dibba, and the fine ladies, 'oo arrived and told us you two 'ad been lost along the way, though they didn't know where. I'd 'a been 'ere sooner, sir, if they'd've given me a place to start searchin'. As it was, they knew nothin' of your, um, departure till they neared the station at Penrith."

"We didn't know where we'd landed, either," I said and swung my legs out of bed.

"Steady on, Cap'n Jack," Guthrie exclaimed, reaching out.

"Oh, I'm all right," I protested, pushing away his help, though feeling more than a bit dizzy. Having been tossed about like a sack of grain by that monster, fighting it hand to hand—or claw, as I should say—had left me spent. "Here, Dupain. Hand me that sword, if you please."

With it as a staff, I stood and walked to the window to look outside. My room faced the front on the second floor, and the sun, though rising above the downs to the east, was about as sullen as it had been the day before.

"Has there been any fresh snow?" I asked.

"Nothin' to speak of, sir," Guthrie answered. "But if you're thinkin' of trackin' that beast, I need to inform you that there's no time. Dr. Raboud insisted that you be brought to Whitefell as soon as possible, sir. 'E wants you there immediately."

A great part of me wanted another day to rest at the White House Inn, for I was tired and had a great many things to think through again, since I'd come to an obviously wrong set of conclusions before. "By the way, from whom did the telegram come alerting you to my—our—presence here?"

"That's just it, sir. It came from Mr. 'Olmes," Guthrie said.

***

Keeping my own counsel around Guthrie and Dupain on our journey north, I pressed Guthrie for news of the gathering at Whitefell Manor.

"I arrived soon after Dr. Raboud and the ladies, and they 'ad been the only thing to cause a commotion, sir, with news of you and the whey-faced lad, 'ere, goin' missin', like."

Dupain scowled at Guthrie for the mild insult, but the lad was that pale. He held his much-abused right arm tenderly and close. Guthrie thought little of injuries while on campaign and had several times urged Dupain to "chuff up."

I myself had begun to look at Dupain with some doubt. In Whitefell's carriage, I asked him how he had managed to remain unaware of the furor in the White House Inn the night before, especially when he had been so recently closeted with Adele, the winsome housemaid.

"I do not know what you mean about me and that girl, sir," he responded with a scowl. I had noted that he'd taken no thought to bid her farewell when we'd boarded the coach.

"There's no shame in it, lad," I replied, "though you would have made a better show of it if you'd taken your leave of her more kindly. Did you not see her standing about, when we got on our way?'

"The servant girl?" Dupain exclaimed. "Why, I'd barely spoken to her."

"Come, come, Dupain. I heard her, with you, in your room, before I went to my bed. You may not have spoken much together, but she claims to have been in your room with you much of the evening and night, before she was frightened by the beast."

"What?" Guthrie asked loudly, glaring at my young charge. "'As 'e been tart-'untin' while on duty, Cap'n?'"

"No, Magnus, nothing like that. I merely thought that the two young people might have fallen into each other's arms, so to speak. Ships in the night, that sort of thing," I explained, somewhat taken aback by Dupain's scowl as I spoke of it. I had been in women's company enough in my time to recognize sighs of pleasure, which I'd heard coming from his room. And Dupain, with his worldly talk, had not seemed the type to deny such a liaison. Still, that was his right. So I dropped the matter, though I found it oddly unsettling.

"Well, then, since we have some time before us, I wish you would let me examine your arm and see how it is coming along," I said.

"I—I'd rather you didn't," he replied, cradling his injured arm close to his chest. "It is too painful."

"Still? In that case, I must certainly see it," I said. "Consider it an order, Dupain."

"Present that arm, young-fella-me-lad, or I'll turn you out of your kit myself," Guthrie growled.

"Very well, but take care. The pain is awful, and I still feel faint," Dupain muttered, surrendering his arm to me.

"Guthrie, kindly—and gently—pull his sleeve away," I said.

Since the coach was closed from the wind but still cold, I had in mind just pulling his arm free and inspecting his knife wound as well as his wrist. The scratches on his hand worried me as a site of infection, though I had bathed them in carbolic. Lacerations from claws are far from clean.

Three shocks ran through me: The knife wound I'd bandaged on the train had bled into the dressing after our falling out of the car. Now, it was only a thin, clean, red line on the boy's pale arm. The lacerations were nearly invisible, and his wrist looked as sound as a bell, with no swelling or bruising.

Worse, for Dupain, he bore a red mark on his neck just under his left jaw. It looked like a love bite, suggesting that he had, indeed, been with Adele.

"Strewth!" Guthrie exclaimed. "You lyin' young frog!" He pushed Dupain back against the carriage seat, whereupon the lad collapsed in seeming agony, holding his bare arm to his chest, his breath coming in sharply. "Cap'n Jack, sir, you 'ad the right of it about 'is actions, an' don' it look like a sham deal?"

"Easy, Guthrie," I said in low tones. "Breaks in bones can be quite painful, even if the joint seems sound. Dupain, lad, put your shirt back on and rest easy. Can you explain what the red mark is on your neck? For, otherwise, you seem quite sound."

"I—I heal quickly, and this other is a rash. I have them often, all over," Dupain answered, as though we were pulling his darkest secrets from him.

"'Eal quickly? A rash?" Guthrie hooted. "It'd make a stuffed bird laugh, Cap'n!"

After several minutes during which I gazed at Dupain, wondering at the seeming change in him, I said only, "Dr. Raboud, no doubt, will be glad to see you sound, after all you have been through."

I wrapped his hand and wrist in the splint again. He would not meet my eyes. Had he lied about Adele? I could think of no reason for him to do so, unless he needed to show himself as pure in his actions, to me, at least. Might he think of me as a father figure? It was true that I had taken care of him as well as I could. But why would he make conspiratorial comments to me about a romantic entanglement with Irene Adler one day and make a rather prudish renouncement of a girl's company the next? Perhaps he feared some reprisal from Raboud for his amorous incident. He would not be the first man to abandon a principle in the need and heat of a moment, I knew too well.

I determined to let him be, for Guthrie was clearly eager to watch for any fault in the lad and had been from the first.

Chapter Seventeen

"Noblesse Oblige."

"What can you tell me, Guthrie, about our host?" I asked as we turned into the grounds of Lord Whitefell's estate on the late afternoon of New Year's Eve.

"'Impressive' does not quite cover the manor or the man, sir," Guthrie said with a wry smile. "I've never met an easier bloke to get along with than that gentleman, sir... nor would I ever wish to get on 'is bad side. I know 'is people love 'im. 'Is 'ouse is as much theirs as 'is own, and you could likely get all of Brighton Beach on 'oliday inside the place."

"You have a cavalier approach to the gentry, do you not, Guthrie?" Dupain added, coming out of his shell.

"I know my betters when I meet 'em, Mr. Viscount Pup," Guthrie returned in a growl. "And there's one now, waitin' for us at 'is own door."

He pointed to a figure in old tweed, standing in the arched doorway of a structure nearly the same size as Buckingham Palace. The wind blew Lord Whitefell's black hair away from his face, but he did not seem to mind the cold. As our carriage rolled through the last row of full, well-tended hedges and up the clean gravel courtyard, he stood with his hands on the shoulders of two men dressed much as he was. Both of these men moved out to meet the coach, and one fellow opened the carriage door for me.

"Dr. John Watson, I believe?" a young dark-haired fellow said to me as he opened the door of the carriage. "My name is Burroughs. Lord Whitefell has put me at your disposal as long as you are at the manor."

"Well met—Burroughs, was it?" I asked, shaking his hand. "I hope not to trouble you much during my stay, but perhaps you could see to my charge, Monsieur Dupain, and take him to his room as soon as can be managed."

"Very good, sir. I shall deliver you into the hands of my lord for safekeeping, shall I?"

"Good man, Burroughs," Lord Whitefell said, coming down the stairs to take my hand. "Dr. Watson, I'm glad to see you looking whole and well. We'd have been after you sooner, had we known that you two had dropped off the train. However did you manage?"

"We had timely help, Lord—"

"Oh, please, sir. In my own home, address me as Fitz, if you will," Whitefell said, drawing me toward the door. "I find the formalities tedious, you see. Welcome, my friend, to my ancestral home. What do you think of it?"

"Indeed, my lord—er, Fitz," I said. "I—I don't know what I expected, really, but it is quite grand."

Indeed, it was a palace, if a homey one, especially with the addition of wreaths and garlands, candles and bright bunting all around. A huge Scotch pine adorned one end of the great hall, a Christmas tree that would have done Prince Albert proud. Small candles winked from the ends of its laden branches, sharing their light with the tinsel and ornaments that graced it.

"I always come back here," Fitz said, "especially this time of year, no matter where I find myself in my wanderings. I take my duties for the locals quite seriously, but much of my time I spend in London and elsewhere."

"Have you business interests there, my lor—Fitz?" I replied, glancing beyond the broad, oak-lined foyer into the hall. The light of a welcoming fire beckoned ahead of us. I saw hunting trophies and tall paintings of Whitefell's ancestors on horseback, at the hunt, or in battle armor. Here, a family of heroes from British history were held as kin.

Burroughs, who had escorted Dupain inside already, returned and said, "Dr. Watson's room is ready, sir," earning a nod of recognition from Lord Whitefell.

"Thank you, Burroughs, and later you might see if you can find some suitable clothing for Dr. Watson and young Dupain. Perhaps some of Johnny's old things?" Burroughs left with a smile and a bow, and his lordship—Fitz—turned back to me.

"Most often, my business in London has me driving a cab," he said, his disarming smile flashing. "Or I work the docks. In Leeds or Manchester, I stoke the gray furnaces of foundries."

He might as well have told me that he could fly. I'm sure my mouth gaped open, fishlike, as I sought some reply. Truth be told, I still harbored some anger at him for his need to have Irene investigate the supposed liaison between Holmes and Mary. That was an anger hard to keep with his generous manner and welcome. No words came to me, though I managed a surprised "Huh-what?" The servants studied his every gesture and grinned at the shock that registered on my face.

Certainly, the man had the physical capacity to do anything he chose, and I did not doubt his ability to handle a coal shovel, a heavy hammer, or the reins of a hansom cab. But as he shook Guthrie's hand and complimented his speed in recovering us, I stammered, "A c-cab? In London, my lord? Was it, perhaps, you in the street the other day—"

"Indeed. I am found out, I see. I wondered if you would recognize me. I should have known that you would," Fitz cried, delighted at my penetrating his disguise. "Aye, and before you ask, yes, you have been my passenger many times, for I will sometimes haunt Baker Street when I hear from Mycroft that his brother has a case on. Might I add, Doctor, that you are one of the most generous men in that fine old town, judging from your gratuities."

His words gave me an awkward moment, thinking that my few shillings' worth of tips had gone into the pocket of a nobleman whose fortune was obviously vast. I couldn't help glancing again at the casual opulence of the place. Whitefell read my agitated confusion in my features.

"Not to worry, Dr. Watson. Your gift to me the other day went into one of the coffers of the institutions I support," Whitefell said. "And Miss Adler informs me that I, er, owe you an apology for my investigation. Sometimes, protocol is best held in abeyance. I am sorry to have been the cause of your separation from Holmes. It is worse than inconvenient, I realize."

"Ah, well, perhaps it was best we did take different paths for now, Holmes and I," I replied, wondering again about Holmes as a werewolf. "In any case, I am deeply honored to be your guest, Fitz," I said, "and I hope that my report of the past two days will help clarify what we are dealing with in this matter, though I doubt it."

"We shall hear it over dinner," Fitz said, placing a broad hand on my shoulder and leading me into yet another grand oaken hall. This one held a table that would seat at least two dozen. There, with Guthrie seated to my right and Burroughs on my left, I drew the smile and light applause of Lord Tennyson, seated at the table's head, and of Whitefell's huntsman, Carl Garrett, seated near him. Next to Garrett sat his dark-haired wife, Lora, who had overseen the meal's preparation, I was told. She regarded me with dark eyes brimming with what seemed to me to be curiosity. Raboud, Dibba, and Irene Adler sat across from me. Three more house servants, whose names I would never learn, were there as well, and Fitz took a seat near them.

I was told that both Dupain and Mary were sleeping. I would have to wait until morning for a much-anticipated reunion with Mary.

No one was "dressed" for dinner, as they would have been in London. No fine china, crystal, or silver adorned our places, and the steaming food on the table—venison, beef, baked game fowl, dishes of country vegetables, and fresh-baked bread—all lay within easy reach of the diners. A large Christmas pudding sat on a sideboard, awaiting its lighting at dessert. Other than the bright Christmas bunting on the walls beneath the winking candles, the room was devoid of opulence. It gave me a sense of home, of family, of equality, that I had never expected in a palace such as Whitefell Manor. All here were equals in the eyes of our host, who gave a homely blessing before encouraging us all to fall to.

While I ate, Tennyson plied me with serious questions, as did Irene, but merriment, even under the strained conditions of our arrival, marked the dinner. Raboud, I found, though he listened with intent to my story of our time apart, said little and offered no critique of my tale, which was a remarkable improvement in our relationship.

The plan was to hold a general meeting the next day, New Year's Day, in the great hall. Mycroft Holmes and Mr. Gladstone were expected early, so it looked as though my New Year's Eve might be one wherein I could rest, finally, after the mad dash out of London.

Whitefell knew the direction of my thoughts. He smiled and said, "Perhaps you should let young Burroughs show you to your room, where you can rest a bit, after we arrange for you to refresh yourself. Then, I assume, you will want to retire. It has been a trying time, I know. I'm sure that Dr. Raboud will benefit from extended rest as well. By the way, I have placed you in a rather special room, one of my favorites; it is my son's room. Lord Tennyson and I will be two rooms away. Dr. Raboud is down the other wing, since memories of his young 'Master Johnny' still haunt him."

After I had taken my leave, availed myself of soap and razor, and robed myself in a dressing gown procured by Burroughs, I did ask him to show me to my room, though I assumed that the rest of the company would be found in the great hall, in the light of the hearth fire and the great tree. Whitefell had been right; I was exhausted, and though Burroughs had done his best to get my suit cleaned and pressed, I did not wish to dress and join them.

"An amazing fellow, his lordship," Burroughs said as we walked down the corridor. "I believe he'd survive under the harshest conditions Mother Nature could offer him."

Burroughs, like the other servants I had met at Whitefell Manor, was quite at home. I wondered aloud whether he had been with Whitefell very long.

When I learned he had, I asked him, "Has Dr. Raboud often been a visitor here?"

"Not as often as we'd like, Doctor, but yes, he is a good friend to his lordship and was a favorite of young Johnny and his bride Miss Alice. Dr. Raboud's late father was often a welcomed guest as well," Burroughs said, opening the door into a room on the second floor which faced the broad gravel drive and the front gardens. It was definitely a young male's room: I was surrounded by sporting items and trophies of the gaming field and the hunt. A relatively small four-poster bed stood in the middle of the room, with several wardrobes arranged on the inside walls and between the high windows that looked out on the wintry landscape.

"Tell me, Burroughs, if you can, what you know of Dr. Raboud and what happened to him in Africa. Thus far, I have learned little about what transpired to practically strip him of his abilities," I said, taking a seat as Whitefell's man took my trousers and shirt and laid them on the bed.

"I gather it was some sort of fever, sir, though I've never known much more than that. His lordship is close-lipped about it, as are his friends. But I imagine that whatever it was kept Dr. Raboud from getting very far on the trail of Master Johnny and his wife."

"No gossip below stairs, then?" I asked. This drew a smile from Burroughs and a shake of his head.

"You won't find that very common here, sir. We are equals at Whitefell Manor. I tell you true that all of us were quite shaken to hear that Dr. Raboud had been taken ill. For myself, I've a suspicion that it had to do with this secret society that brings Lord Tennyson here, under my lord's protection."

"If you are equals, does he not ask you to call him Fitz?"

"He does, actually, but none of us will; he has earned the title of respect. We know our betters, sir," Burroughs said with a smile. "Plus, we observe greater proprieties when his lordship has company."

"Then you should just call me Watson. Though my lads all call me Jack or Captain Jack," I said with a laugh. "Still, I cannot quite bring myself to ask Raboud outright about his African experiences, if only in deference to his standing in the eyes of my associates."

"I will tell you, though, that from what I've heard, it wasn't any sort of natural fever but one brought on by a spell or a hex," Burroughs whispered.

"Good Lord, more magic," I sighed. "I am never to hear the end of it, am I?"

"Nor shall you, if you are around Dr. Raboud, sir. But his fever came immediately upon the death of his father, sir; they were stricken on the same day, as I've understood it. Both were extraordinary men, even by comparison to his lordship and you, sir. And they were like an uncle and a grandfather to Master Johnny when he was growing up. The Rabouds were so close as to know exactly what the other was thinking; I don't think that the son's sudden fever at the same time of his father's passing can be coincidence. They were that linked, sir, mind to mind and heart to heart."

"Thank you, Burroughs," I said as I took up the trousers and shirt and set them on a chair. "You have helped me clear my thoughts."

Burroughs departed after bidding me peace and comfort, but my troubled thoughts continued. When Burroughs had revealed those few details about Raboud and his father, my mind had gone immediately to Dupain. My distrust in the lad was becoming deeper. As I looked back on all I knew, he had been the common denominator in all the equations. Though he'd been Raboud's pupil at the time of the fateful trip to Africa, he had insisted on staying behind with Raboud's father and had been with the father at the time of his death. Perhaps, his painting of himself as an inept young man had been a ruse...

"Watson!" A voice I knew all too well came from under the bed. I started and backed away, but that voice called again. Dropping to my knees, I raised the heavy coverlet and looked into the staring eyes of Sherlock Holmes, who appeared to be as naked as the day he was born.

"Holmes!" I whispered, "What the devil—here! Take these and put them on." I thrust trousers and shirt under the bed. "When did you arrive here? I knew that had to be you who followed us off the train."

211

"Yes. I made sure to keep a close eye on you," he said. Then, showing me the red scar that ran down his chest and abdomen from my sword strike: "Too close, at times."

"Sorry about that, old man," I murmured, "but I was pretty frightened of you in that state, and I owed you, at least, a sore jaw."

"As was warranted. In answer to your other question, I have been here for some hours now, and when I saw the servant set this room in order, I gambled that Whitefell would put you here."

He rose from the other side of the bed, the pants sagging around his slim hips, and began to don the shirt.

"You assumed that he'd do me the honor of letting me stay in his son's room, I suppose?"

"People are predictable about sentiment, Watson, even the great ones, like Whitefell. But tell me, please, that Dupain made it here with you."

"Yes, he is here, resting in his room, wherever that is. I must tell you that I'm beginning to have my doubts about that young man."

"And high time, too. Dupain is the most deceptive murderer I've come across," Holmes declared.

"*Murderer?*" I cried, for though I'd had my doubts about Dupain, Holmes's abrupt claim shocked me.

"Please keep your voice down, Watson. I do not want Dupain to know I am here. I confronted him on the train, and he threatened me with his own knife. I told him to do his worst, that I would disarm him with ease. Then that cunning devil turned the knife on himself," Holmes said. "But wait: I need to brief the others as well."

Taking up a pen and a scrap of paper from a nearby desk, he wrote one word—"*benandanti*"—and handed the note to me. "Please give this to Dr. Raboud. If he is with Dupain, make sure only he reads it and that only he responds to my summons. Then summon the others."

With Burroughs's help, we soon had all the principals in the room. Dibba and Dr. Raboud I had coaxed away from the sleeping Dupain. On our way back to my room, I handed Raboud the note, and he examined it and gasped, "So, that is how he managed it!" But he would say nothing more.

Tennyson and Whitefell were there already when we arrived, and Guthrie had come with them. The Sovereign sat in a wooden desk chair across from Holmes, who sat on the bed, his legs crossed like those of a fakir about to demonstrate a marvel. The rest of us stood. The tension in the room grew palpable.

Burroughs came to the door and whispered to me that Irene and Mary were asleep in the room next to Dupain's. I bade him keep watch in the hall and warn us if Dupain approached.

With the door shut and locked, Raboud broke the silence.

"I assume you learned from your Traveler friends about the benandanti charm," he said to Holmes. "I confess that I did not think of those artifacts as the means of transforming men into werewolves." Turning to Tennyson, he added, "I'm sorry, my lord, that I erred in my thinking."

"Please, Omar," the Sovereign replied in soft tones, "do not take on that burden yourself. We all missed it. Both Fitz and I learned, long ago, that Cameron's people held those charms in trust, and neither of us thought of them in connection with this matter, though we should have. The truth is that I did not speak with Mycroft Holmes about the matter of the thefts and murders in the Travelers' ranks. I thought to wait until this matter had been dealt with, thinking that we faced a different threat from a different foe."

"We were all duped, my lord, by a force that employed one man," Holmes said. "And that man is Jean-Louis Dupain."

I heard several gasps, the loudest from Raboud. He reeled on his feet, and Dibba settled his shocked master into a chair.

"Dupain is a cunning murderer," Holmes went on, "and an adept in the occult arts to a degree none of us imagined. I learned much of what I needed about Dupain shortly before your party boarded the train at Euston Station. In disguise, I made my way aboard and made a haphazard plan to draw you away, Dr. Raboud, but that plan was thwarted by Dr. Watson, who planted me on my backside and knocked the wind out of me, spoiling my hasty actions. I knew well that you would all distrust me, so I confronted Dupain later myself, though he too bested me with his cunning.

"Now, I only lack the identity and motive of the one who set Dupain on this course. For that I came here, after I made sure Watson was safe," Holmes said.

"But what proof do you have that Jean-Louis is a murderer?" Raboud asked in a shaking voice.

"Ah, that is a longer tale," Holmes replied, "about which I need only tell you this: My contact in the Sûreté informed me that Jean-Louis Dupain murdered his own mother, Céline, five years ago. A Parisian magistrate ruled Dupain insane and had him committed to the Charenton asylum. However, he never made it there. He was liberated by a band of Gitanos and disappeared."

"But the Sûreté would have detained him on his arrival in Paris not long ago, would they not?" Whitefell asked.

At this, Raboud's face fell into his hands, and he shook his head.

"Ah, no, they had not the chance," he said. "I traveled to Paris under diplomatic papers, as I always do on Logres Society business, and Dupain was listed only as my ward."

"There is still the matter of how Dupain came to you in the first place, Omar. I have suspicions but no facts. Can you enlighten me?" Holmes asked.

"I can," said Tennyson, with a heavy sigh. "We sent him there at the request of Otto von Bismarck." He closed his eyes and muttered, "I have been so blind."

"We all have, my lord," Whitefell said. "You see, we have sought to influence the Iron Chancellor, Bismarck, for we have seen that he is gathering power in Europe and in the Belgian Congo, an area rich with resources. We have sought to work within his court to learn of his intentions."

"And your son's trip to Africa was part of this," I said, recalling my brief conversation with Burroughs about Raboud's ill-fated attempt to learn the fate of Whitefell's son and daughter-in-law.

"Yes," Tennyson answered, "and because Bismarck's social policies had improved conditions for workers in Germany, we thought that we were succeeding. That's when we—or, I should say, I—made so bold as to offer Bismarck a connection to the Logres Society. When he replied that he had long guessed of our existence, he proposed that he send his protégé, Jean-Louis Dupain, a junior occult advisor, to train with us and act as a liaison between our courts. We... I... thought the plan a success," Tennyson finished weakly.

Holmes nodded. "Which explains the other agents in this matter, those who have sought on several occasions to kill us. I assume that they worked under Bismarck's orders, and I suspect that my great foe, James Moriarty, has been an aid to Bismarck. I know of no other criminal mind able to execute such a complex plan as the one that has baffled us. Watson's bravery and his dogged determination to do his best has been, perhaps, the only thing which has thwarted this plot against us so far. Otherwise, Dupain could have killed us all whenever he wished. Can anyone enlighten me as to what Dupain hopes to accomplish?"

"I can," Raboud said sadly. "Dupain has been learning from me all along about the Mantle of Logres, the power that comes to the Sovereign of Logres at one place, at one time of the year, and gives him the power to rule."

"And he means to stand in my place on Arthur's Seat on Twelfth Night, to take on that power," Tennyson added in a heavy voice.

"I can think of no other reason for his delay. He... used me," Raboud said, his face clouding with pain.

"Then I will go and fetch him here to stand judgment," Whitefell said.

"Not just yet, my lord," Holmes said, "for we will need our greatest weapon in the days to come, and that is Omar Raboud, once we restore his power."

"But how can you?" Raboud pleaded. "I have been..."

"You have been under his control, Omar, for some time. How did he gain your trust?"

"The potions, master," Dibba said from behind Raboud.

"The one thing that you trusted him to do for you and your dear father, all along, was to make the potions to sustain your health."

Raboud gasped and shook his head, tears forming in his eyes.

"How long has it been, Omar, since you ingested one of these potions?" Holmes asked.

"Days, I think, Sherlock, but my thoughts are still so cloudy, I..."

"You are not totally free from their effects, but we do not have time to wait. However, even coming out of those effects, you will be able to see what he has done to you. You, Omar, are the man whom, thus far, Dupain has most injured," Holmes said. "If you will allow yourself to, you can remember what happened to you in Africa."

"No, no, no. I... cannot. Do not make me," Raboud pleaded in fear, as though the terrible memories were beginning to bleed through.

Whatever potions Dupain had given him had kept the memories locked away, I reasoned, and I recognized what Holmes was trying to do. We had used the same technique in an unpublished case that I called "The Strange Adventure of the Vicarage Ghost," in which we rid an old soldier of the crippling horror that had made him prey to a scoundrel's extortion. It had been awful to watch, but forcing the man to remember exactly what had happened, to relive his pain, had been the only way to rid him of the malady that had crippled him and made him prey to another. Raboud would have to face again whatever terrors had beset him. Given that there was likely magic involved, I imagined that they would be worse than combat. I could see in Raboud's anguished face and shaking limbs that the effects of Dupain's draughts were wearing away. He knew what he would have to face, though he fought against it.

"Please, Omar, you must try, for we need you," Tennyson said, and all there grew hushed. The only sound was Raboud sobbing as he fought against whatever terrifying images must have flooded his mind. For him, it would be a matter of feeling everything again, realizing that persons he'd never met had tormented him in order to extinguish his abilities.

"Whatever happened to you was wrong, the work of evil that no one deserves. And it came when? Where?" Holmes prodded in a gentle voice.

"In West Africa, Port Harcourt," Raboud whispered. "You are correct. I traveled with a supply of Dupain's elixirs with me. I took them nightly—to sleep, to ease my worries about my father's failing health, to dull my sorrows about Fitz's missing family. Then, one day after searching many port towns, I found a crew member of the ship on which Fitz's son had sailed. That man said he would take me to... to those who knew how to find Johnny and Alice.

"But no. No, please. I cannot." Raboud shook as though fever chill wracked his limbs. He clutched himself and bent double as though his stomach cramped.

"Dibba, can you help him in any way?" Holmes whispered.

The dweraz, with tears in his own eyes, lay his hands on Raboud's dark head and began a slow chant. At his touch, Raboud sobbed harder and fell to the floor, as though Dibba's charm had released something in him that Raboud could not have released in himself. Dibba followed him to the floor, his chant growing stronger. Part of me wanted to stop the escalation of Raboud's pain, but if we were to have his help, he needed the torment to increase. He needed to find his memories and voice them aloud to ease his mind.

"Then he... took me to an empty warehouse... by the docks," he said at last. "A fever came over me as we went, and try as I might, I could not think. I was pushed inside that awful place, and then it... that vile thing... had me. All like smoke... limbs of foul mists. I knew it for what it was, the Croucher, a demon, and it invaded me, body and soul. It... gloated over me. It told me it would give me what I wanted..."

Raboud's eyes grew wide as he relived the horror of what I could only think of as a physical and psychic rape.

I had seen the kind of entity he spoke of. I knew its horrible strength, for I had helped save Westcott from its coils. My mind reeled at the damage such a thing had obviously done to Raboud's mind and body. He lay on the floor, a quivering image of pain, trying to protect himself with his feeble hands. It was agony to watch.

Holmes went to the floor at his side and called to him, "This thing was sent by Dupain. It cannot control you any longer. Dibba is here protecting you, as am I. You are stronger now, freeing yourself from the concoctions that held you in check. Touch the power that is within you. Cast out this evil now."

Raboud's weeping turned to small cries of effort. I saw his teeth clench. He fought the memory, strengthened and freed by knowing Dupain's deceit. Raboud's anger rose, showing in the fierceness of his gaze. A light grew around him, and he coughed out something like smoke, which settled low to the floor before it faded into nothing, taking with it its stench of corruption.

Whitefell turned and threw open a window to let in fresh, cold air, saying in a harsh whisper, "Dupain will pay for all that he has done."

As we watched and called words of encouragement to Raboud, his coughing subsided and he sucked in clean air. His breathing gradually grew calmer then, though his tears continued to flow.

Holmes patted the man's shoulder and murmured, "I'm sorry, my friend, but it had to be done."

As Dibba helped him up from the floor, Raboud's face strengthened with resolve. "And my father?" he asked Holmes.

"Yes, we can believe that Dupain killed him," Holmes affirmed. "We can only hope that his passing was more peaceful than your ordeal today."

"Omar, my friend, I cannot tell you how sorry I am that you have lost so much," Whitefell whispered. Then he turned to Guthrie and said, "It is time for you—and Dibba—to fetch Dupain and bring him to judgment."

Raboud feebly shook Holmes's hand. "I owe you much, Sherlock, and your efforts to restore me require me to warn you that you bear a dangerous burden in that benandanti amulet you still carry."

"Thank you for your concern, Omar, but I think I should keep it, just until we have Dupain and his confederates in custody," Holmes replied.

"Holmes," I added, "won't you reconsider? Surely, now, with Dupain identified as our foe and here in this house, we can face further challenges as we've always done, side by side."

Truth be told, I worried about what I feared was a dependency problem in Holmes. I'd cajoled him into giving up cocaine, but I feared that the enhancements of the Loup-Garou Curse would be harder to give up, for they courted his every need as a servant of justice.

"I do not personally depend upon it, Watson, if that is your fear," Holmes replied in an affronted tone. "But think, man, about the good that I could do with it. Why, with the aid of this amulet, I could track Moriarty to any lair. No one could hide him from me or overcome me in the effort as long as I have but this simple coin." He lifted the amulet and held it in his clenched fist.

Then a realization hit me so hard I staggered on my feet: Dupain yet had one of the benandanti amulets. That shock was followed hard by Dibba's roaring shouts and the loud reports of Guthrie's revolver from down the hall. Burroughs shouted, "My Lord Whitefell!" Wood splintered, glass shattered, and we heard women screaming. The loudest and last of these screams trailed away into the night.

Mary's scream.

CHAPTER EIGHTEEN

"The Feast of New Year's Day,"
1 January, 1889.

Midnight came and went, and the once quiet walls of Whitefell Manor still seemed to resound with the energy of Mary's last scream, though the minutes and hours dragged by. Dupain had abducted her, making a quick getaway that took all of us by surprise. Clearly, he had known that his ruse was becoming transparent and that with Holmes's arrival he would be found out.

His escape had been bold, brutal, and worst of all, successful. He had bound Mary, though Irene fought him. He buried his knife into Irene's left side as he prepared to escape with Mary as his captive. When our men confronted him, he took on werewolf form and threw Dibba through the solid oak paneling of the hallway. After breaking Guthrie's right arm and most of his ribs on that side, Dupain threw him through a third-floor window.

Dibba had taken little harm from Dupain's rough treatment and had pulled the oak splinters from his own neck and shoulders. I patched Irene's laceration, which would leave a scar. She did not complain. She was focused, angry, ready to fight.

I had eyes and ears only for Magnus Guthrie at this moment. He had borne the worst of it all. He lay on a library table, bleeding from a score of wounds. A compound fracture of his right arm left it at an odd angle from his body. His ribcage on that side was misshapen, and a bloody froth lay on his lips from the damage done to his right lung. He had no more than an hour of life left in him.

Dibba Al-Hassan stood on the other side of the table from me yet again, chanting in the guttural language of the dweraz, plying magic which caused a mild glow to settle on Guthrie. Raboud explained that the dwarf held our patient in a place between the worlds, where he would feel no pain and recall nothing of his attack.

When I first reached Guthrie's side, he managed to whisper, "Don't bother, Cap'n. It's... 'last post' for me."

"Nonsense, man," I bluffed. "I'll see you right, Magnus. Just don't give up. Stay with me." Guthrie gave me a strained smile and a nod and closed his eyes.

As I worked on Guthrie, I learned more of what passed outside my makeshift surgery. Whitefell's gamekeeper, Carl Garrett, had set out on Dupain's track while the rest of us sought to establish a sense of order in the manor. I knew where my work lay, though I had to concentrate to keep thoughts of Mary's plight from intruding on my efforts to save Guthrie.

Garrett found that our foe had stolen a horse, a prized stallion named Tantor, from Whitefell's stable. As Garrett set out on Dupain's trail, the rest of us rallied around Guthrie. As the sun struggled to pierce the heavy cloud of New Year's morning, Garrett came back and made his report to Whitefell, who stood near me as I labored, still, on Guthrie.

"Lord Whitefell, I am sorry to say that the evil young fellow has had help in his escape. Not three miles away on the Penrith road, I saw where he met at least two carriages and two other horsemen. The snow has turned to an icy rain, sir, but it looks as if many men and horses awaited him there. He has made good his escape, sir."

Garrett looked at the floor and was so quiet that even I had to dart a glance in his direction, and I saw tears fall down the huntsman's weathered cheeks.

"He—he murdered the horse, sir," Garrett whispered. "Tantor, well, he was mutilated, sir. Even with the rain, there was blood... everywhere. I don't know how I'll tell the missus, sir. Lora loved that beast." Whitefell embraced the man around the shoulders, and Garrett added in a choked voice, "If you're going after that Dupain fellow, I would like a crack at him, sir."

I thought it a bad idea, but Whitefell told him, "Very well, Carl. Perhaps you and Lora should leave immediately for Edinburgh and head to my rooms in the Pleasance. We'll join you there as quickly as we can, though we may not get there before tomorrow night. Bring in some supplies, for though Lord Tennyson and I have rooms at the Old Waverley, we will need another base of operations. Go swiftly and quietly." Our host departed with his gamekeeper to bring this news to Lord Tennyson.

Dupain, it seemed, had taken thought to do the most damage he could to our party, and I was forced to continue putting my fear for Mary's safety from my mind as I tended Guthrie. He would have been dead by that time had it not been for the wholesome magic of Dibba Al-Hassan. Dibba's hands trembled, and a sweat lay on his wide brow, but whatever he was doing seemed to keep Guthrie breathing. I gave grateful thanks for magic then. Dibba was keeping this good man alive, although apparently not indefinitely. Raboud sat near me, handing me supplies as I needed them, talking softly, although I paid only a quarter of my attention to what he said.

"John, your friend Sherlock has left us. We assume he has gone to hunt Dupain. Miss Adler tells us that Dupain is bound for Edinburgh. He bragged to her of his plans to take the Sovereign's place at midnight on Arthur's Seat on the fifth. He will take on the Mantle of Logres and win control of the power of the Sovereign. He said that he has innumerable allies, so he feels sure of being able to work his will. Lord Whitefell and the Sovereign both assume that Dupain has help from Bismarck's human agents. I think ... a worse thing must be true." Here Raboud paused and I spared him a glance.

"I always suspect the worst. Just tell me," I said and went back to trying to stitch up the cruel lacerations of werewolf claws across Guthrie's chest.

"Dupain must serve a demonic master as well as a political one, though sometimes the difference between the two blurs in my sight," Raboud whispered, holding the edges of Guthrie's skin closed for me with his fine, long fingers. I nodded grimly, willing to think the worst of that young man.

"The benandanti," Raboud went on, "were a sect of people who, from ancient times, sought to help the peasant folk of northern Italy. They possessed amulets that would allow them to shape-shift into powerful beings, most often in werewolf form. They fought the powers of evil that sought to prey upon people. No doubt some of their foes were demonic, though some were of the dark faerie kin, who hate humankind."

"Yes," I muttered, glad that a faerie of the light struggled to keep Guthrie alive even as we spoke. "Why is it that we do not have more faerie aid on our side from the—what did you call it?"

"The Light Court," Raboud replied. "No, they have taken a vow to stay separate from humans, who are dangerous to them. No matter the number of fae from the Dark Court whom Dupain has bribed or tricked into aiding him, those of the Light Court feel that they must not intervene in our struggle, though our victory would aid them, keep them safe. And so I do not know that they will do anything. We shall see.

"However, my point is that Dupain's plan and his connection to the powers of Shaitan, the great Satan, have allowed him to pervert that ancient benandanti power that originally served the greater good, though the Church's Inquisition pronounced it evil. This means, however, that we could use it for good, as Holmes has done, though my plan is still precarious and will delay our apprehension of Dupain. It will save Guthrie's life, if... if I can control it."

I gave him my full attention then and asked, "Can you, sir? I don't presume to know how you can, but if you can do it, do it now!"

"We will need one of those amulets that allowed Dupain to change Holmes and—"

"Hastings!" I cried, leaping to the answer of where to get an amulet of such kind. Dupain must have given one to Hastings: he had turned Hastings as he had turned Holmes.

Raboud nodded.

I begrudged every second we gave to Dupain as he escaped with Mary in his clutches, but I saw the need to gain the power of that amulet before confronting him. I also saw the need of a magic that would heal Guthrie, since I knew all my skill in medicine could not: his wounds were too grave. Dupain would have to wait until the night of the fifth to work his plan. I could only hope we could intercept him by then—and that Mary could be returned safely to me.

I ran from the library to the great hall, where Lord Whitefell and Irene had gone to report to Lord Tennyson and greet Mycroft Holmes, who had arrived during the great press of excitement. I burst in, hands covered in my friend's blood, and ran to Irene.

"Dr. Watson!" Lord Whitefell called. "Mr. Holmes here bears news that, indeed, Dupain has the aid of a coterie of agents from—"

"Yes, yes," I muttered, brushing past him and rushing up to take Irene by the arms. I took no notice of Mycroft Holmes and Mr. Gladstone, who had been in the midst of their report. "Hastings's effects, his belongings that you took from his clothing," I said to her. "Do you have them still?"

"What? Why, yes, John. They are in my luggage now. But I don't—"

"Fetch the lot of them and bring them to Raboud in the library. There is no time to explain, no time to waste," I said. "Just do it now!"

"You lot," I cried to the rest of them, "we might yet save Commander Guthrie, but it will be dangerous. Lord Whitefell, we must have you and your sword with us, in case this goes wrong. And Mycroft, unless I am much mistaken, there is a magical amulet that Scotland Yard holds in evidence. It was last held by Arnold Pinder, and we must suppose that these agents know of it and will try to procure it. Do something about it," I yelled. I took Irene by the arm and half dragged her away. Always ready for an adventure, she made no complaint of my rough handling but went swiftly to find all the things from Hastings's pockets.

I returned in haste to Guthrie's side, thinking about how Dupain had left the Midland Grand immediately before we had.

He must have seen Hastings waiting for Irene and "tipped" him with an amulet. Hastings would have placed it in his pocket and placed himself, unwittingly, under Dupain's influence. A sickening thought.

As we waited for Irene to return with Hastings's effects, Raboud sat with eyes closed, lenses off, his fine features softened by the calm of meditation. I thought it odd how solemn, refined, even beautiful, his face was in that quiet moment. He had always looked so angry, and I saw in his quiet repose how wrong I'd been in assuming that was the core of his character. A quiet confidence came from his calm posture, as though he had shaken off Dupain's evil influence and was once again able to use his powers. I felt hope, then. Guthrie's life depended on Raboud's ability, and perhaps some of that ability still remained.

When Irene placed the pile of coins in front of him, Raboud did not need to seek the amulet by sorting them one by one. Indeed, as she approached, he did not even open his eyes. He placed his right hand above the small assortment of currency that Irene had piled on the table at Guthrie's side. Raboud sighed, and his lips moved in a silent prayer or incantation. The mound of coins jingled and shook. One coin, the size of a sixpence piece, pushed its way above the rest of the change and rose, wobbling as though a tiny, fierce wind moved it. Raboud closed his hand upon it.

"Dr. Watson," he whispered, "please place this on your friend, somewhere that it touches his skin." Taking the small thing in my fingers, I turned to Guthrie. His breathing was so shallow that I thought him seconds away from death. I placed the amulet, with as much calm and reverence as I could, atop Guthrie's chest, where it stuck in a patch of drying blood as though glued there.

Dibba ceased his chanting and stood back on the opposite side of the table from Raboud. I had not seen before, but noted then, that the glow around Guthrie's body emanated from four small, white cubes, bigger than gaming dice and unadorned. I had seen them before in the Alhambra Theatre, where Raboud had proven too weak to use their magic. I could only hope that his new knowledge of Dupain's perfidy gave him enough strength to succeed.

When Raboud extended his hands toward Dibba, the glow increased, making Guthrie's red wounds stand out in sharper contrast to his skin. As I looked, the wounds began to close. The jagged edges found each other and folded together, leaving thin red lines behind.

Yet other things occurred at the same time. The bones of Guthrie's body began to change, and even though he was deeply unconscious, Guthrie suddenly drew in a deep, moaning breath that changed into a guttural growl. Mouth became muzzle. The jagged bone slipped back under the skin, and the broken arm straightened as it added flesh and fur. The clothing still on him ripped away as his torso and limbs swelled with muscle. More deep growls came from his swelling chest, and his lengthened fingers clasped and extended a set of cruel claws. His feet made the oddest change, for they lengthened along the bottom and the heel hardened and grew thicker, making Guthrie's legs appear to hinge backwards. His toes and the ball of each foot broadened, flattened, and became paws.

I saw at once why a werewolf was so quick, for the mechanics of those powerful legs were for running, leaping, and attacking. And I was reminded of why it was so deadly: the claws of its hands would easily shred flesh, and the heavy jaw with its long, bright teeth would tear the throat out of—anything.

Guthrie transformed, though a thing fearful to see, was magnificent to behold. Lost in wonder, I did not even recognize the danger he was to me, who stood so close, until he leaped off the table and faced me, exuding power, red eyes blazing.

Whitefell pushed me aside, his sword before him, though Raboud moved more quickly, rising to snatch the coin from Guthrie's chest. A flash, as of lightning, filled the room, and the glow from Raboud's magical devices faded and went out. The werewolf in our midst uttered no sound but fell into my arms.

Guthrie is a large and heavy man in his natural state, and he had become immensely heavier. I was able to center myself as my sensei had taught me, however, and I guided him to the floor, my arms under his. A tingling sensation, like static shock, prickled between us, but I did not wish to drop him, despite my discomfort. The most volatile jolts made me cry out, but I got him to the floor. Irene, Whitefell, and I stared as the changes back to his normal form came over Guthrie.

I dared ask, "Dr. Raboud, how can a man become ten stone heavier or lighter by virtue of a spell, and what is this viscous discharge that we see on a person whose body transforms back to its natural state?"

"A spell carries force between worlds and has an impact on its object according to the nature of that spell. What it leaves behind as that force goes back to its source is the very mud of creation, Watson. It is a wonderful and natural process, like the change of steam to water," he replied.

"Holmes will be pleased to know that," I mumbled as I rubbed my stinging hands.

"It carries a shock, yes? No?" Dibba added with a wan smile and held up his hands, which I saw were covered with it still. I realized that he must have endured the same shocks I'd felt, and worse, during the hour that he'd held Guthrie in his protective spell.

"You dared all that pain to help him?" I said, just above a whisper. "How could you stand it?"

"Because the grace of Allah is mighty," he replied with a broad smile, "and because I desired to see this man whole again."

Most of his clothing ripped to shreds, Magnus Guthrie sat up, looking at each of us in turn. Wonder shone from his face, and he said, "I feel like a prize bull, ready to fight, but the last thing I recall is that werewolf smashin' my bones and throwin' me about. What in the bleedin' 'ell 'appened to me?"

"You had a touch of the same medicine that cured Sherlock Holmes, Commander," I said. "Now, we must join him in the hunt for Dupain. You were more than right to doubt the lad."

"Strewth! I knew it!" Guthrie cried, springing to his feet and scattering the remains of his clothing upon the floor. "When do we leave?"

"As soon as you acquire clothing, I think," Irene said, giving Guthrie's physique a good looking-over. "You'll make quite the stir in Edinburgh, should you go like that."

***

Still, we were delayed. Raboud and Irene, who would be part of my strike team, were both still weak with wounds and work.

While we waited for them to gain their strength, we gathered what we would need for the journey, beginning with much-needed clothing.

Once we had Guthrie kitted out with some of Johnny's clothes, Whitefell turned to me and examined my clothing, which had taken quite a battering since I'd left London. The clean clothes I'd been provided, I'd given to the naked Holmes after his transformation back to a mortal form.

"Well, Doctor," Whitefell said, "I will not see you turned out on this journey without proper clothing, but we have exhausted most of the options that would fit your heroic frame." I chuckled at his description as I followed him to his room. He, if anyone, could be described as heroic, in both body and mind. There were mysteries wrapped around him, still, in his long-standing relationship with Raboud and in the disappearance of his son and daughter-in-law, but my trust in Whitefell was complete.

He opened a trunk at the foot of the narrow bed he called his own and began to lay out an extraordinary outfit: kilt, hose, heavy sweater, jacket, and balmoral. Beside these, he lay a stag-handled dirk and a *skean dubh*, along with a heavy belt and a sporran.

I started to protest that I was not about to go about dressed like a Jacobite, but Fitz stared at the garments with a look of sadness, mixed with smiles of pleasant memory. Clearly, they were precious to him. Grey woven bands, light and dark, with a blood red stripe at intervals marked the Clayton tartan, and the sweater was black wool, a shade darker than the jacket. He ran the thick, black hose through his hands.

"These were my son's. The kilt is of our family tartan," he

said. "We trekked the Highlands in our kilts a year before we had our—well, a year before he left. They—" Whitefell cleared his throat before he could go on. "Well, I'll be wearing mine, as I do whenever I go to Edinburgh. So we shall match. It befits an Englishman to wear the kilt, when he is half Scots," he claimed in a heartier voice.

"They will keep you warmer than that gabardine suit of yours, and I've a notion that the bird's-eye tweed in that jacket would turn a knife blade, as it might well need to," he added, holding up the jacket to see how well it'd fit me.

I put my obstinate pride away and said, "I shall be happy to wear it to do honor to your son."

Mary would laugh when she saw me, I thought—but then, would she see me? My one hope was that Mary would have the occasion to see me again, dressed in Highland gear or not. I would dare any risk to hold her in my arms again.

***

And yet that hope had to wait. In the late afternoon of New Year's Day, bitter winds swept down from the north, icing everything and layering yet more snow over the slick conditions. An unnatural, nearly arctic cold set in, and we feared that the trip to Penrith would be so slow as to endanger the horses as well as our party. But the Garretts had gotten out earlier and were, we hoped, well on their way by the time the storm hit.

The hours passed as though on broken limbs, dragging themselves along, and Dupain gained distance and time on us. We were all warm enough and well fed, but very little rest was gotten, I think.

I recalled a story of the old days, a tale of the great Sir Gawain. The tale had it that one New Year's Day, King Arthur refused all food, all merriment, until a wonder should appear in his hall. And a wonder did show itself to that fabled king, in the presence of a magical Green Knight, who survived a decapitation. But no such wonder had presented itself to the Sovereign of the Logres Society or to me.

229

Holmes was out there, somewhere, on Dupain's trail. And Mary, God help her, was in the clutches of a monomaniac in the service of a foreign leader who would use him to acquire power over England. If ever there were a need for a wonder, it was on this New Year's Day and the day that followed it, the Feast of St. Basil and St. Gregory, those two mighty friends in faith who had wrought such wonders. They wrought none for us.

All I could do was pace in front of the fire in the great hall and listen to Whitefell, Raboud, and Tennyson reminisce about Fitz's missing son. They talked of his mission in West Africa. And on the night of that feast, with arctic winds howling like loups-garous, Irene shadowed me as I paced about in my kilt. In the shadow of the great Scotch pine, she drew me into talk about Mary.

"John," she said, "Mary will come back to you, if she survives this ordeal. I heard her wish for that while we stood over you, as you lay next to poor Hastings in my kitchen and again as we rested in the berth next to you. She still believes that she and Sherlock were lovers, just that once, but I have seen her, twice now, while she has been in my company, enter that state of utter vacancy that you describe in your reports. Mary admits that such periods cause her a great deal of confusion. Perhaps she has imagined a tryst with Sherlock.

"She does seem clear, though, about one thing: that what you discovered in Anne Prescott, she can never give you."

"I would not ask it of her," I replied. "I never wanted her to be any way but the way she chose to be."

Irene stared at me.

"If you truly want the sort of partnership you dreamed of having with Anne, you will have to find a different sort of woman than Mary is," she said, laying a quivering hand on my arm. "You have a strength about you that is irresistible, and women who dare to dream of an adventurous life are drawn to it."

Turning to look into her eyes, I saw that she was in earnest, and it amazed me. Although she had not said it outright, she had implied much, for I knew that she was such a woman as Anne

Prescott had wanted to be, and I wondered if I should take this as a declaration of Irene's feelings toward me. Yet I did not take her hand as it lay on my arm.

In the light of the hearth fire that played upon the highlights of her hair, her candid gaze and her slightly parted lips beckoned to me, yet I knew that I could not return her desire, though my body wanted to. So powerful was her allure that any man would have given in to it. Any man, that is, who did not know what I knew of myself: I would never make a good partner as long as I bore the burden of the sword I carried and the role I played. I could only hope to try to be the husband I should be to Mary.

I didn't speak any of these thoughts aloud, and after a long moment of us looking into each other's eyes, she turned her gaze away.

"The harsh truth is, though, John," she whispered, "that Mary will not survive this ordeal. I know that you hope to have her return, but you must know, too, that Dupain will do whatever is in his power to hurt any of us. You shall have all my help, though, in trying to save her."

With that, she turned from me, head held high, and walked back to the fire to join the others.

I prayed that she was wrong.

***

By the next morning, the winds had died away, and the temperature rose by slow degrees under a brightening sun. Still, we could not travel the iced-over roads. I stayed apart from the others, meditating, steadying my mind. No fresh snow fell, but that which coated everything nearly blinded our eyes.

By the middle of the Feast of the Holy Name on the third of January, we could begin our slow journey to the station at Penrith. Whitefell was to take another road, a slower road, toward Carlisle and would arrive in Edinburgh after we did. We only had two more days in which to discover Dupain's hiding place in that Athens of the North.

I still chafed at going to Edinburgh, but I knew that it was the place where the questions that drove me could be answered. I would find my answers there, in the city where I was born, or find my death in meeting the challenge of Dupain. I had no idea where Holmes was, yet I believed that he was working toward the same end.

I took comfort in the warmth of my borrowed outfit as we waited in the cold sun to start our journey. Irene said that it suited me. The kilt, of the military or fillebeg kind, was a fraction too long, but it fit around my waist and gave my legs greater freedom of movement. My lumbering boots, with the long wool hose under them, kept my feet snug. Overall, I was a good deal warmer than I had been in my suit, shoes, and greatcoat.

Irene, too, was turned out for adventure, quite eye-catching in her tailored black wool suit and the loose coat she wore atop it. The mass of her auburn hair she had tucked up under a broad-brimmed hat. The wool scarf she wore would mask her lower face so that she could pass for a slender man if one did not look too closely. She was obviously in no mood for male attention; I wondered if that were the reason for her costume. I also wondered if her mood had anything to do with my reaction—or lack of reaction—to her.

Magnus Guthrie joked with her as she stood ready to enter our small coach.

"Why, Miss Adler, you are a vision in that outfit. D'you really think that men will not notice your beauty?"

With hands that moved more quickly than the eye could follow, she drew from under her coat two .45 Colt revolvers, both cocked and aimed at Guthrie's eyes. He could only stare into the two large bores of the tooled barrels that stood motionless before his gaze. Irene met his astonished stare with a frank one of her own, all business, and a deadly business at that.

"Back home, they say that God made all men, but Sam Colt made 'em equals. That makes it a new day for women, too, and I intend that French lad to know it," she said, easing home the hammers and spinning the pistols in her hands to show off their mother-of-pearl grips to Guthrie. Relaxing, he inspected them with a soldier's care. After a brief exchange about the stopping power of a .45 round, she retrieved her pistols and entered our carriage with Raboud.

"Good luck with that one, Cap'n Jack," he said with a wink to me.

He entered the larger carriage with Whitefell, Tennyson, and Dibba Al-Hassan. Since Raboud was to travel with me, I saw that he trusted me—and Irene Adler—with his safety, lending Dibba to the charge of protecting Tennyson, who of us all could least defend himself. We were to travel separately, for, knowing that Bismarck's agents were abroad, we were sure that attacks would come.

PART THREE: "THE LOW ROAD HOME.

CHAPTER NINETEEN

"The Feast of the Holy Name,"
3 January, 1889.

We moved at a snail's pace, it seemed to me, and I fretted every second of the further delay. As we neared Penrith, we encountered our first resistance, even as the conditions of the road improved and allowed us a faster pace. A party of men swept down on us from one of the fells that ran above the road. Burroughs, who drove us, spotted their torches and alerted us to their presence with a series of raps on the carriage roof.

He spurred his team on, and Whitefell's horses broke into a wild gallop as our carriage wheels slewed through the icy slush on the curves of the road. We could hear our pursuers' horses gaining on us and the calls of the men who assailed us, speaking French, I thought. Their numbers and greater speed would allow them to hem us in shortly, and I set my mind to the task of defending my charges as well as I could, though I need not have worried with Irene Adler aboard. I have never seen a woman so capable in a firefight.

They shot at Burroughs, who cursed them for bloody cowards as he hunkered down as low in his seat as he could. I leaned out the right-hand window, revolver drawn, looking for a shot, though they rode in a file behind us. Twin reports of Irene's pistols barked out from the other side of the carriage, and I glanced over at her and had to stare. Having dropped the carriage window, she had hooked her left leg through its opening, set her right foot on the step below the door, leaned out into the wind and rain, and opened fire. I looked on and cheered while Raboud let out a coarse scream and dropped to the carriage floor. The action was on.

Bullets tore through the back of the coach, ripping jagged holes in the upholstery, splintering the wood. Burroughs screamed as a bullet found him, though the speed and control of the carriage never wavered. Four of our attackers fell from their mounts under Irene's fusillade, and if they weren't already dead from her assaults, they were trampled by the mounts of the pursuers behind them as we rattled on.

The other pursuers, masked men in a wide variety of costume, drew to my side of the road, away from Adler's barrage, and I opened fire on them. Two dropped from their mounts, though it was more luck than skill on my part: I had only to fire into the mass of them to hit something. When I looked again, Adler had reloaded and mounted the top of the carriage, even as it pelted along at breakneck speed. She stood high over Burroughs, drawing their fire, which never hit her. Her hat was gone, and her auburn hair streamed around her face in the wind of our passage, but it did not diminish her aim. Of the two who remained, she hit each with several shots. Then she took the reins from Burroughs and whipped up the team again. And within a quarter hour, we tore into Penrith, bound for the train station.

Though our train was boarding, we took a few minutes to see to Burroughs, who had taken one round in his shoulder and one in his right thigh. As I bound his wounds and bade him seek help at the Penrith constabulary, he only had attention for Irene Adler, who held him while I administered aid.

"I will never again, I think, fall in love with a woman as quickly as I have with you today, Miss Adler," he said, through panting breaths. "I pray that you will return and marry me. I will be your devoted servant all the rest of my days."

She smiled at him, kissed him full on the lips, and whispered, "That's as sweet a proposal as I have ever had, and I have had many. If I live to see Epiphany, I will consider it, though I make you no promises." And with that, we sprinted to the platform, threw some money at a startled clerk, grasped our tickets, and boarded the train.

We traveled in relative silence for a while, taking corner

seats in the emptiest of the second-class cars. I could not help but overhear several passengers who passed by us talking in low tones about the beast sightings in Penrith and the surrounding countryside.

"I dursn't stay 'ere a day longer," a woman said to her male companion. "Young 'uns taken like that and killed. It's 'orrible."

"Weren't the Wulver from up Shetland way, though, if you ask me," said the man. "More like Old Stinker from over 'round Whitby, a nasty killer by all accounts."

Another, a young father traveling with two small children, claimed as he entered the car, "'Twere just a pack o' wild dogs, my dears, and you needn't worry. They'll not put up with such in Edinburgh. You'll be safe as houses there, never you fear."

I knew that Edinburgh was anything but as safe as houses, but I could not tell him that. And we heard more such talk, but we added nothing to it and kept our counsel. I wondered, and I saw by the nervous glances of my companions that they wondered, too, whether we were hearing tales of Dupain or Holmes in werewolf form. I thought again of Holmes's hand shaking while he grasped that Italian coin, and I offered a silent prayer for his resolve.

"I trust that they were talking about livestock as the victims," Raboud whispered, "for they only seemed worried, not sickened, as they would be if children were hurt. But if it is Dupain or one of his folk, we cannot look at keeping this secret for too long."

"If it goes on beyond tomorrow night, we can think of it as the new normal, though I doubt we will survive to see that change in this land," I said, earning their silent assent.

After we had ridden for an hour, Raboud broke the silence. I failed to hear him at first, for my thoughts had passed from wondering about Holmes to worrying about Mary. After a while, though, thinking back to the wonder of seeing Irene Adler in action, my thoughts turned, curiously, to Anne Prescott. I imagined that Irene was every inch the woman Anne had dreamt of being, when we dared to think that we could share a life of adventures, and surely would have become. Anne and Irene were both confident, skilled beyond reckoning, perilous, and beautiful beyond the reach of most men. Irene demanded equality from the world and would take it by force of her will. Anne had been much the same, though she'd lacked the opportunities that life had given Irene. Mary, though strong and determined, in her own way, did not have that kind of strength. She needed defending. and I fretted about the distance between us.

"Watson, did you hear me?" Omar Raboud asked. I realized I was gazing at Irene's face as she sat quietly with her own thoughts. I drew my attention away from her.

"I'm sorry, Omar. I was thinking of—marveling at, rather— our companion's skills with her revolvers. Would you please repeat the question?" Irene favored me with a smile.

Raboud nodded and repeated, "I wondered if you had thought much about Dupain's desire to target you," he said, "for as I think back upon it, you and Sherlock Holmes have been his consistent targets. Dupain's pursuit of Holmes makes sense, but if Dupain is in the employ of foreign officials, or if he wishes to do harm to the Logres Society alone, it hardly seems effective to focus on you."

"You and Holmes are the greatest threat to his plans," Irene added. I did not see myself that way, but I gave her a nod of thanks.

"I have had my mind on things other than Dupain's motivations since learning of him as our foe," I replied to Raboud. "It may be, as Miss Adler says, that he learned that Holmes and I would be his main adversaries. However, he targeted you and Irene at the Alhambra, and his willing service to Bismarck may be just an attempt to regain his family fortune, though how or why he would blame the Logres Society for its loss is beyond me."

Raboud's line of thought, however, made me curious about the mental makeup of a young man as twisted as Dupain. He had killed his mother, so I recognized that his madness likely stemmed from some childhood issue, but I knew nothing about him that would explain its onset. Was it some mania about his mother's brief affair with the younger Holmes? I did not think it likely, nor could I imagine why, if it were true, he had turned his vengeful attention upon me.

"Yes, you are right," Raboud said, "though I still struggle to know why he would do all he did. His mind is diseased, certainly. But it is sharp, especially when allied with the powers of evil. And he is cunning. I fear that he plans to use Mary to weaken you."

"What do you mean, Omar?" I asked. I knew that Mary was in danger as long as she was with Dupain, but I'd thought that, like most kidnap victims, she would be used for ransom, though I did not know how.

"Since our last meeting at the Diogenes Club, Dupain has been in dialogue with me about the details of the spell I told you I could use to alter your memory," Raboud confessed with a sigh. "Of course, I thought at the time that his interest was merely academic. Now, having seen and escaped his hold over me, I see his mind more clearly."

Raboud stopped and took off his lenses, leaning closer, to peer at me. I had let myself think about the worst that Dupain could do to Mary; the man was insane and capable of any sort of depravity, I knew. But a dread grew in me that Raboud was about to make my fears worse.

"The worst he can do, he will likely save for you and for Holmes," Raboud whispered, drawing in both myself and Irene, who sat beside him. She would not look at me, and I thought that she might have intuited already what I dreaded to hear.

"I see," I whispered, the words catching in my throat. "He will use that spell to remove me from Mary's mind. It will be as though she has never met me," I said. "Surely, he will wait to do so, until I confront him," I added, closing my eyes as though to keep from seeing that encounter.

"Perhaps, but we do not know the extent of the evil he will dare try," Raboud said in a low voice.

But closing my eyes only prevented me from seeing the approach of Dupain's next attack, if any sign at all preceded that horror. A force like a wind or a wave threw us, all three, together with enough strength to knock the air from my lungs.

Somehow it had found us, that entity of evil from which we had rescued Westcott, that hellish thing that had tortured Raboud. It delighted in working the will of such hate-filled men as Dupain, with both desiring only to torment people.

We were being crushed, and I had none of Dibba's powder, nor could I use my hands, for they were pressed tightly to my sides. It had us and would squeeze the life out of us, constrictor-like, and leave us a shattered amalgam of three bodies on the floor of the train.

I had seconds of awareness left, I knew, before the force broke our bones and ground us into a bloody pulp. Adler's and Raboud's cries melded with mine. Screams from the few people who fled the car reached my ears. Oblivion was seconds away.

A guttural voice using words I could not understand pressed into my head, though not through my ears. Fighting panic, I sought the inner strength my sensei had taught me, but peace that gave me such strength could not come with Irene's screams of pain right in my ear. My awareness shifted to my center, the point of my *ki*, and I could move, could push back at the encircling cloud. But the voice roared in my head in response, angered by my resistance. More like a vibration in my bones than like a voice, it howled over us as Raboud had described, gloating over its victims.

I struggled harder against the smoky coils that crushed us. I managed to push Irene away from my side so that she could breathe. I could move my head freely and saw that the demon cloud pressed against Raboud's mouth like blackened cotton wool, choking him. Everywhere else, I could almost see through the cloud, but it had gone solid over the mage's mouth. His panicked eyes stared back at me and he shifted them toward the mass that covered his mouth. He needed to speak to use his power.

On instinct, I drove my face toward the mass and bit down. My teeth sank into something slimy, foul, and the taste made me want to vomit. But it was solid over Raboud's face, and I bit hard and pulled back by force of will. I heard the shock and rage in the howl that surrounded and passed through me. The stinging sparks lanced through my mouth, sinking into the roots of my teeth, driving me mad with pain. It squeezed harder, but I bit again, deeper, and tore at it, despite the shocks, just because I could do nothing else to harm it. I shook it as a terrier will a rat. My head was the only thing I could move, and I twisted my neck from side to side, up and down, biting at the thing that had silenced Raboud as it had crushed us. The entity's howl turned into a keening scream, and the crushing pressure fell away.

Raboud pulled his head back and cried, "*Ya ashab Allah!*" in a voice as terrible as the entity's voice: it pushed through my flesh and bones.

And the entity screamed one last time and set us free.

We crumpled into the aisle between the seats, rolling free of one another. The strangling tendrils were gone. From somewhere, I heard a scream, then another. Raboud heard it, too, and he turned angry, shocked eyes to me.

"Dupain is on this train," he said urgently. "I felt the power of the protective spell he must have used, knowing the demon might come back on him after he invoked it against us."

Raboud breathed as heavily as I did, but Irene Adler lay on the floor between us, unmoving. Fresh blood seeped through her shirt from the knife wound that Dupain had given her. Her skin had gone grey: she wasn't breathing.

As much as I desired to follow those screams, I would not abandon Irene. As quickly as I could, I took her in my arms, laid her head back, and blew hard into her mouth, hoping to force her lungs to expand. Her pulse was weak, but after my first breath into her, she coughed and dragged in a ragged breath, wincing at the pain in her ribs, which I feared were cracked. She came back to full attention immediately.

"What in hell was that?" Fear showed in her eyes. "And what is that ungodly taste?" For my mouth on hers in that kiss of life had given her a taste of what had sickened me. She spat and pulled a flask from her hip pocket, fumbling with the top. She tipped the flask up and took a long pull, but Raboud raised a hand and said, "Do not swallow, I beg you." Irene nodded and spat the amber liquid onto the floor.

I begged a sip from her and took the fragrant whisky into my mouth, where it burned against the taste that I somehow thought of as metallic bile. But when I spat it out, the sick feeling left me, and I passed the flask to Raboud, who held up his hand. After spitting several times, he said, "I am not allowed. And I have something better." He took one of the white marble cubes from his pocket and placed it within his mouth, rolling it around so that it rattled against his teeth. When he spat it out onto the floor between us, it had gone black, and it disintegrated like a spent coal.

"Come, we must search the train," I said, helping my friends rise to unsteady feet.

As we leaned on one another for another moment, Raboud said, "In answer to your question, Miss Adler, it was indeed something from hell, and you tasted its substance because Dr. Watson dared to attack it to save us. It was a demonic entity, one of the *rabisu*, known as the 'Croucher.' It was likely the one that violated me. It exists in the margins between worlds and serves only the Prince of the Powers of the Air, though it can be invoked, compelled by an evil adept.

"At the very least, this attack reinforces my suspicion that Dupain has made an alliance with the most evil of the enemies of Allah. Only my ability to utter a word of command stopped it. Had it not been for Watson's courage to fight it, to taste its evil, we would be dead now."

Both Raboud and Irene stared at me, and I could only shrug, for I'd had no choice but to taste that horrid evil. "Please, Miss Adler," I asked, "may I have another sip of that—what was it?"

"Kentucky bourbon, one hundred and ten proof," she said, "And I would never have spat it out before today, but I will gladly do so again."

Spitting and wiping our mouths, we set out, and Irene, though she limped from the pain of moving with damaged ribs, took the lead, both revolvers drawn. She whispered over her shoulder to me, "If Dupain is in human form, I will put two rounds through his head, without hesitation."

"Irene," I said, holding her back, "remember that we need

the names of his confederates in the Prussian plot. Shoot him in the knees."

"I like the way you think, John," she said with a wicked grin. She lifted her lips to kiss me but stopped. "No. After more bourbon, maybe."

I dimly remembered people fleeing toward the front of the train when we were attacked. We pushed toward the rear of the train first, for the other cries of alarm came from that direction. As we breached the door of the next car, I saw that it was empty, but a moment later the door at the other end burst open, and a man stood there, raising a rifle to his shoulder. Too slowly, as it turned out. Irene put two shots in him before he had his hand on the trigger. He went down screaming, and Irene dove behind a seat, pistols blazing at the men who had stood behind him. Two more went down, and I rushed the door, pistol drawn.

They were in a mail car, and I smelled the Turkish cigarette in the same instant that I saw the man in the homburg. Dupain was with him. The man in the homburg pushed Dupain toward the yawning side door of the car. Dupain held his hands in front of him; they had been burned, surely by the same demon he'd loosed on us. He turned wild eyes on me.

"*Mon capitaine!*" he cried, in a voice tinged with madness. "I have her, your little madam, and already, she pines for your more manly embraces. Mine must suffer in comparison, though she is as willing as she was with your man Sherlock. But her desire for you will not last long! I take the Low Road!" He was taunting me with the spectre of the spell of forgetfulness I'd been warned about.

I took aim at him, but his well-dressed partner saw my intent and pushed him out the door into the streaming wind and rain. A small figure, dark and bent, materialized at their side and went with them. But they did not drop away. There was a flash of light and then they were gone. I pushed past the men on the floor and flew to that door. The margin onto which they would have dropped was clear. They had escaped.

Before I could stop them, two of the three wounded men threw themselves past me and out of the car. Both fell hard. One rolled away, but the other took an odd bounce off a rise at the side of the tracks and landed under the train. He gave a short cry.

I turned back to the mail car. Irene had the first man she'd wounded under her twin Colts, hammers back and murder in her eyes. He stared at her while I divested him of a German pistol and a stabbing dagger bearing the black cross of the Teutonic Knights. He had no papers in his pockets to identify him and remained mute to our questions. Irene questioned him in German, but all he did was smile and correct her pronunciation.

"Your masters, it seems, are quite willing to abandon you, and I do not think that your Romany co-conspirators will rescue you," said Irene. "You can, perhaps, reduce the severity of the consequences you will face as a spy if you provide us with some information, especially about Edinburgh and the details of Dupain's plans there."

He grinned at me and made a rude gesture, so I added, "Or we can roll you out of that door and let you take your chances. One of your lot was just ground into sausage meat. Perhaps you'd like to join him?"

Dr. Raboud came and knelt in front of the man, who went stiff with dread. My companion said in a voice of icy calm, "That will not be necessary. He will tell us all, and then he will remember nothing, for I can take away his mission, his name, and even the memory of his country. Then we will simply set him free—after pinning a note to him that he might find his way back to the Iron Chancellor."

That opened the floodgates of German, which he spoke with a pronounced Austrian accent. Irene translated. It was not good to hear. Edinburgh was already held against us. An unknown number of foreign assets in league with Bismarck's Prussian allies were already in Edinburgh. Many of these, we were told, were like the men who had wounded Burroughs outside of Penrith: Romany gypsies, not of the Highland Travelers.

This Austrian had also heard that some sort of official police action had been instituted in the form of a warrant for Holmes's arrest, under suspicion of murder, and also for my arrest in the disappearance of Irene Adler. At this, she expressed genuine surprise.

"It must have been taken up by that Gregson fellow," Irene observed, "for both my stage manager and my agent work under the knowledge that I contact them when I have performances scheduled. It is nothing new for me to disappear for days or weeks at a time, often on a mission, though they have no specific knowledge of what I do for the L. S. Neither of them would have reported me missing until another tour started, in two weeks."

"Since Gregson has associated you with Holmes, your reading of the facts seems likely, though if any of this late business with Holmes gets out, you had better divest yourself of connections with him. Otherwise, you might never perform again."

Raboud cut in. "I have now cast an influence on our immediate surroundings," he said. "There are spiritual forces of good that surround us and always stand ready to work for peace, if we only deign to call upon them."

"And at least we will be in Edinburgh before Dupain," Irene said.

"No. He is already there," I replied. They both turned to stare at me. "He took the Low Road, the path that the dead take."

"Dr. Watson," Raboud remarked, with lips quirked in a wry smile, "are you advising us on the occult now?"

"Only in the way a man who has listened many times to 'The Bonny Banks of Loch Lomond' can do," I replied. "In those lyrics, the singer is slated to die, while his friend, to whom he sings, will be ransomed. The song says that the man who dies far from home will get back to the land of his birth along the path of the dead, the Low Road. As he leaped from the train, Dupain boasted to me of taking the Low Road. He is already there."

***

Under Raboud's peaceful "glamor," the frightened passengers forgot the moment that had so terrified them. Still, as passengers got on and off the train at various stops, we heard

247

more and more werewolf reports as we sat among them. These tales became more dire as we approached Edinburgh. At first they were only of sightings, but then they became laced with acts of gratuitous violence: pets, then livestock, mutilated and left for dead or partially consumed. Then, an assault against a woman in the Tweed Valley.

The last report spoke of two "pikies" killed in the Rosslyn Chapel area. Rosslyn is perhaps ten miles south of Edinburgh, so Holmes, in werewolf form, could have killed those gypsies, especially if he'd thought them allied with Dupain.

Raboud had told me that the power of the benandanti charms, though beneficent in design, was likely corrupted by Dupain and the black magic he called upon to use it. Letting Holmes think that he could use the charm safely, to his own good ends, was likely a way to turn Holmes against us. I cursed Holmes's stubbornness and self-confidence. Neither of us knew enough about the magical powers that were in play around us, and I feared as much for Holmes's safety as I did for Mary's.

And Dr. Raboud agreed that Dupain most likely wanted to turn Holmes on us, given his reworking of the amulet's power. True, it was supposed to have happened at Whitefell Manor, as we were told by our captive, Nils Schulte, before I bandaged him up and Raboud took his memory of our encounter away. We put him off the train in the Lowlands as soon as we could, leaving him with complete knowledge of his identity and history, minus our part in his immediate past.

Though wounded, he was better off than we were.

Raboud's lenses were cracked, and though Irene had allowed me the intimacy to wrap her ribs with strips torn from a soft canvas mailbag we liberated, she was in a great deal of pain. Indeed, Raboud said that each of us would suffer more than usual from the slightest impediment, due to our exposure to the substance of that hell-spawn we had turned back upon Dupain.

"Contact with such an entity, however slight, is a poison that must work itself out of our bodies in due course," he warned. "We have all had a touch of it, and our abilities will suffer. It is unavoidable."

We pulled into Edinburgh, disembarked at Waverley Station, and entered Princes Street, weakened and weary, with the knowledge that we had less than twenty-four hours to find Dupain. Provided, of course, that we could avoid the Prussian agents and Romany forces who were deployed there already in addition to the official constabulary.

I knew that we had a place to stay, Lord Whitefell's flat in the Pleasance, and that he and Lord Tennyson had reservations in the Old Waverley, not far from the train station, for the next days, but that way was sure to be watched. It would have been prudent to take a more direct route to the Pleasance, where we could rest. However, I had a more immediate destination, one I had intuited from Dupain's last words to me. His mention of the Low Road, upon which the souls of the dead return to their ancestral homes, had been meant for me. Clearly, he was enticing me—a dead man, in his eyes—back to the place of my origin. We would find him, I thought, at 11 Picardy Place, my childhood home. I planned an immediate assault.

I revealed my plan to my associates; Irene sighed at the thought, and Raboud nodded in his quiet, delicate manner. He knew that we needed his abilities to extend a magical influence over an area. Irene or I would have to lead him, for he could see little in the dark without his lenses. Irene made sure that her Colts were loaded and ready.

Our only other advantage was that we had not far to go to get there, even going in stealth, and I thought our plan unexpected and audacious. Dupain might not expect such guile from me, thinking me the honorable soldier. Yet I saw myself then as an assassin, with but one target. The plan might well secure us an early victory, if we could force our battered bodies into action, though I wondered what effect it would have on my soul.

CHAPTER TWENTY

"The Feast of St. Symeon the Stylite,"
4 January, 1889.

The cold, wet night was, perhaps, our best ally as we left the Waverley Station area. The alleys and side streets of Princes Street had changed little since I'd run them as a child. Shops had come and gone, though I saw a few I recognized: the haberdashery where my father had been wont to buy his meager wardrobe, the artist's supply shop where he'd purchased brushes and paints, even a few pubs he'd frequented when his painting failed to relieve the pressures of home life and the dullness of a surveyor's job.

These were some of the streets I'd wanted most to escape when I was a lad, for they were immediately connected to my father and his "madam," his term—and therefore mine—for my more exacting mother. These were the streets of their failed romance, a crumbling brick and stone memorial to a marriage between two dreamers whose visions of life eventually clashed, each bringing the other low. My brother hid from this life in a bottle, while I sought to escape it with a career in medicine. In a sense, I was still trapped here, and I wanted out.

My plan was to infiltrate the home where I had been born. There, I suspected, clever young Dupain had done his work and found out the one building in Edinburgh that was my least favorite place. He had let slip the word "madam," in reference to Mary, yes, but equally in reference to my mother. And so, I figured, Dupain had baited me. I would take the bait, if only to purchase Mary's freedom—with my life, if necessary.

I realized that in baiting me, Dupain was testing me, testing

250

himself against me, against all I represented. He had seen me as his enemy after I had managed to capture the afreet and had killed the first loup-garou. He had learned to fear and hate me at the same time that he recognized my distaste for things of the occult, for the creatures of faerie whom he compelled as his servants. If possible, he saw me as a greater threat than Omar Raboud, whom he had abused so horribly.

I had to believe that Dupain considered Holmes compromised, since the benandanti charm could be manipulated by infernal power. Making me face Holmes's loss amounted to another insulting challenge to me. Every moment Holmes spent transformed into that awful beast took my friend farther down a dark path that could consume him. Dupain had succeeded in separating me from my strongest ally, and then he had taken my Mary, my one hope of saving something like the ordinary life I had hoped to have. What he didn't realize was that my guile and audacity had grown with each challenge.

However, Dupain had to see now that his plot was exposed, that we had put the pieces of Bismarck's plan in order and knew its intent, knew Dupain's part in it. All the active forces sent by our enemies were drawn here. We exposed him, but Dupain knew we could only fight him on his own field, that we could not hope to mobilize any military or police aid. It was too fantastic a tale to tell to the day-to-day world, and we had no time. His actions amounted to a slap in my face, in the face of England herself, my England, that I would defend to my last breath.

Neither Bismarck nor his confederates mattered as much to me as facing Dupain and ending his threat. Despite seeing the depth of Dupain's insanity, my one thought was to strike him down, in whatever form he appeared before me. To do so would be like destroying a rabid animal, and I would dare anything to make it happen, even killing his human agents.

Our trip from Waverley Station did not take long. Approaching Picardy Place from the north, along Broughton Street, I saw the first of Dupain's watchmen at the next corner. I pulled my companions into a darkened doorway.

"John, how certain are you of this?" Irene asked over my shoulder. "I am exhausted, and Dr. Raboud looks as if he's ready to drop."

"I am more certain now than I was ten seconds ago," I whispered, pointing down the misty block ahead of us on Broughton. There, a man in a slouch hat and heavy coat leaned against the brick of a closed shop, smoking a cigarette in a cupped hand. His eyes scanned the length of Broughton that would take one back to Waverley. We were suspected. At the very least, someone had thought Dupain's plan of using 11 Picardy Place was risky.

"That's just a man smoking a cigarette," Irene claimed, eyes blinking.

"At half past three in the morning, in a freezing drizzle?" I responded.

"It is a bad habit," she murmured. "However, perhaps you're right. But what do we do? I can see no way to approach him without his sounding some alarm. Should I shoot him?"

"That would do as much to get us killed as anything else. I propose that one of you draw his attention by approaching slowly from this direction," I said, "while I try to get past him by going around the other block."

"Please," Raboud whispered. "I will take care of this."

Before we could reply, Dr. Raboud took unsteady steps out onto the cobbled road and started walking toward the smoker. That man started, stood upright, and drew something from his pocket. I heard the cracking sound of a *navaja* opening and saw the glint of its keen blade in the dark, though Raboud had yet to acknowledge the man's presence. With his gait unsteady, in his wet, sagging coat, Raboud might have just been a drunken fool wandering the streets, searching for home.

When he was perhaps ten yards from the man, whose knife twitched in his hand, Omar Raboud lifted his head, fixed his eyes on the fellow, raised his left hand, and mumbled one word, which I could not hear. At once, the fellow sank back, reaching for the wall behind him. Head dropping, he leaned back against the building.

This turned out to be an act of mercy on Raboud's part. Just after working whatever magic he'd just done, Raboud started and stumbled back toward us at a dead run. From the darkness on the other side of the street, a darker shape came at such speed that it blurred. The beast let out a low growl and slashed at the guard's throat. Blood spatter flew out into the misty air and mixed with it. The man on guard died without knowing what had hit him, and the werewolf—the magnificent, deadly loup-garou—rushed past, down Picardy Place.

"Holmes. My God, that was Holmes, I know it," I said to Irene.

Raboud ran to us and practically fell into my arms. His thin hands shook as they gripped the stout tweed of my jacket. "I—I should have sensed him, but he came too quickly, and—and I am so..."

"Did you mention your childhood home to Holmes, John?" Irene whispered.

All three of us were huddled together in fear now, for seeing a werewolf attack, even one so brief, weakens one's knees. "No. That idea only came to me on the train," I replied. "Perhaps Holmes is simply following his nose. It never occurred to me that he would arrive at the same thought."

"I don't imagine he is thinking, Watson," Raboud whispered. "He has a quarry, and he means to track and kill it. That, I think, is proof enough that Dupain has, indeed, manipulated the power of that benandanti charm. The charms are not meant for extended use, even—"

"No. I will not believe it," I said and broke away from them.

At the side of the slain man, whose glassy eyes stared up at the misty sky, I looked at the wound in horror. The man's head remained just barely attached to the ruin of his neck. Dark blood pooled beneath him. There was no hiding his murder, for that is what it was. Unless it rained hard for the rest of the night, blood would remain, and we could do nothing but move on.

"John," Irene said, grasping my shoulder, "we should abandon this plan and get somewhere warm and dry."

"No. I cannot, for if Dupain is here, Mary is here, too," I

said and rose to move down Picardy Place. Irene and Raboud came along behind me, holding to each other, whispering, likely trying to think of a way to change my course. I turned and said to them, "Go. You know the address of Whitefell's flat. Go by way of Calton Hill. Make your way up from Queen's Drive at the base of the Salisbury Crags. You will be out of the main ways. I must go on. Mary and Holmes"—I gulped at the terror that gripped me—"need me."

"As he is now, Holmes will kill you," Raboud said, grasping my sleeve.

"One must take such risks in war, Omar. Send word in the morning to Whitefell and Tennyson. If I can, I will join you," I said, and ran away from them.

While I always craved action, the reality of being at war where Mary's and Holmes's lives stood in the balance sickened me as much as the contact with the demonic "flesh" of the Croucher had done. Yet, because foreign forces were behind Dupain's plan, we were at war, though I hoped our skirmishes would end the threat before any formal declaration were made by those in power.

The Travelers' warning about my life falling into ruin had become my reality, and it looked like coming to a head within 11 Picardy Place. I saw two more slain watchmen at the entry door to that stone tenement that had been my home. They lay in a pile within the doorway that led to the stairs and the second floor, where my parents had raised me, where I'd learned the frustrating reality that I wanted more than the sort of mundane sickness that marked their lives together.

My father, now in a sanitarium, and my mother, dwelling in a cottage on a wealthy friend's estate, were at least far away from the current danger, but thinking of them made me recall how I would escape their quarrels and icy silences by taking the back steps that ran down into the cellar. So I passed the front door of my old home and sought my own entrance.

The building had begun to need many repairs while I was a child. Now, some of the first-floor windows in the back had been boarded up, and the alley was choked with ruined dustbins and discarded furniture. One broken-down chair reminded me of the seat I'd used when our "madam" read us stories of King Arthur and his daring knights. I passed it by, knowing now that deeds of daring, deeds of war, mostly end in death, squalor, and blood. Few and rare are the stories of one man, even a brave and true man, winning against evil.

The wooden cellar door gave in to my pressure to lift its latch, rotten wood sighing as I pulled against the clasp of the lock, and soon I stood in the dark of the same cellar where I had played as a boy. There, I had imagined myself on the field of some martial victory, or on the deck of a ship of war. In my play, I was ever brave and victorious.

Now, my hands shook with fear, for a nightmarish shape rose against me at once from the dark. I stumbled back from it. Dupain had guards everywhere, and not all were human. Whether it was male or female, I could not tell, but its misshapen limbs exuded strength to rend and tear. It stooped under the low ceiling, dripping noxious water as it lurched toward me. Its long, grasping hands reached toward me, and a pale face with staring eyes and ragged teeth came behind them.

I had no time to think, but my sword swept out and took one of the hands off the arm at the elbow. The grasping thing let out a thin, shrill scream and disappeared before my eyes, leaving its twitching limb on the floor. As I looked at it, the hand and bony forearm dissolved into a glistening dampness on the floor.

"Faeries," I muttered. "Father would be so displeased." Faeries, light and airy, had been his delight to paint, and now I hated them worse than before.

As I found the stairs and made my way up them, I recalled stories of such a creature, Meg o' the Marshes, whose sole purpose was to drag innocent victims into a watery grave and gnaw on their rotting flesh. To think that I had just cut the arm off such a creature was almost too much. Fitting, I suppose, that "Meg" had been in the damp cellar, which stank worse than it ever had. I would be glad to leave it, even if that meant confronting Dupain.

The back steps creaked under my feet, and I feared that the

faerie's scream had given further alarm, for light shone down from the second floor and rushing footsteps came toward me. Whitefell's dirk in hand, I stood with my back to the inner wall, ready to surprise anyone who came down the stairs. Someone did, breathless and stumbling. In an instant, I recognized Mary's small cries of fear. Hiding the dirk behind my back, I turned the corner, and Mary, holding a flaring candle, ran into me.

"Mary, Mary!" I cried. "I have you!"

She pushed back from me, and though she looked directly into my face, she screamed in terror. I let her go, and she stumbled back up the steps, crying, "Jean, Jean, oh, someone is there!"

Following her came Jean-Louis Dupain, his hair as wild as though he'd just come from sleep, his eyes wide and wilder. He looked at me in the light of the candle and grinned.

"Ah, have no fear, *ma chérie*, it is only an old soldier," he claimed, letting her bury her face into his shoulder. She was clad only in her shift, and her slender form was all atremble. "You do not recognize him?"

His words knifed through me. He had worked his forgetting charm. This was ruin.

"No," she sobbed. "I only want to get away from this wretched place. Please, Jean-Louis, I know you say you love me, but I am so confused, and I—I just want it all to stop!"

"But surely you recognize him, no?" Dupain whispered in her ear. "He is that awful doctor who has been treating you and making you forget. But he will do no harm, if you face him and tell him to go away."

She did turn to face me, and a pain ran through me at her very glance. My throat was choked with a sob I could not get out, yet she turned her eyes on me as she would a perfect stranger.

Above us, in the home that was once mine, shouts and screams rose. Thumps of bodies hitting the walls and floor shook the stairwell in which we stood. A thought ran through my head that the whole place would come down and crush us. It did not, for the moment, though the noise and pounding went on, with the roaring of a werewolf rising above it.

"M-Mary, please come with me," I stammered, holding out my left hand to her. The ring she had given me caught the light, and she looked at it, too, without recognition. Only horror showed in her eyes.

She begged, "Won't you please let us pass, my husband and—"

"Your husband?" I whispered, horrified that he had held her, been one with her. All the time, Dupain smiled at me with such sick glee that a taste of hatred and sorrow, worse than the flesh of the Croucher, filled my mouth. I could only swallow it.

"Mary, please just look at me, know me," I said, as though I pleaded for my own stained soul at the Judgement Seat. Her brow darkened, and she glanced back at Dupain, who nodded to her. She put out one tentative hand and touched my face, where the tears covered it. Her eyes looked deep into mine.

"Y-you do not look so evil," she whispered, "but Jean-Louis said—"

Behind her, Dupain gave me his widest maniacal smile, held up his charmed amulet, and mouthed words. His face transformed so suddenly that I was forced back a step.

"Mary, Mary, do you not know me?" I repeated, glancing at the monstrous form filling the stairway behind her. She started to turn back to Dupain, and as I put out a hand to keep her from doing so, she looked again into my eyes, as though she were trying hard to remember me, even in the extremity of her fright. Dupain raised both clawed hands above her, red tongue lolling in an evil lupine grin. I saw his intent, having already taken her away from me, to kill her in front of me. Now that he had hurt me, Dupain could be done with her and then kill me.

With a convulsive move, I pulled at her arms in order to get between her and the monster. As I did so, she turned and caught sight of him. Her piercing shriek told me that Mary had seen too much and teetered on the point of going mad. She went on screaming as Dupain swiped almost casually at me and I ducked under a blow that would have ripped away my face. Dupain howled, seemingly with delight, as if he fed off my fear and Mary's screams.

But, in his gloating, he had forgotten Holmes.

A dark hand clutched Dupain's neck, and he was plucked up the stairs into the darkness in less than a heartbeat. Just as quickly, he was sent crashing back down into the wall opposite the steps. Holmes, in magnificent loup-garou form, leapt down upon him, tearing and biting, but Dupain gave back as much damage as he took.

Their combined fury was too much for the shambling wreck of the building, especially the old cellar stairs. At the first jolt under my feet, I wrapped my arms around Mary, and then we fell. Wood and plaster rained down on us with bits of brick and mortar from the outside wall of the old place. Mary landed atop me, and for a moment I thought that might spare her injury, but her cries of dismay turned to groans of pain as she was hit with debris. Snarling and howling at deafening levels still came from above us, and I sought to rise and lift Mary out of the wooden wreck we lay on.

Other hands in the dark cellar reached through the dust of the collapse and dragged her away from me. Her screaming stopped, and I didn't know if she'd been gagged or if she'd seen someone she knew and gone willingly. I fought to extricate myself from the ruin of steps, risers, and plaster dust. By the time I got clear of the rubble, she was gone. Though I'd nearly had her, she had been taken from me again.

Aching with sorrow, still, yet fueled by an overmastering anger, I ran to the front of the building and up the front steps. The door to the flat stood open and all was dark inside. Furniture of the cheapest kind lay scattered and broken around me. I checked each room and saw signs of many people: food scraps and bottles of cheap drink littered every surface in the kitchen. Clothing of various kinds, whether men's or women's I couldn't tell, lay strewn around. I saw the dress in which Mary had traveled hanging over a chair back near a disheveled bed, as though she had placed it there with care. I left the room, thinking about how Dupain had gloated over me, knowing how much he had taken from me. It was as though he knew that I would find the room this way.

I had to look in the small room across the hall, the one that my brother and I had occupied. If my ruin was upon me and I had to face the place that I least wanted to see, I might just as well face it all. There I found the bodies. I never knew how many there were, but I assumed in that moment that they had been the other residents in the building, that Dupain or his men had murdered them so that they could use my old home as their base of operations. Some stabbed, some obviously beaten to death, others mauled into shapeless ruins, these bodies were some of the earliest casualties in the war in which I had been caught up, Holmes's murdered guards having been the first.

There was no other trace of Dupain or Holmes in the flat, so I stumbled out into the darkness. The streets were still quiet. The rain had turned to icy pellets, and a wind whipped them, stinging, into my face. If I'd had a hundred pounds of explosives, I would have planted them in the lower level and blown the whole structure to heaven. Along with my fatigue, the poisons of demonic flesh and of war itself—much the same thing—weighed down on me, and I turned my steps away from that place. My feet dragged as much as my heart labored. I was alive, alone, and had one thing that drove me on: revenge.

CHAPTER TWENTY-ONE

"An Officious Defeat."

It took me forever, it seemed, to make my way to the Pleasance, and I did so by the roads that ran along the base of the Salisbury Crags, that massive upthrust of granite that shielded Edinburgh's view of Arthur's Seat. Though it was Saturday, a market day in Auld Reekie, there was little traffic. Somehow, I needed to get some food in me and find some rest before I made the climb to Arthur's Seat to keep Dupain from laying magical claim to my homeland. But my one intent had little to do with the England I loved. No. I merely wanted to kill him in whatever form he took. A foreign power might impel him, give him support, but he would need to kill me to succeed, magical aid or not, and I was not dead yet.

Though dawn was hours off, my knock on the door to Whitefell's flat was answered by Lora Garrett. She smiled under the mass of her dark curls.

"Oh, I'm terribly sorry to disturb you at this hour," I mumbled.

"Dr. Watson?" a man's voice called out from behind her as Lora reached to draw me in. The man moved to her side and pulled me into the warmth of the entry hall.

"Garrett," I murmured. "I need your help."

"Carl, get the poor man inside quickly," Lora said and moved out of the way to let me stumble in at his side. And it was as though I'd opened a door and stepped into my eternal reward. The poison that was working through me, the blackness of my revenge-heavy heart, had had me walking through a hell on earth since the time I'd arrived in Edinburgh with Omar and Irene. But even the memory of Dupain's leering face dissipated somewhat at the aromas coming from within Whitefell's flat. Fresh-baked bread, some hearty stew simmering on a stove, and the promise of a singing kettle opened a place for rest, and I passed out. I only dimly recall protesting as my boots, hose, jacket, and sweater were removed.

***

When I woke, I lay on a settle in a room whose windows looked east. The first rays of light appeared in the cold, misty air that held Arthur's Seat in its grip. I looked up into the eyes of Lora Garrett. They were brown eyes, as warm as a country kitchen, and they had the power to look deep within a man. I stared back at them, unsure what I might be revealing to a person with such eyes.

But she smiled and said, in smooth tones, "Carl, dear. He wakes," though she never broke the glance between us.

Garrett came and knelt at my side. His weathered face broke into countless lines with his smile and he asked, "Can you sit up, my lord? You need to get some of Lora's victuals into you, I'd warrant."

"Thank you, sir, but you must call me John, or Watson. I am no one's lord," I said. Then I gave my hand to Lora and said, "Dr. John H. Watson, at your service, ma'am. I assume that I must thank you for the doctoring you have been doing on my poor carcass." I could feel bandages on my back, arms, and legs.

"You were full of splinters, sir," she said, "and unless I miss my guess, something worse works on you still. I think you must be some kind of lord, as reckless as you are with your person."

"As for what works on me," I said, "it will pass soon enough, so I'm told, if I take nourishment. Is that stew and fresh bread I smell?"

Whatever Lora Garrett had seen in my eyes didn't stop her from feeding me and treating me often to her smile. In fact, I found it easy to forget my troubles for a time in her presence and in the steady flow of news I got from her husband. Irene Adler and Dr. Raboud had never reached this flat, he said, but had been met by other parties—Garrett did not know whom—and taken to the Old Waverley, where they were given care. The plan had been for me, if I arrived at all, to remain here and rest until our party made its final attempt to stop Dupain tonight.

"Any word about Sherlock Holmes or any news from our friends in London?" I asked. I spooned a healthy amount of stew down my gullet before I began to appreciate its heavenly flavor. Lora smiled at my appetite and brought a tea tray, while I listened to Carl's report. "This stew, by the way, might well revive a dying man, if he could but taste it."

"Yes, my Lora can do things with venison that even the deer approve of," Carl said, helping himself to a cup of tea. "We have not heard any news of either Mr. Holmes. We do not know all the details of this business, but we will provide food and help for anyone who fights at our lord's side."

"I urge both of you to stay locked in this flat when I have gone," I said, studying both earnest faces turned toward me. "In fact, were I able, I might well order you back to Whitefell Manor, for your own safety. Though I think I see in each of you that you would not go. At the very least, you may well have charge of a number of people in as bad a shape as I was when I passed out at the door—"

The sound of many heavy steps in the hallway outside broke my train of thought, and a pounding came on the very same door I had mentioned. Garrett rose to his feet with a scowl on his face and went to the door. I gulped the last of my tea and caught Lora's worried glance at me.

"*Quid leone fortius*: 'What is braver than a lion?'" she said, and I recalled that the phrase was engraved on my belt buckle; it was the motto of the Clayton family, Lord Whitefell's clan, whose tartan I wore. "Pull your clothes on, my lord. I've a knowing about this."

I pulled on my hose and boots and rose to my feet. Garrett backed down the hallway of the flat, hands raised, as was his voice in protest: "This is Scotland, lads, as you know, and a man's freedom in his own home is paramount. Furthermore, I am the representative of Lord John Whitefell, whose home this is, and I did not bid you enter."

Two bayonets were pointed at his face. The rifles behind them were held by two soldiers in uniform, whose hard faces showed no sign of caring about this invasion of privacy. I let my sword lie to the side of the settee and donned my sweater and jacket again. I noted the quick stitching in the back and arms where my hostess had repaired them after she repaired me. She gave me a smile and stood with her hand on my arm as if to protect me or hold me back.

Behind the soldiers came Tobias Gregson, a smile on his face that would have melted butter.

"Have no fear of this jack-in-office, my lord," Lora said, loud enough for Gregson to hear. "There'll be those who know your need."

"And his need will be to come along with me to the garrison, madam," Gregson crooned. "For I bear a warrant for his arrest."

"You are a good way beyond your bailiwick, Inspector," I said, forcing a lightness in my tone. "And your troops here are operating outside civil and military jurisdiction, I think, in this home invasion."

"Oh, I have special circumstances that give me permission to take you into custody, Dr. Watson. Or is it Captain Jack these days?" He handed me a piece of paper he had carried rolled in his hand. It bore the letterhead of the Home Office.

By order of the Home Office, Inspector Tobias Gregson is charged with the apprehension of Dr. John Hamish Watson, suspect in the abduction of Miss Irene Adler with nefarious intent; and for the apprehension of Mr. Sherlock Holmes, on the charge of the heinous murder of Sir Alisdair Scrymgeour. All constabularies, Her Majesty's garrisons, and city or county magistrates are hereby compelled to render him assistance in the matter.

"Note the signature, please," Gregson pointed out, tapping the crabbed penmanship of the Home Office Secretary, Henry Matthews, QC. "That'll hold up anywhere in the realm, I believe. Now, Miss Adler... ?"

"She is not here," I said. If the Home Office had been co-opted in the scheme that Bismarck's forces sought to work in this country, our resistance to Dupain had to succeed, for there were internal threats that remained to be dealt with. And Gregson's use of "Captain Jack" made me suspect that he had questioned other members of Department Zed. If he had, that might mean that our attempts in London to procure the other magical amulet from Scotland Yard had met with failure.

What I said, with as much calmness as I could force into my voice, was, "Feel free to search the premises for Miss Adler. You will not find her here."

"Have you hidden her, then?" Gregson asked.

"The very idea!" Lora Garrett cried, playing the indignant housewife, linking her arm through Carl's. "You have no right to search this home and accuse our guest of involvement with such a crime."

"Why, then, I'll simply take my man here and be on my way," he said with a nod. Gregson was not a bad chap at heart, I think, but it would have been a feather in his cap to bring me and Holmes into custody under such charges, even if we could prove our innocence. It would also be his "thumb in the eye" to Lestrade and the other inspectors who often turned to Holmes for help on hard cases.

"If you are patient, Inspector, I can produce a reasonably healthy and happy Irene Adler, who is here in Edinburgh by her own choice," I said, as they manacled my hands and began to lead me out.

"Well, after you've had a day or two in the garrison prison in yon castle, perhaps you'll get your chance," he said, pulling me out to the stairs.

A day or two, he'd said. That would be too late. I knew that I had to take any chance I could to get away from this incarceration. Yet I could see none. The Garretts, I realized, would send word to Raboud, Whitefell, and Tennyson as quickly as one or both could reach the hotel, and it might be that Irene Adler herself would turn up at the garrison insisting upon my release. But the wheels of legal bureaucracy turn slowly, and even though she might prove my innocence, there would have to be a hearing, and that would take much more time than I had, than we had. My release would certainly not happen today, on a Saturday, with magistrates spending the last of the Christmas season in their homes.

I entered the dark interior of the prison wagon with thoughts black and dangerous.

Above me, from the flat, I heard Lora Garrett's voice ring out, "A Clayton! A Cameron in irons, lads!" She sang it out again and again as we drove away, until I could no longer hear her clear voice. Gregson, who sat opposite me, and the soldier at my side took no notice.

It would take no more than twenty minutes to reach the castle garrison. Once within, an army could not extricate me. Perhaps after nightfall, Holmes in werewolf form would have the strength and speed to climb the south-facing battlements and rip aside the iron bars that would hold me. But Holmes, at present, knew nothing of my plight, and if my fears were accurate, he could know nothing of me at all, if the werewolf madness held him still.

No. I was forced to think of overcoming Gregson and my guard and making my escape. My hands were manacled in front of me, and to judge by his relaxed posture, Gregson did not see me as a physical threat. He smiled at me and carried on a running commentary on my attire. The soldier—a Scot, judging by his disdainful countenance as he listened to the Londoner— was tough and quite strong-looking. His weapon leaned against the inside front corner of the wagon, and his thick hands were clasped in front of him.

A carefully placed elbow strike might put him out of commission, if I hit him cleanly. I imagined he was used to combat, though, and a clean hit was doubtful. Gregson, I would joyously render unconscious with the top of my hard head.

We were going downhill, and I figured that we were still in

the Pleasance and would make for the High Street and directly to the castle. I had to take my chance if I were going to, but my heart turned on me as I thought of harming the soldier next to me, detailed to follow orders that he likely didn't even understand. Yet my chance was better if I struck early, farther away from the castle. I took a deep breath to relax.

"What is braver than a lion?" a man's voice roared out in the street, and the Maria was struck so hard on Gregson's side that he pitched toward me. I only just managed to turn my head aside and let his skull collide with the side of our conveyance. Horses neighed outside as if they were being driven mad. A voice roared "*Efendi! Efendi!*" and the wagon slid to a halt on its side. Dibba Al-Hassan, like a charging bull, had hit the other side of it. I threw myself at the soldier and held his hands tightly to keep him from reaching his weapon. The rear door ripped open and several rifles were pointed within.

"Just be still, lad," I hissed in his ear. "I may well be at war, but I'll swear to the Most High God that it is not with you."

***

The rain had stopped by the time we reached a fishery out beyond Leith Walk, the waters of the Firth lapping at the pilings that held it above the waves. There, I came face to face with Abel and Jamie Cameron again, and I breathed a sigh of relief.

"Well, you're a reckless one and no mistake, Doctor," Jamie claimed with a roguish smile. "Tell me, sir, did you intend to make my prophetic warning come true?"

"Easy, Jamie," his father said. "Few men are able to make the sort of choices he did, given what he knew."

"You're right, Da," Jamie replied, though his glance never shifted from my eyes. "But does any man of us have what it takes to go where he needs to go? You have, I know, and my time's comin', sure. But him? It isn't fair."

"Much in life isn't fair, lad, and yon stout man knows it well," the elder Cameron replied, turning his attention to me. "Do you not?"

"True. I rarely think of life as fair, and of late I have had even less reason to do so. But what is it that I must do, in your eyes, that makes you question what I can do? Whatever I must do, I must do it quickly. The sun will be down in two hours, just before four o'clock. I must meet with the others to assemble a plan for thwarting Dupain. With official forces opposing us, looking for me, Holmes, and Miss Adler, it will be doubly hard to find the others and work out what to do. Time is in short supply. I lack the arms I need. What else must I do first?"

I suppose my frustration showed in my tone, for the elder Cameron, the Traveler King, put his hand on my shoulder as though to soothe me.

"You needn't worry about your sword. That you will have before the need arises, which will be when you take your trip beneath," Abel Cameron said. "There, you must find and bring back with you what you need—indeed, what we all need—to combat this threat. I know that the time is short. Rest assured that your Sovereign and his Court Champion will arrive at Arthur's Seat in time to claim Logres. My men and I will help see to that."

"What of Holmes?" I asked, wondering if the Travelers possessed any means of helping a man who had gone too far under the werewolf curse. "Can you help him? Can I?"

Abel Cameron sighed, shook his head, and looked away. "We... we have tried, and it has been to no avail. We tried early to dissuade him from using the amulet, for we rarely do use such things that have come into our care, and only then to combat a worse evil. For the pull of the wild is strong in all of us, especially those of strong will and determined minds. We have rarely met one with such strength of mind as Sherlock Holmes. We could not dissuade him, not while the need is so great. We would not see England fall to a foreign power, though we will go on, regardless, as we have. Mr. Sherlock Holmes, though, would not be the first man we have lost to the power of the benandanti amulets. It may well be that you—and your sword—have the only cure for him.

"In any case," he went on, "you must take rest now before you go to the bottom of Dùn Èideann. You will need your strength."

267

I knew that Dùn Èideann was the ancient name of Edinburgh, and I assumed that he meant I would need to enter the tunnels beneath the city. The idea stirred memories of old fears I'd learned of those places when I was a boy.

Edinburgh's dark history had many more people residing within the Flodden Walls than could be managed above ground. At first, tenements were built for the poor, but they collapsed or burned down. When bridges were built to traverse the gorge through which the Cowgate ran, far below the level of the castle and its mile-long High Street, the poor and desperate moved below the streets into the chambers and alcoves that were left of the oldest buildings.

As the more raucous members of the wealthy classes looked to London's East End for the fulfillment of dark desires, Edinburgh's revelers went lower, and the stories of dark deeds, murders, illicit trafficking, and riotous living in those dark places multiplied. A good thirty years ago, the tunnels below the High Street and South Bridge were closed by filling them with rubble. Stories of ghosts then rose to prominence, though, for the evil that had been done to the poor by the rich could not be forgotten or put away from people's thoughts.

What I was supposed to bring back that would help us, neither of the Camerons would say. Jamie, who stared longest at me, saw something with his "Sight," I supposed, that caused him doubt, for he only shook his head and walked away from me, murmuring, "I cannot see it clear. We'll have to wait and see what she says."

***

The last, sullen light of the sun still touched the top of the great castle on its mound of granite. Below, in darkness, we approached it from behind the train sheds of Waverley Station. Clouds rolled above the ominous fortress, as though some magic boiled and bubbled within its walled courts. My Traveler band had shrunken to three men: two ready-looking young fellows and Jamie Cameron himself were to set me on my way, once we entered the tunnels.

We ascended the castle mound, where, in some parts, stone stairs ran, though these were tumbled and broken. In some spots, we scrambled through on all fours. As we approached the dark walls near the castle gate, I looked up and saw two figures standing at the top of the stairs. One, I saw from his dress and lean silhouette, was Carl Garrett. The other, wrapped in a billowing cloak, was Lora Garrett, carrying with her a long bundle. As we neared them, she revealed that she bore Mustard Seed in her hands. Her wide eyes were solemn as she handed it to me.

"I am even more in your debt, sir, madam," I said to them, "for otherwise, on this errand, I would go unarmed."

When I placed my hand on the scabbard, Lora did not let it go.

"Only in its appearance and construction is this a sword, my lord," she murmured. In a flash of intuition, I knew that Lora was the "she" to whom Jamie had referred. She was a Traveler, and evidently a powerful one, judging from the deference paid her by my companions.

"I have sat with this since you left us this morning, letting it tell me its story," she went on. "Someday—not now—I must tell you all I know of it. That story is a sad and long one. This blade was made to be sharper than any made before it. Through the accidents of its use, though, it became something else. I bid you take it and think on this: though it defends you in need, it can only belong to one who knows that it is not a sword—"

"But an extension of my heart?" I suggested, having heard the same from my sensei. My interruption caused Lora to give me her smile again, and she dropped her glance away for a second. She went on in a quieter voice.

"No, my lord. It is a border—a boundary, if you will— between two forces at constant war in the human heart: fear and its opposite, love. Take it with this in mind," she said, her smile giving way to a trembling of her lower lip and the dropping of a tear on her fair cheek. "Take the Low Road to the open way, where the walls become thin."

She turned and took her husband's arm. They hurried down

the path we had just climbed; I stared after them. They were soon lost in the dark, and hurrying hands pulled me up toward the castle walls.

Before we reached the cobbled area in front of the castle gates, we turned aside to a small, black door in the brick wall to our right. It was blocked by a rubble of building material, and I'd have sworn it had not been used in decades. Yet, with Cameron's insertion of a key into its lock, it opened with quiet ease. The two Traveler lads entered first, pausing to light torches.

"What way is this? I thought we meant to enter the tunnels below South Bridge," I whispered. "Surely if we find access to the tunnels here, so close to the castle, we will take too long finding our way to the bottom, wherever that may be. After all, the legend of the piper boy..."

On that thought, I was unable to finish, remembering the old story: Once, long ago, a skinny little lad with borrowed kilt and pipes was sent down into the tunnels in front of the castle. Once inside, he was to play upon his pipes so that the men above him, intent on mapping the tunnels, could follow his sound as he worked his way down. They heard him well, until he reached the level of the Tron Kirk and then grew silent. They searched and searched, but the lad was never seen again, and those tunnels took on an even darker reputation. Reports of his ghostly piping below street level were repeated by residents of Old Town Edinburgh and were laughed at, when the sun was above on a cloudless day.

But even after many of the chambers within those tunnels were filled in with rubble, the locals knew that to seek underground Edinburgh was to court an evil death in some form. Only the most desperate, like myself, did so. Now, on this night of skies boiling with the threat of dark magic, I was to follow the lost piper.

"In the descent," Jamie said, "the tradition has it that you must start at the highest level." He then plunged through the door. It was no reason, only ritual, like most magical practices. It made a tight fit for him and a tighter one for me, but I managed it and found that the two lads were already far enough ahead of me in the cellar to have left me in the dark.

Soon, though, we left the cellar, having removed some blocks of masonry so that we might drop down into the tunnel proper, which was damp, low enough to make me stoop. I made ready to bid them goodbye, but Jamie took one of the torches and moved into the lead. "We do not leave you yet. We must see you on your way and do our best to prevent anyone from stopping you. For, unless you are well known to most of the night dwellers down here, you are prey to their cruel whims."

Having them with me, even for a short time, was a boon I had not counted on, and it was called for, as well. Our path had us climbing up and down many times in the short time we'd walked. I marched along in the midst of them and was totally unprepared for the first attack.

It happened when we took the longest descent thus far. I thought that it must be deep enough to put us below South Bridge, but I could not tell. Jamie was knocked aside rolling on the ground with two men, while I stood stunned in the torchlight of the two fellows behind me.

I grabbed one of Jamie's attackers by the back of his coat and pulled him away hard enough to knock his head on the stone of the wall. Jamie got the better of his man, rose, and fetched the man a kick in the crotch that sent him reeling away. That caused shouts from further along the passage, and I heard the sound of running or shuffling feet. We marched on and came into an area of feeble candlelight, where the smells of hard drink and opium smoke dominated. There, in alcoves along the tunnel walls, we saw a myriad of faces peer out at us: male, female, young, old.

My leader announced in a strong voice, "We are the Travelers. I am Jamie Cameron, and any person who is here by force or coercion may come with me now and enjoy the protection of my people."

I heard shouts of protest from grown men. Some few young women and small boys scurried out of alcoves, though hands sought to hold them back, and it seemed to me that many of those grasping hands were clean and well-manicured. A few short fights ensued to release others from captivity. Several well-dressed—if half-clad—gentlemen claimed that they were being

271

robbed by our band, but the Travelers used their hard fists to dissuade those voices, and the protests fell silent when I cuffed one man, who had the look of a city magistrate—well fed to the point of oiliness—to the rough floor.

The Travelers gathered up all who wished to leave and prepared to head back the way we had come.

"From here on, you're on your own, Cap'n Jack," Jamie said to me with a smile. "The way, says my da, is on and down. Be on your guard, for there may be more of this lot around. Beyond that, there'll be other things. You will be challenged, but that is the way of the journey down to the bottom."

He was right. I suffered many such assaults on my journey. I dealt with them as they demanded, thankful that the mere sight of a torch and an unsheathed sword sent terror into the hearts of most of those I happened upon.

I could not help but recall my Homer, and Odysseus's journey to Hades, where the dead fled his living face in terror. Unlike Odysseus, however, I had no question for them. If I made a trough of blood, I wondered, would these shades gather to it, touch their tongues with it, and speak to me their secrets? I could not give in to such a fanciful notion. And these people were not dead, except to opportunity, to a functional life in the world above. Poverty had driven them down to this Hades, and giving them the few coins I had would not suffice to raise them to the land of the living. They needed hope, yet I had none to give them, not knowing what I looked for on this forlorn path.

I lost track of time, and I worried that whatever I was supposed to find in the lowest of lower Edinburgh was beyond my capacity to see. *Take the Low Road to the open way, where the walls thin*, the seer had said, but I could see little hope in the journey. All I'd found was the dark. The way was open, seemingly, as long as I could will my feet to move forward, but the walls around me were as thick and heavy as the earth itself. Mary, Holmes, Raboud, Irene, and our troops might all be dead by now. My torch burned low and gave less and less light. Could I even find my way back up through the rubble and confusion, much less return to them empty-handed?

"No, I'll go on," I said aloud to the dark around me.

But soon, as I moved down a set of narrow steps, light grew in front of me, and I saw before me a shape I knew all too well. My father stood at his easel, in a circle of light that came from no fire or torch. Brush in hand, he smeared something black—was it paint?—on a damp canvas, as my father never would have done. He hummed a tune and turned eyes bright with madness over his shoulder at my cautious approach.

"Well, hello! Aren't you the well-grown boy," he caroled.

"A boy I am no longer, and you are not my father," I said, placing my hand on Mustard Seed's grip.

His smile turned into a leer, and his eyes squinted to points. His mouth dropped open, wider than a human mouth could, and he lunged at me. The shape of my father faded from him and he became something like the creature who had attacked me in the cellar of my old home. More faerie glamor. I stepped into the creature's attack, between arms that grew into nightmarish, skeletal limbs, and I brought the pommel of my sword hard to its face. The shock of the heavy strike knocked the thing back onto its haunches and it bleated, "You took her arm! We'll have you yet! Strong friends we have now, and you and your band will die!"

I made to plant a kick into its sorry excuse for a face, but before I could act, it faded into nothing, leaving me alone in the light of my torch. If only the faeries of the Light Court would come to our aid, I thought, we might well overrun Dupain's forces. But Raboud had claimed that, in general, they would not, choosing to shun involvement with humans. Given what I'd been through just in these tunnels, I could see why.

"Faeries, humph," I said. "No more than a nuisance."

As I took my next steps, I heard sounds of furtive footfalls just beyond the small sphere of my torchlight. Something like whispers I heard too, though I saw nothing. I began to hurry forward, a sense of unreasoning panic setting in, like that I felt when I saw the first werewolf. Whatever things there were in the dark did not menace or growl, but now and then they would laugh—at me, I knew. They returned my derision of their kind. Their laughter, like that of cruel children at games, mocked me, seeming to take delight in my missteps or stumbles. Their laughter told me how foolish I was in their eyes, so I hastened forward, running as best I could in my meager light. I fell forward, dropping my torch, and in its last flash, I saw the stone of a low lintel ahead of me. There was a blinding flash, then darkness.

How long I lay in the dark, I could not tell, but when I awoke, I lay on a damp, stone floor, loose stones pressing jagged edges into me. I heard no voices. But perhaps they could hear me.

"Yes," I said, "I'm a fool for coming here, for thinking that by my efforts I could end the threat of something much bigger than I. Laugh, if you will. I do not care. I am here to find what I need—what we need—and I'll go on until I find it or die in the attempt."

Then, just behind me, I heard a voice so familiar, so dear to me, that I grew weak in the knees at the sound of it.

"That'd be a long, slow death, Jack, not like the mercy you showed me," Anne Prescott said.

"Anne," I breathed, turning to the sound of her voice in the dark. Blindly, I reached out for her. It was a foolish gesture to reach for a spirit, I knew, but I did it anyway, certain that she was there.

And she was there. When her hand took mine, a light grew around her, from her, and I beheld her as first I'd seen her. Her hair, as black as the perpetual night around us, was piled atop her head, and the gray-striped nurse's uniform she wore glowed as though with the light of all the good she had done in her life. Her blue eyes held my gaze as her fingers brushed a smudge on my cheek.

"Shall we go on, then?" Anne asked, taking my arm, as though we were on that London sidewalk where I had first taken her arm to escort her home.

Her very touch acted like a balm to my soul. Looking into those eyes again lifted from me the burden of my descent, my fears and anxieties about what remained for me to do. With her at my side, we walked out of time itself into a place of pure hope.

"You'll need to lead. I don't know where I am going," I said through my smile.

"Weel, Ah do, ye ken, and it isnae verra far," she said with a laugh, treating me for a moment to the soft burr of her home accent. When I'd met her in London, she had sought to make herself sound more like a Londoner, just as I'd done when I arrived in the city.

And so we walked on, and I saw no one, heard nothing as we went, content to be bathed in the light of her presence.

"Anne," I said, remembering that I was here on a mission, "I have come to find... something that will help us rid ourselves of a man bent on evil and domination. I don't have any idea of what that thing might be or why it is to be found here, in the depths under Edinburgh."

"Perhaps it is magic, Jack," she sighed, as though with regret.

"Och, magic," I said in disgust. "I grow sick of having to think about it. It makes no sense to me. I would think that it would make no sense to you, either, you who spent your years learning medicine and patient care to help heal the sick. I would think that believing in magic would not be in your nature."

"Well, I'm dead now, you know. Things that were of my nature run deeper on this side of life, as you'll find one day and for all time."

"One day and for all time?" I asked. "What do you mean? And how is it possible that you are here? That you are not in heaven, as you deserve to be?"

"Can you think that I was bound for the 'streets o' gold' sort of heaven, given all my sins?" she asked, in very odd-sounding, merry tones.

"I... don't know. I was just thinking of what I always believed, that the good who die go to their just rewards."

Her laughter was soft but not mocking, delighted and delightful. "Oh, Jack, everyone and everything belongs here, where I am. The thoughts of men and women can do little to appreciate what it means to be loved eternally, and we—all of us—are."

"All of us?"

"Yes, even those we call evil," she whispered. "Even your worst enemy. We all find ourselves here."

At that moment, our steps took us, somehow, into the heart of London itself. We were walking toward the lights of Piccadilly Circus, its streets and shops bathed now in ethereal light. I saw that she was dressed in an evening gown, and I was dressed as though for the opera. There were no crowds around us as we went. It was as though, for this night, all of that teeming city had become ours alone.

"Do you remember the night we went haring off into the tunnels, looking for clues and enraging Mr. Holmes?" she asked, her smile beaming at me. Her hair lay about her shoulders now, and, as always, we walked in perfect stride together. She glowed with joy.

"I'll say I do," I answered with a laugh. "Holmes was speechless with anger when I saw him later. I had a devil of a time just getting him to hear me out."

"Aye, but you made up, right enough," she added, "and our clues gave us the first break we needed in that case."

"True," I replied. "We should have relied more on what you had to tell us."

"No, I think not, Jack, for I was lost in grief and thirsty for revenge. But for all of that, it was one of the best nights of my life... apart from one."

"The one, in my home, where you came to me?" I asked in a soft voice.

"Aye. Above all the easy days of sunlight and laughter when I was a child, all the hopes and dreams I ever had, that was the best memory I took with me. I'd have gone back to it again, just as we've gone back to London, only it isn't allowed for the dead and the living to be that intimate," she whispered.

"And like as not, I don't deserve it," I said. "After all, I was unable to save you."

She stopped and turned toward me, her eyes shining. "Oh, but you did, Jack. You did save me."

"Anne, I killed you, with this," I said, and I half drew the blade from its scabbard.

"Do you not remember the words of the Traveler woman? You freed me from a path that led to torment, Jack."

Anne turned and started walking again. We had drawn near the center of Piccadilly.

"There at the last, in the Diogenes Club, was the worst moment of my life," I said.

"Worse than the darkness you are in now?" she asked.

"Yes. I would gladly give up any chance for my own happiness to go back to the time where I could have saved you, returned you to the life and freedom you deserved, Anne. Even if it meant that I would never see you again, I would wish that. I would gladly give up this sword, the work I do protecting others, if I could give you that."

Anne stopped walking and turned me to look into her face. Her eyes were sad, but the corners of her mouth turned up as she said, "Mary understood that you are a knight of sorts. But the struggle against the evil that men do, against the dark powers that seek to corrupt men's hearts and minds, is what your life needs to be. Your desire to free people from harm is necessary, though hard, so hard that you cannot think your way through it, but it is what you desired when even as a boy you played those games of battle in your cellar. It was that same desire which freed me.

"Such acts echo through eternity, Jack, through that which connects all of us, even those who are so blinded by hurt and pain that they turn to evil. It is that selflessness that goes through the barriers of the worlds and brings healing, even if it comes through the violence of the sword which stops the evil from spreading. You cannot give that up as long as you live, as long as you love."

"I don't understand," I said, bowing my head. "I don't see how all this fighting, all this struggle for power, has anything to do with love. Surely folks like Moriarty and Dupain are the forces of darkness personified, evil itself."

"Only because they seek a hell on earth, because, apart from the mercy of grace, men are driven by the need for dominance, the need to avenge themselves upon the world they blame for their loss and pain," Anne whispered, lifting my chin so that she could look again into my eyes. "Sometimes, in your world, much is demanded to gain enlightenment. There was a man once who sat atop a pole for thirty-seven years to learn it. You come to it through the burden of that sword that you carry. All that you can do is to be who you are: a true man—a knight, if you will—who serves love with a sword of faith."

"You make it sound as though I need to save someone I think of as evil in this struggle too," I whispered, looking into her eyes. "Who?"

"Dupain, of course," she said, and drew my lips to hers. "And Holmes," she whispered and kissed me again. "And Raboud," she whispered, kissing me a third time, longer, holding me close in her embrace.

When her lips left mine, she buried her face in my neck, and I breathed in her fragrance, for I knew that she was going.

"Anne, can I not stay here, with you?"

"No," she whispered, "for this place where we stand is no more than a faerie glamor—the one mighty gift the Light Court of faerie chose to give you. And here you cannot remain, any more than I can. I must go back to where I belong now. You must go too, for though time runs in wandering channels here, it does pass, and your time to do what is needed is short. We will meet again."

Then her touch on my skin faded away into the mist of the dark place. But before she faded away completely, I heard her say, "As hard as it will seem, you can make the climb, Jack. But before you can succeed, you will have to take to your knees."

Her parting left me in the dark, with an aching in my soul far deeper than the pain in my head from having run into the wall. I swooned at my loss of her and at the weight of the burden that she had placed on my shoulders. Was it more than I could bear? It was as heavy as life itself, and it grew with each breath I took.

**

I woke with the flare of torches making my eyes hurt. Dibba was hauling me to my feet.

"*Efendi*, I am so glad we found you," he said.

Even as groggy as I was, I saw men with him, one carrying a torch high enough to illuminate the room I was in. The light glinted off the black volcanic glass from which the place was carved. A low granite chair sat in the center.

Dibba started to carry me away when I did not respond. My thoughts were still full of Anne, and my head hurt. Pushing away from him, I said, "Thank you for looking for me, Dibba, but I can make it. Where am I, anyway?"

"Under the mountain of celebration. You are in the place where your world and mine overlap, and these, my northern kindred, came to find me when they knew you'd found this place."

"My thanks to you all," I said, turning to face them. Few were as tall as Dibba, but they were all broad, heavily made, and bearded. They bore weapons, ready for battle: maces, clubs, short swords, spears. They were prepared for the war that was coming, the war in which I now knew I had to try to save my enemy.

CHAPTER TWENTY-TWO

"Can War Be Won?"

If what I brought back to the world above was supposed to help in our struggle against Dupain and his allies, I could not see how. Doubting it was no option, though. Anne's words rang in my heart and soul like a bell that tolled out truth. The hour was, indeed, late, and as we made the first stages of the climb up Arthur's Seat, I dreaded the knells from the church towers of Edinburgh that would mark midnight.

Dibba told me that Lord Whitefell and our Sovereign had made the climb to the top earlier, before any activity from Dupain's forces had been seen.

"They intend to hold the summit against all forces," Dibba confided, hurrying me up from Queen's Drive. "Your Magnus, Miss Adler, and Abel Cameron are with them, may Allah bless and treasure them. My master has given them the magical wards to place around them, and Dr. Raboud imbues them with power from below, just here, in St. Anthony's Chapel. The Traveler people ring him with guards."

"Have you any idea where Holmes is?"

"No, *efendi*," he murmured, "but old Abel thinks that Mr. Holmes is too much the wolf."

I could only mutter a curse and follow him. We needed Holmes, but the magic of the curse had him and had taken him from our side. I saw no way to save him as Anne had bade me.

As we approached, I heard the sounds of struggle, human struggle, for men cursed and fought hand to hand. The thudding sound of blows landing made my stomach turn with their ferocity. Dupain's forces fought to kill, as I knew they would. The Travelers would do so at need. Sharp reports of pistol shots rang out, and we doubled our speed. Dibba led us higher on the slope, at the rear of the band of men who sought to overrun the ruins. The only light came from their torches, which danced off the stones of that lone standing corner, its empty windows jet black with night. I imagined that Raboud stayed back in that solitary corner, concentrating on the powerful marble cubes that surrounded Tennyson and Whitefell with his warding spell. And I could only hope that no shot or blow found the delicate fellow. As tired and fatigued as I was, I could not imagine how his slender frame was standing up to the challenge.

I counted at least thirty men in the band that had beset the ten or so Traveler lads who protected Raboud. Yet we gained position on those attackers, gypsy ruffians of the sort who had attacked our carriage outside Penrith, and our band, some dozen strong, fell upon them from the rear. Dibba was foremost in our attack, and I thought at first that his force alone would be enough. Fists swinging, feet stamping, Dibba Al-Hassan waded into them, and it was all the rest of us could do to keep up. Jamie Cameron stood at the fore of his people, his slender form dancing beyond the reach of blows and striking out with lethal precision with his truncheon. If those men in that London bar had seen him, they'd have run in terror. But even while I smashed the heads of two attackers together, I heard the pistol shot that hit Jamie's shoulder and the next two that struck his legs. He went down.

Dibba's northern kin fought silently but with great efficiency. Each bore a small, round shield. They locked these shields together in groups of four across and then threw men down with the combined wall of their weight. And in a breach the dweraz made, I rushed forward, striking around me, and forced my way through to Jamie. Omar Raboud, shivering, stood over the lad, his weak eyes staring, lips moving in the working of his spell.

"No time, John! No time!" Raboud yelled as I bent to Jamie's side. "They will overpower my wards any minute now. The force is too much, and I am too weak."

"Then we must get you closer, though I suspect that the danger to you will increase, my friend," I said.

"Go!" Jamie cried, pushing aside my hands. "Get him near the others. I will be all right. I have men who can help me, and I have charms of my own. But I have seen it! Already the wards fall and Lord Johnny fights before the Sovereign. Go!"

Without debate, I grabbed Raboud's hand and pulled him away. "Dibba Al-Hassan! With me!"

At once, the dweraz dropped the man whose body he smashed into the faces of his enemies. The opposing force was scattered, though, and Dibba came quickly, followed by some four of his kin, while the others fought on near the ruin. Sweeping his master up over his shoulder, Dibba sprinted toward the summit that seemed miles away. A sickly yellow glow lit the summit, making gargantuan, misshapen shadows against the cold mist that hung about it. I heard Adler's twin Colts blasting away.

"He has the fiercest... opposition... flanking him," Raboud cried, bouncing on Dibba's shoulder. "Oh, put me down!"

Stumbling when he hit his feet, Raboud cried, "Go. I'm out of danger here, between the fights. Go quickly to the summit. I'll do what I can with the wards from here."

I had lost my watch, but I knew midnight approached, and we had been seen. Shapes moved down from on high toward us, and I did know what they were. But a stench as of a bog or fen rolled toward us with them, and though their limbs looked ungainly and their heads lolled low, with gaping jaws these faeries, like the Meg o' the Marshes that had attacked me in my old cellar, made great speed.

And there were other creatures, misshapen yet vaguely humanoid, rising from the boggy rills that run from the rock of Arthur's Seat down into The Dasses, that grassy vale screened from Edinburgh's view by the great ridge of the Salisbury Crags. Those things latched onto men's legs as they passed.

With Mustard Seed in both hands, I ran toward the faerie folk that swarmed over Dibba. Where his fists landed, faerie ichor spattered, and creatures fell away from him, though some had trapped his legs. These beasts I scythed through at a dead run, and Dibba sprang forward. His kin rallied around him and formed a wedge with him at its point, pushing ever uphill. I fought to gain his side, and I was gladdened that none of the faeries got past us to harry Raboud.

But midnight was approaching, and so was another line of shambling shapes coming around the side of the great hill. They looked like zombies, but some of them possessed horrid, demonic faces. I thought that these might be revenants, vampires, though they were no match for my dweraz friends.

Dibba Al-Hassan plowed steadily up the hill, fists smashing the faces, limbs, and bodies that pressed around him. I dared hope that his great strength alone would get us to the top. The glow brightened from on high, as though Raboud's wards strove with the sick light of Dupain's incantations.

And in that light, I saw a dreadful sight behind the vampires: the dark, powerful shape of a loup-garou. I knew that Dupain had yet another amulet, and I did not think he'd give up the summit so easily and come toward me. The wolf thing pushed other creatures ahead, screening itself from Dibba's view.

"Werewolf! Ahead of you!" I shouted.

But Dibba's roars filled his own ears as he bashed the revenant creatures down. I cut down faerie beings that clawed at me in my haste to get to him. The loup-garou dashed around the revenants and killed two of Dibba's kin. I was five steps away. It howled as it slashed at Dibba's midsection. Having drawn Dibba's hands down, the wicked thing lunged, snapped its gaping jaws down on Dibba's neck, and bore him to the ground.

I saw from the spray of dark blood that I was too late, though I slashed open the werewolf's back, and it tumbled away from my friend. Dibba was still on the ground when the werewolf turned its blazing eyes toward me, pawing at the long wound on its back. Whoever this was must be in league with Dupain—must be a man who, like Pinder, had taken the coin as a means of doing murder—so I gave it no quarter. It started to lunge at me, claws reaching for my throat, but I gave it a target, then moved to the side, sword high. My cut was strong, and the steel bit harder than its jaws ever could. I left its headless corpse and sprang to Dibba's side.

He held his hands over his throat, but the vicious bite had made his neck a ruin of flesh. Dibba looked up at me and smiled. Blood frothed on his lips, and he pushed away my hands that sought to clamp down on the severed veins and arteries. His lips moved, but his throat was ruined, and he could make only the smallest whispers. I leaned down beside his face.

"Take care of her," he whispered. "She will... be sad..."

And his eyes glassed over.

"Dibba!" I yelled, to no avail.

I bade two of his kin take his body back to Raboud. By this time, a handful of Traveler lads had joined in the fight on our side, and I had no time to ponder which "she" Dibba had meant. Mary? Irene? I had no idea.

But the midnight approached. No bells, but they must be minutes, seconds away, and the summit lay ahead of me. I looked up and saw another swarm of faerie and revenant creatures, perhaps two score of them. I had five Traveler lads, whose pale faces stared up at the oncoming creatures. One of the northern dweraz stood by me, his short sword ready, and I marveled at this people that I'd once dismissed as useless faeries.

But as stout and courageous as these men were, they were not enough to overcome the mass of enemies about to fall on us. I had one thought: do as much damage as we could, and maybe we could pull others away from Dupain at the summit. Then, if Whitefell and my friends were yet alive, we might have a chance.

The howl that rose from behind me and to the right, coming up from The Dasses, sent a shiver of fear through me, but when I spotted the dark shape streaking over the wet grasses, I knew it was Holmes. He had come, even if it was in his madness. With another howl and a great leap, he fell like a thunderbolt on those attacking creatures. Many of them broke and ran, but the lupine Holmes killed with wild power. He tore through their ranks like a storm.

"Up, lads!" I cried, and we formed another wedge, driving our way through the enemies that yet remained between us and the summit. Holmes pursued the rest as they broke and ran toward the other side. I could not waste much time watching him, for the revenants and faerie creatures that remained focused on us and attacked with renewed ferocity. But we forced them back as my lads pushed hard to break their ranks, drawing them off into separate fights so that I could reach the top. Voices I knew rang out from the top: Guthrie and Adler, Old Cameron, and Lord Whitefell fought on. Brave people were giving their all, so I forced my leaden legs to push on, kept my head about me, and fought hard against the nightmare shapes that assailed me.

They parted suddenly, and I saw the smoking tendrils of the Croucher forming ahead of me. Its taste was in my mouth again, making me want to vomit. But I knew that it only called to that bit of itself that tainted me, that slowed me down, and I gave it no quarter. It seemed to wait for me to come to it, but it had never tasted my blade. I remembered Lora Garrett's words about the nature of this magical weapon I bore, and I knew that its edge would bite the Croucher as no other weapon could.

Leaping toward its waiting, misty tendrils, poised to envelop me in its crushing grip, I swept two-handed strokes at it, one straight down and one from side to side. Though I am no religious zealot, I knew that the cross shape, the shape of supreme sacrifice, the shape of pain endured, would cut the infernal evil, especially with the help of Mustard Seed.

And it did. The steel rang as if struck by hammers, but it rang true and brought pain to a thing whose sole reason for existence was to trap others in pain.

"That was for Westcott, Adler, and Raboud!" I yelled, hardly able to hear myself because of its keening cries. The tendrils sought to re-form, but I struck it again and again as it backed up the rocky path to the summit. With one final scream of agonized terror, it fled into the misty night, back to the hell from whence it had come.

I pushed on, scrambling up the rocky path to the summit. I had a clear view of Whitefell standing before Tennyson, facing several faerie creatures who raked at him with long claws. Many more of their kind lay strewn around the summit, dissolving. Dupain stood back, braying a mad laughter. Not far from him, shielding himself from the melee, stood the homburg man, clearly horrified by the nature of Bismarck's alliance with a madman.

Whitefell bled from wounds on his chest, abdomen, arms, and shoulders, but he took a wide stance straddling Tennyson, who had fallen at the point of the summit with a wound across his forehead. Tennyson held a pistol and wiped blood from his eyes as he tried to find a shot. The faeries dodged in and out, like a pack of jackals around a wounded lion. They were cautious and did not stay long in striking range of Galatine's long, shimmering blade. Though I stood in awe of Whitefell's titanic strength, I could see the attacks had weakened him. It would take seconds to get to Whitefell's side, but I was certain he didn't have that much time.

The first bell of midnight tolled in the town below.

Dupain, naked except for a cape that billowed in the gale force winds, stood to one side. Mary lay unconscious at his feet, her tattered clothing and tangled hair also streaming in the wind. Dupain held his *navaja*, ready to spill her blood, his vile sacrifice to his satanic master. An eerie light showed around Dupain, as though it emanated from his skin. The misty air of the cold night filled the light that came from him. He looked like something from an old myth or a faerie tale, a young god—or a monster— awaiting the coming of his power. It would be his when the clock finished striking midnight.

As he looked at me, he smiled and then changed form, with such ease that it looked almost instantaneous. How often had he made this dreadful transformation, that it was so easy for him? Turning his sick, red eyes in my direction, red tongue lolling out of the side of his mouth, he growled a laugh at my expense.

I pushed on, up the summit. My free hand grasped at rocks to keep me steady in the wind. In my other hand, Mustard Seed glittered in the meager light.

I saw the glinting blade of Galatine drop, for Whitefell was spent, and in the next instant, Dupain cuffed him away. Whitefell dropped into the dark, and the werewolf rolled a struggling Lord Tennyson after him. With the second stroke of the midnight bell, Dupain stood at the summit of Arthur's Seat, ready to command the power that would come to him.

I was on him while the second tolling of the bell still rang, and my slashing blade caught the arm of the massive werewolf he had become. He howled and thrashed, but I did not aim a cut at his neck. Dropping below his slashing claws, I hit him with my shoulder hard enough to lift him off his feet and hurl him yards away, into the dark.

The third toll rang through the air, and I sank on my knees to the spot where Tennyson had been, just as Dupain's howl of rage rang out. Putting away all thoughts, I breathed deeply down into my center, as the good Uyeshiba had taught me. I sent my *ki* down into the earth, rooting myself to the summit of Arthur's Seat. I lay my sword flat on the ground before me.

At the fourth ring of the bell, Dupain was back in front of me, his speed prodigious. Other bells joined the tolling then, so it was impossible to tell how many were left until midnight had come and gone.

His red eyes stared into mine, and he howled out his rage. I had taken the lives of faerie creatures and of men who had taken the werewolf charm to do murder. I knew that protecting the people of my homeland would demand that I use my sword again in combat. But I remembered, too, Anne's words that I needed to try to save him.

"Jean-Louis, listen to me," I called to him. "You are far gone, yes, but even now, it is not too late to undo what you have done. Give up this madness. You have talents that could help heal all this, help heal you, too. Can you not forgive the hurts done to you? Put aside your anger at Holmes, at me. Don't do any more harm to Mary. We can protect you from those men who have used you."

With my blade flat before me and my *ki* connecting me to Arthur's Seat, I knew that I was anchored, and no force could move me. The energy of that ancient place, the telluric currents that culminated there, poured into me as though the old volcanic power had reached up and pulled down on my feeble energy, joining me to the land.

And I did not move, though Dupain sprang upon me and pulled with a strength that ripped my clothes apart. His howling, louder than the wind, drowned out every other sound. Claws bit into the flesh of my shoulders as the bells tolled on, but I did not move, though Dupain sought only to replace me on that summit of power.

Only when the bells fell silent, their last vibrations passing in the gale, did he think to kill me. I knew that he would kill me just for spite. He would kill Mary, too, just out of hatred. But as he stood tall over me and looked down, I saw his eyes dim in what looked, perhaps, like puzzlement.

"You can yet choose to turn aside, Dupain," I said. "You once said that not all losses can be restored with a single stroke of good fortune, but this one can, Jean-Louis. A great evil has been averted here, and you can yet walk away from it, if you choose."

Doubt clouded his features further, and his glowing eyes closed. I thought he might just relent, having heard his own words repeated back to him. I realized that he'd lied in saying those words, lied every minute of his time in our midst, just to bring about this end, his revenge. He opened his glowing eyes again, lifted his hand on high, claws ready to rip out my life.

Then a dark shape bolted from behind me and struck Dupain hard. The man in the homburg, having seen his plan go to ruin, ran screaming down the path of the summit. Twining, fur-matted bodies tumbled across the rocks. It had to be Holmes. I seized Mary and pulled her into my arms, as limp as she was. I knew that she was lost to me, but I would not just leave her exposed to the elements and to the peril of dying where the werewolves fought.

And fight they did.

They were well matched, but the werewolf without the ripped ruin of a cloak about his shoulders, Holmes, was by far the more ferocious. Dupain, though lost in his madness, retained too much of himself in werewolf form. He thought too much, relied too much on controlling the strength and speed of the wolf. Holmes as a werewolf, though, simply sought Dupain's death. His transformation, as Dupain had planned it, was complete, and he was lost to his former self. His one thought was to kill his quarry. Every move drove home a lethal stroke that would have killed a man. I thought back to Dibba's heroic defiance against the other werewolf, but even that would have been insufficient to keep the Holmes wolf at bay.

It ended with a sudden lunge by Holmes. He took Dupain by the throat, shaking him in mad exultation, then hurling him away to fall in a crumpled pile of blood-matted fur. Holmes howled then with a fury unabated, and I looked on him with a fear unequaled. He was lost and deadly.

And when he turned in my direction, I saw his nostrils flare as the wind blew the scent of my blood into his nose. His eyes became slits, and his tongue lolled over teeth that Holmes wanted to sink into any living flesh, mine or Mary's.

"Holmes! Think, man!" I bellowed at him, and on instinct I stood and picked up the sword from the stones of the summit. Killing Holmes would have been unthinkable, even to save my own life, but I could not let him kill Mary. Though she did not know me, she was mine to defend, even from Holmes, whose sterling mind had become lost in the wilderness of feral bloodlust. Dupain's blood dripped from his claws, still, as he stalked toward me, growling.

Then I saw my chance, the slimmest of chances, shown to me by the rain that poured down on us. The copper chain holding the amulet around Holmes's neck caught the drops that ran down its length.

Holmes sprang, but time slowed for me. I saw the muscles in his great legs twitch. I stepped toward his lunge, moving off to his left, and struck—but did not slice through his neck. His claws tore the front of my coat, but the chisel tip of my sword only cut the chain that held the amulet to him, barely nicking the skin below it.

A howl broke from Holmes's throat as he fell toward the

spot where I would have been. He clutched at the amulet in midair and missed. I caught it, chain and all, and held it. Like a cold that burns skin, it hurt me, but I would not let it go until I could give it to Abel Cameron, whom I saw beside Tennyson, each wounded and leaning one on the other. The kings of their respective peoples looked on my struggle with wonder in their eyes, for I had not killed a foe but saved him.

Holmes dropped to the ground as though I had hit him with a sledgehammer. As a werewolf, he had shimmered with power in the cold mist. As a man, he shivered with weakness, like the rest of us. His howl turned into a man's cry, and in seconds to anguished moans. Holmes lay helpless at my feet beside Mary on the summit of Arthur's Seat.

But when I had kneeled at the summit as midnight passed, I had claimed Logres, and England, for my Sovereign, of course. And the telluric power that flowed up into me from Arthur's Seat had shown me things. It had allowed me to claim my identity and my ancestral home of Edinburgh. While I could not see the agents themselves, I saw the occult and political threats of the Iron Chancellor fade away. That threat had ended, for a time.

The man in the homburg would remain unaccounted for, but I knew his face and what he stood for. I would also know when he returned, if he dared. The people of Romany, those who hadn't been killed, would fade into our very midst, moving, always moving. But I knew, too, that though the Travelers would also disappear, they would weave themselves all around and through my efforts to protect those who could not protect themselves, which is the very heart of Logres.

Dupain, I had not saved, though I'd tried. He had chosen his death when he gave that amulet to Sherlock Holmes in order to use him as a weapon. Dupain's failure lay in not seeing that such a weapon can turn against the one who wields it. Holmes was too deadly to be used by any man. Even if Holmes as a werewolf was the most perfect weapon on Earth, I would never countenance putting another of those amulets in his hand. It was Holmes the man, not the weapon, whom I had saved.

And as my thoughts turned to the others around me, I saw

Raboud trudge up the slope, aided by one of Dibba's northern kin. His face was a mask of grief for his faithful Dibba Al-Hassan. Still, he turned to help those who had been wounded, of whom Lord Whitefell had taken the most hurt. Magnus Guthrie, having been shot and stabbed, would be whole again with my doctoring, as would Irene Adler, who had been rendered unconscious. She was wakeful, though in pain, not the least of which was caused by looking on Holmes's pitiful condition.

Raboud knelt over Whitefell, weeping. Tennyson was there, too, stanching the cuts that his Court Champion had taken on his behalf. But since the power of the mountain of Logres flowed through me still, I saw things clearly and knew that to save Raboud, all I had to do was keep a secret. I knew secrets now, and some would remain secret. I also knew that we would live to see another morning, and for the moment, that was enough.

EPILOGUE

On our way back down from the summit, I took Holmes's arm to help him over the rugged trail. Guthrie had given Holmes his greatcoat, but Holmes stumbled as jagged granite dug into the soles of his feet.

"Please, old man, lean on me," I encouraged him. "I will—"

"Watson, please," Holmes snapped, pushing away from me and falling to the trail. I extended a hand to him, but he waved it away and turned his eyes from me. "Please, sir. Just, leave... me be." He would take no one's help until Abel Cameron put his arm around Holmes's waist and helped him limp along.

Mary, too, rejected my help, remembering me only from the falling staircase on Picardy Place. I had no idea what to do for her or for Holmes, so I helped the Travelers, many women and children now, to treat the wounded and, alas, carry away those humans who had been killed. By first light, there would only be muddied grass from the skirmishes, and the winter rain would soon wash their blood away.

It took all of Epiphany day to get the wounded sorted out and moved to Whitefell Manor, under the direction of the Garretts, clearly some of the most capable people I will ever have the privilege to call friends. Tennyson would stay there until a suitable escort could be found to take him home, what with Whitefell in need of healing. Tennyson, though nursing a cut on his forehead and a bruised, if not fractured, rib or two, needed rest and the opportunity to discuss the event of the Christmastide past with the leaders of the Logres Society. Such political allies as Gladstone could call upon would travel to Whitefell Manor.

Holmes had retreated no farther than Whitefell's flat in the Pleasance. He held some talk with Mrs. Garrett before she returned with Carl to Whitefell Manor. When I asked her for news of Holmes, she would only tell me, "He needs rest for his heart and his head, my lord, though he is as hale in his body as is possible for a mortal man to be. I have left him with victuals aplenty, enough to last a week, if he will just eat, but he will require your trust to help heal what plagues him. His power, even without the aid of magic, is hard to fathom, as is his stubbornness. He asks after Miss Adler, and I do not know what to tell him, for they are too much alike. Time, I think, will help them both as much or more than medicine or magic."

"You hold a great store of each in your keen mind and generous heart, madam," I said. "I hope we shall meet again soon, for I intend to come back north and see to Lord Whitefell, after my business in London is complete." My Sovereign had asked me to return to London to take charge of the missing amulet, which had been hard won, but thereon hangs another tale.[2]

***

I could hear the strains of a violin from Whitefell's flat even as I entered the outer door. I passed into the apartment on quiet steps and stood watching Holmes play. My very bones were tired, so I helped myself to a stiff whisky from Whitefell's ample supply and sat to listen. Though he was dressed in cast-off clothing—procured from Cameron's people, I thought by its make and cut—Holmes was the picture of physical health, except for the bandage on the left side of his neck. Only the manner in which he tore away at the difficult runs of the piece he played showed me his inner turmoil. The violin sounded as though it would break under the strain of the music he wrung from it.

"Not your usual attire, and certainly not your usual instrument, I see, but you look like the very picture of health,

---

[2] "The Fog of Fear" short story can be found at www.MJDowningsPlace.com

Holmes," I remarked at a breaking point in his music. "I don't recognize the piece, though."

"Improvisations on a failure in character," he muttered, "in B flat. And the instrument is on loan from one of Cameron's people, an Amati copy, I think, of good construction though inferior wood. Watson, I—"

"You need not explain anything, Holmes. You saved me from Dupain. The people of this land should erect a statue of you to honor your victory."

"My actions over the past two days—those I remember with any clarity—are inexcusable," he said but added, with a wry grin, "If such a statue were made, it should bear a wolf's print."

"Holmes, without you, we would have failed. I would never have made it past Dupain's forces, and no one from the Logres Society would have been at the summit of Arthur's Seat, if you had not made it possible. As for Dupain, well, his rampant monomania forced him past the point of being saved. I will hear nothing more about failure on your part."

He nodded, stared at the floor, and fingered the neck of the fiddle in an absentminded way.

"But you were right about my ability to control that... that device," he said. "It took me over completely. I did not know myself much of the time, and when I did, I panicked that I would never be able to rid myself of that amulet."

"Nonsense, Holmes. You attacked our enemies at precisely the time we needed you," I said.

"And you risked your life to save me when I charged you."

"A risk, yes, but Holmes, you were inflamed with the heat of battle," I explained, "and I doubt you knew me at all."

"Oh, but I did, Watson. I knew you. I knew your smell and your skill, and with the last parts of what I retained as my mind, I attacked you, for I knew that if anyone could free me, you could. I—I counted on it."

The terrible weight of his words caused my throat to close. Finally I managed to say, "I simply had to risk taking that thing off of you, whatever befell after."

We both sat in silence for a long moment, staring at the

carpet, glad to have passed that point. He stood to resume playing, but before he drew the bow across the strings, he said, "I do hope that you believe that I was not... with Mary... before. I only wish I knew why she would say that."

"I do believe you, old man," I replied. "But about Mary, we, well..."

"Yes, Mrs. Garrett told me. And now Miss Adler will not see me."

"Then we shall simply soldier on, eh, Holmes?" I said, forcing a note of joviality into my voice. I rose and turned to leave.

Before I reached the flat's door, Holmes called out to me, "I say, Watson, Joseph Joachim will be playing Bach's Sonatas and Partitas for Solo Violin at the Royal Albert. Would you see about tickets when you get back to the flat, please?"

"Of course, old man. Wouldn't miss it," I said and left him to heal.

***

I took my leave of him and spent my last night in Edinburgh, for a time, at the Old Waverley, in the suite that Tennyson had been meant to occupy for yet another day. My own weakness was slow to pass, but it left me restless, so I wandered through the Old Town and wound back around to Leith Walk, past Picardy Place. The old residence there no longer haunted my imagination, but I knew that when I returned in another week or so, I would look up my parents and see to their welfare as best I could. In the meantime, I also visited a kiltmaker and got measured for my own Highland outfit in the Watson family tartan. Arranging to have it sent to me at Baker Street, I took my leave for the Old Waverley and an early dinner.

As I took the steps up, a voice called to me. "Excuse me, Dr. Watson, may I have a word with you?"

Tobias Gregson stood below me with his hat in his hands. His deferential posture—and the lack of armed men in his company—helped me know that he no longer pursued me. I went down the steps with my hand extended.

295

"I've been waiting around much of the day for you," he said, "and some fellow in the Pleasance told me I would find you here. I, er—that is—it would appear that an apology of sorts is due to you. Miss Adler cleared things up here, just yesterday at the magistrate's office, and my superiors inform me that they have received several corroborating statements giving Mr. Holmes a strong alibi for the time during which Sir Alisdair was murdered."

Garrett, I assumed, had kept Gregson out of Whitefell's flat where Holmes hid himself, and I was grateful for that. I gave Gregson the best smile I could gather and said, "I am glad to hear this news. I think I told you that Holmes could not possibly have had any involvement in such a thing."

"Only, sir, I learned that Miss Adler was with your missus on the night of the murder," Gregson added, letting a wry smile play about his lips. "I note that Mrs. Watson is not here with you now, sir. Isn't that right?"

"Ah, Inspector, there is no hiding the truth from you," I said with a sigh and a wry smile of my own. "I must confess that my wife is estranged from me, perhaps permanently so. She will be residing for the foreseeable future at Whitefell Manor, under the protection of Lord John Whitefell. She seeks to forget me, sir, and I think she is succeeding in her endeavors. I will also confide in you, Tobias, that I am done with matrimonial love. I hope to go on living as a bachelor, alongside my friend, Mr. Sherlock Holmes. I think that we are the only fit company for each other. We might, each of us, have an affinity for the ladies, but we make bad husbands, don't you think, Inspector?"

I doubt that my question was what he was looking for. It stymied him, I think, because it was as honest as I could be.

"As you say, sir," he replied, sketching me a short bow and then hurrying away toward Waverley Station.

***

The next evening, rather late, I let myself into the flat at Baker Street, looking forward to an early meeting the next morning to receive O'Hara's report and, of course, the missing amulet. Mrs. Hudson was out, so I stopped long enough in her kitchen to set a copper of water to boil, seeing evidence that someone had used it earlier. I thought nothing of it, but went about my business on quiet steps, glad to be home.

Taking the stairs on tired feet, I eased into the dark sitting room, making for my chamber, intent on having a shave and crawling into my own bed. As I turned the knob and eased open the door to my bedroom, so as not to spill my water, I heard the sound of water splashing within.

The door swung open, and Dr. Raboud gasped in surprise, standing naked in front of the washbasin. I turned away and shut the door. I had known, of course, while I stood in the flow of the mountain's power. However, I had said nothing and had sworn to myself, as I was to swear later to Dr. Raboud, that I would say nothing. As it was, I pulled the door closed for her. With all that she had been through, Dr. Raboud deserved her privacy.

The End

ABOUT THE AUTHOR

M.J. Downing is a native of Louisville, Kentucky. Born in Shively in the spring of 1954, he was raised in Okolona. M.J. resided in the Highlands for twenty years before marrying his wife, Amy, and moving to Valley Station.

M.J.'s interests are in this order: God, who is *the* Mystery; family, Amy and daughter Mackenna; writing stories; reading, everything from comics to criticism; playing guitar, all things Celtic; working out; walking; watching movies; travelling; and the comforts of home. He is a certifiable Tolkien geek and will wear you out with it, if given any encouragement.

For employment, M.J. has been a firefighter, a construction worker, a tobacconist, and many other things. Since 1983, he has taught college writing and literature classes, spending the last quarter century doing so at Jefferson Community and Technical College, Southwest.

FOR A FREE, EXCLUSIVE, SHORT STORY BY MJ DOWNING, VISIT HIS WEBSITE AT

http://www.MJDowningsPlace.com/

FOLLOW MJ DOWNING ON FACEBOOK

https://www.facebook.com/markstories54/

ALSO BY M.J. DOWNING

SHERLOCK HOLMES AND THE
CASE OF THE UNDEAD CLIENT

Sherlock Holmes has only been deceased a month when Dr. John Watson, still grieving, recounts his final case with Holmes. A terrifying mystery, it sends Watson and Holmes into the dark reaches of London's back alleys—and the human soul.

It begins when Anne Prescott, a lovely Scottish nurse, begs Sherlock Holmes and Watson to help her find her fiancé and her sister, who have gone missing in the teeming streets of London. Immediately, Watsonfeels an attraction to her that shocks him. Newly married to Mary, and deeply in love with her, he struggles to put Anne out of his mind.

As Watson and Holmes dig into the slums and sewers of London looking for Anne's fiancé and sister,they uncover a deadly web of bloody murders, horrific medical experiments, and even voodoo ritualthat threatens not only London, but the entire British empire, and beyond.

Watson must call on his unique combination of expertise in the medical sciences, as well as his military training to stop this killer before London—and Anne—are lost to the killer's bloody plan.

But time is short and the mystery ever more complex. How can he manage his feelings for Anne? What about his loyalty to Mary? He can't have both.

PRAISE FOR M.J. DOWNING

"*Sherlock Holmes and the Case of the Undead Client*breathes new life into a classic series. Even Arthur Conan Doyle would be a fan of this stellar mystery that would make him wish he'd done it himself. A must-read for all mystery fans in general and Sherlock Holmes fans in particular."

—Jon Land,*USA Today*bestselling author of
MURDER, SHE WROTE: A Date with Murder

"Entertaining as hell. Highly recommended!"

—Jay Bonansinga, the*New York Times*bestselling author of
*Robert Kirkman's*The*Walking Dead: Return to Woodbury*

"…brisk action and pitch-perfect Sherlock-ian aplomb make for a page-turner"

—*Kirkus Reviews*

BurnsandLeaBooks.com